# The Voidwalker Collection

## (The Voidwalker Novellas Books 1-8)

Derek Bailey

*This is a work of fiction. All characters, locations, and events are products of the author's imagination and any connections that can be made to the real world are up to the reader's interpretation. Opinions of the various characters within this story do not necessarily reflect those of the author and are only in place to define their character or to build the world they exist in.*

Edited by Jeff Macmillan and Nathaniel Mellor

ISBN: 978-1-958380-01-7

# DEDICATION

To Neal, Taylor, Keith, Al, Ed B, Cassie, Jim, Doug, Kendra, Sean, Brian, Diana, Ed M, and, of course, my parents for mentoring and shaping me into the person that I am today. While I have learned so much from all the classmates, colleagues, friends, managers, and family members that I have been blessed enough to have in my life, I am especially grateful for everything I learned from you about servant leadership, embracing my strengths, improving my weaknesses, and finding opportunity within adversity. It is safe to say I would not be who I am today without your example.

# CONTENTS

**Book 1: The Manor of My Dreams**

Chapter 1 ...................................................................3

Chapter 2 .................................................................20

Chapter 3 .................................................................32

Chapter 4 .................................................................40

Epilogue ..................................................................54

**Book 2: Paradise's Vexation**

Chapter 1 .................................................................59

Chapter 2 .................................................................69

Chapter 3 .................................................................83

Chapter 4 .................................................................97

Epilogue ................................................................109

**Book 3: Dark Horizon**

Chapter 1 ...............................................................113

Chapter 2 ...............................................................124

Chapter 3 ...............................................................133

Chapter 4 ...............................................................142

Epilogue ................................................................161

**Book 4: A Deadly Crescendo**

Chapter 1 ...............................................................165

Chapter 2 ...............................................................172

Chapter 3 ...............................................................185

Chapter 4 ...............................................................193

Epilogue ................................................................212

**Book 5: Haunted**

Chapter 1 ................................................................ 217

Chapter 2 ................................................................ 221

Chapter 3 ................................................................ 233

Chapter 4 ................................................................ 245

Chapter 5 ................................................................ 254

Epilogue ................................................................ 268

**Book 6: The Hands of Time**

Chapter 1 ................................................................ 273

Chapter 2 ................................................................ 283

Chapter 3 ................................................................ 297

Chapter 4 ................................................................ 308

Epilogue ................................................................ 326

**Book 7: Memory's Graveyard**

Chapter 1 ................................................................ 331

Chapter 2 ................................................................ 337

Chapter 3 ................................................................ 356

Chapter 4 ................................................................ 366

Chapter 5 ................................................................ 384

Epilogue ................................................................ 400

**Book 8: The Fate of a Soul**

Chapter 1 ................................................................ 405

Chapter 2 ................................................................ 414

Chapter 3 ................................................................ 433

Chapter 4 ................................................................ 458

Epilogue ................................................................ 463

# PREFACE

I started <u>The Voidwalker Novellas</u> back in 2015 after launching my debut novel, <u>Digitarum</u> earlier that year via Amazon's Kindle Direct Program (KDP). The idea behind this project was to create a reading experience that felt similar to watching a high-budget show on one of the popular streaming platforms. I knew right away that I wanted each installment to feel bite-sized, but ultimately build to something more epic.

From an authorship perspective, this seemed like a great way to tell a larger story in manageable pieces, however I greatly underestimated the logistics of essentially releasing eight separate books in short succession of one another. I had the initial drafts for all eight parts finished by the time the first two entries in the series were released in 2016 and things seemed to be moving along nicely. I was even able to get the manuscripts for third and fourth parts into a mostly finished state before I was pulled away from this project by some challenges I faced with my primary career that would later turn into an amazing opportunity—followed by a lot of changes in both my personal and professional life.

Fast forward to 2022 where I found myself feeling a lot more established in my professional life, settled personally in a new location, and having been through all the adjustments resulting from COVID-19 such as learning to work from home. I realized there was never going to be a perfect time to resume efforts on my writing endeavors, but that the present was as good a time as any considering all the change I had been through in the past few years. With my former editor, Jeff, seemingly no longer in business, I scrambled to find a new one as I worked feverishly to clean up the remaining four manuscripts in the series. I am so grateful to have found Nathaniel on the freelancing site, *Fiverr.* He did such an amazing job jumping in at the middle of the series and working with me to ensure that those four novellas were the best they possibly could be.

With the manuscripts polished up to the best of our collective abilities, covers created, and a desire to finally release this story into the wild, I finished up the eBook files and set them to release weekly via

KDP. With the remaining six installments all set and ready to release, the one thing I felt was missing was a print edition of these novellas. While I'd initially written the series with the Kindle platform in mind, there's also something special about being able to hold a physical copy.

Since each novella is so tiny (each is approximately 20,000-25,000 words which is on the shorter end of a standard novella word count) it wouldn't have made sense to release individual paperbacks and I had already learned that doing individual mini-releases creates a lot of logical overhead anyway. This meant that I would have to do a collection of some sort. It took me a little while to decide whether I wanted to have two separate collections for each half of the series or go with one large compilation. Of course, I ultimately landed upon the latter since that seemed like the bookish equivalent to a "binge watch" option.

And so, here we are with The Voidwalker Collection which compiles all eight entries of this psycho-spiritual fantasy thriller. I am so excited to see this series finally finished in both electronic and print editions and I hope you enjoy this adventure down a very dark rabbit hole!

# Book 1:

# The Manor of My Dreams

*To everyone who ever made me feel welcome,*
*even if I didn't belong.*

# Chapter 1

My eyes pop open to the sound of silverware lightly scraping against dishes. A mild din of conversation floods my ears and I start to panic because I'm not sure who all of these voices belong to. It doesn't help that when I look at the crowd before me, there are nothing but blurry blobs of color. I blink a few times and can make out that I'm sitting at an enormous dinner table. On either side of it sits fifteen people-shaped color swathes. I'm at one of the head spaces and in the other is a dark figure. I think by the shape of the colors that it's a man on the other side and it seems like he's staring at me. I'm not sure, of course, since I can't really see his eyes. Then I realize that it might be me who's staring at him so I quickly avert my gaze.

Thankfully, my close-up vision begins to improve. To my left is a man with rich brown hair combed neatly over his brow. He also has a spectacular moustache waxed into elegant twin curls. He shoots me a sideways grin and tips his crystal wine glass up towards me. There's an air of confidence in the gesture, one that suggests that this is a man who is afraid of nothing. To my right is a slightly older woman, or perhaps just one who has greyed a little early in life. She gives me a pearly smirk and raises a brow at me, but says nothing. Seeing her fills me with a certain warmth that one doesn't often get from a stranger, but I'm grateful for it all the same.

As my vision continues to sharpen, I can see that everyone around me is wearing stylish suits or elegant evening gowns. They all look relatively young – averaging at around thirty, I'd say. The ladies either have their hair done-up in elaborate buns or falling in silky waves. The gentlemen all sport different hair styles and some have facial hair to go with it, but all are exceptionally well-groomed. I notice too that the plates and bowls before us are all made of fine chinaware. The silverware seems finely polished and is adorned with intricate floral patterns. Every glass and water pitcher on the table is crafted from polished crystal and even the mahogany tabletop is free of blemishes.

I suddenly feel very self-conscious. In spite of how ridiculous it might be, I don't actually remember what I look like. I decide that I must look at least a little attractive since everyone at this table is appealing in some way. I look down and see that I'm in a navy suit coat and white dress pants with black shoes. Without being too conspicuous about it, I look down further to find a white collared shirt and black bow tie beneath my coat. Next, I reach for my wine glass and slosh its contents about as if to scrutinize it. While doing so, I catch the reflection of a square-jawed man with neatly combed dust-brown hair. It's a distorted image, but enough to convince me that I belong in a place like this. I'm coming to this decision when the man at the other end of the table rises with his wine glass in one hand and a silver spoon in the other. I turn my attention to him, finding that I still can't quite perceive his facial features at this distance. I can see most of the table's occupants fairly well now, but not this man. He pauses for a slow breath and dings the side of his glass three times with the spoon.

"Good evening, everyone," his voice rings out in a deep, soothing tone. He has an accent, though not one I recognize. It sounds proper, but also … *ancient* … somehow.

"Good evening, Shirun," all of the guests reply in unison.

I'm the only one who remains silent which makes me even more nervous. I try to guess at why I'm the only one confused here, but come up with no logical answer. I don't think I know any Shiruns. I'm not even sure what nationality that name is.

"Thank you all for being here with me tonight," Shirun continues, showing the white of his smile as he speaks. "As you all know, tonight is a very special night. Tonight, we welcome Bryan Daley to our table. Please join me in greeting him formally right now."

All heads turn from Shirun's end of the table to mine and a resounding "Welcome Bryan!" careens into me.

"T-thank you," I manage with a forced smile. "It's great to be here," I add. I haven't the faintest idea of where *here* is, but I don't want to be rude.

The guests all give me approving grins, curt nods, or tips of their wine glasses. I try and put on as happy a face as I can muster,

4

hoping that they will turn back to our host soon. Thankfully, that's just what they do.

Once eyes are back on him, Shirun concludes, "As always, my friends, I hope you enjoy the meal. Afterwards, Jeremy and Natasha will be treating us to a series of cello duets."

Upon making this announcement, Shirun returns to his seat. The guests break into dainty applause which I join in on. Their attentions turn to a man and a woman sitting beside each other toward Shirun's end of the table on my left. They're looking around with toothy grins and slow head bobs so I can only assume that they are Jeremy and Natasha. Jeremy looks like a tall man since his torso and arms are so long. His face is pale and narrow, but the dark brown hair that falls in curls shapes it nicely. Natasha looks like a woman of average height, but very petit. Her shining blonde hair is pulled back into a cylindrical ballerina bun with some pointy strands draped around her high cheeks. Both are wearing silver attire that shimmers a little when light hits it in a certain way.

While studying the pair, I notice that Shirun is most definitely staring at me now if he wasn't before. At least I can finally see him in full detail. He's wearing a black collared shirt with a dark blue vest over it. He has long, ebony bangs carefully swept across his brow and eyebrows that sit low over his piercing eyes in perfect arches. I can't make heads or tails of what ethnic background this man comes from. His skin looks like a sort of Arabian bronze while his dark hair has an East Asian luster to it. His eyes are a crystalline blue color which makes me think he might be part German. His jawline looks strong and shapely like a Spaniard's while his thick nose and plump lips would befit a French gentleman. The more I study him, the more I wonder if his tanned skin isn't South American, if his hair might not be English, or his eyes Russian. The entirety of this man is an enigma. His appearance, his odd name, and his unidentifiable accent all leave me baffled and flustered. What's more is that I still have no idea as to why or how I now find myself at this man's table – at this man's party – in this man's house. I'd also like to know why his sapphire gaze remains fixated upon me. It's rather unnerving and I get an unsteady feeling that this Shirun knows some things that I do not. I'm left to question just what those things might be and whether or not I'm able to trust

5

him.

Eventually, Shirun raises his glass to me with a warm grin and turns his focus back to the meal before him. It's unclear as to what just passed between us. Perhaps we were sizing each other up, or simply taking each other in. Whatever the event, I'm quite grateful to be released from my host's scrutiny. I look down to my own plate and notice for the first time the feast that is set before me – the source of the extravagant holiday aroma which has flooded my senses ever since I came into conscious thought. The spread is so lavish that I'm not quite sure where to start. It's like a multi-course meal was just set upon the table all at once. Feeling overwhelmed again, I look around to the other dinner guests for direction. From the look of things, everyone was picking at a crisp Caesar Salad before Shirun made his announcement. Snatching up my short fork, I nimbly stab into the leafy mix and devour it while trying to also maintain good etiquette. It's mostly just fresh lettuce which while crunchy, isn't too hard to ingest with haste. It helps that the dressing has a tangy kick to it, making me crave another bite as soon as I have swallowed a mouthful. But before I know it, the salad is gone and I am caught up to the others. Lamenting the loss of this appetizer, I set aside the short fork in exchange for a wide soup spoon and scoop up hearty mouthfuls of a warm chicken and basil broth which while light, also has a rich, creamy texture to it along with a delightful herbal scent. After sipping this patiently, we come to the still sizzling slab of stake which is smothered in caramelized onions and peppers. All sorts of aromatic juices seep out as my knife splits open the cut and I feel myself salivate as I take in the sight and smell of this main course.

The steak is as good as it looks. The meat is thick, but not chewy and the sautéed garnish practically melts as soon as it makes contact with my tongue. I savor each bite while trying to keep all of the drool to myself. Time seems to swirl around me protectively until I finish the last bitter-sweet bits of it. Coming back to my surroundings, I see that the others are finishing up as well so I cool my pallet with the orange sherbet that waits behind the rest of my dishes. I'm not quite sure how it has retained the perfect consistency of being partially melted while still fully solid, but I can hardly complain about it. The creamy treat slides down my throat and I realize that I haven't so much as touched my wine. First, I down the cup of ice water before me, and then I take up the wine and start my sociable sipping. It's a warming white wine, a White Zinfandel, perhaps.

"Did you enjoy everything, my dear?" asks the woman to my immediate right.

The question gives me a slight start, but I try not to let that show. It's a little embarrassing that I let myself get so absorbed in the meal, but the lady gives me a knowing smile, which puts some of my anxieties to rest.

"It was overwhelmingly delicious," I tell her.

She chuckles and lightly slaps the tips of her fingers against the table. "Oh yes, everything is always quite marvelous! Shirun's parties serve only the most fulfilling food and drinks."

"I'm glad to have experienced it," I say with the first genuine smile of the evening.

I'm still very confused about all of this, but having shared such an exquisite meal with these people does give me something to discuss with them and I can build on that. What now troubles me is the fact that no cooks or servers are anywhere in sight. It's also strange that the woman made a compliment only to Shirun, not the cooks behind this meal. But surely he didn't put this all together on his own did he? I would hardly expect her to know which chef made what dish, but saying something about the head chef seems far more appropriate than gratifying the host who dined as well as we did.

"Have you been to many of these events then?" I ask her, trying to shoo my ponderings away.

"Oh yes indeed. More than I can count, I should think. We all have, in fact. After all, once you've been to one party, you're bound to come to any that should follow."

Now I find myself uneasy for two new reasons. Firstly, in spite of how warm the welcome is, I feel afraid that I'm to be left out of conversations on account of not having any prior relationship with these people. Secondly, there's the bit about attending any parties that should follow. It almost makes this place sound like a kind of trap, but I'm sure the lady just means that they are so good that no one can refuse an invitation to return to subsequent events.

"So you all must know each other rather well then?" I prod,

hoping to hear about at least one or two other relative newcomers to this crowd.

"I don't know if I'd say that, my dear. I'm far better acquainted with some than with others. The faces are, of course, all familiar – as are the names – but I dare not claim to know or even associate myself with them all."

This brings me some relief to hear. From the sound of it, there are various friend groups within this gathering of people. Perhaps if I am not welcomed into one, I'll find a greater measure of success with another. Out of the corner of my vision, I can see Shirun addressing Jeremy and Natasha. Shortly after, they arise and depart from the table. Shirun, swings his attention towards me so I turn my head a little in order to avoid making further eye contact, however indirect it might be.

"Ah, it seems the entertainment portion of our night is upon us," the lady comments, seeming to notice the development as well. Gently, she lays her somewhat wrinkled hand over mine and stares excitedly at me with her bright eyes. Let me show you around to the others, introduce you properly," she offers.

"I'd like that."

Together we arise and she brings me first to the man who sits immediately to my left – the one with the knightly moustache.

"Bryan, this is Mister Myles Westerly," she says. "He's been a dear friend for as long as memory permits me to recall."

"Hello there, old chap!" Myles bellows as he snatches up my hand and gives it a forceful shake.

"A pleasure," I return while trying to match the gusto of this man's greeting

Myles has a charming grin and a warm twinkle in his eyes, but he's also the sort of man one would do best not to upset. He stands tall, nearly a foot taller than myself, and his physique is an intimidating one indeed.

"How are you enjoying the party so far?" Myles asks once he's released my hand.

"Everything and everyone here is quite incredible I'd say."

"I'd have to agree with that!" He says while giving my arm a brotherly slap.

Retaining his smiling countenance, Myles steps back and

crosses his arms, giving me an odd look all the while. There's something in his gaze that unnerves me, something behind the happy front. It seems to me then that perhaps Myles distrusts me. He seems skeptical, maybe even suspicious of me. It's then that I remember that I am in an utterly unfamiliar place with no notion of how I came to be here. It's quite possible, even very probable, that this is as strange an event for them as it is for me. But before I can think on this too hard, my guide speaks up.

"Myles, I was just about to show Bryan around to some of our better acquaintances. Would you care to join us?"

"Oh, no. Thank you kindly though," Myles hums.

He leans back on his heels and his gaze on me lightens a little. As his mood recovers, so does mine so I send him as enthusiastic a grin as I can muster. The lady beside me slides her arm under and around mine as Myles moves to depart.

"You two enjoy yourselves now," he says while he strides by us. Stopping for a moment and looking back to us he adds, "Should you need to find me again, I'll be on the dancefloor with Miss Shelly Simmons."

"Ah, yes," the lady hums. "You promised her a dance last time, did you not?"

"I sure did," Myles replies, his grin widening a bit. "After all, you never know which dance shall be your last and this one is long overdue."

Without another word, Myles strolls off and the lady tugs me along. Suddenly I realize that I never caught this woman's name. It is a mighty fine thing for her to walk me around like this, but it seems she has neglected the most basic of courtesies. We pass by a man and a woman who appear to be related. They, like my escort, are slightly older in age, but between their neatly kept, dark hair and stylish crimson outfits, they hardly look old at all. They give me an unfriendly glance as we walk by. Thankfully, no introductions are made, but I do wonder how my guide doesn't know them well since they all seem so close in age. In fact, these two are some of the only other people in the room who look even remotely aged. I quickly decide that it doesn't matter. I need to remedy the awkwardness of not knowing my new friend's name before we come upon someone she *does* know.

Not knowing how to politely broach the subject, I blurt out, "One moment, my lady."

She brings us to a halt and turns to me with a gentle smirk. "Everything alright, my dear," she questions.

"Well it's just that while I'm grateful to you for touring me around like this, I am afraid that I must ask you to hold off on all further introductions until you have first introduced me to yourself. Please do forgive me if my manner in this is too abrupt, I simply must know your name before I meet another soul."

I pause for a moment, afraid she'll be offended, but she laughs and pats my wrist with her free hand. "Oh, I'm terribly sorry! I'm Margaret Pembrook."

Before I can say, "*Thank you, Lady Margaret*," she is tugging me along again.

"You'll have to excuse my haste," she explains as we walk. "There are just so many people to meet here and I fear there may be a trifle too little time to meet them all."

I can't help but grin a bit at Margaret's enthusiasm. But before I can comment further, we arrive at Shirun's end of the table where a young man has lingered. There are few others still standing around here as most are now migrated over to the open part of the dining hall which consists of a wide, ivory floor surrounded by long tables covered in silver platters and purple, velvet table cloths. Upon a small stage, I can see Jeremy and Natasha preparing themselves for their performance. Shirun is with them, apparently helping to ensure that they're ready to begin, and a large cluster of people forms nearby. I presume these are people that intend to dance once the music begins. Myles is probably there right now with Shelly.

"William, how are you, my love?" Margaret exclaims as we come up to the man who's staring absently at the scene which I've been studying.

He turns to us with a confused haze over his eyes at first, but his face sparks to life at the sight of Margaret. She releases my arm and snatches up the sides of his cheeks to pull him down for a kiss on each side of his face. When she's done, he takes up her hand and plants a kiss atop it. He looks quite young, perhaps a bit younger than myself. There's also an inescapable flamboyance to his appearance. All of the guests here are certainly well groomed and elegantly dressed, but this man has somehow managed to stand out more than the rest. His hair is combed across his forehead in regular, gentlemanly fashion, but he's apparently taken the time to part his bangs in a series of pointy swathes. This style combined with his hair's rusty brown color rather reminds me of some sort of ancient weapon. His pale blue eyes look equally sharp. His jaw is pronounced, but also narrow whereas his brow is broad. Most striking is how his eyebrows look plucked in a sharp, sloping manner that a woman might sport. He stands at average height with a slender build and pale skin. I can't help but think that he might be quite handsome if not for having such a rigidly composed face.

"How are things with you, Madame Pembrook?" he asks her with his somewhat weaselly sounding voice. For some reason I don't think it fits with his carefully arranged features. I suppose I anticipated a deep, sultry tone, not one that's anxious or hyper.

"Well, I asked you that same question first," she chuckles, giving him a soft pat against his arm. "But I'm quite well, thank you. I'm showing Mister Daley around and thought it might be lovely to introduce him to you."

"It's lovely indeed to make your acquaintance, Sir," he says to me as we shake hands. His grip isn't feeble or dainty by any means, but it does lack a sense of any real vigor or strength. It's a cold, absent-minded sort of greeting.

"It's nice to catch you away from the others," Margaret comments, "But why are you over here instead of enjoying the party? It looks as though the music is about to begin."

"Oh, you know me…" William says a little weakly. He stuffs his hands into the pockets of his statin, blue trousers and turns his frozen gaze down to his white loafers. "Never really much for this part of the party." He looks back up at Margaret like a nervous little boy.

"You stop that!" Margaret scolds, sounding rather motherly in her doing so. "After all, you never know which party could be the last."

William nods, but I feel my stomach drop at this last comment. Why should she say a thing like that? Didn't Myles just make a similar comment as well? Surely there will be more parties for a good long while! Everyone here is all quite young after all, including our host. If the man doesn't feel much like socializing, then he should be allowed to enjoy the evening in his own way.

"Excuse me for just one moment," Margaret chirps before I can say anything in William's defense.

She shuffles off, the ruffled train of her green gown swaying behind her. I turn my attention back to William who's giving me a disinterested, sidelong glance.

"She's a lovely woman," I say — my voice a tad strained.

He simply nods and I start to fear that we will fall into an awkward silence. Then he says, "She worries about me." He steps up to the edge of the table and places a finger over the edge of an empty wine glass. "I try to convince her that I'm perfectly fine and decent, but I imagine she finds me strange all the same." William's attention remains on the glass as he slides his finger in a circular pattern over the crystal's edge.

"It seems to me that Lady Margaret accepts you wholly as you are," I reply, attempting to sound consoling.

He lets out a loud snicker and turns to look at me with a less distant look in his eyes. "No, I know she accepts me, but I doubt very much she understands me and I'm even less convinced that she approves."

I'm quite puzzled by what he means and can only assume we're talking about his obsession with his own appearance — or perhaps his social aloofness. His gaze turns back to the wine glass. It seems to me that he's looking into it regretfully — wishing that there might be a bit more to drink from it. In addition to his unusual choices for shoes and pants, he's wearing a ruffled white shirt which dips rather tastelessly at the chest. It's interesting to me that he shows this part of himself off with so little reserve. His utter hairlessness in that region suggests he might even spend some time shaving it. Maybe he fancies that his body is like a Greek sculpture and endeavors for others to think the same of it. I can't quite tell what the shirt is made of, but guess that it's silk. Over it is a velvet vest in a blue hue, a few shades darker than his pants. Beneath the shirt, I think I also spot the glint of a silver chain. I'm about done scrutinizing William's gaudy dress and mopey demeanor when Margaret returns with someone new in tow.

She's holding the hand of a younger woman and apparently

dragging her along towards us. The woman's arm is pulled taught while she sluggishly follows Madame Pembrook's lead. As they come closer, I see too that this other woman's brow is creased and her pale green eyes stare off into the distance as if to avoid acknowledging myself or perhaps this gentleman beside me. I do hope that it's William she so loathes seeing since I've not been here nearly long enough to have someone dread my company in this manner. Or perhaps it's simply company of any kind which she is averse to.

"Bryan, this is Miss Joanna Turner. William, you've spoken with Joanna on a number of occasions before haven't you?" Margaret's voice is chipper as she and Joanna come to a stop beside us.

I begin to reach out my hand, but Joanna takes a step back and gives me a curtsy. As she does so, I realize that she too has a rather odd appearance about her. Her amber hair is cut in a short bob, not boyishly so, but also not of the common lady fashion from what I've seen so far. She wears a midnight blue dress of shockingly short length. The sparkling silver tassels that hang from its bottom bring the garment down to her calves, but whenever she moves I daresay I can see half of this woman's legs! Much to my shame, I find this as thrilling as I do distasteful.

"A pleasure," she says in a mousy voice as she arises from her curtsy.

I'm struck again by the gaudiness of her silver jewelry and how it compares to her meek voice and disposition. "A pleasure," I return, not wanting to delay in my response.

"I do believe Miss Joanna and I have met on several occasions," William's voice cracks out from behind me.

"Yes, that's right," Joanna confirms and now I'm stuck with the dreadful thought that I'm caught between weasel-man and mouse-lady.

Thankfully, Margaret cuts in with, "You two should go join the others for dancing!"

"Madame, please," William nervously chuckles. "Miss Joanna and I know how to have fun at a party. We don't need you fussing about over us. We're both adults after all."

"Nonsense!" Margaret exclaims with a gentle toss of her

arms into the air. "You may be adults, but you cower from socializing like shy little school children. I do verily insist that you march over there at once and enjoy a good dance, or two, or three!"

Without further argument, William and Joanna give Margaret sheepish grins and follow her instructions. I'm watching them reluctantly take their place on the dance floor when I feel Margaret's arm lock with my own. Again we're meandering along, this time toward one of the long serving tables which line the dance floor. It seems curious to me that I hadn't noticed all of this out here before. It's even stranger that all of the food looks so fresh. Rolls are still steaming and bowls of sorbet haven't melted one bit. But if this was all set out prior to the dinner, then how could this be so? No, this had to have been prepared while we ate, but where are the people that put it all out? Does Master Shirun employ little dinner elves that come and go unseen? Is he some sort of party wizard? I'm about to scold myself for having such ridiculous thoughts, but then I realize that it's the party which is ridiculous, not I.

The music hums out to us from where Jeremy and Natasha play. It's a moaning sort of melody that calms some of my worries. This is just as well too since I'd rather not spend the evening fretting, even if there *is* something amiss. We come up to another young man who seems to be entertaining himself with a platter of eclairs. Because of his slender frame and bright reddish hair, I wonder if he's little more than a boy. His back is turned to us so I can't be sure, but it would certainly be odd to see a child at an event like this so I assume this is just a trick of the eye.

"That's Jack," Margaret whispers to me. "He may seem a bit out of place at these parties, but he's a sweetheart, just a bit shy is all."

I turn my head a little to find that she has her face angled toward me as well. From the glint in her sea-green eyes, I can tell that she is quite fond of this person and I guess that I'll be introduced to him next.

"Jack, darling, I was wondering where you've been hiding!" Margaret pips.

Jack twists around with a surprised spark in his eyes. He sucks the rest of the eclair into his mouth and sends us a puffed-up smile. The chipmunk grin makes his thin, boyish features all the more exaggerated. I can immediately see why Margaret likes him. It's a little surprising though, to see someone so young here. He looks so small, frail even. His Adam's apple bobs as the pastry sinks down his throat, but a smile remains plastered on his face. The grin pulls his freckles over his nose and narrows his already slim eyes.

He takes one last gulp to ensure his mouth is cleared before replying, "Hi, Madame Pembrook!" Even his voice is quite small.

Margaret releases her hold on me and scoots over to Jack with her arms spread wide. She wraps him up in a motherly hug and plants a kiss on his forehead. It's a very casual moment, free of the pomp and circumstance that has marked much of this evening so far. They hold the embrace for a moment before disengaging and turning to me. Margaret opens her mouth to make the introduction when Jack comes up to me with his hand extended.

"Jack Fleming, it's nice to meet you, Mister Daley."

"And a sincere pleasure to meet you, Mister Fleming," I return.

I shake his hand a bit more cautiously than with Myles or William for fear of hurting Jack's slender arm. The boy's grip is strong enough, but even with his square-shouldered suitcoat, his frame still looks quite slim. He also has a different sort of look in his eyes. Whereas Myles looked to me with distrust and William's gaze seemed disinterested, Jack's is more of the wholeheartedly trusting and completely engaged sort. There's something pleasing, comforting even, about having someone look at you like that. In this moment, I feel perfect. I feel that I never have nor ever could do any wrong.

"How are the eclairs?" I ask him as the handshake is released.

His grin drops into a more sheepish one and he glances back to the serving table with some apparent embarrassment. "They're my favorite," he tells me. Already, I can see a look of longing fill his eyes.

"Well I daresay you've had your fill tonight!" Margaret exclaims, her attention drawn to the disturbed platter.

Jack turns to her with a low giggle. He gives her a little shrug when her eyes meet his.

"A few treats won't hurt the boy, I'm sure," I cut in.

I'm not quite sure why anyone would harass such a scrawny boy for eating, unless of course he has a habit of making himself sick with the stuff.

"Let's you and I go and dance for a bit, hmm?" Margaret suggests to him. By the time he can nod in assent, she's already leading him along. "Why don't you sample some of the deserts yourself, Mister Daley," she calls back – giving me what I think is a teasing look over her shoulder. "There's more wine too."

"I'll try to leave some eclairs for you, Jack."

"You better!" he calls back.

I watch as the oldest and youngest of the guests meld in with the crowd which is now twirling and strutting to the aching cello duet. As I look out to the crowd, I catch a glimpse of Myles dancing with a woman who I presume must be Miss Shelly Simmons. She's a pretty, young thing with long blonde curls, sapphire eyes, and is wearing a flowing, snow-white ball gown. Myles is looking intently at her. It's the sort of look which suggests that he is aware of nothing and no one else in that moment. His body moves effortlessly in sync with Shelly's every motion and his face looks utterly serene. It's a scene that warms my heart in a way I can't explain and makes me long to enjoy such a moment with a woman dear to myself. Not wanting to get caught staring, I try to look elsewhere in the room. While most are presently dancing there are some who also entertain themselves with the refreshments so I don't feel entirely left out of the party. Most notably, I spot Shirun at the other end of the room. I can only see him when there's an opening in the sea of dancing figures, but from what glimpses I get, it appears as though he's conversing with a woman. Their conversation seems intense as they are leaning in close and I imagine that they're speaking in low voices.

When I finally get a good look at the lady, I see that she has jet-black hair which falls straight down to her shoulders. Her face is of a fair complexion and is speckled with light freckles. Her light blue eyes meet mine for a moment before another wave of dancers disrupts our line of sight. I note a certain hardness in the way this woman looks at me. A firm purpose fills those eyes, the design of which I cannot begin to guess at. Looking a couple of tables down to my left, I spot the older pair from before – the ones dressed in crimson. They're helping themselves to cannolis and wine, but also seem to have some of their attention directed towards me. They're too far off to hear over the humming music, but I get the unsteady feeling that they're talking about me. Suspicion soon leads to irritation as I stew over how rudely they look and gesture at me. I understand that introductions can be uncomfortable, but this type of behavior is just unseemly, especially for people their age.

Perturbed, I snatch up an eclair and turn away from them. It smells of rich chocolate and feels silky, yet firm in my hand. I'm not sure if I will treasure these as much as Jack does, but they certainly do seem like magnificent little morsels. As I bite into it, I find that the pastry is a perfect balance between flaky and smooth. The chocolate frosting on top is the best that I have ever tried and the cream filling tastes smooth and cool, almost like vanilla iced cream. There's really no comparison to how delectable this treat is and I suddenly understand why Jack eats them by the half-dozen. Then I come to another discovery. On the front portion of the silver platter where eclairs no longer lay, I catch a reflection of my own face. It's instantly familiar to me and I feel ashamed for ever forgetting it.

It's a distorted image, but enough to help me recall my angled forehead, thick nose, square jaw, and shallow cheeks. Even though I'd suspected that I was a handsome enough man to fit in here, having this confirmed for me does wonders for easing any insecurities regarding this matter. From what I can tell, my thick, brown hair is indeed neatly arranged and my face is clean shaven. In spite of all the relief that I feel, I can't help but remain a little uneasy that I ever forgot my own appearance to begin with. Wouldn't it have been *I* that shaved my face and combed my hair? Wouldn't I remember doing these things? What sort of place is this where one can forget their own face and glorious helpings of food can be set without mention of a chef or the presence of any servers?

"Wonderful aren't they?" a voice behind me proclaims.

My body freezes up with a start and my head twists to find that Shirun has somehow come up beside me without my notice. I nod my head quickly and then put on a smile, trying to be polite in concealing my surprise.

"Everything here is positively exquisite, Mister Shirun," I tell him honestly.

Shirun's expression brightens a little and he releases a light, but hearty laugh. "That's very kind of you to say, but you can't have all good and no bad, can you? Surely there is someone or something here you are less than fond of."

I consider telling him about the pair to our left and their rudeness, but that would be a bit inconsiderate, not to mention cause for needless hubbub. I think about discussing how odd of a fellow William is, but it occurs to me that to do so would be cruel since I hardly know the man. Then there's the matter of the chefs and servants, or lack thereof. This last topic is one that I am burning to broach with someone, but looking into Shirun's piercing – almost mesmerizing – eyes, I decide not to bring this up either. Looking to the table where the food is set, I swear that the eclair platter has somehow been refilled. At no point did I notice or hear anyone come by to restock it, yet in the time it took me to turn to Shirun and turn back to the table, the once half-empty platter is now brimming with eclairs again. Now I really wonder if Shirun isn't a magician of sorts and conclude that I should most definitely not make mention of my noticing these strange goings on.

"This is simply the best party I have ever attended," I explain, finally – turning my focus away from the magic platter and back to Shirun.

I'm satisfied with this answer since it rings true to how I actually feel. But then it occurs to me that I have no recollection of any parties that came before. In fact, I have no memory of anything at all. I don't have any notion of what I do for work. I don't know where I live or whether I have any family to speak of. I don't really know anything about myself or my relation to Shirun. As I ponder over these things, I find that the éclair is now a far less agreeable presence in my stomach and can feel a heat start to build up around my temples. Shirun appears pleased with my prior statement so I try to hide the panic that now swells up within me. Not seeming to notice my distress, Shirun throws an arm around the back of my shoulders and leads me along to the table's end where rows of Champaign glasses are set up.

"I'd to like to hold a private toast," he explains, "Just you and I."

With a light touch, he takes up one of the glasses and hands it to me. Then he picks up another, keeping his hold on me all the while. Looking around I see that we are indeed in a rather private spot here in the back left corner of this hall. At the center of this back wall is the small stage where Jeremy and Natasha's performance keeps our voices from going very far. Most of the guests are a few paces off and wrapped up in the steps of their dance. I don't know why it bothers me to be so isolated from the others, but I feel a distinct sense of vulnerability in being secluded here with only Shirun in my company. It's not that I don't like Shirun, but it does feel as though there is a great deal he's hiding from me. A part of me wants for it to remain that way. If Mister Shirun tells me too much, then the magic of this place might fall apart. But if I don't get some answers from someone soon, I might explode with anxiety.

"To having you here with us," Shirun begins, holding a glass aloft. "May you find yourself anew in our company. May we face adversities together and show one another support throughout the darkest of moments."

"To you and your fine guests and your exemplary refreshments," I add, finding this whole toast to be a tad heavy, and rather odd in its nature.

"Welcome to the manor," Shirun finishes as we clink the tips of our glasses together.

Before I can take a sip, the ringing from the glass grows louder in my ears. I look to Shirun with a furrowed brow and unsteady knees. The ringing starts to pierce into my brain and my balance feels as though it may shatter at any moment. My visions blurs, but I feel Shirun's tight hold supporting me. A blinding white light then engulfs me and all other sensations slowly slip away save for the feeling that I am slowly being lowered down further and further into this glowing abyss.

# Chapter 2

My eyes snap open only to see more white. I can hear myself panting and feel my heart thumping inside of my chest. But then I realize that I'm just looking at a ceiling – my ceiling. I'm at home, in my apartment bedroom. Chiming next to me is my alarm clock, also known as my cell phone. I roll over in bed and snatch it up. The sound isn't quite the same as the ringing that filled my ears while I was asleep, but it's close enough to make my head ache so I frantically swipe the screen to make it go away. I roll over onto my back and toss the device down beside me. Pinching the bridge of my nose, I try to block out the images from my bizarre dream.

Nothing makes sense to me while I think about it. What was with the prim and proper Oxford accents? Why would I dream up such an old-school sort of party and why were all of my thoughts like something from a Jane Austen novel? Am I honestly still offended that that lady, Joanna, wore a dress that showed off her ankles and teased her calves? More importantly, why do I remember it so vividly? Everything from Shirun's confusing appearance to Margaret's soothing voice is stuck in my mind. Aren't these kinds of things supposed to be fuzzy when you wake up? But every second I spent in the dream and every "person" I met there feel as real as anything I've come across in real life. For a while, I just lay there, waiting to see if those memories will become more ... well more dreamy. But they don't. So I pull off the covers and notice that they are a little warmer than I'd expect. I pat the sides of my black boxer briefs and feel the front of my forehead and decide that I've neither been sweating, nor am I feverish so I can't for the life of me explain why I had such a weird dream.

My head is still spinning by the time I wander into the bathroom so I decide that it's going to be a long shower for me this morning. Turning the faucet up to hot, I wait for the steam to start rising, pull off my boxers and climb in. Even with the smell of shampoo and body wash in the air and the warm water beating against my skin, I can't bring myself to relax. The faces of all the people from last night still fill my mind – their voices echo through my ears. It all feels way too real for a dream. But the thing is, I'm not some crazy person or anything. I don't think people actually have out-of-body experiences, I don't believe in ghosts or spirits, and I'm not even meditative in any way. I never have nor will I ever adopt a religion of any kind so I don't have any of that mumbo-jumbo running through my head either. Call me a jerk, but I just don't take any of that kind of stuff seriously. This dream though, *that* I'm taking *very* seriously.

I'm also getting annoyed with myself so I rinse the suds out of my hair and decide to cut the Roman shower down to a normal one. I've only just reached for the towel hanging on its hook when my phone goes off on the sink counter. I do a haphazard towel off before wrapping the cloth around my waist and picking the phone up. While I'm well aware that I could just continue drying off, there's something that seems wrong about talking to someone while you're naked, even if the person on the other end of the line would never know. I see that it's Kayla calling so I swipe the answer icon just as the last ring is about to finish.

"Hey babe," I answer.

"God, there you are, I thought you'd never pick up!"

Her voice sounds like one of those TV detectives as they're about to break the suspect and solve the crime. It's not exactly what I need on a morning like this, but I know better than to snap back – that would drive her from overzealous detective to full on ice queen in about half a second. Instead I wonder if she likes to talk on the phone naked…I hope she does.

"Was just hopping out of the shower," I explain.

"Running late then?" She asks, though the question sounds a lot more like an accusation.

I pull the phone away from my ear and check the time to see that I'm definitely running a bit behind. I figure I must have just laid in bed a little longer than I meant to and now I'm even more annoyed with how this morning is going.

"Yeah," I reply. "Guess I didn't sleep very well."

"Alright, well I'm feeling dinner at Zarello's tonight. Gonna be a long day for me, I think, so I just wanted to make sure you keep your schedule clear. But yeah, I'll let you go now. I don't want to wait around for you to get out because you got in late. Alright well, love ya, byee!"

With that, she hangs up. There's nothing left to say, so I lay the phone back down on the counter. I suddenly find myself feeling angry as I finish drying off. Angry that I mentioned something was off with me and all she worried about was me being late for dinner. Then there was the way she hung up. She dropped her typical "love ya, byee!" thing and cut me off before I could say goodbye too. How many times has she done that to me? When was the last time *I* got to say goodbye? When was the last chance *I* got to tell Kayla that I love her?

I try to just focus on getting myself dressed. Black shirt, grey pants, black shoes, silver tie, and my navy fall jacket. Even by the time I've slid on my silver Kolex watch and clipped my black belt in place, I'm still pissed off. It occurs to me that I can't remember the last time that *I* made the dinner plans…or *any* plans. I head down the open-design curling staircase of my apartment suite and rush through my living room into the kitchen. Like most mornings, there isn't much time to just hang around, so I just snatch up my laptop bag from beside the kitchen island counter and sling the strap over my shoulder. I give the lower floor of my suite a quick look-over before heading out the door – shutting it harder than I mean to. As I walk down the complex hall, my thoughts alternate between the fancy party in my dreams and the aggravation I feel towards Kayla. This continues as I take the gold colored elevator down to the parking garage and hop into my silver Wersedes sedan. The drive to the office is long since I failed to get in before the morning traffic. By the time I pull into the company parking garage, I'm not really looking forward to doing much at all. As crazy as it is, all I really want to do is go to another one of Shirun's parties. I wonder if I might go to one tonight. But I know that's ridiculous. It was just a dream. You don't really get to go back into a dream.

I try to keep my head down as I make my way into the office. For the most part, no one really bothers me. I only get a "Good morning," from our receptionist, Ronda.

"Hello," I chime back. I may be in a pissy mood, but I could never be rude to old Ronda.

She has her long, silver hair in supermodel curls and wears magenta lipstick that complements her blue mascara. At first glance, someone might get the impression that she's a woman who didn't get the memo that she's almost into her sixties. But you spend about five seconds with her and you realize that she's just a sweetheart trying to age with style. Her greeting brings a light smile to my face – it always does. I pass through the lobby and into the office space where I eventually come to my workstation. It might be a cubicle, but it has taller walls than most and is way more spacious. It's one of the perks of being a Manager, but it's still not a real office. I'm young enough though, so I think I can get there eventually.

I snap my laptop into its docking station and boot it up. The framed pictures of Kayla and I in various places around the city remind me that I'm mad at her. I wonder why I have all of this sudden hurt. Kayla didn't do anything bad necessarily. So, why do I feel so angry? Where is it all coming from and why now? When my desktop loads up, I immediately open up my email. It's not like I don't check it at home, but there's nothing quite like the morning email rush. Normally I enjoy it with some coffee, but I managed to slip in without much notice and I'd rather people didn't catch on to my late arrival this morning. So I indulge in my email, but hold off on the coffee for now. Scanning through, it's a calmer morning than I expected. There's a blood drive on Thursday that HR is pleased to remind us all about. I hate needles, so I'll definitely be skipping that. Some activist committee wants volunteers for … nope don't care – just some shmucks with *way* too much time to waste during operational hours. Kayden Packard is being a douchebag again. No Idea what he's got up his ass this week, but he's already my worst nightmare and it's only Tuesday. Kelly Parke wants to know if she can sign up for a training seminar, sure Kelly – approved. Then there are all the random awareness emails which I skim through before I hear a light tapping at the back of my cube-office.

I spin in my chair to see that it's David. We started at the same time and hit it off well, but now he's got a real office and thinks he's a cool shit because of it. I think the ass-wipe just got lucky.

"Hey Bryan," he says swiping his arching bangs with a thumb.

The man's hair is so thick that not a strand would drift out of place if it wanted to so he looks ridiculous every time he does this.

"What's going on, David?" I greet him, trying to sound happy about his standing in my cube.

"Just wanted to swing by and let you know that the post-production patch seems to have eliminated the worst of those bugs. I'll send out a formal thanks to you and your team, but I figured I'd give you the news first thing."

He's upbeat and smiley about it all, but he and I both know I was a couple of days away from getting thrown under the bus by him. He's only been above me for about half a year and he's never actually made a scapegoat out of me, but this last software package got released with some pretty substantial bugs. If my team hadn't pulled together and got it ironed out, we'd have been roasted for sure.

I try to put on a convincing grin for him and say, "Thanks, I appreciate you coming by to let me know." As if I need him to tell me how my software package is doing…having the official word is nice, yeah, but it's like this guy thinks he just brought me breaking news or something. Instead of being a jerk, I just say, "I know my team will be happy to see that email since they've been working overtime to get this thing sorted out. We were all a little apprehensive about the product release date leaving such a short QA window and it's been no small thing to compensate for that."

I know it's completely unnecessary to throw that last bit in there considering all the heat that David's taken from higher-level leadership. But I can't help but toss this little dig in here since it's his job to protect us from executive bullshit like this. He's probably still adjusting to the new role and all of its responsibilities, but that's not my problem, it's his – it's what comes with getting a fancy little office and an even fancier pay raise. So my sympathy for him is pretty thin, all things considered. There's something about the way that he's timidly standing at the entrance to my cube, though. Maybe it's the downtrodden glaze over his normally bright brown eyes. Or it could be the way he's rubbing the back of his cropped brown hair that makes me feel like *I'm* the one terrorizing *him*. This makes me all the more irate since I've been the one putting up with his constant status checks and offers to pull in other resources. *Other resources!* He might as well just tell us that we suck and should find new jobs. What I better be detecting is guilt. He also better be grateful because with or without tossing us into the lion's pit, he'd still have been in deep shit with the higher-ups he reports to. He's got to know this because he hasn't said anything yet. He's just nodding with some semblance of a smile still on his face.

"I'll be sure to emphasize how grateful I am for their performance under less than flexible circumstances," he announces finally.

I assume this is as close to an apology as I can hope for. David pivots on his heel as if he's about to leave, but then turns back toward me. His jaw looks slack as though he's about to say something so I cock my eyebrow and wait patiently for whatever else he's got to tell me.

"Kevin, Erin, and Devon bumped into me last night," he starts. "They were filling up with gas after a movie and I'd been here late so the timing was just sort of by chance. Anyway, they invited me to come with them out to The Commons for a live performance or something tonight. They mentioned that they'd like to see you too if you're free."

I pause for a minute. I'm a little stunned since David and I haven't really been social in almost a year's time. I also feel bad since there's probably no chance Kayla will change plans to eat at her favorite restaurant.

"I told Kayla I'd meet her for dinner at Zarello's. What time are you guys meeting?"

"Six-thirty I think. The show is at seven, but Devon and I will probably grab a couple of drinks first."

"Not sure I'll be able to make it. The restaurant is on the other end of the city."

"Sure, no biggie, of course. It's just a last minute thing – they didn't even know they were going until about an hour or two before they ran into me. I just wanted to make sure you got the invitation too."

"I appreciate that," I state coolly. Catching my indifference, I follow up with, "If Kayla's fine with changing the plans, then maybe we could both head there after eating somewhere closer to

The Commons."

"Yeah, just let me know," David says, his full smile reforming. "I should get to that email now, thanks again for working so hard."

With that, David springs out of my cube and is out of sight. I think about returning to my email, but now feels like a really good time for a coffee, so I lock my screen and head into the break room. When I'm back at my desk—with a steaming foam cup in hand—I decide that I'd like to call Kayla. The sooner I catch her in her day, the more likely she is to be flexible with the plans. I pick her out of my recent contacts, but hesitate. My thumb hovers over the call button and I wonder why I suddenly dread this conversation so much. Maybe it's because I know she has her heart set on Zarello's. It could be that I've been reamed out for this kind of thing before, or maybe I'm just being a little bitch. Pushing aside my reluctance, I tap the screen and bring the phone up to my ear. It rings for a little while and I start to think that Kayla isn't going to pick up – maybe her showing has already started. Then the ring tone clicks off and I hear Kayla's voice come through.

"Hey Bryan," she answers. For some reason, it seems to me like she's surprised I called.

"Hi babe, sorry, are you doing the showing yet?"

"The buyers should be just about here, why what's up?"

"David stopped by my cube this morning –"

"Oh how is he? Has it been a while since you guys talked? I thought you were in the same group and stuff."

I feel myself cringe a little. I guess that I've never really told her about my new working relationship with him. I think she knows that he got a promotion while I did not, but apparently she has no idea that I report up to him now. And she clearly has no notion of how he's been on the edge of selling me and my team out for the last month. I feel guilty at first.

I silently ask myself, *"Am I a bad boyfriend? Am I shutting Kayla out of my life?"*

But then I have to wonder: does she not know because I'm hiding things or does she not know because she doesn't care to know? I'm not sure where this idea comes from, but it starts to gnaw away at me.

"Things have definitely been different between us," I reply, trying to mask my newfound irritation. "Anyway, he mentioned that he and some of our old friends are meeting up at The Commons tonight at six-thirty to see a show of some kind that starts at seven."

"And he invited you to join them…" she finishes flatly.

"Right. That's obviously not doable if we're eating at Zarello's since we'd be across the city so I told him I'd probably need to decline. But I wanted to call and see if maybe you'd like to do Zarello's tomorrow night and find someplace closer to The Commons tonight. It might be fun to try and catch the show. I know I'd really like to see some of the old crew again. Then we could head over to my apartment afterwards. I'm pretty much right there anyway. Plus it's been a while since you've been over to my place so it'd be cool to have you with *me* for a night."

There's an uncomfortably long pause on the other end. At first, I hope that there is just an interruption in the cell service, but then I hear a muffled sigh and a sinking feeling formulates inside of my chest.

"We made plans, Bryan," she reminds me coolly.

"I know – I know that. I'm not saying we should change them. I just wanted to see if you'd like to mix things up a little. Just be different for a night and catch up with some old friends. I don't mean to try and back out of anything, just wanted to let you know about a different option."

"Listen, Bryan," Kayla snaps. "I think this is the buyers rolling in now, so here's the deal. I'm under the gun to get this house sold and if anyone's gonna buy it, it's this couple. I'm going to be tired and stressed so I want to go to Zarello's and then we'll go to *my* apartment, like we normally do. Honestly, I think you're a little selfish to suggest that we do otherwise. As for mixing it up, I don't think we need to. I'm happy with the way things are and I'm happy with the plans. If you feel differently, then maybe we need to talk about that, but I gotta go so I'll see you at Zarello's tonight."

"Okay, wait, I didn't mean any –"

"Bry, I gotta go," she whines.

"Right, sorry, see you at Zarello's then. I lo –" I stammer when the line clicks off.

There that is again – me getting cut off before I can say

"goodbye" or "love you." Losing all interest in my phone, I just toss it onto my neatly kept desk. It makes a bit of a thud when it hits which probably startles a couple of my direct reports, but it's got a protective case so I don't really care. I just sit there for a while looking through but not actually reading my emails. I think maybe I should be angry about that exchange, but I just feel cold instead. There's this sort of apathy that takes over. I do wonder whether I deserved to get chewed out like that, but I'm not necessarily bothered that it happened. My thoughts drift, instead, back to my dream. I feel a sense of longing for the "people" I met there. I want to have my arm linked with Madame Margaret's. I want her to lead me along and introduce me to all sorts of strange and interesting characters. I also wish that people – real people – would look at me the way Jack did. When his baby blue eyes met mine, I could only see love and trust in them. I didn't get the sense that he wanted to be anywhere else with anyone else. He didn't ask anything of me nor did he seem to have his own agenda. In that moment, the company of Margaret and I were his whole world. That's a feeling I will never forget, even if it wasn't real.

I'm forced to compare this to how David looked at me a few minutes ago. It was a far more hardened look. One that didn't really convey joy for being in my presence and certainly didn't indicate trust of any kind. But I, of course, don't trust him either so I guess that makes us even. Come to think of it, it's possible that I *never* trusted him to begin with. It's true that we came in as equals. We both came in as twenty-two-year-old new graduates with bright minds and eager attitudes. We shared common interests, common goals, and identical challenges to face. Some coworkers nicknamed us "the dynamic duo" and sometimes joked about how much time outside of work we spent together. Obviously things feel different now, but I wonder if we weren't always at odds with each other and just didn't realize it. Were we always competing – racing to see who could get on top the fastest? Was it only a matter of time before one of us overcame the other?

As if on cue, a notification appears on my screen indicating that David's thank you message has come through. I open it to find that it's basically the same as what he said to me before. I'm not really sure what I expected, but for some reason I'm surprised by the level of sincerity in the way the message reads. It makes me think of the mild tone David used before. Then I recall the hesitant way in which he brought up the invitation to join him tonight. I wonder why he'd have such a change of attitude towards me after all the hell he put me through. Then I question whether he was ever my enemy at all during this past month. This doubt burrows into my mind until I impulsively start to go through old emails. I pour through all the status requests and examine all the meeting invitations, but find nothing to justify how I feel towards David. In each and every message, he sounds nothing but supportive. He's borderline fatherly in the way he prods us for updates and asks if we need assistance.

I'm left to ask myself, *"Am I just being crazy?"*

I try to think because I know I'm not crazy. I wouldn't just choose to imagine slights like the ones I know David is guilty of. And I know that I'm not simply wrong about this. There had to have been some things said during meetings or maybe just the cool and calculated way that he conducted himself. It's easy to sound civil – even kind – in an email. Anyone can do it, especially in the cutthroat software industry where we're all pros with electronic interaction. And ultimately, nice words alone won't cut it when you fail to protect the people beneath you from the telltale red flags in software development. In this industry, it's all about coming up with unique and worthwhile ideas and then making those concepts into a technical reality. But there's a lot that goes into it. There are business needs to define, designs to develop, prototypes to build and test, and then a whole lot of coding voodoo that's got to happen before you can actually sell something. Marketing, sales, usage stats, and technical support all come into play as well. The bottom line is that the process takes a lot of time and it really mucks things up when a bunch of executives decide they want to push up our production release in order to beat a competitor to the market. This is what happened with my team's product.

Parson International creates cutting edge financial, accounting, and managerial software solutions. It's a niche industry, but a very competitive one and there's a lot of revenue on the line. I wouldn't say that every product we come out with is insanely original or inspired. A lot of the time we're releasing a superior version of something that already exists or taking the idea of a competitor's product and recreating it in a different way. My team was tasked with creating a new addition to our project management package called TrackRite. We made an extension which allows users to view and track team members' planned days off right within the program proper, whereas that sort of thing is generally stored on each person's calendars and shared only when a manager either looks for it or asks their direct reports to send it to them. It also runs automated calculations for how many hours the team has available within a given period of time based on prior input from the people involved in a project team. We packaged this, along with several other smaller extensions, into our newest version of TrackRite, TrackRite VII.

Because Parson is known for doing things first, we came up with the brilliant plan of rushing this thing out the door. My team's extension was entirely unique in terms of competitor offerings and served as the major selling point of our new version so we would've been fine releasing on time. Apparently a couple of our other additions are similar to features included in the latest versions of our competitors' products and this just wouldn't do. Now maybe David really was just a messenger for this change, but I almost guarantee he made some type of moronic promise to his superiors that my team could make the new deadline without major issues. Either way, our testing window got downsized and an embarrassing number of errors showed up in the finished product. Maybe I shouldn't be so sour about it all, it's not like our group was the only one with bugs to fix. We just had most of them. *Shockingly* enough, we got almost all of them ironed out by the time we were *supposed* to have everything ready for originally. This makes a nice case for the company not pulling this type of crap again and gives me some "I told you so" rights, though I'll want to be careful about how I exercise them, of course. David probably knows this too which is why he's playing so nice. But I should play along. I click the "reply all" button on David's message and compose a simple follow up:

David,

I agree with all of your points completely! I'm very grateful to the team for all their hard work. We really pulled through under less than favorable circumstances and I think we finally have a product that the company can be proud of.

As always, your support is very much appreciated.

Sincerely,
Bryan Daley
Manager, Organizational Software Solutions
Parson International

I give it a once over and decide that I'm happy enough with it. The message is gracious, but doesn't ignore the point that my team completed our objectives in spite of him and the odds stacked up against us. Five patches after the release and a solid week of long shifts and weekend hours later and I can finally breathe. I have a number of personal thank you notes to send to the people on my staff as well as managers of other teams that meddled with our shit … I mean leant us a hand. A few minor bug reports come in as I'm crafting my messages which keep my staff occupied, but not overly busy. It's a relatively easy day compared to how the last couple of weeks went. Eventually, the end of the workday rolls around and I start to get an uneasy feeling that dinner will not go as smoothly.

# Chapter 3

I arrive at Zarello's at 4:45 PM and take a seat. The hostess knows not to send anyone to wait on me until Kayla arrives so I have a bit of solitude for now. It feels good to be out of the office. There's a light din of conversation buzzing about the room which keeps things from feeling too lonely. It's strange how good it feels to just sit here by myself. It's stranger still how little I want my state of isolation to change. I don't even try to listen to the dialogue around me. I notice a few of the people at the surrounding tables, sure. There's a pair of women – sisters maybe – dressed up in business attire, a table of four older gentlemen – all in suits, a man and a woman, seemingly early along in their relationship and both dressed in casual, but clearly designer attire, and a party of three women taking their seats at a booth, all wearing fancy jackets and sparkling smiles. I'm sure any one of these tables would be interesting enough to eavesdrop on, especially one with the three ladies, but for some reason, I just don't want to. I want to sit here, with myself and no one else in my company, not on my mind, not in my ear, and not even really in my sight. The world around me seems to fade out of focus. It all just blurs into the delicate haze of the restaurant and I fall into my own thoughts.

I think back to the party in my dream and can't seem to shake the desire to be back there. In spite of all the strangeness there was something enchanting about that place – something perfect even. Maybe it's just that things there felt so different from my normal life, my typical routine. Every day its work, then dinner with Kayla, then us hanging out, then the gym unless I ran that morning, then some chores around the apartment before I finally go to sleep – assuming I don't need to get something done for work. It's a good life, I think, but apparently it's not enough. I mean if I really want to live in a dream that I will probably never have again, then something must be missing, right?

David's invitation crosses my mind again. The guy's single,

has been for a while. While my life is probably a lot better than his overall, I can't help but feel jealous of him tonight. I haven't seen Kevin, Erin, or Devon in what feels like forever. I used to see Erin every now and then since she'd join David and I for lunch. She worked nearby, can't remember the name of the place now, but it was literally a block or two down from The Parson Tower. Her and David might still meet up every now and then, but I don't think so, I'm pretty sure she got a job someplace else in the city or maybe her office just moved, yeah I think that's it. And even *that* bit of news I think I got from Friendbook – it's been a while since I've talked to her in person. And what about Devon and Kevin and … well, I guess I never really want to see Julie again, but what's been keeping me from seeing the rest of them? Am I really just that busy? Or is someone or something keeping me from them? It's probably not fair to blame Kayla for this in general, but it's certainly her fault that I'm not seeing them tonight.

My anger towards Kayla thickens when I see her step into Zarello's reception area. Everything comes back into detail for me. The light hum of conversation, the rich smell of marinara and garlic, and the wide room of neatly arranged tables. Beyond it all is my woman scanning the scene skeptically as if expecting not to find me. She turns her attention to the young redhead working as a hostess. The girl points in my direction and Kayla's expression softens as her blue eyes finally fall upon where I sit. She departs from the hostess without turning back and saunters towards my table. Her steps are long and deliberate. With each stride, her hips sway in wide, purposeful arches. Her business skirt is wrapped tightly around her legs, but doesn't seem to impede her at all. The aisle becomes her catwalk and I, her mesmerized audience. The hazy light of the restaurant falls upon her in an enchanting way – the effect enhanced by how the crystal chandeliers give off a small sparkle. It all creates a brilliant sheen over her midnight hair which trails behind her like a silk veil. These short moments stretch out gloriously and all I can do is smile as she reaches the table and twists down into the seat opposite mine. She slings her black purse over the top of her chair and flips her long hair so that it is pulled over her shoulder on one side. It hangs like satin along the side of her face in a way that she must know drives me wild.

"Hey," she hums sweetly.

"Hey," I return – a smile in my heart to match the one on my face.

She scoops up the menu and begins scrutinizing its contents, even though I'm sure she already knows what she wants. I suddenly feel my face drop and a sour taste forms in my mouth. How many times has she walked in like an angel and greeted me with her honey voice? How many times have I been ticked off at her only to have my temper soften into putty?

"How was your day," I ask, craning my head up so as to peek at her over the menu she's got covering her face.

She taps the smooth back of it with an opal fingernail. There's silence for a moment as though I'm interrupting her. Then she slaps the menu shut and sets it down over our circular table.

"It went alright," she sighs. There's another pause as her eyes meet mine. "I think the showing went okay, as good as it could have gone, really. It's just that the sellers are trying to get above market value for the home. If anyone's going to make a purchase, it'll definitely be the Kensons. They've got the money, they don't want to be too close to neighbors or the road, and they'd like to have a decently large house. The Madbury Place meets all of those things, but this couple is smart and I think they know the home's overpriced. They liked it and I think they think it's nice, but we all know it's not *that* nice."

She lets out another sigh and taps her fingers on the menu. I look down at mine for a moment which is spread open on the table before me.

"I'm sure you gave it the best showing possible," I offer.

"I know I did, but I can only upsell an older house like that so much. It's really going to come down to how much they want the location's unique perks. I tried to focus on those. That way, even if they choose to walk away, they'll at least feel conflicted about it. It just sucks because my branch coordinator is demanding that I close this sale and the Kensons are pretty much my only shot of making that happen.

"Yeah, you were saying that before, but can you really get in trouble for not selling a home that's more than it's worth?"

Immediately after I ask this, I feel kind of stupid. If I can get grilled alive for not making a deadline that is earlier than the pre-agreed upon one, then she can probably get in trouble for this kind of thing. Real Estate may not be Software Development, but it's all the same shit, just a different industry.

"Well no, not exactly I guess," Kayla admits, leaning back in her chair. "Like, I can't really get fired or anything, but it seems like this is my best shot to impress him — my branch manager that is. If I can sell this thing then he'll probably start trusting me with bigger sales, meaning better commissions for me, but if I muck this up, then it's back down to the little leagues. Hell, I'll probably be lucky to get the mediocre single-family units that I got when I first started."

Her bottom lip droops into a pout. In spite of the purple lip gloss and onyx eyeliner, I can't help but think that Kayla looks remarkably childish right now. I force myself to grin as I search for something reassuring to tell her.

At last I reply, "Whatever happens, you can at least say you did your best. If the house doesn't sell, I'm sure Frank will understand. You may even be able to make a case for the owners to lower their price and then maybe a sale will be a more reasonable undertaking."

Before Kayla can respond, a tall, skinny, blonde lady arrives at our table. She has rich brown eyes, plump pink lips, and breasts much larger than I'd expect from someone with such a slight build. Her uniform is conservative enough, a black blouse with grey slacks, and black flats, but she manages to make it seem skimpy, the way she fills it out.

"How are the two of you doing today," she chirps. I'd guess that she's at least a couple of years out of college.

"We're doing good," I tell her, even though that's probably not true. It strikes me as funny that I can so habitually lie when answering this question.

"Great!" she sings as though we could possibly give her any other answer. "Can I start you off with something to drink?"

"Strawberry Margarita for me," Kayla orders without delay.

When our server looks to me, I hesitate. Normally I just get a draft beer of some kind — an IPA or Lager usually. But tonight, I'd like something a little stronger than that.

"Sorry," I say as I snatch up the drink menu. "I typically just get a beer, but I'd like to try something else now that I think about it."

"No worries," the waitress replies, patting the air with her hand. "Our House Spiked Iced Teas and Rum and Cokes are pretty successful crowd pleasers most of the time. If either of those sounds good, I can get you one or I can just circle back in a few once you've had a look at our menu."

"The Iced Tea sounds good, let's give that a shot."

I see Kayla cock a sculpted eyebrow at me as I set the drink menu back down. Our waitress scribbles down my drink and looks back at us brightly.

"Alrighty, would you like an appetizer or anything?"

"Actually I think we're ready to just go ahead and order now," Kayla tells her. There's a snotty sort of superiority in her reply that sounds like she's partially talking through her nose.

"Oh, good, okay. What will it be for you then?" The waitress stands poised with her pen and notepad in hand. I can't help but notice then that her butt is extremely defined – it's just the way she's standing with her hips twisted to one side that brings this to my attention.

"I'll take an Emperor's Caesar Salad with a side of Pallamero Spinach Dip," she recites.

"Great, now is that the regular Caesar or the Chicken Caesar?"

"No, the regular one."

"And you?" the waitress asks turning to me.

"Could I get the Chicken and Pastina Bowl?"

"Sure thing," she says as she notes it down.

She stuffs the notepad into her apron pock which bears the loopy "Z" shape that appears in the company logo. Our menus are gingerly scooped up and then the woman zips off as quickly as she came. During the order I'd dreaded the continuation of my initial conversation with Kayla. I haven't told her about *my* day yet and while it wasn't a bad day, I'm not sure I want to revisit it either. But the question of how things are with me never comes. Instead I hear about the other realtors at her branch and the gems of properties they've been assigned to. Literally a few seconds is all it takes for me to check out of this monologue. I'm hearing the general gist of what she's saying, but we've had this same sort of *"conversation"* hundreds of times already. Our drinks arrive and she's still going on about how unfair it all is, then the topic drifts to more socially oriented gossip about her coworkers. I guess some lady named Madison, who's a bitch and has been getting properties over in the Westminster Estates, is about to come out of the closet. There's Jimmy who I guess people have discovered used to be a porn star – though the details of how this discovery was made have not been divulged. Suffice it to say that several people, Kayla included, validated this claim. There's a bunch more bla bla bla and then something about how she has it on good authority that a senior realtor named Julianne is cheating on her husband. How Kayla always manages to find out all of these things is something I've never gathered from these talks. She's only really been working at this place for eight months, but you'd never know it if you overheard these rants of hers.

As the monologue drones on, I start to get a conflicting pair of emotions. On one hand, I feel let off the hook for not having to share my day. On the other, I'm pissed that she hasn't cared to ask. I need to wonder if she knows *anything* about what I have going on in my life when I'm not with her.

"*Of course she does,*" I tell myself, but I'm not entirely convinced.

I'm sure I've at least mentioned that things have been rough lately or that she's maybe picked up on it, but I definitely haven't talked about it in detail with her. Finally, our meal arrives, cutting off the flow of *"dialogue."* Our table falls quiet when the waitress leaves us again. I take another sip from my drink while my eyes follow the waitress down the aisle until she's gone. It's then that I realize that the beverage is already half gone. It also dawns on me that I'm not really sure that I've tasted a single sip of it. So I take another to find that it's definitely good. It has a sweet, but not too sugary flavor to it and there's a hint of lemony bitterness mixed in, which I love. It's smooth and tangy and I definitely do not regret giving this a try. Kayla's margarita is already demolished and she's now sipping from ice water in between bites of her salad. Looking down at my own plate, I feel a disturbing lack of desire to eat. The warm Italian aroma that made my stomach groan before no longer has much appeal.

"Things have been a bit better for me," I announce before taking a bite of my pasta.

"Oh good!" she hums. For a brief moment, I feel relieved that she does know what's been going on at my job, but then she asks, "Have things been a little stressful for you then?"

My heart skips a beat as I hear her ask this. But then a bitter thought crosses my mind – that I shouldn't be surprised by this at all. It takes everything I have to contain myself.

"Yeah," I respond simply, but there's an unmistakable edge to my tone.

"Well it's good that it's better now right?"

"Right"

I turn back to my dinner without another word. A cool silence falls between us as I force myself to eat. Fortunately the soft elbow noodles are warm and the tomato sauce is thick. Glancing back up at Kayla, I see that the icy frustration I feel isn't shared. She's munching happily at her salad and scooping up blobs of the spinach dip with pita chips. I guess I've never really seen her in a bad mood once dinner is served at Zarello's. A part of me doesn't want to break that trend, but another part can't just sit here and quietly eat. Without meaning to, I drop my fork and it clangs against my plate. The sound is light, but loud enough to draw Kayla's glance up to me and it probably wins the attention of a few others in the room as well.

"Bryan?"

"I want to be able to say 'I love you.'"

She stares at me for a moment, a little stunned. I realize then that I probably sound like a crazy person.

"I don't…" she trails off, both eyebrows raised.

"I tried to say it twice today on the phone. But both times you hung up before I could. I don't think today's the first time either, it's just all I can think of right now."

"I'm sorry, Bry," she says softly. She pushes her salad bowl aside and slides her hand over to me. I sort of want to resist taking it, but lay mine out for her anyway. I do feel better once my palm is beneath hers. I can even sense my heart rate slowing.

"You know I've been busy lately. And I know you love me. But I'll wait from now on, okay. I won't hang up until you've said it."

I bob my head and tighten my grip on her hand a little. Maybe we're both just in a rough spot right now. It could be that neither of us is quite ourselves lately. Yeah that might be it. It's hard to say really, but for now my anger melts away. My dinner starts to taste better and Kayla's company suddenly feels warmer. After dinner, we head out into the bustling North End downtown area where we walk around for a while in the cool night breeze. To this day, we tell ourselves that we're just wandering around the blocks yet we always somehow manage to find ourselves at either Sandy's Snack House, a little shop that sells organic fruit pastries and treats, or The Silver Nugget, a frozen yogurt place where I normally get made fun of for having more toppings than yogurt. Tonight we find ourselves at The Silver Nugget where I am chastised for all of the chocolate chips that somehow find their way into my cup.

After a couple of hours, we go our separate ways. I take off and go to the gym. Today is a back and bi day, thank God. I tend to zone out when I'm at the gym. I'm aware of the people around me and can feel the passing of time, but it's also like I slip away into a different reality. It helps me unwind and it makes me forget any shit that I dealt with that day. The rest of the night rolls on like this — me in my own little world. By the time I'm home and showered, all I can think about is sleep. I've hardly slipped into a pair of trunks when I crash into bed. I flip the light switch beside me and let my head sink into my foam pillow. Everything is dark. Everything is cool. Everything is silent. And then I slip away.

# Chapter 4

Light orchestral music mixed with a small bit of continual chatter fills my ears. I find myself in darkness for a moment before my vision is filled with a flurry of bright colors. At first I find it all rather disagreeable, painful even. But the noxious blur soon sharpens into a full picture. I'm in a large ballroom from the look of things. At the end of it stands a wide, empty stage. Red velvet drapes curl around tall, gothic windows which look rather striking when set against the pristinely white walls. The dancefloor is pure hardwood, stained in an auburn color and is filled with people in lavish attire spinning and stepping to the whimsical harmony that plays.

It's then that I realize that I must be back in Shirun's mansion, but I can't quite remember what I've been up to since the last party I attended. I can't even rightly remember how long ago that party was, nor do I recall leaving it or receiving an invitation to this one. I wonder if perhaps this is a different party at all. Maybe I fell into a spell of imagination whilst we moved into a different room, is all. This hope is instantly dashed once I look down to see that my white pants and blue coat are replaced with a silver evening suit. A rush of panic slams into me. I wonder how I can fall into such a queer mood every time I find myself in this place. Is there perhaps some sort of foul magic at play after all — a dastardly trick of the mind? Have I simply formed a habit of indulgence when it comes to beverages? Whatever the case, it won't do for me to idly stand by myself like this so I peer about in search of some familiar faces.

I spot a skinny red-headed figure over at the long serving tables and can only guess that this is Jack. It really is astonishing how he can eat so much yet gain so little. Unfortunately for me, he's nearly on the other side of the room so I try to find someone closer. I think I spot William and Joanna among the crowd of swirling dancers. Upon a moment's thought, I realize that I'd rather not engage them in conversation anyway. I suppose I don't really know Joanna, but William has already proven to possess rather dreadful communication skills. Suddenly I realize that my position has been noticed. The older pair from before approach me and I get a sinking feeling in my stomach at their arrival. Both are now dressed in smoky-grey – a suit for the gentleman and a gown for the lady. The woman pushes past her companion by a few steps.

"Good evening, Mister Daley," she chimes.

She smiles widely, but not necessarily sweetly. One hand is placed on her wide hip and another rests over her black shawl.

"It's a pleasure, Madame," I reply with some hesitation.

"Carolyn – Carolyn Baxter," she declares. There's a sourness in her tone which gives me the impression that she expected I would already know her name. "This is my brother, Charles Baxter," she removes the hand on her hip to gesture to the man now standing beside her.

"A pleasure to meet you both," I return, my hand extended.

Charles takes it and gives me a docile handshake. When I notice that Carolyn has no inkling to do the same, I pull it back. Up close, I can see that they are certainly nearer to Margaret's age than anyone else here, but are still a good ten years younger. They are also far less lively than Margaret unless first impressions deceive me. Furthermore, there is an air about them which gives me unease. I have to wonder why exactly they bothered to engage me in conversation if they intended to be this dull. I also can't help but remain vexed over their rude stares and gestures toward me during the previous gathering.

"We thought we might come to meet you ourselves," Carolyn explains as though reading my thoughts. "There has been much talk about who and *what* you are, you know. We thought it best to come and see if we can't sort fact from fiction. Isn't that right Charles?"

"Certainly is, Carolyn," Charles replies gruffly.

Immediately after hearing Charles' reply, Carolyn's plump cheeks rise up into a wrinkled grin. I notice that much of the skin on her face is pulled taught by how tightly her bun is tied and can't help but presume that this effect is intentional. In that short flicker of what she must think is a smile, I am able to see how worn her features really are.

"Is there that much talk about me?" I ask. It's my hope to sound as innocent as possible in my doing so.

"Oh there is always talk!" she titters. "But yes, you especially are of great interest to this crowd."

"I only just arrived, though," I protest.

"Yes, well true as this might be, what you fail to understand is that this is precisely the reason why you have garnered so much attention. It's been a good long while since anyone new has made our acquaintance."

"I see," Is all I can manage in my perplexed state of mind.

"Do you?" Charles interjects. "I mean, do you *really* see?"

"I, I'm not quite sure anymore. I admit that you have me all out of sorts in regards to your meaning."

Charles's lips purse together as he strokes his gentleman's beard. I note that the warm brown color of it is flecked with strands of grey. He eyes me for a moment, perhaps scrutinizing me, perhaps searching for something to say. His thick eyebrows pinch together, bringing out his own age marks.

"Yes, now I can see that you haven't the faintest idea of what we are talking about," he says at last.

"Perhaps we shouldn't bother the poor man, then," Carolyn suggests.

"Now, now, Carolyn," Charles scolds, tossing a hand up into the air. I find this exclamation funny since I take him for the younger of the two. "Let me ask you this then, Mister Daley…" he continues. "…Do you feel like you belong here?"

It takes me a moment to recover from the question, but eventually I reply, "Why, yes, of course! Miss Margaret went through great pains to introduce me to some folks that frequent these gatherings and Shirun's toast to me was quite welcoming as well."

"I think you misunderstood my brother," Carolyn stops me. She shakes her head and explains, "He did not ask you if you felt welcomed. He asked if you felt like you belong. Does it feel right and natural for you to be here? Or does something seem amiss to you?"

Both of their gazes fall harder upon me. Any unease I felt

before has multiplied tenfold. Of course there are things that feel off to me. There are large spreads of food set out that seem to replenish themselves. A delightful melody plays, yet I see no orchestra of any kind. I realize then that even the party's host is nowhere in sight. My eyes scan the room, but find no sign of Mister Shirun. In a crowd like this, I'd surely be able to find him if he was indeed present. Turning my focus back to the Baxters, I fear telling them this truth. Something about them doesn't sit right with me one bit. I long more than ever to be free of their oppressive company and prying eyes.

"I –"

"Bryan, there you are!" Margaret's voice swoops in behind me, cutting off my reply.

"Madame Margaret," I return shakily as I turn and open my arms to her.

She takes me into an embrace and I hold her a little stronger than what is really considered appropriate. She indulges me for longer than I'd expect before pulling away.

"Ah, I see you've met the Baxters, my dear, how lovely!" There's something about how her pitch rings a little higher that makes me think her greeting to them is less than genuine.

"Lady Margaret, always a pleasure to stumble across you," Carolyn returns in an equally disingenuous tone.

"Do, forgive me then, I have been looking all over for Mister Daley here. I've missed his company dreadfully you see and was hoping you might permit me to steal him away from you."

Carolyn opens her mouth when Charles interjects, "But of course, you may, Madame Pembrook. Carolyn and I should be making our rounds as well before people start to think us rude. Do enjoy the rest of your evening now."

Without a parting gesture of any kind, the Baxters turn around and head off away from us. I then find my arm entangled with Margaret's and I'm led along in the opposite direction. There are a lot of things I want to ask Margaret right now, but I'm too grateful to be free of the Baxters to say anything. She leads me around the dancefloor to a back corner of the ballroom where tables are set.

"Some wine, Mister Daley," she offers, gesturing a hand

toward where crystal glasses sit on a platter. I can't help but think that I might like something a tad stiffer, but nod in assent anyway. I'm released from her hold and take up two glasses of the deep, aromatic, red wine.

"Thank you, my dear," she says as I hand a glass over to her.

"I'm the one that really ought to be thanking you," I return before taking a sip.

"Oh dear, those Baxters don't have you all up in a tizzy do they?"

She reaches to me and gives the side of my arm a tender brushing. I know that if there's anyone here I can trust, it's Margaret, but I still don't know how much I should really tell her. It's even harder to judge this since tonight she looks especially pure. She wears a white ball gown with a pearl necklace and matching pearl earrings. Her silver hair is pulled around her face and over her right shoulder — falling elegantly down the side of her chest in a lazy spiral. In her sea-green gaze, I can see nothing but love and compassion. I decide that I want to trust her — that I *need* to trust her.

"They were asking me … some odd questions," I start. "And they said that people have been talking about me."

Margaret takes a thoughtful sip before replying, "It's true that there's been a bit of talk. But there are always rumors and speculation whenever someone new comes to Shirun's parties."

"They also said that it's been a long time since Shirun welcomed anyone new here."

"That is true as well," she admits.

There's a silence between us as Margaret takes a couple of long pulls of wine. Her brow creases and her eyes drift about the room. Whereas the Baxters seemed to be trying to expose something, Margaret appears to want to shelter me from it. She opens her mouth as if to speak, but snaps it shut and turns about. I look off in the same direction and realize that Myles is marching toward us. Shelly trails behind him, her golden curls bouncing about. Though I can't quite make out what they're saying over the music, I gather that they are bickering over something.

"Mister Westerly, Miss Simmons, whatever is the matter with the two of you?" Margaret calls to them as they draw nearer.

"Madame Pembrook, can you kindly tell Myles to settle down?" Shelly asks – a little breathlessly. This combined with the reddish glow on her face suggests to me that she and Myles have been at odds with one another for quite some time this evening.

"Myles, good heavens!" Margaret exclaims. "Your face is flush and you have a wild look about your eyes. I daresay you need to calm down at once! A little fresh air and some ice water are also an order."

"I'll not settle down, Madame," Myles hisses, thrusting an index finger toward the floor. "This is an absolute outrage and you know it!"

"What is?" I ask this perhaps a bit out of turn.

Myles's head turns sharply towards me and the hard expression he wears softens just a little. "Mister Shriun is the outrage," he explains, still looking me in the eye. His voice struggles to keep an even tone and I wonder if he isn't also trying to protect me from something.

"I think you're just blowing this far out of proportion," Shelly argues. Her voice is sweet and light, just like what I'd expect it to sound like.

"No, just listen to me, both of you," Myles snaps, turning his attention back to Shelly and Margaret who now stand side by side. "He cannot just disappear like this, not now. Not when we have so many questions. He was aloof all night last time and now he doesn't so much as show up."

"I'm quite sure there is a good explanation for everything," Margaret soothes.

"I think you know better than that," Myles retorts.

He crosses his arms and looks to the ladies for a reply. I'm left to just stand here and wonder what precisely they're talking about. Could all of this truly be about me? Could my appearance at the last party really have been so troublesome? Is it a foul omen of some kind for these people?

"I don't know anything for sure," Margaret says in a weary tone.

"That's exactly it though, isn't it!" Myles's voice is raised again. "None of us know what's going on and we deserve answers. He does too, especially if he is who we think he is," he bristles as he shoves a hand in my direction.

"And what do you intend to do about it then?" Shelly challenges.

"I *intend* to find him. I'll find him and then demand that he tell us what's happening here. I'll not stand to be left in the dark like this. We could all be in grave danger without even knowing it." Myles raises his chin defiantly once he's finished with his tirade.

"Do what you must then," Shelly replies in a rather bitter tone. "But don't complain to me if you anger Mister Shirun. He's always been good to us – you should try and trust him a little more now."

Myles grunts and spins about on his heel. Without another word, he storms off toward the exits. I now feel an insatiable desire to flee from this place. Whatever trouble I bring with me, I certainly don't wish it upon these fine people. Furthermore, a deep guilt bears down on me for causing them so much distress. I decide that I really ought to head home now, but then I'm reminded of something dreadful, something I have not suffered the full gravity of just yet. I haven't the faintest idea of just where home might be. For that matter, I'm not even sure where *here* is! I try to think on the roads I took to arrive wherein I now stand, but I can't. I know I came to this realization the last time I was here as well, but now – now this lapse in memory seems so much more haunting.

"Are you alright, my dear?" I hear Margaret ask.

She has a hand on Shelly's shoulder. Teardrops grow fatter in the corners of the younger woman's crystalline eyes. She's looking to where Myles exits the ballroom and her lips quiver as he shuts the door behind him.

"It's all just so much to take in," she whimpers. "And I hate to see him angry like that." The way she looks at the doors to the ballroom shows me how deeply she loves and longs for Myles. She's certainly a patient woman to put up with someone with such a temperament as his. "Please excuse me, I think I just need a bit of fresh air," she concludes.

"Of course, dear. Go catch your breath for a bit." Margaret gives the side of Shelly's face a soft pat as she says this.

Shelly gives each of us a brief curtsy and takes off for the other side of the room. I watch as she glides away, her purple dress swaying behind her. She leaves the room through a small door I hadn't previously noticed. I surmise that there must be some sort of patio beyond it, perhaps a garden as well. I shift my gaze to Margaret, finding that she too looks in Shelly's direction. She turns to me with a smile, but there's a somber haze that falls over her normally bright eyes.

"Let's have a dance shall we?"

"I'm not quite sure I know how," I reply.

"Just follow my lead and I'm sure the steps will come to you easily enough."

Looking to the mass of dancers, I see how they all stride and turn and spin in unison. It all looks far more complicated than Margaret suggests. In spite of these doubts, I allow her to take my hand and lead me out onto the floor. Nerves build up as Margaret takes her place in front of me. One of my hands curls around her back and the other interlocks with one of hers. She rocks us to the right and I step in line with the motion. Then we take a step back and two forward. Suddenly I no longer think about the steps. It feels as though the music has taken over control. We step and we sway to its command. When the string instruments rise into shrill crescendos, we are even compelled to spin about. It's an odd feeling to move about so involuntarily. One more thing to add to the list of oddities this place has to offer, I suppose. As we move along a bit more, I start to find it a little relaxing to be guided along like this. Each step and every sway comes as easily as drifting down a gentle current. Then a horrible thought crosses my mind:

"*Is this place a trap?*"

I have to wonder what all this strangeness is really about. Could it be that this mansion is slowly assuming control over me? Perhaps all of these guests are really pawns, prisoners, or puppets of some wicked scheme. After all, I continue to notice things that are wrong yet make no motion to leave. I can't even be sure that I'm able to leave. If I can't recall where I came from, or how I got here, or even where I am presently, then perhaps the trap is already sprung. Then another notion strikes me:

"*Is any of this real?*"

It's a fair question to ask, all things considered. It is definitely a place that seems far more surreal than real, but this is of little comfort. It *feels* real right now and that is enough for me to perceive a real threat to my well-being. But as we dance, I see that I'm not the only one in this room who's frightened. All over the dance floor, I receive skeptical glances from those dancing nearby. Many come from faces who have already been introduced to me. William and Joanna shoot me beady looks, the Baxters frown in my direction, and then there are the performers from the last party – Jeremy and Natasha. They don't glare so much as look to me with concern. Everyone seems to know – or think they know – what is afoot, but I'm utterly ignorant to it all. My heart lightens some when I meet eyes with Jack. The boy is dancing with a young blonde woman who looks like she's around Shelly's age. I only hold Jack's gaze for a moment, but his wide, boyish grin makes everything else subside for that brief pause in time. Clearly all that is on this boy's mind is how pretty his dancing partner is. I see no fear or doubt written on his face – only genuine and unhindered glee. Then he and his partner step behind another twirling couple and the lightness leaves my spirit.

When I look back to my own dancing partner, I'm struck with even more heaviness. It's not exactly a frown that Margaret wears, but it's certainly not a smile of any kind either. Her eyes look dry and her face is a bit pale, but there's still an enchanting quality to her. It's just the way that the dazzling light of the ballroom falls upon her as we twirl. It shimmers off of her silver hair, sparkles off of her pearl jewelry and reflects off of the soft white of her dress in a way that looks almost divine. She looks lovely in a regal sort of way which makes her uneasiness seem all the more tragic. I know that she can tell me what's going on here. She can feign ignorance if she wishes, but it's clear to me that she *does* know something, even if it doesn't answer everything. I think she wants to tell me too. If I can just find a way to get through to her, perhaps I'll get my answers. But how should I approach this? Margaret's resolve might be worn down, but what can I say to crack through the last bit of it? She's a kind soul and perhaps therein is where her weakness lies. Ever since I met her, she's done nothing but try to help people. She spent a whole evening touring me around which is proof enough that she's got a tenderness about her, but that's certainly not where her benevolence ended. Along the way she found a dance partner for

William and Joanna, saving them from their own dullness. Then she danced with Jack. Now tonight, she's saved me from the Baxters and tried to intervene with Myles's outburst. It's perhaps the noblest kind of chink in one's armor and I am a wicked man for exploiting it, but I really need to know what's happening here – what's happening to me.

"None of this makes any sense to me," I start, keeping my tone hushed and low.

"It doesn't make much sense to any of us, dear" she replies, her voice equally faint.

We glide along thoughtlessly to the hum of the music around us. I'm sure that those around us are listening closely in spite of our attempts to stay quiet and I hope that the orchestral rhythm is enough to keep their ears in the dark. Though I'm not looking, I know other couples are drifting closer. I can feel them dancing nearer to Margaret and myself.

"Why do they look at me like that?" I continue, nearly whimpering. "Who do they think I am?"

I'm suddenly tugged inward, scandalously close to Margaret. Our feet are almost touching with each stride and her nose is nearly poking mine.

"No one is sure, but if you are what we think you are then you're not supposed to be here. We may all be overreacting – letting our imaginations get the better of us. But we all have to ask, '*what if we're not?*'"

The crowd around us drops out of focus. The only thing that seems real to me right now is Margaret's furrowed countenance and hushed voice. Even the music all but dwindles into a light echo.

"What do you think I am?"

"There was no precedent ... no warning ... no introduction," she babbles.

I worry that she's about to fall into hysterics. If that happens, I won't be getting what I need. I have to pull her worry away from herself and back to me.

"I need your help Margaret..."

My eyes fixate on hers, holding them captive. I hope she can hear my desperation. Her eyelids flutter and I see the faintest quiver in her red lips.

"I have to know what I am to you people. Why are you all so afraid of me?" I press on.

She averts my gaze for a moment, but I keep her held close. She looks around us before bringing her lips to my ear.

"We think you are the source," she whispers. "Either that or the collective. But if you are the collective, then the rest of us wouldn't be here. And if you are the source, then you *shouldn't* be here. Whatever you are, I'm quite sure that you are *not* one of us."

She pulls her head back and looks to me with bloodshot eyes.

"None – none of this makes any sense," I stammer.

She tilts her head and asks, "Do things feel strange to you here?"

I realize that this is the same question that the Baxters tried to pry from me, but I don't care. I need to trust Margaret, I'm in too deep to consider doing otherwise.

So I say, "There are a lot of things strange to me here."

"Shhh, quietly now!" She scolds.

I can see those dancing around us in my peripheral vision and suddenly get the feeling that I'm in great peril. So I drop my volume to a whisper and speak directly into her ear.

"When I awoke here, I had no recollection of who I was or even what I looked like. I say 'awoke' because it was as though I was asleep and came back into consciousness only moments before Shirun declared my presence at the table. Furthermore, I still have no notion of where I live, how I got here, or even where here is."

Margaret makes no immediate reply or reaction upon my finishing. She just absorbs what I said for a moment "Go on," she invites.

"It's this place in general," I continue. "There's all this food laid out for us, but no servers. The food is exquisite yet no one pays a compliment to the chef. Then there's this lovely music. The harmony plays without one soul manning an instrument."

I pull my head back a little to see that Margaret looks at me with an even expression. I can't quite get a read on how my comments have affected her which makes my hands feel a bit clammy.

*"Did I tell her too much?"*

"All of these things feel peculiar to you?" She asks this as though she cannot grasp the fact that none of this makes any logical sense.

"Immensely," I reply, realizing that I'm beyond the point of being able to take any of it back.

"Then you will have to forgive me, my dear," she responds in a wavering tone. "All of the things which you experienced and observed are undoubtedly valid, however the fact that you find any of these things strange is of great concern. The mere fact that some of it has even drawn your notice is even more worrisome. These are things that none of us have ever pondered or questioned before and many of these notions make little sense to me. It's proof enough that although you are most welcome here, you certainly do not belong."

*Belong*, that's the exact word that the Baxters used. How in good sense can I be welcome, yet not belong? How can Margaret, a shrewd and sensible woman not see the peculiarity of any of this? Has she never heard of servers or cooks? Is she quite accustomed to music playing out of thin air? My mind spins as I try and piece it all together.

"I can only conclude that you are here under the gravest of circumstances." Margaret's words cuts into my thoughts. "Whatever happens next will be most unpleasant for us all. More tragically, it will be beyond anyone's ability to anticipate."

"I don't —"

I'm cut off by a sudden and shrill cry. It's the sort of shriek that halts words as they roll off of one's tongue and makes the heart skip a beat. The ballroom falls utterly silent. Even the symphony played by an unseen orchestra comes to a complete stop. My limbs are released from the transient hold which the music has had on me so I step back from Margaret to look around. So far as I can tell, everyone in the room is unharmed and they're all looking around curiously as I now do. Then I realize where the noise came from.

Margaret and I twist to face each other in unison and announce, "Shelly!"

Immediately we break for the ballroom's side exit. The thick crowd wanders aimlessly, trying to guess at the disturbance's source and a few heads turn our way as we trot rudely through. I push my way across the floor with Margaret close at my heels. Before I'm quite halfway through it, I hear my name called in a squeaky voice. I decide that it must belong to Jack but press on without acknowledging him. By the time I reach the thin door, I can feel all of the eyes in the room bearing down on me. I'm not sure whether it is confusion or cowardice that holds the party's attendants where they stand, but I push the thought aside and toss open the door. It slams against the wall as I step through. A chilly blast of air greets me when I walk onto the stone patio. Not a star can be seen in the pitch-black sky above us, making our only sources of light the ballroom's windows and the tall lampposts which are set throughout the manor's rose garden. To my great horror, my eyes finally discover the source of the scream. Shelly's body lays strewn across the shimmering stone walkway which weaves through the tall bushes. Her limbs are tossed wildly about as if she were in the middle of desperately fleeing from something. Then I notice the dark pool of blood which spills out from her neck and gathers around her pale face.

"Oh, Good Lord!" Margaret gasps from behind me.

"Shelly!" I hear another woman exclaim.

Jack and the blonde woman whom he danced with rush forward to the corpse. They roll her over onto her back and it's then that I can clearly see the deep gashes of flesh pulled out of her throat. It makes me feel rather sick to see such a pretty young thing so grotesquely mangled like this. The wound appears to be suffered from some kind of beast. But what sort of a creature could climb over the iron-barred fence which surrounds this garden? What could have entered in so quietly yet caused such a gruesome, bloody mess? Out of the corner of my eye, I see curious shadows dancing like ribbons. Without thinking, I dash off towards them.

"Bryan!" I hear Margaret call, but this only makes me charge off with greater haste. Whatever is running from the scene of the crime might just be the key to whatever trouble is afoot here. And if that's the case, I need to catch it. I curl into one of the narrow pathways through the garden and drop from their sight. I see a pair of hind legs like those of a hound duck sharply around a bush and wonder if I should really be chasing after something that just killed someone – especially since it's not a human being. It's too dark to see what I'm chasing for sure, even under the gentle glow of the lanterns. In spite of my doubts, I continue to sprint through the aromatic corridors after the strange ribbon-like shadows.

After rounding a corner, I get a clearer glimpse of the canine killer. It bounds down a straight path toward a large shed. The thing runs like a bear and is large enough that it might actually be one. But instead of fur, the thing seems to have tendrils swaying off the top of its back. By now, I know I should promptly cease my pursuit of this creature. It is clearly something of unnatural means and unholy intentions. But something drives me to it — keeps me from ending the chase even though I want very badly to give it up.

I come up to the shed's door when I see it suddenly open. Out from it swings a large greyish blur. Whatever the object is, it collides sharply with my skull. My body is instantly flattened against the ground, my vision grows dark, and my senses fall numb.

# Epilogue

I snap upright in bed. My hands clutch my sweaty forehead and my bare chest heaves in a desperate effort to catch my breath. For a minute, dark flecks cloud my vision, but they clear as soon as my breathing calms. I realize that I'm back in my apartment, back in reality. But for some reason *this* doesn't feel real. The images from my time at the party still flood my mind – still feel like the *real* world. The sensation of having my steps be controlled by the music, the ominous ring of Margaret's voice, it all feels like something that happened – I mean *really* happened – only seconds before now. I can't find any injury on my forehead, but my head pounds in a way that I have never felt before.

"It was just a dream – only a dream," I whisper to myself.

But I can't seem to make that idea stick. My hands quake and my breathing is still a little strained. I can't get the image of Shelly's corpse out of my mind. I can't seem to comprehend that I'm no longer chasing that weird demon-dog. I wait and wait for the nightmare to fade out of my mind, but it doesn't. I look at my phone and see that it's only 4:00 AM.I should try to get back to sleep, but the way my heart thumps tells me that will probably be a futile effort. So I get out of bed and stumble through my room into the bathroom. My eyes sting once I flip the light on and my headache only gets stronger. Once I can properly see, I'm struck by how awful I look. My hair is damp and matted, my complexion is pasty white, and my eyes make it look like I've been smoking something all night long. And this crackhead look is all thanks to a dream, just a little dream – because that's all it was…*just* a dream.

"Only a dream," I say out loud.

My voice is scratchy, so much so, that it sounds like someone else's. I put my hands on the sink counter and let my head drop down to my chest. I'm really not sure what the hell could be happening to me. I don't get why something as stupid as a nightmare could have such a strong effect on me. And it makes my head hurt even more to think about it, so I try not to.

"It was just a dream – *only a dream,*" I whisper.

DEREK BAILEY

# Book 2:

# Paradise's Vexation

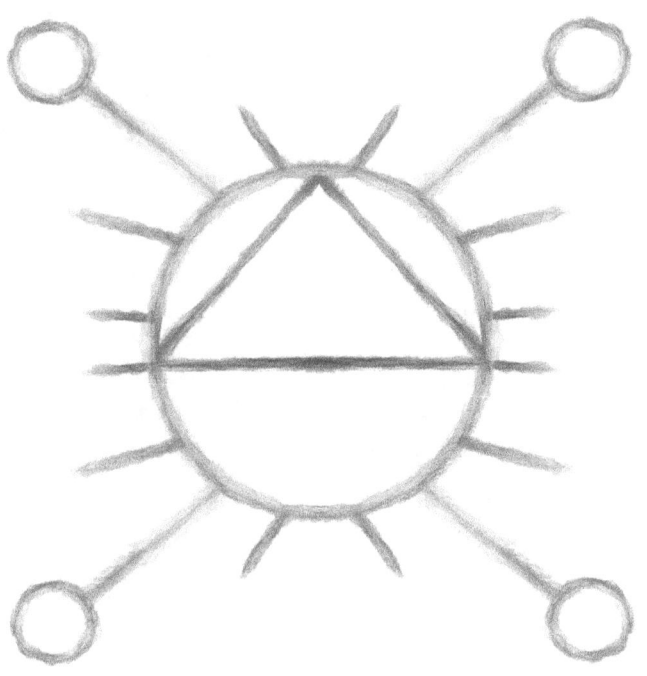

*To those no longer in my life – the people who'll
stay with me, if only in memory.*

# Chapter 1

Parts of that dream still flash through my mind. The hypnotic quality of the music, the concern written across Margaret's face, the ominous tone in her voice, it all feels so close to reality, but it *can't* be real. Yet the images, and sounds, and sensations feel so much closer to memories than dreams. All of it feels disturbingly vivid, but what stands out the most is the bloody mess of Shelly Simmons' corpse lying strewn across the garden path. Then there was my pursuit of that weird shadow hound and the hit I took to the head. My breathing picks up as the last images run through my mind again. What gives me the most anxiety is the fact that my head actually hurts, right in the front corner of my skull where I got whacked in my dream. I pull my head up to face myself in the mirror. Aside from the beads of sweat running down my face, my matted hair, and a pasty quality in my complexion, I don't look so bad. Still I can't resist the urge to examine where I took the hit – in my dream that is. I know it's a crazy thing to do, but without being able to calm myself any other way, I pull myself upright and tilt the left side of my head toward the mirror. I don't see anything right off the bat so I cautiously pull aside my damp bangs. There's nothing. No bruising or cuts or any sign that anyone so much as slapped me in that spot. I don't know why this surprises me – maybe because my head throbs as though I took a mean blow to it. I guess I'd hoped that I actually bashed my head against the wall or thrashed so violently that my skull connected with a bedpost. But it looks like I won't be able to explain this pain so easily. Fortunately, a simple headache is an easy enough thing to fix so I leave the bathroom and head down the dark staircase.

I know I should just turn the lights on, but I'm afraid it will hurt too much. The bathroom light behind me gives off an easy glow that lights my way until I'm halfway down the curling steps. Then I guide myself down using the railing until I finally have to flip the switch for my living room lights. Even though I shut my eyes to it, the light still sears into my brain. It stings for a good few minutes until I can squint into the room. For some reason, I notice how empty it looks. There's a widescreen TV mounted to the wall and a plush set of a couch and two chairs with sleek black end tables in between, but the floor between the furniture and television is fairly bare. Back when I first moved in here, I tried to keep this space clear. I held parties all the time with friends, friends of friends, and even friends of friends of friends. I'd push the furniture to the back edge of the floor which left a nice space for people to get together. We all drank and laughed, and talked, and sometimes a few of us went home and got lucky. I got lucky a couple times myself with chicks that weren't so eager to leave the party with everyone else. Whatever the outcome, it was always a fun time and we tried to mix things up as much as we could. On a couple special occasions, we had a DJ come in and make the night more about dancing. Sometimes we'd have drunken potlucks. And with the right crew, we'd even do weird things like replace drinking games with those PlayCube games that make you dance or sing in order to win.

The room itself is denoted by a six inch depression in the floor which is all that separates it from the kitchen. This made for a nice wide open area where drinks and snacks were only a few steps away from the heart of the party. I feel a smirk come on as I picture this place filled with people from my past. This is where I met Kayla too. She was one of those friends of a friend of a friend. Those times feel both so close and yet so far passed. Things are just different now, I guess. But there are definitely times that I think about it and I miss it – like now for example. A kick from my headache pulls me out of the past and reminds me what I came down here for. So I head into the kitchen and choose not to flip on the lights even though my eyes are adjusted. A plastic BestAid bag sits on the kitchen table from several nights ago. I guess I couldn't be bothered to unpack it at the time. After fishing through it, I find my bottle of aspirin and throw a couple pills back with some orange juice from the fridge. Then I brew a pot of coffee and check the time on my microwave. It's still only 4:15 AM so I pack myself up a lunch, something I rarely give myself time for. It's nothing fancy, just a ham sandwich, granola bar, and a red apple. By the time I've put that together, stashed it in the refrigerator, and downed a cup of coffee, it's still only 4:34 AM. Now I'm really not sure what to do with myself. I consider heading back to bed and maybe getting another hour or so of sleep, but what if I end up at the manor again? I feel like such a child. I'm actually scared of going back to bed for fear of having a bad dream. Is this really real life right now? Whatever, I don't really care. I've had enough of that "*place*" for now. I'm not taking the chance of going back there so I'm going to be ridiculous and just wait around until it's time to leave for work.

With my headache subsided and a whole mess of time on my hands, I can think of only one thing to do so early in the morning. So I head back through the living space to where my office door is. The office is the one room on this floor that is actually surrounded by walls and a door. It's not like I'm in need of that much privacy or peace and quiet here, but having a door does help when I need to shut myself in and get some work done. It's a nice setup too. The computer desk is wide, taking up the entire back wall of the small room. I have two screens set up and run a tower that has way more processing power than I will ever need. If I was a gamer, I might get *some* use out of what it can do, but I pretty much only ever use a fraction of its capabilities. I certainly don't need it, but at the time I guess I just bought it because I could. I don't even turn it on much either, since I mostly bring my work laptop in and hook it up to the monitors. This last week – hell, more like this last month – this room proved to be a lifesaver. I sat down, enjoyed the space of a full workstation, and just hashed things out as they came up. Now that I think of it, it might be safe to say that this room is partly how I even got to where I am since there have been many a night when I used it as an office outside of the office.

I may be thirty two, but that's fairly young for a Manager. Getting there took a combination of rubbing the right elbows, putting time in after hours, and making it known that I was putting time in after hours. A bit of well-timed luck never hurts either. It's pretty much the same story with David. He either just rubbed those elbows a little smoother or got a little luckier. Besides that, I'm not quite sure how he could have managed to get ahead of me. It annoys me just to think about it so I try not to. I jab my finger into my tower's power button and boot up my desktop. Once things have loaded up and I've logged in, I open Platinum, my browser of choice and navigate to FriendBook. Usually I just check it on my phone so there is a certain sense of luxury I feel now that I'm checking my newsfeed on a big screen. I'm also very glad it still has my login stored because I honestly don't remember what my password is. This is where the luck ends for me, though. Immediately I spot a set of photos at the top of the page. They belong to my friend, Erin May and are accompanied by a short statement about how great it was to see all of the people who show up in the photos with her. I don't really read it in full, but notice that Kevin Rousey, Devon Canavan, Julie Carson, and David Jones are all tagged in the post. These names bring back a rush of memories.

My eyes drift down to the thumbnails displayed and see the shrunken versions of familiar faces which accompany these unforgettable names. They all seem to be together at The Commons where they met up last night. I feel a rush of anger at seeing them together without me, but realize that this is stupid since I was technically invited to join them. Still, I feel a twisting in my stomach. Maybe it's guilt or maybe I'm just feeling irrationally left out. It could be that I simply miss these people. I can't actually remember the last time I saw all of them at once. Despite my better judgement, I click on the album which opens up across my screen to an image of David and Devon tipping their beer bottles together and grinning widely. I guess they went to a bar at some point, probably before heading over to The Commons – I think I remember David saying something about them possibly doing that. The two of them were roommates back in the days when we all lived at Pinnacle, an apartment complex downtown on the south end near Parson International. I'd met David first, of course, when we had training together. It was a while before I met Devon in the laundry room. I was bound to run into him eventually and I sort of knew him through David anyway. He was – probably still is – a quiet, shy guy, but I could tell right away that he was fiercely smart. I also had a theory that he would make a very happy drunk. When David and I finally convinced him to come out with us one night, it so happened that he proved me right. He seemed embarrassed about it at first – as if the rest of us weren't acting like jackasses too – but after a while I think he felt more comfortable around us. In time, he felt like any other member of the group and started to loosen up a bit.

I remember teasing them because they looked like brothers. They cut their dark brown hair in a similar, short style, share a warm glint in their brown eyes, and even have approximately the same height and build. They could easily be mistaken for twins if seen at a distance. And just like a real pair of twins they were always very different. David always favored the business causal look, even outside of work. Devon worked as an Associate Marketing Rep. at a startup that recently found success and were looking to expand their brand. I can't remember what they sell or even what they call themselves, but I do recall them having that more relaxed, small business dress code. I remember Devon always dressing nice for work, not business-like, but well enough to look presentable and not push the boundaries of what was or wasn't okay to wear into work. This is pretty much the sort of look that he went for in his social life as well. I found it funny that such a quiet and generally reserved guy could have a career in marketing, but I guess nowadays there are all sorts of digital walls between marketers and the people they're marketing to. It's very possible that he's just a way more charismatic and confident person online. After all, it was on the internet that he and David met. Good old, RoomateFinder.net! It's not the way I would have guessed that they met each other, but when you're moving to a new city you do what you have to.

Admittedly, I met my roommate online as well, but that was a bit different since I met Kevin on Parson International's onboarding website where new employees could meet and find housing. The site even pulled a list of apartment listings in whatever area you wanted. Some would probably not think of living with a coworker as a good idea, but the perfect thing about Kevin was that I would never actually work with him. I went into Digital Solutions and he came on with an entry-level job in our Sales department. His face shows up in the next picture. He's with Erin in front of an elaborate fountain where a merman and a mermaid are back to back, water pouring from their hearts. It looks like they took this picture a little later in the evening since there's a rich orange glow descending upon them. It leaves brilliant highlights in their jet black hair and makes their blue eyes look as though they're on fire. It's an amazing picture in all respects. He and Erin have been crazy about each other since they first met and from the way they still cling to one another so earnestly, I'd say that the spark has only grown brighter.

I guess I'm glad to see him like this – happy that is. We were never super close in spite of being in the same friend group, but I always liked him. He has the best manners ever and his politeness never felt insincere. He's always had a sort of dreamy, Romeo-esque air about him. It's like the only thing he ever wanted out of life was to love and be loved. From the looks of this picture, I'd say he got just that. I can't say I'm surprised to see them like this now, though. He and Erin were the perfect pair right from the beginning. Erin lived in the same apartment complex as us, just a few doors down the hall. I remember how Kevin and I met her in the mail room and can't help but smile now as I recall how abruptly he invited her to get drinks with us as she was about to walk away. Then he gave her this ridiculous, pouty, lover-boy look like he'd die if she said "no." Fortunately for him, she agreed to come out. She didn't seem weirded out by it at all, even. I think she might have actually found him charming. Either that or she just felt bad shutting him down.

Kevin became unbearable afterwards. He paced around in a fit of boyish nerves that got worse the closer we came to going out. After a solid hour of Kevin asking me if he looked good or not in an assortment of shirts, I found myself ready to commit roommate murder. Fortunately, Erin came knocking on our door and spared his life. Then I led us out to a nearby bar and into an evening that they would never look back from. They hit it off nicely, maybe too nicely. It went so well for them that I actually wound up slipping away to meet David and Devon at a different bar. It seriously felt like I was sitting in on a fifth date the way they talked – never a moment where one of them wasn't speaking with excitement, nor any point where one cut the other off. From day one, they always just seemed so in sync. And here they are now, still the happiest couple I can think of. It's hard to move on from this beautiful picture of them together, but I'm starting to feel like a creep so I click onward. There are some pictures of the folk band that performed, a couple of two-person selfies taken by Erin with David and Devon. There's also a shot of all four of them together on a park bench. Then comes one that I'm not prepared for. The four of them are on the marble steps that lead up to the park's giant gazebo and standing in the middle of them is Julie. I don't know why seeing her in this picture makes my stomach drop. I saw her name in the post, but I guess it didn't fully register with me.

Her azure gaze pierces through the computer screen and into me. I suddenly get the ridiculous sensation that she's looking at me. It must be the intensity in those eyes – the drive – the indomitable purpose. It's the same striking look that captivated me those years ago. I find myself helpless against them even now, even though this is just a picture, a moment frozen in time. Her golden hair is longer now, it falls at shoulder length and it looks good, she's always looked good. Part of me is glad I wasn't there with them now. I don't know if I could face her after all this time. The way this picture of her hits me now tells me that I never would have been able to handle it.

She was Erin's roommate back when we all lived at Pinnacle. Erin and her were friends from college that applied to jobs in this area so that they could stick together. Erin found one at Image-In-Nation Graphic Solutions as a Junior Designer and Julie started as an Associate Financial Analyst for Johnson & Co. Financial Consulting. Once Erin began to join us for weekend fun, it was only a matter of time before she brought Julie along. They weren't attached at the hip precisely, but they did do an awful lot together and never seemed to want to leave the other behind. Once Erin and Kevin became an item, which took all of a couple of dates' time, they told us that we would be introduced to Julie. I'd expected her to be similar to Erin – thought she'd be sweet and mild mannered. But Julie ... Julie was something else entirely. I wouldn't say that she ever came off as rude or blunt or terse, just intense. She attacked life with a passion I have yet to see rivalled. She never did anything halfway and I can't think of a time when she didn't do something she said she would.

I remember that first night she showed up with Erin at Sinbad's Bar and Grill as clearly as what I did five seconds ago. The sight of her walking into the place would have knocked me on my ass if I wasn't already sitting down. The fierce look in her eyes, the soft glow of her skin, the silky sheen of her ear-length hair, it was all too much to take in at once. But I tried to play it cool for fear of coming on strong, or worse, coming off as awkward. After a few nights out I discovered that she was, in fact, single and decided that she was as lovely internally as I found her to be on the outside, albeit the intimidation factor. She proved herself to be brilliantly decisive in each and every decision, right down to when she wanted to do something, where she wanted to go, and even what she wanted to eat or drink. She made life appear so simple. For her, everything was abundantly clear – even things no one else would consider to be obvious. Given this, I should not have been surprised that she'd been onto me the whole time. I thought that I'd been pretty coy with my feelings, but one night I found out that they were no mystery to her at all.

We found ourselves alone then, waiting for the others to get themselves ready for a night out. I caught her giving me a good hard look. At first I tried to make it seem like I didn't notice, but eventually I had to acknowledge her gaze and when we made eye contact, I felt as though I stood completely naked to her. In that moment, nothing felt secret. All I could do was stand there, held captive by the mesmerizing blue of her irises. Then she said something that shattered my entire charade.

Her exact words were, "If you're going to ask someone out, then it's better just to ask them. If you do, they'll probably say 'yes'. If you don't then they'll never get a chance to. Nothing's more unattractive than indecision."

She said it so calmly, so smoothly, as though it was just a thought she needed to whimsically air out. I stood completely stunned after she said it, unable to form any kind of reply. Fortunately, our friends swooped in before I bumbled something stupid out. The rest of that night went on like any other, but her words continued to rattle through my brain. The next day I took her advice and she tossed an approving quip of some sort my way. I even came to her with a set time and place for our first date: Juanito's restaurant at 5:00 PM that night. She looked even more impressed with me when I rattled off these details and it occurred to me then that I'd never before had such a concrete plan in my life. I suppose we've always been opposites in that way. She, the woman with a swift answer to every choice, be it big or small. And me, the man who struggles to figure out what he even wants for lunch. In spite of this, things went well enough on our first date. A few more nights out together formed us into a FriendBook official couple and the two years that followed were the clearest I'd ever had. With her, everything felt simple and nothing seemed impossible.

The time that passed during those years remains the best I've ever had. Our group was inseparable and the fun never seemed to stop. We celebrated each other's promotions, our birthdays, all of the holidays, and most often, we celebrated just to celebrate. As I sit here now, I'm forced to recognize that this obviously didn't last. Not the nights out at the bars, not the excitement of being young upstarts in our respective careers, not even the relationship that brought me so much clarity. There are often times when I try to think about where it all went wrong – why I can't still have what I had then. But it's not something I really want to think about right now – not this early in the morning. Not while I'm at my computer by myself looking at pictures of other people having fun like some lonely creep. Maybe it's just that we all eventually moved into nicer places. Possibly it's just that we all became busier and more responsible. But looking at this photo of them all together, all looking so happy, I kind of wonder if maybe it's just me that feels like this. Maybe somewhere along the line, I got screwed. I know I was invited to this little reunion, but for some reason I can't help but feel like I've been left out for some time now.

Suddenly I can't stand to look at this picture anymore so I move on to see what's next and the album loops back to where I started with David and Devon happily clinking their beer bottles together. Even when I close out of my browser, a pang of jealousy clutches my heart, making it throb. I don't want to think about any of this anymore – about any of them anymore. There's still a solid hour until I can really get ready for work, which sucks since the internet is a dangerous place for drudging up old memories. I guess I'll just watch some shitty early morning TV. With any luck there'll be a rerun of one of the million crime dramas the networks have to offer or at least a particularly weird infomercial to keep my mind occupied. I retreat to my living room couch and spend about ten minutes scanning my assortment of mostly worthless channels and find nothing interesting. I finally come across one that I stop at. An infomercial on Slender-Bra it is. For some reason it's funny or at least ironic to see a bunch of skinny chicks model an undergarment meant to create a more flattering waistline for not-so-skinny women.

# Chapter 2

It's another slow day at the office, but I'm not sure if that's a good or a bad thing. On one hand, my head is so foggy that I think it would be impossible to get anything done anyway. On the other, I feel like I could really use something to keep my mind busy. Emails, meeting invitations, and checking the news works for a little while, but eventually I realize that there is no ignoring this dream issue forever. I *really* want to believe that it's no big deal. It could be that all the stress at work is catching up with me. Being overtired is another possibility. There's even a chance that there's nothing going on at all. It could just be a fluke. But two nights... *two* nights in a row with the same dream. No – not even the same dream – a continuation of one dream. And with such a stark level of detail. I remember every second of the time I spent in that fictional mansion. I can recall all the faces, the voices, even the taste of the food that I never actually ate. Food that I'm almost positive I've never had before – at least not like that – and faces that look nothing like people from my real life. It makes my head spin just to consider it and the more I do, the more I psyche myself out. So I finally cave into my burning need for answers. I open up Platinum and run an Ogle search for "dream interpretations."

I'm well aware that the information I'm about to find is probably almost entirely bullshit, but I don't care. I don't want to see a shrink and I don't think I can wait for professional help anyway. I need answers now, even if it's in the fishy, internet variety. I ignore the first two results: dreamz.net and thedreamoracle.com since they're paid ads and probably charge a premium for use of their site. The next two down are dreamindex.org and thedreamguru.me. I right click on both, opening each in a new tab of the browser and start with The Dream Index. It's supposedly put together by a bunch of dream enthusiasts, but the indexed definitions are less than enthusiastic.

The first one reads "**A** – suggests the dreamer feels satisfied with a recent deed or accomplishment."

Then there is the next entry, "**Abacus** – suggests something in the dreamer's life is counting up or down."

I mean these are fine and all, just a bit generic. And they seem limiting. Like what if I'm seeing the letter "A" in a creepy or bad context, what does that mean? I give the other site, The Dream Guru, a look and I'm a lot more impressed by it. For starters, the web site is actually styled as opposed to a drab, plain white page that reeks of sadness. I don't know if the guy who made this used one of those site building services, hired someone to make it, or is just a whiz at web design, but this thing looks slick. It's got this midnight blue background with stars speckled across it and the logo is a cartoon crescent moon with his eye closed and "z's" rising up from his mouth. It's a little cheesy, sure, but obviously made with a degree of care. From the look of things, this site was apparently created by a psychology student, though they don't give their name or say what school their degree is from. The message on the home page states that they had a special focus in the human subconscious and were always particularly passionate about dreams. That passion led them to build the site as a side project just for fun … *yep, yep*, should not be taken seriously or used as a means of self-treatment … *sure, sure*, is constantly being updated and added to and contributions in the form of new ideas are always welcome. Okay, so I think this is what I'm looking for. The site's creator seems pretty humble and down to earth and the site is well crafted so these are all good signs. The button for Dream Symbols A-Z on the main menu even twinkles when I hover over it.

The index page of different dream symbols also looks nice. There's pages upon pages of this stuff and fortunately a quick search bar to look specific things up as well as a dropdown that filters by the first letter of the item's first word. Just giving this a quick glance, I see that the explanations are quite detailed and allow for different possible meanings so I don't even bother to read through a couple before searching for "evil demon dog." This doesn't turn up any results so I figure the search terms must need to be an exact or partial match to something on the list. I try "demon dog" and "devil dog" with still no success. At last, I get a hit with "evil dog." The list of possible interpretations seems pretty extensive so I feel hopeful that something will fit. The listing reads:

### Evil Dog

Seeing or being attacked by an evil or demonic dog or hound-like creature can represent a number of potential fears or insecurities.

1. Seeing a dog as evil may indicate a subconscious fear of anything in the canine species or even a general fear of the animal kingdom.

2. A dream in which you are attacked, bitten, or chased by a malicious dog might be a means of coping with a traumatic incident involving either yourself or a loved one suffering an injury from a dog.

3. Depending on the situation, encountering an evil dog that is causing injury, death, or destruction could indicate that there is an uncontrollable force in your life which is threatening to or actively causing destruction to something you consider valuable.

4. To see a dog that belongs to or is otherwise familiar to you acting in an evil way may indicate that you are losing your grip on something precious. This can be a manner in which your brain represents children, peers, pets, or people you see yourself as a mentor to who are behaving in a way that's troubling you.

◊ Alternatively: this can be something more abstract like one's career path

This is as detailed an explanation as I could hope for. Unfortunately, I'm not really sure if any of these actually apply. Maybe I *am* afraid that something's devouring or destroying my life, but that seems like a question that demands way more reflection than I'm willing to spend energy on now. When I think about it though, that dog was a very small part of what I found so unsettling about these dreams. No, what really unnerves me about them is their overall atmosphere. All the things that seemed missing or wrong – all of the confusion and suspicion I encountered on that second night – I need to know what these things mean. I search for "fancy party" and luckily, something shows up right away.

### Fancy Party

Dreaming that you are at a fancy or elaborate party or general sort of gathering most often indicates one of two scenarios:

1. Dreaming about fancy parties can be a sign that you are satisfied with your wealth and general social standing. It is generally a good indicator that you feel loved, wanted, and successful in life.

2. Another possibility is that you are actually dissatisfied with your life on an unconscious level. Being at a large and/or expensive party would then be a representation of the kind of life you want, but do not currently have.

◊ See also: Ruined Party/Event

This one seems a bit closer to the mark. I used to have parties with friends all the time so it's possible that I miss having that. Now it's mostly just me and Kayla. I still go out on weekends, but it's always with *Kayla's* friends, a group that I swear is different from month to month. Still, I want to know more so I click on the hyperlink for Ruined Party/Event to see what this other symbol includes.

### Ruined Party/Event

To be at a party, event, or gathering of some sort which ends poorly is most frequently indicative that something in your life is either not going as planned or not living up to your expectations.

When dreaming about a party or event that is utterly ruined either in a figurative or literal sense, this is typically the mind's way of trying to sort out an outcome in your waking life which you perceive as having gone catastrophically wrong.

◊ Alternatively: having a party ruined due to a guest leaving can be a sign that you feel abandoned or rejected by someone in your life, or even by a group of people.

◊ Alternatively: a dream where a single guest or small group of guests is causing a disturbance or destroying something can mean that there are some people in your life who are preventing your happiness. These guests may be invited or uninvited, but often this detail is not specified in such a dream or at least not recalled by the dreamer.

At this point, I'm getting the vibe that I'm definitely-maybe a bit bummed out about life. I don't have my old friends or my old partying routine and I'm not even sure I'm happy with my relationship with Kayla. Is this really all that's going on? I'm just sad? I'm not sure if it's my pride or a sincere gut feeling, but I can't quite accept that this is all there is to it. I decide that the next word I want to search for is "Murder," but in the interest of not wanting the internet gods to think that I'm dreaming of killing people, I just filter for the letter, "M" and scroll down until I've reached the word.

## Murder

A dream in which a murder takes place could be symbolic of various things. Some possibilities are:

1. That someone in your life was literally murdered and their death is haunting you on a subconscious level.

2. That a recent death of someone close to you was sudden or suspicious in some way and seeing them murdered is your brain's way of trying to deal with those fears and suspicions.

3. That you are afraid of losing someone near to you.

4. That someone or something near to you was recently lost in some way, though this can be a more abstract form of loss as with friends who you have fallen out of contact with, but are still very much alive to the best of your knowledge.

I think I've had enough of this now. This is all good and maybe sort of helpful, but I think what bugs me the most about these dreams is how vividly I remember them even now and the fact that they occurred in sequence. Maybe it's just chance or coincidence, but I need some answers. There's nothing on The Dream Guru website about this so I head back to Ogle and run a search for "vivid dreams." There are a bunch of articles on how the relevance to one's conscious thoughts, hopes, and fears can make dreams more memorable. There's also a couple of neurological papers which are cited repeatedly in these web write-ups, but nothing that really hits home for me. I run searches on "repeat dreams," "episodic dreams," and "consecutive dreams" but don't get much out of the results for these either. It does seem like it's reasonably common for the mind to replay the same dreams or at least dreams with the same narrative patterns. And it seems like instances of this can feasibly occur on back to back nights so maybe I'm just jumping the gun on worrying about this. On this note, I close out my browser and turn my attention back to email.

I'm slowly opening the first couple of new messages when I hear, "Bryan."

I jump a little in my seat and twist around to find David standing at the entrance to my cube. His brow immediately furrows and he gets a bleak sort of look in his eyes. He's got the side of his hand resting against the metal rim of the cube wall-piece which makes me wonder how long he stood there tapping it with his knuckle before calling my name. The hand drops to his side and he takes two urgent strides into my workspace.

"Bryan, are you okay?" he asks in a hushed tone.

I develop a strange nausea, though I'm not sure if it's brought on by the concern in David's voice or the fact that this is the closest he's stood beside me in a good long while.

"Yeah, I'm fine. Why?" I shoot back at him but I sound hoarse for some reason.

He leans back a little and replies, "Nothing. I guess you just look a little tired is all."

"*That's a sweet way of putting it,*" I think to myself. Because what he probably means to say is "*Holy hell! You look like you got hit by a truck and then that truck rolled over you a couple of times before taking a giant truck crap on you.*"

"I haven't been sleeping very well." I admit this a bit begrudgingly since I'm annoyed at him for calling me out.

He gives me a slow nod and his features freeze for a moment before he says, "Right, well you've had a lot on your plate lately. Is everything else okay though?"

Hearing him talk to me like this definitely makes me a little sick to my stomach. He's talking the way he did when we were friends, but he has no right to do that now. Or does he? Is he right? I mean how awful do I actually look?

"Bryan?"

He cuts into my thoughts. I realize he's looking at me with even wider eyes and a more scrunched forehead. Have I been making weird faces or something? Or maybe it's just that I keep zoning out on him – that's it most likely.

"No, I don't think so." It's a struggle to get this out.

"Everything's not okay?" He confirms and I realize that I just gave the exact opposite answer of what I meant to say. Or perhaps it was a Freudian slip…

"No, no, I think everything is fine," I counter as quickly as I can, though I stumble over the words.

"Are you sure?" David cocks his head to the side as he asks this.

"Yes, I'm sure." I try to sound as decisive as I can.

"Okay, well you've done good work, so if you need to take off for a day or two to get some rest then just do it. Don't even worry about meetings or anything like that. If you're really needed then we can just call you in, otherwise I'm happy to cover for you. You've been putting in a *lot* of extra hours so if you don't want to spend a personal day, I could probably pull some strings to get you a couple of freebies."

The offer catches me off guard. It's weird to hear him say nice things about me after he ... I find myself at a loss for moments when he put me down recently. I know it happened, but still can't remember anything specific for some reason. Maybe the memories are just getting jumbled because of how chaotic these lasts weeks have been. But I know these moments of injustice happened, they must have...

"I appreciate that man." My voice sounds soft, maybe even weak. I also realize that I let that "man" slip through as though we were just chatting at a bar. He doesn't seem to make note of it though so I continue by saying, "I think I'm okay though, really." I'll just try to relax a little more tonight before going to bed.

"Sure, just let me know how things are tomorrow. You've definitely earned yourself a break, so everyone will understand if you need to take off. How has Kayla been by the way?"

*Again, with the compliments and the understanding!* Where is all this coming from? And asking about Kayla — switching the subject so I don't have to awkwardly thank him again — what is *that*? How does he have all the right moves and manners today? Is there some kind of angle I'm missing here? What's he really about?

"She's well," I reply, trying not to seem too surprised at his asking. "She's been pretty busy with trying to sell this one house that's a bit troublesome, but other than that she's been good. She just puts a lot of pressure on herself sometimes."

"Guess you two are in the same boat on that one then," he chuckles.

Same boat? *Really?* He's the one that's been putting pressure on me, not *myself*. In the interest of keeping this chummy civility going, I try to calm myself. He does have influence over any promotions I shoot for now, after all.

"How was it meeting up with the old crew last night?" Since I've already poured through the photos, I guess I don't really need to ask this, but he doesn't know about my creeping and it would be rude not to ask at this point.

"Oh, it was good, thanks. I've tried to stay in touch with most of them, but it's been forever since I got to see all of them in one place like that."

"Sounds like a good time for sure," I reply absently.

"Yeah a couple of them asked about you and I told them about some of what we've been up to here."

A sharp, sting suddenly runs through my body as I realize that I haven't been talking with any of them, not even Kevin. I wonder why they've stayed in touch with David, but not me. I was their friend too, *wasn't I?*

"Yeah, I can't remember the last time I head from any of them," I return coolly.

This breaks his composure for a moment. He just stands over me like I'm some kind of wounded puppy.

"Well they definitely miss you," he says at last. "We talked a lot about our times at Pinnacle – seems so long ago now, but not *that* much time has really gone by. We all agreed that we should try to do a night out like the old days sometime soon."

"That definitely sounds nice," I return, a little dispassionately.

"Only if you'd like to," he quickly adds. "We obviously don't want to intrude on your personal space or anything. We respect that you've got a pretty full life, but it would be real nice to have you join us sometime. Anyway, just try and take it easy today, get some rest tonight and let me know if you need a little break or anything."

"Thanks, David," I say as he's leaving my cubicle.

The second he's gone, I start stewing again. *"Intrude on your personal space,"* what's that about? How does he always manage to make *me* feel like the bad guy? You'd think that I told them at some point that I was too busy for them. But that's complete bullshit. They were my friends and I'd obviously make time for them if they wanted to see me. Or would I? I guess I didn't last night... I decide that I'm done thinking about this. Done thinking about all of it. I just want to find something to keep me busy for the rest of the day and not worry about anything else. Unfortunately, I don't really find any one thing to hone in on so I just putter through the rest of my day by completing little tasks here and there.

After work, I go over to Kayla's for dinner. She can cook a mean meal when she wants to, but most nights, tonight included, it winds up being some type of salad with garlic bread and wine. Tonight it's a chicken salad that includes chopped strawberries, canned mandarin oranges, blueberries, dried cranberries, and diced almonds. It's drizzled with a sweet Poppy Seed dressing and is accompanied by a White Zinfandel wine. It's an unusually sweet ensemble, but I like it.

"What inspired this?" I ask, looking up from my plate.

"Oh," she chirps as though suddenly noticing my presence. "Well, I had a salad just like this one the other day for lunch when I met with my friend, Annie. This week I've been craving it and it's been driving me crazy cause I don't even remember where I had it. I asked Annie, of course, but she's being a real bitch this week and she didn't remember either. So I just got the makings and did it myself."

She finishes with a quick bob of her head before returning to her dinner. She seems pleased with the fact that I asked about it, but I never got a chance to say that I liked it, only that I was intrigued by its origins. I feel defeated for a moment. Do I really have to fight to say something nice to my own girlfriend? I know I've already made her happy, but maybe this isn't just about her, maybe *I* want to be happy too.

"Well, it's really good. I'm kind of glad you had to resort to making it yourself."

"Oh thanks babe, that's really sweet."

I catch her grin, but she doesn't look up. She clearly didn't need such a spelled out compliment, but it makes me feel better to have made it. I take this win and let the rest of dinner carry on in silence. Afterwards I sit patiently while Kayla cleans the dishes off the table. Anyone watching this unfold would probably find it pretty sexist, but I gave up trying to help with the dishes a long time ago. One broken glass and you'd think I shattered this woman's whole world. After the catastrophic meltdown that ensued, I was surprised that I even got to use her dishes for eating ever again. Eventually, I thought it might be safe to offer to help clean, but the look I received in answer made the room temperature drop. There was no mistaking then that nothing was forgiven and certainly not forgotten. I made the mistake of offering a couple more times before I learned to just let it go. Now I try to think of it as being let off the hook, but I'll always know that's not really the case.

Once Kayla restores the kitchen and dining space to a spotless state, I instinctually rise from my chair, slide it back to where it belongs, and head over to the living room where I sit on the right, not the left, end of it. Kayla takes the middle cushion and retrieves the television remote from where it always sits in the middle of the glass coffee table. She surfs through the channels for a couple of minutes, but I know where we'll end up. Sure enough, the remote is set down once we reach TVS which is predictably playing <u>Fashion Bitches,</u> a competition where aspiring designers get challenges to design an outfit based on a theme and must then not only construct it, but also model it. Naturally, they only let the prettiest skinny girls on the show and always seem to give them a theme that inspires some sort of skanky getup. As one might guess from the show's title, they also only pick the most conniving, bitchy women they can find. I'll admit that it's an interesting concept to have fashion designers actually have to wear and model what they create. It's also neat that they bring in expert shoemakers and jewelers to compliment the contestant's designs with accessories that enhance their appeal. But I guess that alone doesn't make a good show, you need half naked women getting into catfights to make things really entertaining. Not that I'm complaining though, I love psycho women being psycho in small clothes just as much as anyone – I guess that makes me part of the problem.

I understand why Kayla likes the show too. She's always had a certain affinity for fashion and glamor. Between the sparkling apartment and her myriad of unique outfits, I guess she can be a bit of a diva in her own way. I'm her boyfriend and I don't think I've ever seen her in the same ensemble twice. Even her "comfy" clothes seem like a carefully constructed look. When we first started dating, I thought she did it all for me, but after we'd been together for a while, I realized she wasn't trying to impress anyone. She did it only for herself. It's not a problem that this is the case. She has a right to look as good as she wants to after all. But sometimes she looks so good that it's almost like she's distant or somehow unreachable. Like right now. We're sitting close to one another, but the slim space in between us makes me feel like I'm a world away. I slowly put my arm over the top of the couch behind her and realize I'm about to put high-school moves on my girlfriend of three years. But I don't care, I let my hand slip down to her shoulder and pull her in towards me with one motion.

"Babe," she lightly protests, but doesn't resist.

She feels tense against me like she'd rather not be in this position. We don't say anything for a little while and I realize that the silence feels uncomfortable. I try to focus on one of the particularly bitchy bitches screaming her head off at the passive aggressive bitch. While I sit here, I get a hollow sort of remorse well up inside of me. The picture of Kevin and Erin together under the sunset comes to mind. It's the way their eyes sparkle and how bright their smiles glow that makes me feel jealous even as I'm here with my own partner. Do Kayla and I have pictures like that? Have we had moments like that? I need to believe that we have, but at the moment, I'm really just not sure. And why haven't we moved in together yet? It's not because we're saving ourselves until marriage, that's for sure. And it definitely isn't cheaper to rent out two separate places. We could do a lot with the money saved from sharing a place. But then maybe it's that we just don't want to live under one roof. I like my apartment and I think she likes hers so maybe there's no point. Even still, I can't help but feel like something's missing here. I also decide that we aren't involved enough in each other's lives. Kayla has no idea what I've been going through at work and I had no idea she was mad at her friend Annie. Actually, I'm not even sure I knew she had a friend named Annie.

"So what happened with Annie?" I ask since I might be as much to blame for this problem as Kayla is.

"What do you mean?" she replies after a pause. She sounds disinterested and her eyes are fixed on the television.

I try to keep my voice steady as I say, "At dinner, when you were talking about the salad, you mentioned that Annie's been giving you problems."

"Oh, no, she's just being a bitch this week."

"What did she do, or say?"

"Huh? Nothing, babe, she's just being bitchy is all. Now, shhh. I'm trying to listen to this. Angelica hasn't been this crazy for weeks."

I'm about to ask when I realize Angelica is the woman who's been screeching for the last few minutes. If Kayla's honestly more interested in TV drama than what's going on in her own life, then I guess her issue with Annie can't be that bad. Still, I can't help but feel pissed for being put off like that. I know a good boyfriend would just let her watch her show, but I guess I'm in a fighting mood tonight.

"Sorry for caring," I mutter, making sure I'm just loud enough to hear.

"What's gotten into you?" Kayla snaps, pulling herself upright and away from me.

I'm left a little stunned by the viciousness in her reaction so I just shrug.

"You're all needy and weird this week, why?"

Again I'm at a loss for words so I just say, "I've been tired I guess."

"Alright, well head home and get some sleep then."

That's it? "*Go home and get some sleep!*" I mean can she be any colder? My last month at work has been complete shit, I've been missing my old friends, this relationship is pissing me off, and all she has for me is "*get some sleep!*" Maybe some of this is my fault for not outright saying these things, but I think it's mostly on her for not giving a shit about any of it.

"Okay," is all I can manage as I try to contain myself. "Have a good night, Kayla," I add before getting up and heading for the door.

"Good night, and get some rest," she calls to me as I put on my shoes and jacket.

By the time I'm heading through the door, her attention has already returned to <u>Fashion Bitches</u>. Making note of this, I shut the door a little more forcefully than I should and march out to my car. I hit the gym before I go home. It's leg day – can't skip it, no matter how tempting it might be. I would have rather worked out any other muscle group, but at least the workout does calm me down a bit. Unfortunately, it doesn't tire me out nearly enough. By the time I'm home and showered, I'm still pretty wired. Only now it's my dreams that have me on edge. What if I go back to the mansion? Twice is just a coincidence, but three times…three times is a pattern…three times is a problem.

I find myself hesitant to even go up into my bedroom. But I can't just not sleep. I'm exhausted enough already so losing rest isn't really an option. Not sure what else I can do, I withdraw a bottle of Merlot from my refrigerator. There's only about a fourth of it left, so I don't bother to pour myself a glass. I take the bottle over to the living room and sit sideways in a chair. Leaving the TV off, I just stare out the window while I drain the wine bottle. The more I drink, the more the city lights seem to sparkle. Eventually I notice that there's a pleasant warmth running through my body and a profound sense of calm that swims around my mind. Obviously, I'm not drunk, but I feel buzzed enough to be able to slip into bed without any worries or cares on my mind. So I drag myself up the stairs and into my room. All that my mind remembers to do is peel off my clothes and shut off the lights before collapsing into bed. I let out a deep sigh as I shut my eyes and then my mind falls into the black.

# Chapter 3

I open my eyes to find a crowd of people around me. Everyone is dressed in black. We're outside in a wide field of neatly kept grass and in the middle of us is a single gravestone. Before I can even wonder who it might belong to, I realize that this is a grave for Miss Shelly Simmons. Sure enough, this is the name I see etched into the stone once my vision clears. And that means I'm back.

*"Wait, back...back from what?"* I silently ask myself.

I start with the basics. I'm at Shirun's estate, a place I have been twice before. But I don't know the name of the manor or if it even has a name. I've met this Mister Shirun, but I don't know whether Shirun is a fist name or a surname. I have no idea how he came upon such wealth or how it is I made his acquaintance such that I came to be on his invitation list. I also don't see him here among us. And he should be here. Not only because this is his property, but also since Shelly was *his* guest who died at *his* party. But what happened in between her getting killed by the beast and now? Where am I back from? I rack my brain for the answers to these questions. At first, I have not so much as a notion as to what's going on, but then it all comes to me.

I'm Bryan Daley. I'm employed at Parson International. I work on a team that creates computer software – something I doubt the people here have any ability to use. I live at Spyre Apartments, Unit 616. I'm dreaming. But if this is a dream, then how could I know that I'm dreaming. That's not supposed to happen, that simply shouldn't be happening. If I know that none of this is real, then I should be awake, but I'm not. I'm still asleep and I'm still here without even the slightest clue of how to get out. This realization causes my head to throb so I bring my fingertips up to my temple where the pain is most severe and feel a soft padding of fabric. Startled, I feel around a bit more and discover that my head is wrapped in a soft, cotton cloth. Before I can identify the full extent of the bandaging, my hand is taken hold of. It's a gentle grasp, so gentle that I look over expecting to see Margaret, but it's not her, it's Jack that's holding me by my wrist.

"I know it hurts, but try not to play with that," he says, soft and whisper-like.

"Sorry," I return and drop my other hand down to my side, hoping to show him that I won't meddle with the bandage any further.

I expect him to release his grip on me, but instead he tugs me along toward the grave. I allow him to lead me even though I'd prefer to hang back in the thick of the crowd. There's a certain strength to the boy's stride and I can't help but feel that it seems odd given his slight build. He also looks skinnier somehow. I'm not sure if maybe his suitcoat is just a bit too big for him or perhaps he has somehow managed to actually get smaller. We come up next to the grave where Jack stops and turns to look at me. His blue eyes are shimmering and his complexion looks paler than usual – even his freckles seem faded. His hair is combed, but there are some stray locks hanging over his brow so I reach out and try to arrange them back into order. Jack stays perfectly still while I do this, his eyes never leaving my face. He's still gripping my wrist too. It's not a strong squeeze, but it seems to me that he doesn't want to let go. I can see the fearful look upon his face, the tensed jaw, and wide eyes. And he should be afraid, after what we saw.

But we didn't actually *see* anything because none of this is real. It can't be real which means that Jack can't be real. But the throbbing in my skull *feels* real. The grip that Jack has on me seems real. And the softness of his red hair as I push it back into place is as genuine a sensation as any. Is Jack a boy or some kind of cruel phantom playing a trick on me? His eyes fall toward the ground and I realize that I must be troubling him with my hard stare. So I reach a hand behind his neck and pull him into an engulfing hug. His figure feels cold and I detect a constant shiver racking his skinny frame. It's these details in the embrace that make it much harder to question the reality of his existence. I'd almost rather that he slip through my arms or at least feel somewhat ethereal in my grasp. But he's not that at all. He's solid and fragile, and he trembles violently. If he's not real, then he's at least real enough.

Yet there's still something about this place that isn't right. I look out into a vast field beyond the headstone. Every inch is trimmed and vibrantly green, but it's wrong somehow. It's too perfect. And there is far too much of it. The terrain looks endless and entirely isolated. As far as I can see out into the horizon, there's nothing but hills that roll on forever. I see no roads or rocks or trees, just an endless field. While I know there could certainly be a road on the other side of the estate, it's still troubling to have so much nothing before me. The same is true for even the air around us. The light here is dim, giving everything a gray sort of shroud, but there's not a cloud in the sky. It's just dim, like some of the soft blue has been sucked out of it. And I can't find the sun. It's just...missing...somehow it simply isn't there. Is any of this even possible? While Jack might feel real, the space around us is equally surreal, and yet there's a stark vividness to it as well. The air is not just inexplicably gray, but also bitterly cold. So cold that it stings, the way the cold does when the wind is fierce, yet the air is utterly still.

It's troubling in a way that I have never experienced before and more horrifying still is that Miss Simmons has been buried on the estate grounds. Hers is but a single, lonely grave sitting upon a vast, seemingly endless expanse of grass. Come to think of it, her headstone, footstone, and the mound of dirt in between are the only blemishes upon this entire field. Why here? There's no cemetery, not even a private one. There's just this one grave, all alone and inescapably out of place. To the best of my knowledge, Miss Simmons is not kin to Mister Shirun. And even if she were and even if it was the family's habit to bury one another on privately owned grounds, it's still strange that she is not deposited into a formal burial place.

"Mister Daley," Jack's weak voice bursts through the fog of my confusion.

I quickly release the boy and reply, "I'm so sorry for all of this, Jack."

"It wasn't your fault." I catch a few heads turning my way as he says this and feel the accusatory glances that make me wonder if I might actually be to blame for this somehow. I'm the newcomer to this place, after all, and things seemed to be going splendidly untill I came along. I imagine they are as unsettled by me as I am of this place.

"Do we know where it went?" I ask, turning my focus back to Jack who now has his arms crossed in a sort of self-hug.

"Where what went?" He sounds a little startled by my question.

"The creature that killed Shelly — the one I ran after," I explain.

"We didn't find any creatures, human or beast," a woman's voice from beside us cuts in.

I turn to my right to see a woman on her knees beside the grave. Her back is to us and her voice is not one I recognize. She has a small frame and I think she has blonde hair beneath the black lace veil that covers it.

"All we found was you lying back down against the walkway with a terrible gash across your forehead. You were lucky we came when we did because whoever struck you must have also been scared off."

The lady rises to her feet and smooths out the front of her dress. When she turns around, I recognize her as the woman Jack danced with last night ... at the last party ... or my last visit here. Her blue eyes meet mine for an intense moment that seems to last longer than it probably does.

"I'm very grateful then," I say at last. "I don't quite know what I was thinking, running after someone or something that just committed murder."

"You were being brave," she steps in as she says this and places a hand over my chest. "Shelly was my friend, I should have been the first to charge after her killer, but I —"

"You were in shock," I finish for her. Calling what I did "*brave*" is a generous approximation of my actions. Deep down, I know that I chased that thing in the interest of gaining answers, not to avenge anyone's untimely end.

"Perhaps," she concedes. "But what I wouldn't do now to catch whoever did this!" Her voice is low and bitter, filled with loathing for herself as well as the perpetrator of this violence.

I remain silent for a moment before saying, "I'm very sorry for your loss. I wish I could have done more."

"You did enough, more than enough." She says, much softer

now, but she pulls away from me and turns to the grave. A piercing chill seethes through my body in spite of there still being not even the slightest breeze to speak of. The space around me feels starkly silent again. I want to say something to someone, but there's not much of anything to say.

"Jasmine Cooper," Jack whispers to me. His voice is small, but manages to give me a start. "She and Shelly…they were the best of friends," he explains as I twist my head towards him. "You should find Myles, he'll be hurting too."

Jack leaves me with this thought and walks up beside Jasmine who has fallen to her knees again. He places a hand tenderly upon her shoulder and together they look to the gravestone – the only thing that remains of the late Shelly Simmons. I know I never really got to know her, but standing here now, I can't help but feel a sense of loss still. I can tell from the weight of all the mourning souls around me that she was someone precious to this group. And maybe it's my imagination, but I also believe I sense a bit of fear here. It's the uneasy silence that surrounds me, the way that people barely even move that makes me think that Shelly's death is not only tragic, but also a bad omen for us all.

After all, the beast from that night and whoever hit me are still very much at large. And if they were willing to kill one seemingly innocent young woman, then anyone else could be next. But judging from the way we're all just standing here, I'd say no one has the fire in their bellies to do anything about what's going on. I understand entirely that this loss is cause for great distress, but if we fail to take action then the number of bodies we need to bury may very well grow. Then something horrible suddenly occurs to me. On the night of Shelly's murder, I noted Shirun's absence from the party. While I may not have done a headcount of all the guests, it certainly seemed as though everyone else was present. And even if one or two others didn't make an appearance, is his absence not the most peculiar? In spite of my better judgement, I start to look around at who is present right now.

Scanning through the crowd, there are almost thirty people here including myself, but no Mister Shirun. I peer through the crowd twice, then a third time, but I'm certain after the first check that he's not here. I'd be able to pick his face out in any gathering, but if I'm to suspect him of being involved in a murder, then it's only right that I double and triple check myself. Finally I spot him. He's not among the crowd, but rather standing up upon a balcony that juts out from the third floor of the mansion. It's hard to see him from this position, but I'm sure it's him. Even though I'm too distant to make out his face, I can see his bronze complexion just fine. It also appears as though he's not even looking down at us – more like gazing over or beyond where we're gathered. It feels more than odd to have him perched above us like this. It feels wrong, in fact. And it certainly does little to ease my suspicions about him. Is this place some kind of a trap for us? Is Shirun a wolf disguised as a shepherd? Are we just being herded for the slaughter?

I realize that I'm getting some odd looks from those around me. I'm sure they're all wondering about Shirun as well, but I really should exercise a bit more discretion. I try and think fast in spite of how badly my head aches. Thankfully, I spot Myles and Margaret before I have to come up with anything particularly clever. Trying to make it seem like I was looking for them all along, I rush over to where they stand. I'm sure not everyone is convinced that this was my intention the whole time, but at least I no longer feel the burning sensation of a crowd-full of eyeballs bearing down on me. When I reach Miles, I see that he looks ghastly pale. His eyes are trained on the grass in front of his feet and seem to be locked there.

He doesn't look up or so much as flinch when I say, "Hello Margaret, Myles." I even send a curt nod in his direction, but he doesn't appear to see me.

"Oh hello, my dear!" Margaret coos. Before I can say anything else, I'm snatched up in her arms and she begins fussing over my bandages. "How are you feeling, Darling?" Her fingers flutter over the wrapping but never really touch it.

"I'm okay, Margaret," I assure her, but all of this attention suddenly makes me dizzy so I put a hand on her shoulder for balance.

"You sure, dear? You seem rather dazed?"

"My head just hurts still. And everything seems so strange, so wrong."

"It's a strange time for us all," Myles states quickly.

His voice isn't harsh, but it is quite loud and makes me jump a little. I realize that I might have said too much. And here I am supposed to be checking on Myles, but instead I've come for my own purposes and he's covering for my verbal carelessness.

"I know," I agree, hoping to abate any suspicion I might have aroused. "How are you dealing with all of this?"

"I'm angry." His eyes are still affixed to the ground. "I should have been there...I...I shouldn't have left. Maybe I could ha –"

"Shhh, Mister Westerly, do try not to do that to yourself," Margaret cuts in. Keeping one hand against my cheek, she puts the other up against his back and strokes it lightly.

"I tried to catch it," I offer absently.

"Catch what?" Margaret asks in a sort of gasp as she turns back to me.

"The beast that killed Shelly. It was a hound of some kind, a big one. I had a hard time seeing it in the dark, but I caught glimpses of its hind legs as I chased it through the garden."

"Dear, I don't think there were any beasts here. You got the knock on your head from a very human attacker and I think it must have your mind a bit jumbled."

"Enough, Margaret," Myles hisses. "You and I saw the wound to her neck, no person could have done that. No matter what Shirun wants us to believe, the facts are the facts."

Myles' tone is low, but it echoes through my mind. The mention of Shirun makes me feel desperate to share my fears about him. I'm quite sure this isn't the time or place to do that, but I need some answers and I need them this instant.

"I think –"

"I have a fine idea of what you think, my boy, but let's save those thoughts for the reception, yes?"

Myles' eyes shoot up to meet mine as he cuts me off. My senses feel frozen in place and an overwhelming feeling of embarrassment washes over me. I manage a brief nod before falling into absolute stillness. I stay with them like this until the group begins to depart from the grave. It's unclear what initiates this exodus. I myself feel only a sudden compulsion to withdraw. So I follow Margaret and Myles toward the manor like sheep herded into a barn. Looking back, I see Jasmine and Jack still kneeling beside

Shelly's burial spot and imagine they will be the last to answer the silent call. The procession heads through a modest back door, down a narrow hall, and lands in a grand lounge area where tall, round tables of food are set up. By this point, the absence of servers or attendants no longer fazes me much. There are much larger oddities to fret over now, after all. I follow my companions toward a table covered in crystal wine glasses where each of us takes one in hand. Then they lead me over to a back corner of the room where three chairs encircle a small end table. Not wanting to dull my senses, I set my glass down upon the table and look to each of them expectantly.

For a few minutes, no one says a word. Myles eyes the room suspiciously as people settle in. I join in observing the crowd around us and notice that this is an event where it seems one is not expected to mingle much. The crowd splits into smaller groups of people that appear to take no notice of anything outside of their immediate circle. Jeremy and Natasha fall into a group of five while William and Joanna shrink away onto a small sofa. They're not snuggled up against each other, but there's certainly a kind of intimacy between them that I didn't detect before. Perhaps it's the way they just sit there absent of any conversation and abstaining from refreshment of any kind. They're just two souls, trying to block out everything around them. The Baxters shoot me an unkind glare from across the room before they disappear into the largest circle of people. Jasmine and Jack amble into the lounge after a few minutes. I see them for only a few brief moments as they gather up a plate of crackers and cheese and then slip away into some corner of the room invisible to me. It's a somber scene indeed. As I notice that nearly everyone has food or drink in hand, I can't help but see us as being fattened for our inevitable harvest. He may possess magic trays that refill themselves and rooms of extravagant comfort, but Mister Shirun may very well not be as benevolent a host as he appears. No, perhaps it's this pampering that will be our undoing.

"It should be fine to talk now," Myles announces. A light din of conversation does indeed fill the room and there seems to be no one within immediate earshot so I expect that he's right.

"Where would you say we should begin?" I reply.

"You said you saw it, the thing that…the monster that killed

Shelly?" Myles' voice is deep and low. It's not shaky, but there's a certain strain on it, a hint of desperation, I'd say.

"It looked like a dog of some kind, a big one – almost as large as a bear. But I didn't get a good look at it and it was giving off strange shadows," I explain.

Myles tugs on the right curl of his moustache and eyes me very carefully as he replies, "But it wasn't the hound that gave you the blow to your head was it?"

"No, I don't know what hit me. I had the hound's hind legs in my sight and then suddenly a piece of metal swung in front of me. Then it all went black…"

I almost mention that I awoke after, but it seems distasteful somehow to tell them that I think this is all some twisted dream. No, for the moment I ought to treat this like reality, especially since I can feel pain here which is about as believable as anything. Plus, there aren't many in this place who I can count as friends so manners are of the essence with these two.

"You see, Margaret, what did I tell you?" Myles groans. "We both know what we saw, why do you insist on buying into Shirun's fiction?"

"Oh, I don't know, Mister Westerly," she snaps back. She has a distant sort of look about her and the bright veneer of her eyes seems dulled. "Perhaps this is all too much. None of us really knows what's happening, but I can't stand the thought of some devilish creature on the prowl. Still worse, I can't bear the thought that such a creature is aided by a person, perhaps someone who we've come into close acquaintance with."

"Is it…" I falter, not sure I really ought to ask what's on my mind.

"Go on, my boy. If you've got a thought, let's hear it."

"I'm not sure I should."

Myles looks at me with an iron gaze and the weight of his impatience bears down on me without relent.

"Is it possible… that maybe…" My voice sinks to a low whisper as I finish with "…Mister Shirun is somehow involved in this?"

Myles leans back in his chair and Margaret brings a hand up to her mouth. It's quite possible that she lets out a small gasp, but if she does, it's too quiet to hear. My heart sinks at the realization that I have most certainly gone too far so I quickly try to come up with a recovery.

"Wh-what I mean is..." I sputter, "...Mister Shirun was missing from the party. To the best I could tell, all other individuals could be accounted for that night save for him. And if everyone else was at the party, then he is the only person that could have sprung me in the garden. Unless you think that someone could have been intruding on the grounds."

"Oh no, my dear," Margaret chimes, dropping her hand down to the arm rest. "People do not simply intrude upon these grounds, it isn't possible. If you are here, then it is because you are invited." Thinking about the vast emptiness around us, I imagine that this is an entirely accurate statement.

"So it must have been Shirun then?" I conclude.

"Not quite," Myles corrects, leaning forward in his chair and keeping his voice down. "When I went looking for him that night, I found him in his chambers, the doors wide open. He was pacing back and forth whilst muttering to himself all the while."

Myles drops his head and fiddles with the left curl of his moustache. Looking to Margaret, I see that she wears a sullen expression which deepens the creases upon her face. It seems to me then that she looks quite old and perhaps unwell.

But before I can inquire into her well-being, Myles continues. "It was the queerest thing I ever did see, my boy, especially coming from our Mister Shirun. Seeing him like that held me at bay for a fair while, but eventually I remembered the anger which brought me to that spot. So I interrupted his mad ramblings and demanded the answers which I sought."

"And what answers were those?" I butt in, though I'm already quite sure that I know.

"It's – I..." he grimaces a bit as he stumbles to find the right words, "See I was asking about you, my boy. I wanted to know the nature of your arrival. I don't mean to be cruel, but you're not like us, you see. We all realized this after your first party with us. It was like you were with us one moment and the next, you...were somewhere else."

"Do not all the guests take leave of the party at some point?"

I challenge.

It fills me with a sickly horror to know that my coming and going is noticed here. And I wonder what sort of dream involves the dream people acknowledging the dreamer as an outsider. This is *my* dream after all…isn't it?

"We don't mean to frighten you, dear," Margaret answers softly.

"I know, you warned me that I was different," I say wearily.

"Still you look even more spooked than when you and I last spoke."

"Right enough, my boy, sorry if I've gone and alarmed you," Myles adds leaning in toward me. "It's just unprecedented is all. And what's more is that Shirun never warned us of your coming nor did he offer any explanation upon your arrival. He gave us no inkling as to who you might be or what your presence might mean."

"But we don't think any of this is to be blamed on you," Margaret assures me. She reaches out to give my knee a soft pat.

It occurs to me that I must look terrified in my present state. My jaw is clenched, my breathing tight, and I find myself holding onto the armchair as though some great force might come and sweep me out of it.

"No, not at all, my boy," Myles promises. "So far as we can tell, you are a blameless participant in whatever discord has befallen us. A bad omen, perhaps, but hardly the source of our problems."

"*The Source*," isn't that one of the things Margaret said I might be? What if I *am* the cause of all of this? Are they being entirely honest with me right now?

"So what did Shirun say about me?" I ask, trying to sound a little more relaxed, but maintaining a firm grip on the armchair.

"Nothing to abate any of our anxieties…"

There's a tinge of frustration in Myles' tone. I can hardly blame him for it. It's disappointing to hear that Shirun had nothing helpful to say, but perhaps the fact that he and Myles were speaking rules out Shirun as a potential suspect in Shelly's murder.

"There was just a lot more wild rambling on his part," Myles continues. "He babbled on about how I couldn't understand what's going on, but that he would need me to act as one of his *'champions'* when the time came. I kept on him for some real answers, but all he would tell me was that my support would be crucial to him – critical to us all really. And he apologized incessantly. What for, I cannot really say. I *can* tell you one thing for sure, though: Shirun is not the person that attacked you in the garden. He was with me still when we heard Shelly's screams and he came down with me to find her mangled corpse. When we got there we heard Jack's cries for help. He must have found you shortly after you were rendered unconscious."

"And *I* can tell you for certain that Shirun was not the only person missing from that party," Margaret adds. "Miss Olivia Kristov was notably absent as well."

"You're sure," Myles asks, snapping his attention over to Margaret.

"In your anger you must not have had your wits about you, my dear. You as well as I know for certain whenever someone is out of place. We're old enough to know every face, and have little trouble noticing when even one guest is not in our company."

I get the sense that Margaret is saying these things more for my benefit than for Myles', but he gives her a few nods of acknowledgement. I do have to wonder why she counts Myles as being as old as her when he looks only a little older than myself. And even then, he may actually appear younger if not for the prominence of his moustache.

"But Olivia though!" Myles sighs. He places his hands over his knees and lets his head hang below his shoulders. "I suppose I really should try and keep a closer eye on things then. Now that I think of it, I don't recall seeing her there myself. But of all the members of this assembly, she is one of the last I could imagine causing even minor mischief, never mind an act as heinous as what has been committed."

"Is she here with us now?" I ask hopefully.

"No, dear, I daresay she isn't," Margaret answers without hesitation. Myles instantly scans the room and Margaret gives what I see as an obligatory look around – I'm certain that she noted Olivia's absence long before now.

"We'll need to be finding her then," Myles concludes.

"Shouldn't we be asking Mister Shirun for his help?" I wonder aloud. "This is his estate, after all."

Myles shakes his head. "He may not have been the one who attacked you nor do I think he's involved in Shelly's death, but I'm also not inclined to trust in his assistance. Whatever's happening has him pretty spooked too and he knows far more than he's letting on. He's outright lying and hiding things from us, even. Like with Shelly's death, he tried to convince us all that it was done by the hands of a person despite her wound clearly being the work of some foul beast. I'd reckon that he's more interested in trying to keep people from getting too panicked to really be of use in solving this crime. And another thing: this isn't his house, he was just here first."

This last bit leaves me more stunned than anything else that has been said so far. How could this not be Shirun's house? What does it mean that he just got here first? And why did my question about guests leaving get ignored? Is anyone really a "guest" except for me?

"We will also want to exercise discretion in taking our leave," Margaret points out.

"Right you are, let's exit one-by-one out this way."

Myles gives a slight gesture towards an open concept doorway near our back corner of the room. Looking around it seems like many of the "guests" have sufficiently drowned their sorrows and fears in wine. I see Myles do a similar check around the room before getting up and casually strolling over to the exit. I watch anxiously as he leaves, but no one appears to take notice. When I turn back to Margaret, she flashes me a weary smile.

"It'll all be alright, you know," she says to me in her motherly voice. "Things might seem bleak right now, but we'll have it sorted in the end. You'll see. You're in good hands, too. Myles and I will take good care of you."

"And you *trust me*?" I ask, but I'm not sure if this is fair.

Margaret's grin widens as she replies, "You've got a good heart, Mister Daley, even if you don't yet think so – even if you do not yet know how to let it lead you. But yes, we trust you. Before this is all over, I imagine we'll all need to rely on you a great deal. You are the key to arriving at a resolution, of that I'm certain. I'm not afraid in the slightest either, I believe in you. I just pray that you will believe in us as well, that when you need us, you will trust us to come through for you."

"Marg —"

"It's alright, my dear. Just think on it is all. Should be about time for you to join Mister Westerly, I'll be along in just a bit."

I give the room several look-overs before cautiously arising from my seat. I know I need to proceed with care, but each stride is made with urgency and by the time I reach the hallway where Myles waits, I realize that I've been holding my breath.

"Smooth escape, my boy?" Myles greets me with an expression that has to be some kind of amused smirk. He's leaning up against the wall with one hand in his pant pocket and the other adjusting the curls of his facial hair.

"I think so."

"No worries, old chap, was just a joke. Normally all eyes would have seen you leave, but I'd say everyone is far too pickled presently to have noticed if you hopped up on a table and did a little jig."

The very picture of something like that happening brings a light smile to my face. It's nice that he can still joke, even at a dark time like this. I don't know the full extent of his relationship with Shelly, but they were undoubtedly close and I'm sure this loss has him in a lot of pain. Now here he is consoling my worries and I've done nothing for his. I truly am the most useless whelp in existence. I mull this over while we wait in silence. Eventually, Margaret comes through the doorway like the final tail of a wave sliding up onto the shore.

"So, what now?" I ask

"Now we find us some answers," Myles replies, pulling himself away from the wall.

# Chapter 4

"If there's any place someone might go to hide, it's the second floor," Myles explains as we ascend the wide staircase. One side of it is exposed to the foyer space so we try to ascend it with as much haste as we can. "Most of us spend all of our time on the first floor, you see," he continues though I feel as though we really ought to be a little more silent. "That's where most of the party rooms are, not all, but most. The second floor contains a good number of littler rooms and chambers and the top floor is mostly for storage, more bedchambers, and of course, Shirun's room. Above that is the observatory which is much less of a floor than it is a great room which sits atop the manor."

"Few of us even know how to find our way around the upper floors," Margaret adds as we reach the top of the steps.

"Who else aside from you two are among those few?"

"There's Carolyn and Charles Baxter, Olivia, and Jack," Myles answers.

Having Jack included in this list seems a bit odd given his age. So I comment, "So you've shown young Jack around as well then?"

"Young!" Margaret titters. "Oh no, darling, none of us are especially young, some are just older than others. But little Jack is one of our oldest and dearest friends."

I decide that this place is just never going to make any sense to me. And why should it? If it's just a dream then it should be of no surprise to me that everything is backwards. Yet the longer I stay here, the less like a dream it feels and the more afraid I become.

"Let's put a pause on that chatter now, shall we," Myles suggests.

He stuffs a hand into his suitcoat and withdraws a shining revolver. I don't quite know why, but the sight of this man makes me think of Mr. Green from <u>Clue</u>, a board game I enjoyed as a child. And if he's Mr. Green, then Margaret could be Ms. White. I'm a bit young to be Col. Mustard, so I guess I'm stuck with Prof. Plum. And we've got ourselves a murder, a revolver, and a suspect. I then have the dastardly hope that Olivia will be as lovely as Clue's Scarlet. But the good news is that perhaps this crazy dream is just a product of my subconscious childhood memories. Maybe I ought to relax and have a bit of fun with it all.

"Mister Westerly!" Margaret gasps, interrupting my thoughts. "Wherever did you find a nasty little thing like that?"

"It's been in my possession for a good long while, Madame Pembrook," he replies, perhaps a bit mockingly.

"But whatever do you have it for?"

Myles shakes his head at her continued protest and retorts, "We can't very well confront a murderess and her hellhound without some protection now can we?"

"Just try not to do anything too rash, who knows what we'll find up here." Margaret goes quiet after saying this. Even her footsteps barely make any sound.

Most prominently heard is the sound of Myles' controlled, but forceful breathing. Occasionally there's a crack or a groan from a floorboard, but the hall down which we walk is mostly still. The floor is stained in a deep burgundy and a thick crimson carpet lines the center of it. The walls are painted in a sparkling white and stretch continuously down into the mansion, broken up only by burgundy support beams and gold picture frames. Inside these frames are a variety of classically painted portraits and landscapes. They are of no place I know, nor any face I recognize, but are all equally lovely to behold. We proceed through this space using a wordless process. First I fling open a door then Myles leans inside with his revolver held out in front of him. Margaret trails close behind. She may not be an active participant in this search, but it feels safer to have her with us. Maybe it's because she's so steady and secure while this hall is…well it's not precisely dangerous, but there's something rather unsettling about being here. It might be how quiet it is or how empty these rooms are. Whatever the cause, there's an unmistakable eeriness in the air.

The first few rooms we enter are small, but elaborately furnished bedrooms. Either the people staying here keep these rooms immaculate or no one actually spends the night in them.

Given what I know about the mansion so far, my guess would be the latter. I'd normally ask myself what kind of people don't use bedrooms when there's more than enough for everyone, but these are dream-people so there's probably no sense in them sleeping and even less sense in my questioning it. As we move along, we come upon other types of rooms. There are a couple of lavatories, a billiards room, a lounge, and a cocktail room amidst the endless string of bedrooms – all of which are starkly empty. The constant and methodical process of searching through each room starts to wear down my resolve. A part of me still dreads the impending confrontation with Olivia and perhaps her pet as well. The other aches to just be through with this affair. We're closing the door to yet another room when Margaret lets out a dainty huff and stumbles against the wall.

"Madame Pembrook," are you alright? Myles gasps as he rushes over to support her.

"Oh my!" she groans as though a great weight has just befallen her. "It's just that I have a sudden aching in my bones and a terrible knot in my belly. I don't think we should go any further. No, I think we ought to turn back right now and get some help from the others."

I've remained frozen in place this whole while, unsure of what precisely has befallen this normally calm woman. Has she had a premonition of some kind or has she simply lost her nerve? Given how very near I am to experiencing a break in my own composure, it would hardly be surprising for a lady of her age to experience a breakdown of sorts.

"It'll be alright, Lady Margaret," Myles assures her. He tugs her away from the wall and has her lean against him. "We must press on though. I'd warrant that we're getting close to catching our killer, we have to be. But if you need to retire, I'm sure both Mister Daley and myself will more than understand."

"No, no I will press on," she declares, pulling away from Myles to stand on her own. "I just have the sudden fear that we are about to stumble upon far more than we have accounted for."

Myles gives her a tender pat on the back of her arm and marches back to where I am still just standing. He holds his gun steadily at his side and gives me a brief nod as he passes by. Margaret and I follow his lead down the hall as it comes to a U-shaped curve. On either corner is a winding staircase just like the one we came up. On our right is a wall, unbroken by doors and to our left are large bay windows which let in rays of gray light from the outside. It's a nice stretch to walk down since there are no rooms to examine here. I can just look out the windows and see what lies outside. Below us is the massive rose garden which is now tainted with the fruits of a horrible crime. Beyond it is another field of endlessly perfect grass. It's of little surprise to me that this is so, but still a bit disheartening. To see so much emptiness creates a sense of dire loneliness so I take my attention away from this landscape and observe the paintings we pass by instead. After we've rounded the corner around to the second half of the floor, we come upon a whole host of empty rooms which we search. It all seems calm, but a deep chill floods through me. It's not quite an aching as Margaret described, but rather a sort of biting cold which penetrates my skin and wraps around my bones. This chill slows my steps and stirs up a poignant nausea in my gut. It's not long after that I notice a change in Myles' pace as well.

An "Oh my!" escapes Margaret's lips.

I turn to find that she has frozen in place a few steps behind where I come to a stop. Her eyes look sunken and a sickly pallor overcomes the rosy complexion of her face. Turning to Myles, I see him standing tense with this gun held aloft – pointing at the open door which I just now notice a little ways down the hall. It's not only peculiar in that it's open, but also because a dark gray fog rolls – no, writhes – out of its archway. It's a ghastly sight for sure and it behooves me to wonder what could cause such a wicked sort of vapor to spill out. The stuff is far too thin to be smoke, yet much too dark to be steam, so I am left without much of a guess as to what it is. If not for these fumes, the door would not look particularly different from any other in the hall. It's the same size, design, and color as all the rest, yet it manages to still be dreadfully ominous.

"This door was never here before," I hear Myles say.

I walk up next to him and ask, "What do you mean? How could a new door just appear? Are you quite sure that you simply don't remember it? There are a great many doors on this floor, after all."

"Oh I'm quite sure, old chap! I remember this spot well. It was always a mere stretch of wall, strangely bare in a hall of neatly spaced doors. If ever a door existed here before, I would know about it."

I have nothing else to say on the matter. This turn of events is far too strange for me to comprehend. One thing is abundantly clear to me, however…we should turn back. Yes, we ought to turn back and do so right this moment.

But then Myles says, "It's no matter, I think we've found our mark, now's the time to act."

"What if Margaret's right? I think we ought to turn back."

"Oh no, old chap, that won't do at all! Let's not lose our courage now, not when we're so close to getting this sorted! So close to getting Shelly's murderess brought to justice!"

There's an indomitable certainty in Myles' tone. His words don't seem at all negotiable. They're not a suggestion or a request…they're a mandate, a demand. For some absurd reason, I'm compelled to follow his command without further protest. Myles must know that his assertions have this effect because he marches off toward the mysterious entrance without waiting for a reply. I hesitate only to glance back at Margaret who moves past me with unsteady steps. I follow her down the hall and watch as Myles enters the room with his weapon at the ready. We quicken our pace as he disappears through the doorway, but when we turn into it ourselves, we freeze in horror.

The room is shrouded in the same thick fumes which spill out into the hall. Perhaps it's this unnatural vapor creating a sinister effect, but the room appears to be shades darker than the rest of the house. The walls look like they are painted in a hazy ebony and even the wooden supports are stained in a dingy gray. A crimson rug covers most of the floor, but the shade of red is so deep that I almost mistake it for being black. There are no real lights in the room, only twisted candelabras which sit upon triangular golden tables. The combination of this sparse lighting and sharp reflections create an uneasy and spotty atmosphere that does little to actually brighten the space. Even eerier are the long shadows cast from a myriad of oddly shaped bottles, coin stacks, and statues of nude women.

These statues depict ladies in a selection of different poses: some flailing their arms dramatically, some swooning with one hand over their brow and the other cast aside, and the rest are sprawled daintily over the white marble bases which support them. Each of these statues also has a small bowl placed upon it. In some, the women are holding a copper tray and in others it is set by their feet. A sort of incense rises up from them which is apparently the source of the knee-high cloud of smoke which swims around us. The bottles come in peculiar S-shapes, pyramids, and long tubes with spherical protrusions bubbling outward. When I walk up to one of the tables, I pick up a coin for further inspection. It's a relatively plain object with only a thick outer rim and a beveled eyeball shape popping out from its base on the front side. On its backside is the profile of a crowned person looking off into the distance. From the flowing hair and plump lips, I first take the face to be that of a woman's but when I notice the square jaw and pronounced eyebrows, I realize that it could also be a man's face. It's a strange little thing that's ice cold to the touch so I set it back down where I found it. In fact, the entire room is cold, so cold that we can see our own breath. Save for all the weird artifacts, it's also empty. Neither Olivia nor anyone else is hiding out here. So what might this place be? Some kind of perverted shrine? A horde of bizarre treasures?

"What is this place?" I ask out loud, hoping either Margaret or Myles will have some inclination toward the nature of it.

"Not a clue, my boy. I only know that there's no other room in the house quite like this one and that it's not supposed to be here."

"Perhaps we were just never meant to find it," I offer.

"No darling," Margaret sighs. "In this house, things that wish to remain hidden, will remain hidden. Things that wish to be found leave the door open unto any that might come along."

I'm about to question her on what she means when a small tremor rumbles though the mansion and disturbs my balance. There's a groaning sound which floods the space around us, likely from the building itself. Then an arid stench fills my nose that stings like smoke. I see that the back wall of this room is indeed burning, but not necessarily on fire. There are thin lines of sparks which singe the paint and leave a horrific burning red symbol on the wall. It's not entirely demonic so far as I can tell, but I'd guess that it's also not representative of anything holy. The glyph is comprised of a triangle in the center where each point on it intersects with a circle which surrounds it. From this circle shoots strange, spikey projections. If not for the center triangle, this circle and its spikes might look like a child's depiction of the sun. But then, of course, there are also the four orbs surrounding this main shape. Each connects with one of the spikes and forms a sort of box pattern around the main portion of the symbol. It's a simple, yet curiously striking design which I'm quite sure I've never seen before, yet I can't help but feel certain that such an icon cannot belong to anything good.

Then there's another rumbling through the house which makes the stacks of strange coins chatter. When the tremor subsides, I suddenly notice that a bed draped in silver curtains is set in a back corner of this chamber. From beneath the shadows of it is a pair of glowing green eyes. They're not a pretty sea-green like Margaret's, but rather a sickly, pale, lime-like shade. What's more is that they are not human eyes, but rather more like those of a serpent where the pupils are narrow slits cutting through large irises. Immediately I'm left to question if those harrowing eyes have been trained on us this whole time or if they're a new presence in the room.

"Myles," I croak, finding it hard to speak.

But Myles already has his revolver aimed at the bed. The three of us remain still, our attentions given to whoever or whatever is in that bed. Could it be that those eyes belong to the beast? Does this room belong to it? Before any of these questions can be posed, there is a deep, clanging cackle that comes from the creature concealed in the shadows.

"Hello there, little ones," it says through the laughter.

I can't quite tell what gender this being might be since its voice is neither masculine nor feminine. It has a sharp, industrial sound to it instead, like two pieces of metal scraping against each other. The sound of it sends goosebumps down my back and fills me with a sick feeling at the base of my throat.

"I've been expecting you," it continues, no longer laughing.

The thought of this thing waiting for us makes me shiver. "So many curious little bees in this house! So foolish of you all to think you have any say in what's happening here."

"Who are you?" Myles demands, "Are you the one that killed Shelly?"

"Oh my dear Mister Westerly, you're a brave one, I'll give that to you, but I daresay you're not altogether bright."

"Answer me!" Myles shouts this time. It gives me some comfort to see him so unafraid of whatever peers out at us from the darkness – whatever thing already knows our names.

"I'm a guest here, same as you," the creature responds, keeping the same, even tone. It's a tone that sounds either incredibly patient or entirely dispassionate.

"You're not a guest any of us know of," Margaret challenges. "If you were, I'd certainly have made your acquaintance by now."

"Indeed, but how naïve of you to think that you know all there is to know about this place. No, I'd say you are aware of but a fraction of what exists here, a mere nugget of what there is to know."

"I'd say you're an intruder, an unwelcomed guest if you're a guest at all," Myles snarls.

The creature lets out another cackle before replying, "I can assure you that I am *quite* welcome here."

"Is that so?" Myles steadies his aim with his free hand and squints a little.

"Quite, why not just ask Mister Daley? It's upon his invitation, or should I say *invitations* that I have come here."

"Impossible!" I snap back. "I've only just got here a little while ago and can promise I have not been sending invitations of any kind to anyone."

I'm not sure if I'm trying to convince myself or my companions of the falsity of the creature's claims. It is my dream after all, which means that this thing is indeed as much a construct of my imagination as anything else here. All I know for certain is that I'm no longer having fun. This dream is hardly like playing a game at all.

"Dear Mister Daley, how very little you really understand. You will come to discover that a great many wrongs are because of the working of your hands, my existence is but one of them. It will be delightful to see how you choose to become engaged in this little affair."

The creature behind those burning eyes laughs a loud, shrieking laugh. It's a sound that careens into us viciously like a brutal gust of ice cold wind. Every fiber of my being shudders to think of what this evil thing's meaning might be.

"What are you?" I hear Margaret utter.

"Your doom," the thing states simply.

Then the manor shakes again and the red-hot glyph radiating off the wall starts to spin. The center triangle turns in one direction and the rest of it goes in the other. The light coming off of it becomes blinding and a low growl comes from it.

"We need to leave here now!" I practically scream.

As I do so, a shadowy beast pops out from the glyph as though it's some kind of doorway. In that instant, I'm sure that this is the monster from before. Its eyes match the fiery color of the symbol and flicker inside its eye sockets like some kind of flame. It has a long canine snout with a sparkling set of ivory teeth that drip with saliva. Its features seem like they're stuck in a permanent snarl and a deep, throaty growl echoes out without pause. Even more harrowing still is the way that its entire body seems to be made up of steaming black ribbons all tangled up into an apparently solid figure. Strips float in tattered sections up off of its back and at the end of its tail like fur. It's some kind of demonic, smoking, mummy-dog which is tenfold as horrible as I ever could have imagined. I feel immediate regret for being unlucky enough to witness the sight of this thing up close.

"Go!" Myles bellows as he fires a couple shots toward the dog.

The bullets find their target, but have no effect on the beast. They just enter its body with a snap and a sizzle, but the dog doesn't so much as flinch. It's as though the ammunition is either absorbed into it or melted before its ribbon-like skin can be penetrated. Before I can marvel at it much longer, Margaret takes my hand and pulls me along behind her outside of the room. We race down the hall toward the staircase at its end. Evenly spaced wall lamps whizz by as our feet propel us forward faster than I imagined they could.

I'm surprised at how nimble Margaret is given her age. I'm sprinting with all my speed yet Margaret is nearly dragging me behind her. She's going so fast that I worry she's going to cause me to trip. She must be fast for Myles too because I can hear his pounding feet and heavy breathing as he struggles to stay on our heels.

Then a voice floods through the hall, the clanging voice of whatever creature sits in the shadows of that bed. It says, "Run little ones, run! Flee from your destruction as though there is any escape. Soon enough, you will see that there is nowhere you have to run to." I can hear the being as clearly as I did before.

Is it here with us now somehow? Does its voice just carry with supernatural power? Or has it somehow burrowed its way into my mind? Margaret tries to move us along with even greater haste so I surmise that she must have heard the echoing voice as well.

"Faster," she commands.

"I can't!"

Behind us I hear Myles fire off another couple of shots. By my count, that's four now, leaving only two rounds left in his revolver. And still the hideous growl from that devilish hound grows louder. Its steps, which were previously inaudible, can now be heard in a soft, rhythmic pattern. One more gunshot cracks through the air then another shortly after and now I know that this beast can't be stopped. All I can do is desperately hope that we can outrun it. It feels like a devil is nipping on our heels as the top of the staircase finally comes into view. Myles catches up to us and it looks like we're going to make it, but then what? This thing isn't going to just stop chasing us. Even if we make it downstairs to where the others are, how can we stop this thing? Will it simply devour everyone in the mansion? What purpose would that serve? To what end does the creature in the bed hope to bring us to? A quickening in Margaret's pace pulls me out of the what-if's and brings my attention to how loud the growling behind us has become. Myles is now nearly beside us, but I'm not certain any of us will evade the beast. The thing's footsteps sound like they are right on top of us.

In a sudden turn, Margaret comes to a complete stop with her leg planted in front of me. Unable to react in time, I trip over her and tumble toward the stairs, my hand no longer held by hers. I twist around on the floor to see Myles bringing himself to a stop beside me. Margaret stands firm a few paces away, her back to us. She's just waiting there, ready to embrace the beast's bite.

"Margaret!" Myles bellows, but it's far too late.

The dog leaps on top of Margaret who never flinches away as it pins her down and sinks its teeth into her shoulder. She lets out a pain-filled screech as a sickeningly large chunk of flesh is ripped off of her and swallowed by the monster. I remain stuck in place as I see the blood pouring out of the lady. But not Myles, he charges fearlessly at the creature.

"Get off of her," he howls.

Then, further down the hall, I think I see it – the creature from the bed. It's figure is obscured by a large, flowing cloak, but I immediately recognize its glowing green eyes. I still can't discern its gender as its shoulders are as wide as its hips, its face is hidden in shadow, and it walks with an animalistic gait like a predatory feline. Myles is about to tackle the dog when the hooded being flicks its arm to the side, the long flap of its sleeve waving like a black flag. In that instant, a cylindrical field of iridescent black light appears around Margaret and the beast. Myles slams into it with all the force intended for the dog, but is repelled backward. He lies beside me on his back as I watch in horror while the dog bites Margaret's entire hand off – a hand thrown out to defend herself. The blood from this amputation spills down her arm and dribbles onto her contorted face.

"What are you doing? Come help me!" Myles growls as he recovers from his dazed state and stumbles to his feet.

I get up and follow him toward the strange force field. As we bang on it, the beast swipes its claw across Margaret's face. Blood oozes out of the gashes across her previously comely features. Is this to be all of our fates? To lie pinned down by this creature, writhing and screaming while it tears us apart!

"Run!" she shrieks as we continue to bang on the unbreakable shell.

A cackle vibrates through the hall and the cloaked being giggles, "Yes little ones, go along. Mine is a methodical genocide, not a single massacre. You will meet your ends soon enough, do not be so eager to die just yet. After all, I have so much more in store that I'm just dying to share with you both!"

The beast takes one last bite out of Margaret, this time tearing out her throat just like it did to Shelly. Margaret gurgles a little before the life leaves her tear-filled eyes. Her body still spills out more blood than I have ever seen in my life. Then the beast looks up at us and I swear it smiles. It's snout is smothered in Margaret's blood and the red smoke rising from it eyes intensifies. Myles and I take a step back from the dark wall around the beast and I have to wonder what will happen now. Without warning, the swirling light-field brightens and the spinning intensifies. A high pitched hissing noise floods my ears and pierces my brain.

"That will do for today, little ones!" the hooded figure snickers. "Now, begone!"

I notice that the hooded creature looks quite tall, even at the distance it stands behind its mutt. Then the force field bursts, flinging Myles and I backward through the air. I see Myles smash back-first against the wall, knocking a picture off of its hanging. He falls limply against the floor. Then I collide with the carpet, its thickness doing little to soften how hard the back of my head bashes against it. A sharp jolt of pain rushes through me. But the force of the explosion rolls me over my head and onto my side. My shoulder bangs against the edge of the top step and then I roll down the hardwood staircase uncontrollably. Every part of my body is racked with pain as I tumble downward, but it's the blows to my head that fill me with pain so intense that my vision blurs. Finally, I take a sharp hit to my left temple and everything goes dark.

# Epilogue

My eyes snap open and I let out a sharp gasp. Where am I? What the hell just happened? At first the light is too bright. It stings my eyes and makes my head ache. But then I realize that I'm at home. I'm in my bedroom, but not in my bed. Scrambling into a crouched position, I realize I'm on the floor. At some point I rolled off of my bed, maybe that's why my whole body feels sore. And I'm also feeling pretty pissed. How could I have had this dream again? It's been the same, continual narrative for not just two, but three consecutive nights. How could it have been so intense that I rolled out of bed? Why am I breathing heavy? Is this really just a dream? If it was a dream then how did I figure out I was inside of it? How is it possible that I could remember reality? What was all of that bullshit the creepy creature talked about? Am I possessed or something? Haunted maybe? Mentally ill? Why were all of my thoughts still in a weird oxford-proper affect? What the hell could possibly be happening?

When I try to stand, I feel dizzy, so I slowly lower myself back onto my ass. I run my hand through my hair and find that it's damp. I touch my chest with the other to discover that it's greased with sweat. Then I become unpleasantly aware of my own body odor. There's something else too, a sort of metallic, salty taste in my mouth. Without thinking about how I just touched my chest-sweat, I stick two fingers into my mouth. When I pull them out there's a thin layer of blood coating them.

"What kind of a dream makes you bleed?" I ask myself out loud, finding that my throat's dry and my voice sounds scratchy.

Then one last question dawns on me, "*Why is it so bright in here?*"

I twist my head to the end table where I leave my cell phone and scramble over to it on my hands and knees. When I snatch it up from its resting place, yanking it free of the charging cord, I realize that it's 8:45 AM. I'm forty-five minutes late to work and I have a 9:30 AM meeting. I'm too sweaty to just throw a suit on and head out and even if I did, I'm betting I'd hit some nasty traffic.

"I'm so screwed!" I huff as I scramble to my feet and lurch toward the bedroom door.

But my head is still reeling and I immediately crash face-down against the floor.

"*Shit!*" is all I can manage to hiss as I deal with a whole new wave of pain and disorientation. No amount of panicking or hastiness is going to save me so I just lower my forehead to the carpet and whisper, "Whatever this is it has to stop, *please* just stop…"

But I know better than to think that I can just wish this away. Whatever this mess is, I'm probably going to have to sort it out myself.

# *Book 3:*

# Dark Horizon

*To all the people who were ever patient with me.*

# Chapter 1

I've never stopped to appreciate just how soft and cushiony my bedroom carpet is until now. It's a damn good thing too because I'm going to be here for a while. Whatever this violent spinning sensation is, it's way worse than any hangover I've ever had. The pain pulses through my entire body, making it impossible to do anything but lay here. I know I didn't really fall down any stairs, but it certainly feels like I did. It's unnerving to think about this because dreams aren't supposed to hurt you, right? I've never heard of dreams doing something like this to a person and what's worse is that I really don't have time for this. What am I supposed to tell management when I burst in late to a project closeout meeting?

"*Oh hey, sorry guys, I had a really bad dream,*" I bet that would go over great with everyone!

The average person would probably have the sense to call in sick, but that's not me – that's never been an option – not when I can get some facetime with the higher-ups. So I let out a savage groan and lift myself up to my elbows and knees. Then I snatch up my cell phone lying beside me and crawl off towards the bathroom.

"Hey Sapphire," I say to the phone as I edge my way across the room.

There's a playful little ding as my phone's artificial "intelligence" comes to life, ready to listen to my commands.

"Cady's Cabs," I order.

Hearing my voice followed by my phone's chime of acknowledgement sends a shockwave of hurt through my skull. After a few seconds of loading, I see the search results come up. I give the address a quick check before hitting the click-to-call link and bring my crawling to a halt as the dial tone resounds like thunder into my ears.

"Cady's Cabs, how can I help you?" the woman on the other end answers in a twangy accent.

"I need a cab at 502 Covington Way in twenty minutes, can

you guys do that?"

"Oh, sure, sure, hon. I can send one right on over. Could I get a name and phone number?"

"It's Bryan Daley, thank you so much," I reply before clicking the phone off and resuming my infantile march to the bathroom.

Was it a douchebag move to hang up on her like that? Yeah, but get with the times, woman! There's this thing called caller ID and there's a 99% chance that I want a callback on the number that I just called you on. Plus there's no way I'm reciting my full number twice (they always ask for it twice), not while I'm like this, not while she can take ten seconds to check the ID and jot my number down. I just hope that she doesn't get pissed and choose not to send a cab because there's no way that I'm driving to work in this state. Hell, I can't even walk! I can't even stand, really. I pull myself up into the shower over the tub wall and manage to sit myself up tall enough to twist the knob.

After a blast of cold water, it eventually warms to a nice, steaming hot. The feeling of it crashing down on me is one of the most glorious things I think I've ever felt. I try not to let the fact that I never slipped out of my underwear diminish the utter bliss of this moment. It's my moment – mine and for some reason it feels like the first thing that's my own in a good long while. But I know it can't last too long so I reach for the shampoo bottle and squirt some into my hair. Tilting my head back, I let it wash out and then dump a bunch of body wash all over me. This I don't bother to wash off. I just lay back and let the shower head do all the work. All of this clears my head a little, but it still feels heavy as a rock.

With every bit of resolve I have, I pull myself to a seated position and turn the magnificent flow of water off. I know I need to move so I support myself on the tub wall and step out. At least I can kind of stand now. My knees still feel like they're about to buckle beneath me, but as long as I prop myself against the bathroom wall, I manage not to come crashing down to the floor. I try and breathe easily as I open the closet door and fish for a towel, though my heart still thumps a little faster than I'd like. I'm not sure what time it is, but if I miss that cab, I'm screwed, so I dry myself off and check my phone.

"Nine, eleven," I read out loud. "Nine more minutes..."

Since I've got no time to just hang out here, I walk myself out along the wall and reach my dresser. With a lot of crafty leaning, I manage to change into a new pair of underwear, pull on a white undershirt, and slip on some gray socks.

"Nine, thirteen," I tell myself.

That leaves just seven more minutes until my ass needs to be outside. I scramble along the wall to my closet where I pull out a white shirt and throw it over my shoulders. Then I get into a pair of navy pants and a matching coat. There's not enough time to get all tucked in, so I just slip my feet into black loafers and snatch up a black tie.

"Nine, fifteen...**shit**!"

I slide out of my room and make a sort of leap from one side of the hall to the other. Then I curl around the corner where I cling to the stair rail for dear life. What I'd love to describe as a "walk" down the stairs is really much more like a slide since most of my weight is on the railing. Either way, I do eventually make it down to the living room. But now comes the hard part of stumbling across it into the kitchen. The result isn't pretty. I get a few steps in and then I crash to my knees. A few more steps, then back to my knees. Then I give up and crawl the rest of the way to my kitchen island where I have my computer bag propped up.

"Nine, nineteen," I read, taking a knee by the bag.

No call from the cab driver yet, that's a good sign...maybe. It means I either have a couple of extra minutes, or that no driver is coming at all. Either way, I think that I'm an actual psychopath for trying to get to work at this point. But I don't care. I sling the bag's strap over my shoulder and reach up to the edge of the countertop to pull myself up. I let my weight rest on it as I step through the kitchen and eye the door. After a deep breath, I heave my body toward it, crashing against the wall beside the exit. Snatching up my keys from their hook, I open my door and slink through. My hands rattle as I slip the key into the lock. Now I'm out – just have to get to the elevators and down to the streets.

It's a dishearteningly long skid down the hall and I'm sure the sound of someone sliding along spooks more than a couple of the residents here, but they'll get over it. By the time I'm at the elevators and have pushed the button, a bigger concern is upon me. It's 9:25 AM now and there's still no call from the cab company. Even if I make it down right as my ride gets here, I'll definitely be rolling in late to my meeting. But what if the cab just doesn't come? The very idea gets my heart racing again. But then my ringtone goes off and my breathing comes to a halt.

It's not from a number I have in my contacts so a flurry of hope rushes over me. "Hello," I answer.

"Eh, Mista Daley, I'm out front."

The elevator dings, but it feels like an eternity before the doors finally slide open. "Alright, I'm in the elevator right now, be out in just a moment."

"Can't be out ere too long Mista Daley, this ain't a spot for parking."

"I know, it will literally just be one minute."

"Ohkay sir, see ya in one minute," he replies before hanging up.

I slap the elevator wall a couple of times as though it will make the doors close any faster. When it lurches downward, my stomach feels out of sorts all over again. By the time it groans to a halt, I feel a little dazed by the sudden stop. But I've got to hold it together. Taking a deep breath, I force myself out of the elevator and across the lobby. In spite of my best efforts, I'm sure I'm walking like a drunk, but I try not to think about that. I just focus on each step I take and tense all of my muscles in hopes that I can keep my balance.

By some act of God, I make it to the golden revolving door and see my cab still waiting for me right in front. Using the last of my balance and grace, I stumble over to it and run into the back door a little harder than I meant to. No longer trying to keep up appearances, I scramble to fling open the door and toss myself into the back seat. I get a funny look from the cab driver in his rearview mirror, but try to ignore him. Safe at last, I pull the car door shut and dump my bag in the seat beside me with a sort of grunt.

"The Parson Tower, Sunbury Ave."

"Yes, yes, I know where dat is, Mista Daley."

The cab scoots forward without another word, the sudden change in motion making me even more nauseous than before. My hand flies instantly to the bottom of my abdomen, the pressure somehow making it all feel less dramatic. It's then that I remember that I'm all untucked still. Looking down at myself, I see that while I might be in dress clothes, I'm definitely not looking very dressed up. My dress shirt is barely buttoned, my coat is flapping wide open and my belt...oh God! I don't have a belt! We're only a couple of blocks away from my apartment, but it's way too late to go back there now. I'll just have to try and conceal the absence of a belt using the flaps of my suit coat. The main thing that's flawed about my plan is that the jacket parts right where a belt buckle should be. Maybe if I just walk with my computer bag hanging in front of me and keep my arms crossed once I've settled in at the office, I can keep anyone from noticing. Trying to keep this hope in mind, I button both my shirt and overcoat up and tuck in my button-up as tightly as I can. Then I snatch up my tie which is draped over my computer bag and proceed to put it on. All I can think of as I do so is how savage I must have looked getting into this cab. This driver has got to hate me for being an entitled slob or something. Not that his opinion is relevant, but still, there's no getting around the fact that I am an absolute mess right now. I try to calm down once I have myself sorted, though it's hard to be this disheveled and play it cool.

Even at this late hour, traffic is still horrendous. I try not to look at the clock on the cab's radio and I shove my phone into my pant pocket. I'll be late to this meeting for sure, but I don't want to know how late, there's no use in that after all. Instead of fretting, I let the side of my forehead press against the window and look out into the streets as they roll by ever so slowly. It's like the little bit of calm right before a big storm. I try to enjoy the present since I know the future won't be all that much fun. Right now, my problems seem so small, so irrelevant and that somehow feels amazing. But naturally, it doesn't last. Eventually the cab does come to a stop in front of the Parson Tower. When it does, I have a moment of panic where I realize that I forgot my wallet. Fortunately, I keep my gift cards stashed inside of my phone case so I scramble to pull it out and pry the case apart where I find a VistaCard prepaid gift card with fifty dollars loaded on it. It's signed and I'm sure I've activated it already, so I go ahead and slide it through the cab's billing console.

I even pick the highest tip, though I don't actually read the amount. I'm grateful to have had such a lucky break, though the cab driver is definitely twice as disgusted judging by the way he's staring at me in the mirror.

"Alrighty then, Mista Daley, ave a nice day," he says as I hurriedly shove the rest of my gift cards back into my phone case.

I reach into my coat and slip the VistaCard into my shirt pocket. Before leaving the cab, I take one last deep breath in preparation for the coming walk of shame. That's of course assuming I'll be able to walk at all, but I try not to dwell on that. I'm feeling much better now, not great, but I should be good enough to pull this off. So I sling my bag onto my shoulder and shove the cab door open. I feel a little shaky stepping out of the vehicle and my legs don't cooperate much on the first couple of steps. After that though, I have a bit of a rhythm down. I'm still dizzy and sore and am probably walking a little criss-crossed, but I don't think I'm in danger of falling over. Even coming out of the revolving door is fine so I stride with a little more ease over to the elevators, which are fortunately pretty empty since it's so late in the morning.

By the time I make it up to the eleventh floor, I've still managed not to see the time so I have no idea as to what I'm about to step into. Once I'm out and in front of Ronda's desk, it's impossible to ignore the large digital clock that sits on the wall behind her. It's 9:56 AM now making me twenty-six minutes late to my meeting – I only planned to be five to ten. I can't remember whether it was scheduled for a half an hour or an hour, but at this point, it's really just a matter of two different degrees of awful. Just when I think that I'm in as rough a place as I can be, Ronda stands up at her desk with her mouth agape. Now I am faced with the horrible truth that I still look like a disaster, even after my efforts to straighten myself out.

"Oh no, hunny, come here," she greets me in a hushed tone while waving me over to her. Like a scorned child, I meander along and come to a stop beside her desk. She licks her thumb and uses it to smooth my hair across my brow. I manage not to cringe even though I find the whole finger-licking, hair-fixing trick gross – it's got to be a generational thing. Next she straightens out my collar and tugs on the center of my suitcoat. Then she moves on to adjusting my tie before stepping back and looking me over. Her eyes narrow and she pushes my bag to the side, exposing my beltlessness.

"One sec, Bryan," she huffs before swinging around and ripping open one of her desk drawers.

When she turns back, she presents me with a black leather belt.

"Ronda, you're an angel! Thank you."

"No worries," she chimes, throwing a hand through the air. "You aren't the first I've seen in this pickle and I'll bet you won't be the last."

"You just have this on hand?" I ask, shoving the belt into my bag and positioning it back in front of where my belt should be.

"That one, a couple other sizes, a few black and white ties, a few shawls, and some assorted feminine products," she explains.

"Look, this is awesome, thank you so much again. I'll bring this back with me tomorrow. You're a lifesaver."

"Don't even mention it, dear. Back when I was your age I had some of the *craziest* nights! It was seriously a wonder I was able to stay employed during those years of my life."

Ronda's smiling and giggling at the memories. As much as I'd love to explain to her that I don't look like this because of partying, it's better that I just bite my tongue. This woman really is an absolute sweetheart.

She must notice me nervously eyeing the office space, because she says, "Go on, now, you're looking good enough for whatever you're running late for."

"Thank you, Ronda," I repeat before scurrying off.

I weave through the rows of cubicles and duck into mine. Once I've set my bag down, I pull out the borrowed belt and slip it through the belt loops of my pants. I'm as put together as I'm going to be so I pull my laptop from its bag and emerge from my cube to see David and our executive sponsors leave the conference room at the other end of the office. I missed it! I missed it completely. Suddenly the living hell that I made it through this morning seems utterly meaningless. I don't really know why I forced myself to come in. Now I just have more egg on my face than I would have otherwise. It occurs to me that I can still duck back into my cube and either slip away or find a way to recover from this, but then

David and I lock eyes. It only lasts a moment, but it's enough to make my hairs stand on end. As David turns his head he waves me after him with a subtle flick of his wrist.

Looking around, I find that the executives are retreating to the elevators, probably returning to the top of the tower or running off to some other meeting. With the coast clear, I follow David toward his office. I try and walk with as much pride as I can, but I feel like a teenage shithead getting summoned to the principal's office. It's worse when the "principal" used to be a good friend. Fortunately, no one is up and about so I skulk in through David's door unnoticed – so far as I know at least.

"*Not smart, Bryan,*" I think to myself as I come in.

David is closing the blinds on his inner windows so I close the door behind me and take a seat in front of his desk. When I hear the blinds on the door drop, I know I'm about to get the third degree. It's probably what I'd do if I was in his position, but this actually isn't what it looks like so it sucks to get reamed out for what I'm sure David thinks is irresponsibility. He walks around to the back of his desk and pulls his chair back. Before lowering himself into it, he puts his hands on the desk and leans in to look me over. I say nothing and do nothing – I don't want to give him the satisfaction of my sniveling or squirming. I don't look at him either so I'm sure he's probably having a hard time reading me.

"I'm – I don't – I'm wondering if you're okay, Bryan," he stutters as he eases into his seat.

It's a weird way to open up a scream session and it brings my eyes up to meet his. I'm too stunned at first to reply. Why would he start like this? It's like he thinks I'm some kind of child – this is almost worse than getting chewed out.

"What I mean is, this obviously isn't like you. Since we started I think I can count all of your sick days on one hand and you've never come in at a time that most would consider early." He chuckles at this and leans back in his seat.

I don't know why he's laughing, there's nothing about this moment that's funny unless it's amusing to him that I've finally screwed up. "It's not what you think," I tell him and jump a little at how scratchy my voice still sounds.

"I'm not thinking anything, man," he replies, leaning back in and returning his features to a more even expression. "I'm just worried. You're never late, you take only enough vacation time to avoid losing any, and you work longer hours than anyone else I know both in the office and at home. Now here you are. You've missed a stakeholder closeout meeting, your hair isn't styled, your eyes are red, and you're wearing one of Ronda's emergency belts."

"What?" I burst out. "How do you know this is Ronda's belt?"

"Because I recognize it from borrowing it once," he smirks a little as he says this. "It was a couple years ago when I was trying to stop drinking so much coffee and I came in so tired that I didn't even know I was missing a belt until she pulled me aside."

I just nod, vaguely remembering that point in time. I wonder how many people old Ronda's saved with this belt or one of those ties.

"I just want to know what's going on with you. Why do you look like hell? Why do you seem so pissed off? Why are you even here? You could have just called in."

I guess this is it, the big blowup. This is all I get. On one hand, I should be touched that David has taken such a gentle tone with me. But on the other, this makes me feel so much more stupid than if he just yelled at me.

"I don't know," I say flatly, but realize I can't go with that so I correct myself, stating, "I don't know if you'll believe me if I tell you."

"I don't have to believe you, Bryan. I've known you for long enough to know if you're telling the truth or not. Whatever it is, you can just tell me."

"I – I haven't really been sleeping," I explain. "I mean, I have, but not well … there are these dreams I'm having and they're messed up and it's been going on for the last three nights and this morning they made me sleep right through my alarm. I just woke up, I felt like death and I panicked that I'd miss the meeting so I showered and dressed and got a cab, but it was too late. I tried to be here, but I was too late…" My voice drifts off and I realize that I either sound like a complete psychopath or a total cry-baby.

I can't really tell which conclusion David has arrived on. His face isn't stone cold so much as it is contemplative.

"What kind of dreams?"

"Not nightmares, something worse – more elaborate. I don't know, I get that this sounds stupid, but it's the truth and I don't really want to talk about it here."

I say "*here*" but what I really mean is, "*I don't want to talk about it with you.*" David just nods, slowly and repeatedly. Did he hear the sharpness in my tone? Does he think I'm insane or maybe just that I'm full of shit?

"You said you took a cab right?" he confirms.

"I didn't feel good about driving," I admit, "I felt dizzy and –"

"No, that's good, that was smart at least. But I would have preferred that you just stayed home. You don't have to come in if you're not well. You do know that, right?"

"I'm fine!" I hiss, slamming a fist on the table.

David shifts back away from the blow. He looks to me with a furrowed brow and now I know he thinks I'm a psycho. But he corrects himself, finding it in him somehow to soften his features.

"Can I take you home then?"

"What?"

"Well, I know you'll probably want to work the rest of the day now that you're here, but let's bug out a littler early and hit up a happy hour someplace. We can get dinner there too – my treat on all of it. Then we can talk and I'll get you back to your place after. I've been thinking about a way to say thank you for all of your long hours lately and this seems like as good a way as any."

I sit forward with my fist still on David's desk and my mouth slightly agape. Did I just blow up on him only to have him offer to buy me dinner? Why won't he yell at me back? I know he wants to. Just because he's a big fancy man in a spiffy little office doesn't mean he's suddenly above it all. So I glare at him good and hard. I don't know if I buy into any of this crap, but at this point I'm not in much of a position to really decline. He's making me look like a complete asshole and I can't have that, not now, not from him.

"Alright," I say in defeat. "Yeah that'd be great," I add, trying to sound a little more grateful.

I may not know what David's real play is, but I should try to be nice. He's the only one that seems to have my back right now.

"Good, at four I'll come grab you. Until then, I told our sponsors that you weren't feeling well so if you could just lay low for the day and not sign into OfficeSync that would be great."

"You didn't have to cover for me," I say, my stomach dropping.

"We've always covered for each other — it's what we do, right?"

Maybe I really am just a piece of shit. I can't remember the last time having his back crossed my mind. I guess that always was our way as we moved up through the ranks, but I'd figured we were done with that. Apparently he never stopped. Now I'm more embarrassed than ever, so I force a smile and nod as I get up out of my seat. He grins back, but I leave him without another word between us. There isn't much left to say anyway.

# Chapter 2

At 4:00 PM sharp, David swings by my cube. Normally I'd feel lousy about leaving early after coming in late – or just leaving early at all, but I've accomplished nothing today anyway. Another hour or two in the office won't change that. Plus, I guess if your boss is the reason for leaving, then it's all fine and good anyway. It still doesn't feel that great though. I make my protest by packing up as slowly as I can, but David makes no complaint. He just sits in the extra chair in my cube and waits. When I'm done, he rises – still without saying anything – and leads me towards the lobby. I send a gracious nod Ronda's way as David and I wait for the elevator. She gives me a little wave back as though just saying "*have a good evening.*"

A light ding and swoosh of the elevator doors beckons me into the cart. There are three other people inside which makes the silence between David and I much less awkward. The ground floor button is already lit up so David and I just take up our places and wait for the elevator to make its descent. We pick up a currier on floor seven, lose two and pick up one on five, and then lose two on the second floor. As we're arriving at ground level I can't help but think about how this elevator trip is a lot like life. People just kind of come and go out of it, some you know well while others you never really know at all. I wonder if this is all life really is, just a constant dance of meeting new people and then saying goodbye. I try to cast this idea aside as we get out and stroll across the main lobby toward the parking garage elevators. We only have to take this down one floor, but already I'm starting to feel like spending time alone with David will be beyond uncomfortable. Fortunately, he's always in so early that he gets a good spot in the basement garage. I do too normally, but most get stuck parking in the side garage, a block down the street.

I'm led to David's car. He drives a Wersedes as well, a different model than mine though. I have the VX750 and he drives a M700. We bought them around the same time a year or two ago.

Mine has a better growl when you kick it into ignition, but his rides a little smoother. This model also has cool, futuristic headlights that make the front of his vehicle light up like a spaceship every time he starts it up.

In spite of the awkwardness between us, it's a relaxing drive out through the city. We're heading toward where I live and an ungrateful part of me hopes he'll just skip dinner and drop me off. But I don't think I've ever known David to back out of something he said he'd do. As we get closer to where we live, my heart starts to thump inside of my chest because I think I know where we're going. Sure enough, we find a spot along Werther St. and I can see it from where I sit. On the corner of Werther and St. Andrews there's an upscale pub called The Golden Clove. It's a charming little spot to get a high quality meal and enjoy a wide variety of unusual craft beers. It's also where David and I started hanging out outside of work. We've celebrated promotions and birthdays here and it's a place that I haven't been to in a long time. I feel a sudden pang of guilt for not taking David here when he became my manager. Maybe that's why I get the feeling that I've been avoiding this place somehow.

"This work for you?" David asks, looking over to me.

"Yeah," I say, trying to recover, but I'm sure he's noticed my lapse in composure.

We get out and walk in through the front door where a young man stands in waiting at the host's podium. I'm thrown off by it being a guy. I know it's not that out of the ordinary, but it's also not as usual as having a hostess waiting there with a wide smile. Maybe I was looking forward to being greeted by a hostess rather than a host.

"Ello there, ow many today?" he chirps.

It's then that I realize why he's the acting greeter. He has an authentic-sounding Irish accent! Looking more carefully, I notice his light brown hair, pale freckled skin, and light blue eyes. The boy is about as Irish as you can get without going to Ireland and snatching one of their youths up. Then again he could also just look Irish. Some ethnically inspired places have been known to recruit workers from the Avánt School of Theatrics. I've got to wonder if this boy is an actor or the real deal.

"Two please," David says

"Alrighty. Ight this way if you would please," the host instructs as he snatches up two menus and leads us into the dining area.

He could be an actor. He's short and has a strong jaw as well as a build that may not be athletic exactly, but also isn't scrawny. Or maybe he's actually just from Ireland studying abroad or something. I'm not sure why I'm harping on this so much. I guess if I can't tell it doesn't really matter. Fortunately, he leaves our sight once we're seated at a high table for two and I no longer have to think about it. Moments later, a girl arrives.

"Hey there, I'm Amy, I'll be taking care of you today. Can I start you off with anything to drink?"

There's no accent on this one and she's not exactly the type you'd stick out front. She's a bit thicker — big boned is the polite description, I think. But at least she's well endowed, making what would be a loose-fitting T-shirt a bit taut. She's got a nice enough face too, or at least knows how to apply makeup in an elegant manner.

"Two Dark Clouds, please," David answers. "And could we get some cheesy breadsticks as well?"

"Sure thing, I'll put those in and be right out with those drinks."

She shuffles off and heads straight into the kitchen. Since it's so early, the place is just about dead which will keep things moving a little quicker. Then I look to David and it strikes me that things are moving in slow motion for him right now. He's scanning the room — probably just taking it all in. And then I have to wonder how long it's been since he's been here. It's close to where I live, sure, but there are a whole mess of other places we could have gone. Did he really have to be weird and pick this one? It's almost like taking your girl back to the place where you had your first date. For couples, that cheesy kind of shit is cute, not so much for a couple of buddies. At least I don't think so. And it's kind of messed up, the way he's in this really distant disposition. It's like he's in a different time, seeing things that aren't there anymore.

"I've missed this place," he says at last. "Have you been here recently?"

I shake my head. In complete truth, I can't really remember the last time I came here.

"Me neither. I've thought about it a couple of times, but could never bring myself to actually go. It's kind of out of the way for me now, you know?"

I nod. He really is a bit of a drive away now. I can't recall exactly where he moved to after his big promotion, but I know it's closer to where Kayla is. It's kind of strange to me that he misses it so much though. It's just a restaurant we're talking about, right? I haven't really thought about it at all myself. Thankfully our waitress returns with our drinks before I have to say anything.

"Here we are then. Are you ready to order or do you want me to give you a couple more minutes?"

Neither David nor I have opened our menus yet, but he asks, "Could I get the Bangers and Mash?"

I remember now that this was always his favorite plate. I think I have a favorite too, but I can't think of what it's called now.

"And what about you?" our waitress asks, turning to me.

Tossing open the menu, I thankfully find what I'm looking for. "I'll do the Gentleman's Corner Club Sandwich." It's a Corned Beef Rueben sandwich that I can't believe I forgot about.

"Great!" she pips. "I'll take those from you and be back with the appetizer."

We hand her our menus and she takes off again. Now comes the awkward silence, soothed only by the light strumming sound of instrumental Irish folk music. Not knowing what to say or do, I cup both my hands around my tall beer glass and turn my gaze into the dark, frothy lager. It smells rich with hops and spices as well as a hint of coffee, but I don't take a sip. This is a great place filled with fantastic food and even better memories, but I don't really want to be here. It's just too uncomfortable to sit in this place with David now.

"So," he hums and I remember why we came here in the first place.

"You sure you don't want to ask her to spit the check?" I ask in desperate hopes of avoiding the coming conversation.

"I'm sure," he says deeply and firmly. "I just want to hear about what's going on with you. I need to know how you're doing."

"I'm fine, really." My eyes remain fixated on my beer.

"Bryan, I don't want to sound cruel, but you're a mess right now. I mean none of this is like you. I just want to know what's going on and if I can help."

The worst part of this conversation is that I can't just get up and leave if he pisses me off. I'm close to home, but it would be a pretty long walk to get there from here. I don't want to be an ass to David, but I also don't want to have this talk with him. He's my boss, not my mother.

"Fine," I snarl. "I am a mess, but I don't know what's happening to me. That's the truth." My eyes dart up to him defiantly.

David shrinks a little in his chair before he replies, "You said you weren't sleeping well – something about dreams that were bothering you."

"I don't know how to explain it in a way that makes any sense." The edge in my voice is gone, now I just sound defeated.

"Have you told Kayla about them?"

The question gives me pause. I guess she should know about them, but if she stopped talking about herself for more than five minutes, maybe I'd have had a chance to share them with her.

"No," I tell him.

The waitress comes sailing in with a plate of breadsticks in hand. "Here you go," she sings as she sets it on the table.

"Thank you," he tells her before she's off again. Turning back to me, he asks, "Have you talked to *anyone* about this?"

Now I feel really uncomfortable so I just shake my head – guessing he already knew the answers to these questions. He bobs his head in thought a few times and then takes a long sip of his beer. I drain a little from my own glass and find some comfort in the thick, bittersweet texture. When I put my glass down, David's looking at me with wide eyes and a slack jaw. This isn't really his problem so I don't know why he's trying to get involved in any of this.

David's jaw tightens and loosens again before he says, "I know it's been hard for you with me as your boss and it's been weird for me too. But I'm not here as your boss right now, I'm here to be your friend. I don't want to see you struggle and if you need

128

someone to talk to, then I want you to be able to talk to me."

*Friend*, it's been a while since I've thought of him in that way, but I guess he never got that memo. Still, it's a nice offer, I just feel strange taking him up on it. Then again, maybe I should. He's right that I don't have anyone to bounce things off of, sad as that fact might be. And looking at David now, under the warm glow of the restaurant's lighting, I can almost see the friend that I used to share everything with.

"They started three nights ago – Monday night," I begin. I was in this fancy mansion with all of these fancy people and I ate the most incredible dinner I've ever had. But things were weird, like how I couldn't remember who I was or how I got to the party, or even what I look like. And then there was all this food that seemed like it had been set without any servers buzzing around. The host was really odd too. He was a bizarre and indistinguishable mix of different races and had kind of a strange manner about him. Oh, and there were these desert and wine platters that appeared to magically refill themselves."

"Well, at least a couple of those things sound pretty nice," David chuckles. It's then that I also see the easy-going grin that he always used to wear – one that I haven't seen in a long time.

"I thought so too, but then I was back in that same mansion the next night. It wasn't the same dream, but definitely the exact same place with the exact same people. Only this time they all looked afraid of me. They were worried that my presence might mean something bad for all of them. And sure enough, one of the women there ended up dead. I tried to catch the demon-dog that did it, but got jumped by someone who hit me upside the head."

David looks at me a little more seriously now. I can't tell if he thinks I'm crazy yet and I don't know if I should continue.

"That's definitely a little unsettling," he says. His voice is smooth and sounds encouraging, but I'm not really sure how much more I can tell him comfortably.

"Then last night, it was worse." My voice is no longer as steady as I'd like.

David reaches for one of the bread sticks and I do the same. Eating the warm, fluffy, cheesy bread buys me a satisfying moment of quiet time. Trying to stall a little longer, I take another sip of beer as well.

"Did you go back to that same mansion?" David prods.

"Yes, and they were having a funeral for the girl who died, but it was weird because they buried her in the mansion's backyard, not a cemetery. And then I was finally able to remember who I am."

"You mean who you are in real life?"

"That's right, and I recognized I was in a dream which is weird because I don't think that's supposed to happen."

"I've never heard of that, no." I'd forgotten how active a listener David is. He could always keep even the most difficult or awkward conversations moving forward. "What happened to you next?"

For a moment, I hesitate since what comes next is easily the most bizarre part of it all – maybe bizarre enough to earn me a nice straight-jacket. Eventually, I say, "Well there are two – I'll call them people – that befriended me right away on that first night. I teamed up with them to try and find the woman they thought might be behind the murder. What we found instead was this creepy room in the manor that no one knew about and a shadowy … creature … inside. It said a bunch of weird stuff, basically blaming me for everything bad that happened and would happen and then sicked the demon-dog on us. The thing tore one of my friends apart and then a weird magical explosion knocked me out, or woke me up I guess. I'd fallen out of my bed, felt dizzy and sore, was sweating, and had blood in my mouth. It's all still so clear in my head and I know it's not real, but these dreams have been a pretty real headache."

David doesn't respond right away. He takes another breadstick and chews on it while he chews on what I've said. Did I go too far – say too much? I probably shouldn't have shared this with him of all people. What if this gets me fired?

"It sounds like you've been having a rough couple of days then," he concludes after finishing the breadstick. "I'm sorry that I didn't notice the extent of how off you were sooner. But I *did* tell you that you should take some time off – a suggestion which you ignored. Why?"

"I was fine."

"But you're not now…"

I feel myself getting heated so I pick up my beer and take long gulps of it. It's hard to look David in the eye. He knows I can't just take a break like that. Hell, he's the reason I needed to work so hard.

"I made some arrangements today… for you," he tells me, cocking his head to the side in a vain attempt to make eye contact.

"What kind of *arrangements*?" My stomach twists into a knot and I continue to stare off into space.

"Starting right now, you've been granted a temporary leave. From tomorrow until Friday of next week you are going to be given time off, time that won't be deducted from your vacation time balance. It's not a lot, but I want you to make the most of it. Do not come into the office for any reason, do not think about work, and definitely do not so much as log on to your work computer. Just relax, recover, and try to come back refreshed."

My blood boils at listening to this and I can feel my face getting red hot. He has no right to do this to me. I've never been anything but excellent for this company. If I wanted time off, I would have asked for it. But instead he's gone and put in a formal request for my leave which means that now I really have to take it. If this is his idea of a reward then he's a sicker man than I thought.

"If you need more time after that then just call me, but you will likely need to spend some vacation days at that point," he adds as if this will make me any less pissed.

"You had no right," I hiss.

I turn back to face him with a scalding frown and steaming eyes. Our conversation falls into icy silence for a while. It takes everything I have not to go off on him and he makes it worse by just sitting there. All he does is look at me with a creased brow and puffy eyes. It's like he's trying to make himself out to be the innocent party in this and to my great frustration, he's kind of succeeding.

"I'm just trying to look out for you…even if for some reason you don't want to look out for yourself," he says in a quivering tone. "It's what we do, remember?"

"Yeah is that what you're doing? Are you really looking out for me as my friend then or are you doing this as my boss?"

"Why can't it be something that I did as both? Why do I

always have to be one or the other?"

His voice sounds especially frail now. If I didn't know better, I'd feel bad for him. But I *do* know better. He can never be both because he chooses to act as one or the other. And mostly he just chooses to act like my boss. He's fooling himself if he's been any kind of friend to me lately. I just shake my head at him and try to avoid his misty gaze. A few minutes later, our food comes which makes the silence between us a bit more palatable. As I eat, I wonder if maybe I should feel a little bit bad about upsetting him. He's giving me a ride home, buying me dinner, and he scored me some free vacation days. But I just don't feel bad at all. He ended our friendship when he got promoted, not me. He fell short on his duties as a director and *he* pushed me to the spot that I'm in now. Any mental or emotional issues that I'm having are all on him. I'm not sorry – not for anything.

# Chapter 3

David drives us into the complex's garage. He could have just dropped me out front, but this is more convenient for me so I don't complain. He comes to a stop right in front of the elevators and shifts his car into park.

"I should be able to oversee the post-project work," he says, but he's looking straight ahead. "If anything does come up, I will let you know myself, but I'll try not to have it come to that."

"Thank you, David," I reply. I do get that he's trying to be nice, it's just too little, too late.

"Try to get some rest," he tells me as I pop open the door and unbuckle my seatbelt.

"I will," I promise him before closing it and heading toward the elevators.

David's car rolls off behind me as I summon the elevator. While I wait, I get this feeling like I've lived a whole week in this one day. And it's not even 6:00 PM yet. This sensation wears me down a little. It's exhausting to think about how ridiculous my day has been from start to finish and the worst part is that I don't want to go to bed. The very idea that I might wind up back in Shirun's mansion terrifies me. I'm so on edge that I jump back a little when the elevator dings. My whole body kind of shakes now and I start to feel sort of paranoid to be here alone. The second the doors swoosh open, I hop in and smash the button for the tenth and topmost floor. I'm fidgety the whole way up, both reluctant and eager to get back to my apartment suite.

When the doors finally slide back open, I don't have anywhere else to go, so I just amble along to my door, unlock it, step inside, lock it again, put my bag on the island counter and then go double check that the door is locked. It's a pretty standard routine, but for some reason it feels very tedious tonight. I also get the sinking feeling that everything is wrong somehow.

"Just relax Bryan," I tell myself.

I take a few deep breaths and close my eyes, but then I suddenly remember that I haven't talked to Kayla all day. I rip my phone out of my pocket and find that I have three missed calls from her. Normally this is where I'd swear under my breath or something, but I don't have it in me to care tonight. I just drag myself over to the sofa where I plop down and let my thumb reluctantly hover over the callback button. I'm really not in the mood for a fight right now, but it will also be ten times worse later on if I don't call her now. So I let my thumb fall onto the screen and bring the phone up near my ear.

"Bryan, I called you like six times!" she answers almost immediately.

"Hi, I know," I groan wearily.

"What have you been doing?" she presses me.

I don't want to snap at her, but I also don't have the patience for this, so I just say, "Look, I had a bad day and I don't feel well and I'm sorry that I missed your calls. Do you think you could just come over here for tonight? I don't really feel up to being out."

"Ew, no, if you don't feel good, that's fine. Just stay in, get some sleep and be better by tomorrow night."

I shudder at the thought of having to head out for Friday night festivities while I have all of this crap going on. I have a sneaking suspicion that one day off of work isn't going to fix everything. I'm also annoyed that she didn't bother to ask me any details on how I feel unwell. She's just assuming I have a cold or something.

So I make a point of saying, "Okay, but I'm not exactly sick, babe, I just feel run down and weird and maybe a little angry is all."

"Sorry Bry, but those can all be telltale signs that something nasty's about to come on and I want no part of that. Get some fluids in you, go to bed early, and just call in sick to work. Oh and give me a call tomorrow to let me know how you're doing. This weekend is a club weekend I'm thinking, so I need you good and ready to go. Got it?"

"Got it," I sigh.

I should probably tell her about the dreams, about my morning, and about my forced vacation, but I don't think she'd care. And why should she, it's not like we're dating or anything…oh wait...

"Have a good night, Bry."

"Good night," I huff.

I hang up and toss my phone onto the coffee table in front of me. I feel bitter as hell toward Kayla. Does she actually just not give a shit about me? Am I some kind of trophy boyfriend that she wants to come out with her on the weekends – someone to keep her company during the week? Is our relationship even something that's real or is it something we do just because it feels good? Is it all for show? These questions gnaw at my soul. Of course there must have been some good times. There had to have been moments where we were there for each other or situations where we got to know each other on a deeper level. It's been years after all, there's no way we would have made it that far without that kind of stuff, right? But I can't bring anything to mind. All I know is that loving Kayla has always been so easy. Now it's not and I really don't know why. All I can think of is that picture of Kevin and Erin in the park. I know it's just an image, but where are *my* pictures like that? Why don't Kayla and I look that good together? I realize that thinking about this isn't helping the situation so I try and think back to my early days with Kayla.

~*~

*It was right in this room that I'm sitting in now. I had it filled with people. I got music going, people talked and danced, and I'd stocked up with enough booze to keep the drinks flowing. I used to try and have parties like this at least once a month starting right around the time I'd moved into this place. David and I had both just been promoted to a Senior level we'd all decided to finally move out of Pinnacle. He chose a more sensible place uptown while I went for this suite at Spyre Apartments. Kevin moved in with Erin into a spacious apartment above a coffee shop while Devon found a nice loft on the outskirts of the city. I'm not sure where Julie went.*

*David, Devon, Erin, and Kevin all came to my fancy new place for a housewarming party to break it in. There was this awkward tension in the air since I didn't invite Julie, but I think we all had an alright time. Fortunately, things grew from there. I started inviting other people from Parson over as well as some of my neighbors and any friends of those friends who decided to show.*

*On one of those nights, I met Kayla. She'd come with a woman named Denise. Denise used to live one door down with an older guy who was maybe her husband, maybe her sugar-daddy, or maybe a combination of the two. In any case, she was taken. Hot, but taken. She was also friends with a woman I knew at Parson which is how I first met her. Kayla knew her somehow and came along to my party. I first spotted them on the couch talking and I immediately realized that I'd never laid eyes on anyone as gorgeous as Kayla. But I wanted to play it cool so I ignored her at first.*

*Retreating to the kitchen, I wondered if I should bring them out some drinks. But when I looked back into the living room, I saw that they both had one in hand so I decided to just be patient. I struck up a conversation with anyone who entered the kitchen, made them a drink if they wanted me to, and kept my eyes on the prize. Eventually, my waiting paid off. When I saw them get up off the couch, my heart started to thump inside of my chest. Kayla wore one of those ruffled tube dresses that chicks rock in the clubs. It was made of a soft-looking, sparkling blue fabric. I'd seen a lot of girls in a dress like that, but none of them wore it like Kayla did. It hugged her every curve and stretched effortlessly with each and every movement. It even managed to perfectly contain her bulging breasts — not once did I see her have to do that little wormy shuffle that so many women do to keep everything in place.*

*And then there was her dark hair, pin straight and floating through the air like a satin cloth. She had it styled like an Egyptian princess back then with elegant bangs falling down to her sculpted eyebrows. Her piercing blue eyes instantly demanded my attention — their enchanting hue highlighted by dark eye makeup. The way she strolled over with Denise at her side and the cool way that she seemed not to notice anything or anyone was just out of control. My core melted for this woman, it burned for her. They came up to where I stood at the kitchen island and that's when I knew I was done for.*

*"Can I get you ladies a drink?" I asked in as suave a manner as I could.*

*I must have channeled my inner gentleman-spy pretty well too because both women instantly broke into a smile. The moment that Kayla's indigo lips pulled back to reveal her snow-white teeth, I knew I needed her. If she was the fox, then I was the witless hare caught in her trap — hers to devour as she pleased. And prey on me, she did. First, she graciously took my drink. I didn't make anything special, just some vodka mixed with fruit juice, but she sipped it like something mixed by an experienced bartender. Next she demanded I make one for myself. Normally I'm more of a whiskey or rum sort of guy, but in that moment, the thought of refusing her never even occurred to me. So I poured a little extra vodka into my glass and let her pull me out into the living room.*

*She took us to the sofa, leaving Denise to do whatever Denise does with herself at a party. From there we just talked for a while. Damned if I can remember anything that we said now though. I think we mostly just talked about her life: where she's from, what she did for work, where she went to school, and things like that. I couldn't help but hang on every word she spoke, always waiting for more, always needing to hear whatever might come next. Once we'd finished our drinks, she led us into something I enjoy far more than talking. We stepped into the middle of my living room where a few people danced. It's not like I threw wild parties or anything, but I liked to clear enough space for the drunk ladies to shake it out. Every so often, a lucky guy or two would find themselves in the mix at some point that night. This time, the lucky guy was me. And the longer I danced there the luckier I got. I could always get down with the rhythm of a beat — just letting the music flow through my body, but tonight "dancing" was a rather generous term for what I did. Kayla did most of the work. She went up on me, down on me, and all around me. I mostly just needed to be there. It all felt so right, so clean, so easy.*

*We had this unspoken understanding between us. Somehow we both knew that we wanted the same things. When I was with her, the rest of the world blurred away. Only one thing mattered. I could think of only one person I wanted to be with, and that was her. I'm sure I did a horrible job of hosting my guests that night, but everyone deserves to act a little selfishly every now and then, right? I knew I'd never have another shot like this one. A girl like Kayla doesn't wait around, not for me, not for anyone. She hit me like a perfect storm and I just wanted to be in the eye of it. As my guests slowly funneled out, Kayla remained. I don't think I ever even asked her to stay. I never had to.*

*The second that the last person shut my door behind them, she gave me a coy look and locked up my door for me. Then I took her up the stairs with her hand in mine. Before we even made it to my room, she had me back against the wall, my lips locked with hers. We remained interlocked as I scooped her up by the back of her thighs and carried her to my bed. We kissed the whole way down as I slowly lowered her onto the mattress and then she began to delicately pop open the buttons on my shirt. Our desires flared as we peeled off the other's clothing and a flame burned in between us as our bodies interlocked. It's a sensation that I'd never forget, but also something that I haven't felt in recent memory.*

~\*~

The fire isn't burning anymore. Now it's just a little tongue of flame lapping the air in a desperate attempt not to die. I don't know what happened to it, but I'd do anything to get it roaring again. I try to push this all aside. Sure, I could use some passion right now, but what I mostly need is some rest. Of course, rest doesn't come without sleep and I can't sleep real well when my sleep isn't restful. As much as I'd love to hold out hope that I won't be seeing that haunted mansion again, I know better than that. *Three* times I've been there. Three nights *in a row!* This—whatever's happening to me—is no mere coincidence, it's a pattern and patterns always repeat. So now I'm left to wonder about what I should do, what I *can* do.

But maybe David's right. It's very possible that it is just stress at work that's doing this to me. Since I don't have work for a while, I should try to get all thoughts of it out of my head. Maybe then I can finally get some rest. This is easier said than done though. I'm used to being busy. Maybe I *need* to be busy. The longer I sit here, the more I realize that I'm not going to stop my mind from racing, not without a little help at least. So I get up and go into the kitchen. In an upper cabinet, I find my collection of alcoholic beverage options. On a little wire rack there is a bottle of Merlot and a bottle of White Zinfandel, both unopened, but I don't think tonight is a wine night. Beside this rack is a fifth of Krystof Vodka, a bottle of black raspberry brandy, and a handle of Jack Dean honey whiskey. At first the choices seem overwhelming, but my eyes keep settling on the whiskey so I pull that out and set it down on the counter. It's an elegant container that's mainly shaped like a box, but is adorned with curvy ridges that give way to its cylindrical neck. It's a handle without the actual handle which I suppose makes it more of a large bottle.

It may be a fine thing to look at, but it's what's on the inside that matters most to me, so I go into another cupboard and retrieve a short, wide glass and bring it back to the bottle where I twist off the cap and pour the sweet liquid into my glass until it's nearly overflowing. It's a rather large portion to sip on casually, but I feel as though I deserve it. Maybe I even deserve a refill. With this thought in mind, I put the cap back on, but leave the bottle out. Then I return to my seat on the couch where I snatch up the remote and turn on my television.

Clicking through the channels, I'm reminded of how little value my cable subscription really provides me. There are a bunch of sports talk shows and newscasts on, but I really only care about watching the games – could never get into listening to the opinions and predictions of a bunch of salty men who look like they never got picked first in gym class, much less look like they have any real experience with professional sports. Sure, you've got the retired athletes on some of them and the highlight reels are fun, sometimes there's even a blond bombshell around that occasionally gets to have a word or two, but I pass these channels by without much remorse. There are a couple of action movies on, but I've seen these probably a dozen times over already. I could watch this show where they tear the inside of a house apart and make it look fancy when they reconstruct it, but I'm trying to *not* think about a certain house, so I steer clear of this program.

Eventually, I land on <u>Superstar in the Rough</u>, a new kind of singing competition. I know there are a thousand of these things on TV, but I kind of like them. A lot of the contestants are young, some as young as sixteen, and all of them are really passionate about music. They all just want to make something of themselves and I can get behind that. It's fun to watch the really talented ones rise above the contestants that aren't as good. In a way, it reminds me of my earlier years at Parson. I think this particular episode is a re-run of what aired earlier this week which is fine since I missed it. And this is how I spend the rest of my night – trying to relax with some booze and reality TV. My glass drains pretty quickly and it isn't long before I start to get that warm, fuzzy feeling all over. Looking at what little is left of my drink, I contemplate a refill, but the more my head swoons with the alcohol, the more I fear falling asleep.

I do end up standing and walking crookedly over to the kitchen where I pour my glass to the halfway mark – or maybe more like the three-quarter mark. Either way, I take it back and try to sip a little slower this time. The singing show gives way to a trivia show and then comes a sitcom. But I'm not fully watching any of it. More than once, I feel my eyes droop, but I fight to keep them open no matter how badly they sting in protest. It's an unpleasant battle. Certainly the foggy state of my mind isn't helping. I want very badly to give into my fatigue, but at the same time I also want to resist it with every ounce of resolve that I can muster.

Then there's a sudden chill that washes over me. It cuts through the warmth of my alcoholic buzz and sends a shiver down my spine. I get the inescapable sensation that something's wrong. It's an awful feeling to have and I'm not sure I can make any sense of it. All I can think of is that it feels as though I'm being watched. It's like an unwelcomed presence is suddenly with me – looking at me – scrutinizing me – waiting for me to make a move.

"It's just the booze," I try to tell myself, but drinking has never made me paranoid so I know this isn't the case.

The sensation becomes oppressive and makes me feel even more tired than before. All I want to do is curl up on this couch and fall asleep. I'm scared to leave the sofa and I'm even more afraid of shutting my eyes. I know this is stupid. Obviously there's nothing and no one in here with me. But in my mind's eye, all I can see is that horrible hooded figure with the clanging voice and glowing eyes. I know it's not real. I know none of it is real. I just want to shut it all out. I want it to go away.

"*Come back,*" echoes through my ears. At first, I don't recognize the voice, but then I realize it's Shirun's.

"Come back Jessica!" I hear, but this time I discover the voice is coming from outside my apartment.

It's just Carl, a man who lives down the hall with his girlfriend, Jessica. Every so often, they get into a fight. While I'm not close enough to their apartment to hear the actual fight take place, I will sometimes catch wind of Jessica storming out and Carl chasing after her, demanding that she return. They're a dysfunctional couple to say the least and the fact that they are so juvenile in their mid-thirties says a lot about why I've never bothered to get to know them even though they've been here almost as long as me. While their antics are normally a nuisance, they're a welcome clamor tonight. The sound of Carl's repeated pleas to Jessica and her shouted chastisements ground me somehow. They remind me that there is nothing mystical going on in my life. The only thing to fear is how mundane life can be. And with that thought, I sprawl out over the couch, situate my head on some pillows, shut my eyes, and fade away from this sad, strange little world.

# Chapter 4

When I open my eyes, bright light pours into my vision. It makes my eyes sting so I snap them shut again. I hear a groan ring through my ears — it takes me a second to realize that it belongs to me. I try to roll myself over and away from the light, but my body doesn't cooperate with me. Maybe I could have done with just a little less whiskey. It's a disheartening sensation to be so pinned down, so utterly helpless. It gets worse when I feel a pair of hands take hold of my arms. This sends me into a deeper panic. My breathing comes in sharp bursts and I try wriggling myself free.

"Bryan," a voice coos.

I don't recognize it. It's soft and soothing and it belongs to a woman. Perhaps it's Kayla's? No, I don't think it could be her. I'd recognize her voice without a second's delay. And I don't feel familiar with this woman's touch. Her hold on me is secure, but not brutish by any means. It occurs to me that this is the type of grasp which protects, not one that traps. I allow my limbs to relax and let my breathing slow. The light starts to soften on me as well. After another moment, I'm able to open up my eyes. When I do, I see a lovely chestnut-shaped face with fair skin and light freckles that dot her cheeks and roll over the bridge of her nose. Sparkling blue eyes look down at me. They're cool, but fill me with a comforting warmth. Dark hair falls around the sides of her face as it hovers over me.

"It's alright, Bryan," she tells me.

"Who —" I croak, my voice failing to serve me.

"My name's Olivia, you're saf—"

I gasp at the name and shuffle away from her on my back. This is Olivia? She withdraws from me with her hands held up. My breathing picks up again and my heart pounds. I don't know Olivia, I don't know if she's dangerous, and I don't know if it's really wise to trust her although she seems to be taking care of me. All I know is that I'd much rather awake with nearly anyone else by my side.

"Don't' lie to the poor boy," a gruff voice calls from somewhere else in the room, drawing Olivia's attention.

"He needs to know that he's among friends." Looking back to me, she says, "I'm not going to hurt you, I'm on your side."

"Right as that may be, there aren't a great many spots we can say are safe right now," the man's voice counters.

"Myles?" I ask hoarsely.

"Hey there, old chap," he replies.

I pull my torso up, propping myself against my elbows and then I see him. Myles stands poised at the doorway to whatever room in the mansion I've found myself in tonight. His revolver is gripped firmly in his hand. I presume it's been reloaded, but given how ineffective it proved to be against that hound, it looks like a useless little toy. Still, there's a certain comfort to see him there holding it. Perhaps it's just that I see it as a sort of symbol – one that that says he's still willing to fight, still trying to defend. He sounds so tired though. And he should be – after what we've been through. I wonder how long he's been up and guarding the door while I've just been lying here. He's still wearing the same clothes as the last time I was here, so I'm guessing he's been guarding me while I've been asleep… or awake… He's removed his suitcoat and rolled up his sleeves. His shirt is creased and one of his suspenders is a little crooked. It's a ragged look to be sure, but I think he still appears as daunting as ever. Looking down at myself, I see that I'm also wearing the same dark pants, shoes, and white shirt as before. My suitcoat lies at the foot of the bed and seems to be tattered from my violent fall down the steps.

"Where are we?" I barely manage to choke out the words, my mouth is so dry.

"You're in the infirmary," Olivia informs me.

Her tone is still sweet, but it's much quieter than before. She holds a glass of water out toward me. I suppose that she must have gone to grab it while I was focused on Myles though I didn't hear her move at all. She sounds so timid all of a sudden and I think I have myself to blame for that. I also feel bad to see her standing there so withdrawn. One arm is wrapped around her abdomen and the other is fully extended toward where I lay. Yes, I'd say I've offended her a great deal. She's undoubtedly been taking care of me, perhaps she even rescued Myles and I from those creatures. But I can't really know anything for sure. She could still be involved in this somehow in spite of how innocent she seems right now. There's something unsettling about how she is so undaunted by our current predicament.

"Thank you," I say, taking the cup from her hand.

A corner of her mouth briefly curls upward and then she takes a couple of steps back. I take a sip of the cool water. It streams down my throat and washes out the scratchy sensation that ails me. It has a loosening effect on my whole body, in fact. My muscles relax and my mind clears. I try to make eye contact with Myles, but his attentions are fixed on the hall that lies beyond the open doorway. So I look around the room to find that this is indeed an infirmary and not of the makeshift variety. Its walls are lined with anatomical diagrams and glass-doored medicine cabinets stocked full with little white bottles.

I'm atop a surgical cot. Two more just like it are set up to my right. Olivia takes a seat on the one immediately beside me. Her crystalline eyes settle upon me while she smooths out the length of her white dress. She looks sort of like a nurse and her white heels add to this effect. But I don't think this is her normal getup or usual place of occupation. I realize now that I *have* seen this woman before. She spoke with Mister Shirun during the first party that I attended. She stood with him only moments before he approached me. Now I know that I'm right to be suspicious of her. She and Shirun conferred on something that night. Both of them know something about what's going on here – something I deserve to be clued in on.

*Here!* Why do I still think of this as a place? Why must I return to wherever or whatever this is night after night? In spite of myself, I really did hope I could evade this creepy dream space if only I just relaxed a little. If I can just bring this insanity to a close then maybe I'll be free of it. But I know this is not a task that'll be easily accomplished. From what I know so far, when I'm "here" in this mansion, nothing works the way I think it ought to. Everything is off in a surreal sort of way like how the house has its own infirmary. What house, however fancy it might be, has that? There is a shadowy fiend that's invaded this estate's walls and it has a flesh-eating hound at its beck and call. Now both are on the loose and this woman knows something about that. She might be helping me right now, but if she doesn't tell me the truth – the whole truth – then she's as good as my enemy.

"What do you know?"

"I beg your pardon," she replies, setting her gaze firmly upon me.

"It's alright, old chap," Myles interrupts us, his attentions pulled into the room. "She's not what we thought. She found us after…well…you know…"

"I awoke Myles and he carried you here where I tended to you," she picks up after Myles' train of thought falters.

"You just found us without incident?" I challenge.

"That's right," she replies. She sounds much sterner now though I don't much care if I've offended her.

"Why?" My voice cracks as I ask, "Why would that…thing…just leave us there? After what it did to –"

There's a moment of silence that hangs in the air. I can feel the tears well in my eyes as I meet Myles' gaze. The word, the name, the question hangs in the air. Could there be any chance that Margaret is still alive, maimed as she might be? Myles must see the hope that swells within me. With a slow shake of his head, he does me the greatest kindness and most extreme cruelty all at once.

"Margaret, why did you have to die?"

I don't know why I ask this out loud. I already have my answer and I know very well that nothing will change it. It's perhaps the most selfish thing I have ever said, but I can't seem to process this loss. It feels like a piece of me has been ripped out and I can never really replace it. I just can't believe that she's gone. She was far too good – she did far too much good for everyone around her. Stupidly, I wish this was all just a bad dream, which of course it is, but the sentiment remains. My heart sinks when I see all of the remaining vigor fade from Myles' eyes. His shoulders slump and his features contort into a weary grimace. He takes a parting glance down the hall before closing the door and wandering over to where I lay. As he comes closer, I get a better look at how utterly defeated he appears. His eyes are red and droopy and thick bags hang beneath them. Even his magnanimous moustache seems a bit out of sorts.

It's still curled, but little strands of hair poke out from it making it look a bit scraggly.

"She's not gone for nothing, my boy," he tells me – his voice is barely audible. "She died so we could live."

"Why? Why her? Why **only** her?" I feel foolish for voicing these questions, yet I ask them all the same.

Myles' brow creases and his eyes get puffier. He takes my hand in his and clutches it firmly. For a second, his grip actually makes me feel safer.

"She was a message." Myles pauses. His eyes search the room before he continues, "Whatever that thing in the robe was, it took her and left us because it wants us to know that it can take whatever's most precious to us. It wants the whole house to know that nothing and no one is safe. It wants us to tremble in terror, wondering when it will send that devilish hound to come and devour us. Somehow, Margaret understood this, that's why she offered herself instead of running. She must have believed that we could make this right."

"Where is it?"

"We don't know," Olivia laments.

"But you do know something!" I snap, my eyes locked on hers.

"Easy there, old chap," Myles soothes, giving my hand a squeeze.

"She spoke with Shirun on the first night," I persist. "He told you something then, didn't he?"

Olivia slides off the cot and strides over to us with her arms crossed. For a little while there is a tense silence between us. The way that she glares at me is a strong indicator that she thinks I'm the most ungrateful creature in the world, but I don't much care right now. This whole thing is absurd and if I'm to overcome this magical devil-thing then she needs to start talking.

At last she explains herself. "Yes, he told me that something – a wicked presence of some kind – would be released within the mansion. He gave no details as to what it might be. He only said that it would surprise us all and attack with a ferocity the likes of which none of us have seen before. He told me that I should withdraw from the others and be watchful."

"What exactly did you watch?" I sneer, "Because two people have died while you've been *watching*."

"You."

"What?"

"I've been watching you, Bryan. I was in the garden with you when that beast murdered Shelly. While you chased after it, I slipped through the paths and made it to the shed before you. I'm the one that got the jump on you."

"Why," I ask, utterly exasperated at her explanation.

"Because Shirun said that you're not ready to face this darkness just yet. Its power over us is too great presently."

"Then why was that hound running away from me? Why would it not have just killed everyone at the party if it's so powerful?"

"Weren't you listening to what that freakish thing told us?" Myles cuts in. "It's not trying to just kill you, it wants to destroy you."

I'm a bit perplexed by all of this — even more so than before. What is this "presence" and why is it out to destroy me? How is destroying me any different than tearing me to pieces? Why am I even here at all? None of it makes any sense and I need it to start making some sense if I'm going to beat this thing. I heave myself into a seated position and let my shoulders hunch forward.

"What happens next then?" I ask, bringing a hand up to my forehead. I realize then that my head is no longer bandaged.

"We must get to Shirun," Olivia tells me. Her tone has softened again.

I look to Myles and ask, "Is this what you'd advise as well then?"

His eyes shimmer with uncertainty as he replies, "I think that in as dire a situation as this, we must put our trust in him. He may not be open about what he knows, but the mere fact that he knows anything at all makes him our best chance at preventing further death from cursing these halls."

"Alright," I concede as I slide myself off of the cot.

My legs wobble a little, but I soon gain a sure footing. In spite of my tumble down the steps, I feel remarkably spry. There's no pain in my joints, no aching in my brain, or even a hint of fatigue that I can feel. Even though I got better in the real world, I still expected to be hurting here.

"What have you done to me?" I ask before I realize how rude this sounds.

Olivia grins and her complexion reddens. "It is a skill I simply have. I cannot explain it to you as I don't fully understand it myself, but you were quite battered when we brought you here so I did my best to get you back to whole again."

"Thank you," I state simply.

By now, I know not to question things here too much. The fact of the matter is that I feel rejuvenated and I'm quite grateful for it no matter how nonsensical this recovery might be. I'm also feeling guilty for how I've spoken to this woman. She's done me a great service and I've treated her like an enemy. People behave strangely here, but perhaps I should start trusting them a little more. I certainly won't be taking down that hooded being by myself so I'll take whatever aid I can find. I also need to stop trying to write these people off as characters in a dream. If this is a dream, then it's a very serious one indeed. I can feel things here and when I do, the sensations come back with me to the waking world. That could mean that dying here comes back with me as well. It's a grave matter to be sure, so I'll want to proceed with the utmost caution.

"We ready to get going then, old chap?" Myles asks – some of his usual vigor restored.

"I think it's high time that Shirun explains himself."

"Just give me a moment to pack up some things," Olivia requests.

Myles answers her with a slow bob of his head. She sails off across the room and snatches up a satchel that hangs from the wall. She fills it with rolls of cloth bandages, various medical instruments found across the room, and bottles pillaged from the medicine cabinets. As she does this, Myles returns to his post beside the door, though he leaves it shut for the time being. I just stand between the cots like a useless little child. Myles has his gun, Olivia has her medical supplies, and I have nothing. I'm an allegedly big piece in these events yet not once have I managed to pull my own weight. It feels like I'm just along for the ride without any power to steer our course. It's my deepest hope that this will change once we've reached Shirun. Maybe then, I will be equipped with the knowledge to understand my role in all of this and finally be empowered to take appropriate action.

"Are you ready Miss Kristov?" Myles asks.

Olivia's goes through the pack, reviewing its contents. "Ready," she declares as she fastens the bag shut.

"Right then, come along, my boy." Myles makes a sweeping wave to beckon me over.

I walk toward the exit and take up a place behind where Myles is planted. Olivia joins by my side and Myles sets his jaw firmly before turning toward the door. He flings it open, immediately shoving his gun out through the doorway. My chest tightens and then unwinds as this plays out. There's nothing in this section of the manor except for us. This is a fact that should give me some measure of comfort, but leaves me with unease instead. My feet are heavy as I follow Myles out into the hall. If I didn't know that something dreadful stalked this place, then I'd find nothing scary about being here. It's brightly lit and perfumed with the scent of flowers. Not a picture frame is out of alignment, nor an end table knocked over, nor any lamps disturbed. Had I not the good sense otherwise, I'd say that everything's perfect here.

But everything is also horribly silent. No footsteps can be heard save for our own and not a single voice reaches our ears. This utter stillness makes the air around us feel heavy. It's a sort of scene that's seemingly made to be broken – a perfection that cannot last. My muscles tighten in anticipation of something unexpected and my eyes dart around in search of anything that might be out of place. Without warning, Olivia slips her arm around mine, linking us together. It's exactly like the way that Margaret liked to lead me around. At first, I guess that she does this out of her own anxiety, but when I look over and see how purposefully she looks ahead, I realize that it's *me* she's aiming to comfort.

While I appreciate the gesture, I'm also embarrassed that my nerves were great enough to draw her notice. I try to recover some of my dignity by turning my attentions to the path before us and attempting to relax as we move along. Myles leads us down the long hall and into the foyer where one of the large, arching staircases sits. This tells me that we've been on the ground floor of the mansion.

While it's nice to gain my bearings, it's also a little unfortunate that we are so distant from where Shirun waits. Anxiety grips me as we ascend the steps. I may not have been fully conscious when I first saw it, but I'm certain this is the staircase that our attacker hurled me down. When I spot a little dried blood on several of the steps, my suppositions are confirmed. And if we are climbing the stairs which I fell down, then we are also fast approaching where that creature ripped Margaret apart.

My breath quickens and my stomach grows queasy. I find myself pulling Olivia closer and I feel like a scared little boy for doing so. But I'm loath to imagine what I will find in just a moment. Is the bloodied corpse still there? Did that dog leave only a trail of innards? Did someone have the decency to clean up the mess? I want to shut my eyes before we reach the top step, but I can't bring myself to do so. To my great relief, I find nothing once the hall comes into view. There's no body, no leftover entrails, only blood stains across the already red carpet and against the white walls. It's not the most pleasant sight, but it's also not nearly as gruesome as I feared it might be.

To our right is the base of the staircase to the third floor. As we reach the top of the one we are on presently, we round the corner and head to the base of this next one. As we do so, I notice something wholly unnerving. Sitting along the corner where the wall meets the floor is a pile of dark, ribbon-like goo. Little bits of it writhe in the air and over the floor like a pile of snakes all huddled together. But then I realize that they remind me of something else – the fur-like material that hung off of the beast's back. Is this some sort of fur it shed and left behind? If it is, then that is most horrifying. I try to ignore it as we rise up the steps. Unlike the first staircase's semi-circular arch, this one shoots straight up. It also feels far more confined since white walls line either side and the steps themselves are a little narrower.

"Watch your footing," Myles instructs as he sidesteps something.

I see that it's another heap of that ribbon-goop. Olivia and I stop short in front of it and realize that the stuff is all around us in concentrated little piles. We unlink our arms and Olivia ushers me up the steps in front of her. The pile's tendrils reach out toward us desperately, longingly even. There are a couple of blobs on either side of us plastered to the walls. We avoid several more on the steps and when we finally reach the top, I discover that there is even more of this vile substance on the third floor. Some of it is even stuck to the ceiling. It's immeasurably disturbing how the little black ribbons reach for us like arms whenever we draw near. Myles leads us slowly down the hall, keeping his gun trained on whichever goo pile is closest. It's a nice feeling to have him protect us like this though I doubt the weapon will have any effect on whatever this is, especially if it did come off of that hellhound.

After heading all the way to the back of the mansion, we eventually come to a large archway which houses a pair of twin doors. Unlike the rich burgundy color which most doors are stained in, these are painted in a deep red that matches the hall carpet.

Myles reaches for the golden knobs when Olivia says, "Wait."

"What for?" he retorts.

His head twists towards us with a look of genuine confusion across his face. I feel a little bad for him. It must be tiring to act as everyone's protector. I think I can hear the fatigue in his voice and I definitely take notice of the bleak haze over his eyes.

"Shirun wants only to speak with him," she answers, motioning to me.

"What?" Myles snaps. "After all that's happened, he really thinks he can just continue keeping secrets? They're dead, Olivia! Shelly is dead. Margaret is dead. And they're just the start if we don't do something. It will get so much worse unless Shirun opens up to us – to *all* of us!"

"I know that," Olivia replies softly. "What Shirun has to say is for Bryan to hear." She walks up to Myles and takes hold of his wrist, but he clutches the doorknob tighter. "I can't pretend to know what Shriun is about or what is really going on, but he has asked that we trust in him. This is a dire time for us all which means that we need Shirun, now more than ever. And Bryan … Bryan is the key to resolving the vexation that is upon us. Whatever Shriun wants to tell him in confidence must be important to that cause, else he'd happily include us all in the conversation."

Silence hangs in the air momentarily before Myles releases

his grip on the door. He gives me a steady nod and backs away from the entrance. I have to wonder if they'll be alright out here what with all this dark matter lying about.

"We'll be fine, my boy," Myles assures me.

I hesitate briefly before approaching the doors and taking hold of both knobs. Twisting them in opposite directions, I push the doors open to reveal the expanse of Shriun's chamber. The sight of it leaves me standing at the entryway rather breathlessly. The ceiling is no taller than other rooms, but the sheer width and depth of this "bedroom" is staggering. An impossibly large golden carpet is laid down, but the walls and support beams share the same color scheme as the rest of the house. In spite of the magnificence in its size, there is also a distinct drabness to this space. Perhaps it is in how sparsely furnished it is. Against one wall stands a set of triplet wardrobes which look quite ornate in their design. The craftsmanship that went into carving out the elegant curves on the bases and indentations in the doors is hard not to admire for a minute.

There are a number of less extravagant end tables scattered about, some accompanied by cushioned wooden chairs. On the side of the room opposite the wardrobes is a bed of tremendous size, accented with bright red drapes that hang around it. Like all the other beds in this building, it appears to be completely undisturbed. It strikes me that it is far more a decoration than an actual piece of furniture. It's an odd thing to consider that Mister Shirun probably doesn't make use of any of the furniture in this room except for maybe the wardrobes. Even more odd still is that not a single painting hangs off of the walls. They're utterly bare which makes the room seem that much emptier. So far as I can recall, this is the only room I've encountered so far which is so poorly filled. It gives me a hollow feeling to step through it, though what perturbs me the most at this moment is that my thoughts still do not *sound* like my thoughts. This leads me to question whether they really belong to me at all. Are they being fed into my mind? Controlled, perhaps, like my steps were when I danced with Margaret?

I try to push my doubts aside and remind myself that things are simply different here. A more pressing concern takes over my mind instead: I can't find Shirun. Is he not here? Surely this must be the right room, but are we too late? Did that *thing* get here before us?

"Bryan," Shirun's smooth, rolling tone reaches my ears.

It's then that I finally notice him. Looking through the door in the back of the room, I spot him standing out on the balcony. His back is turned to me so he must have heard me come in. But who knows with this gentleman, he could have just as well sensed my entry with magic of some sort. I also take notice of the banners that hang on either side of the open doorway. The one on the right shows a slender figure lurching forward with a golden sword held out to the side. The figure is comprised entirely of white swirls that seem to shine off the surface of the tapestry. I can't quite tell if the creature is naked or clothed, nor can I discern whether it is a man or a woman. Its shape seems more abstract and less human the longer I look at it. The banner on the left shows a very similar sort of image except that this body is formed with black swirls and wields a scalding red whip tipped with a spearhead. Whereas the right tapestry seems to glow, the one on the left does the opposite in that it appears to devour the light that surrounds it.

Of all the fine artwork Shirun could have picked to adorn these walls, he picks these two flags. It's a rather unsettling choice and I don't much care to dwell on what these images might represent. I try not to even look at them directly as I move through the doorway and join Shirun on his balcony. He remains perfectly still as I come up behind him. His hands clutch the railing and his gaze is set on the night sky. But it, of course, is not a night sky. There are no stars, no moon, and no clouds or fog that might excuse their absence. No, this is just air – just open space that's devoid of any brightness. It's the absence of a sky that just so happens to take a shade of midnight blue. The seemingly endless landscape may very well be just that – *endless*. There is nothing else in this world, only the mansion and all of the people inside of it.

There are also those who are in it no longer. I'm reminded of this when my vision rests upon the two headstones that shoot out from the earth. It relieves me somehow to know that one of them has Margaret's name etched upon it. If anyone ever deserved a proper grave, it was that woman. I'm not sure that much ceremony went into placing her body in the ground given the circumstances, but at least her corpse isn't lying around the manor. It's this thought that makes the sight of these lonely graves bearable. I even have to wonder if these ladies aren't the lucky ones somehow. Then, beyond where the headstones glitter, I see something flash. My eyes are drawn to where a dark purple haze looms in the horizon. From it springs stark white bolts of lightning that occasionally strike the ground. Are we about to be hit with a literal storm? And if this is supposed to be the calm that comes before then I'd protest that this is really not a very calm time at all.

"You must have a lot of questions," Shirun says. He doesn't turn his head toward me.

He looks a bit like a statue – so still, so serene. He also looks very different tonight. At first I thought he wore a suit just like any other, but now I see that it's not at all ordinary. There's a thick collar on it that rises up the back of his neck and curls around to the front where it dips down to the top of his chest like waterfalls. It's made of a fabric that looks stiff and soft at the same time. Deep ridges dig into it, leaving large, blocky lines sticking out that resemble plates of armor. It sports some kind of bold, oceanic blue that makes his crystalline eyes shine brighter than usual. Then I realize that his pants are strange as well. They simply conform to his legs too perfectly, as though every inch of the garment is tailored to his exact dimensions. Aside from having a shimmering, white velvet veneer and skin-like perfection, they are otherwise unremarkable. They tuck into glossy black boots at the calf. It's an otherworldly look that while not unbefitting a gentleman, also seems rather appropriate for a warrior.

I want to ask whether we are at war, but instead I just ask, "What is it? What is the creature that killed Shelly and Margaret?"

"It's a foreign presence here, summoned here by a terrible power and hungry for devastation."

"It's master then? That creature in the cloak?"

Shirun inhales deeply before replying, "There are a great many things you could call it, I suppose. For now, let's just call it Sin."

"As in the seven deadly sins?" I ask incredulously. His response makes no sense! If this is the way our conversation is going to go then my temper will be lost very quickly indeed.

"Not exactly, no," Shirun clarifies in an even tone. "I don't expect that you will understand very much of all this just yet nor do I believe that you are ready for the full truth."

"Then make me understand," I snap, turning toward him with my hand draped over the balcony rail. "What is Sin? Why is it here and what does it really want?"

"It wants you, Bryan. It's here for you." Shirun doesn't sound as steady as before. He turns his head to me with his eyebrows pinched together. "It wants to devour or corrupt every last part of you until there is nothing left. It wants to empty you and then it wants to kill you."

There's a glimmer in Shirun's eyes that I can only take for fear. Whatever is he going on about? I know Sin is a magical creature of some kind but how does it plan to empty me? And more importantly, what can be done to stop it?

"How can we kill it?"

Shirun's eyes widen as though this is some kind of preposterous question. "Oh, no," he hums, "It doesn't die, it can only be diminished."

"You're not making any sense," I grumble. "How do we stop it, what do we do? Olivia said I am the key to ending this so just tell me how I might end it."

Shirun turns his face back to the horizon and shakes his head. "What comes next, I cannot predict. This is a situation unlike any other I have heard of before. All I can say is that you must learn the difference between friend and foe and learn it quickly. Other than that, all you can do is fight. Fight for your life. Fight for the lives of those around you. Fight with all the passion you can muster."

The lack of clarity that this conversation has provided me is making me furious. This was supposed to be the big revelation, not another series of senseless riddles.

"That's it?" I fume, "That's all you have to tell me."

"No." Shirun winces and pinches his eyes shut. "I have to tell you that I'm sorry, so very sorry for everything that has happened to you and everything that is to come."

This confuses me tremendously. Is Shirun behind this whole affair after all? Silence falls between us only to be broken by a sharp and chilling gust of air that tussles Shirun's dark hair and cuts into my flesh. Once it has passed Shirun's eyes pop back open. I'm left shivering, but he seems largely unfazed. His shimmering eyes stare out into the endless field before us with an intensity that makes me turn toward it myself. I see that the purple fog has come much closer. I can now see the bolts of lightning more clearly and it seems to me that they strike with greater frequency.

"I don't understand. Why should you apologize?" I don't turn to face him as I ask this. I'm afraid that if I take my eyes off the storm again then it will nearly be upon us.

"All of this is happening because of a choice I made," he confesses, his tone sounding quite feeble. "You have to understand that Sin has always been a part of the manor. It's just that before it was locked away. Only I knew of its existence and only I ever had any contact with it. We are linked, the two of us."

"You and Sin?"

"Yes," Shirun replies with a sluggish nod. "We are so different, yet also the same. We two were the first to arrive at the mansion, but I was far stronger than Sin. I locked it up in a secret room – the room which you had the misfortune of discovering – with it locked away, I then hid the door. I needed it to be gone before the next guest arrived."

"You mean the guests that never leave?"

He sighs through his nose and lets his head hang below his shoulders. "It's true that guests never leave, but what else can you call us if we are not owners of this house?"

"If you got here first wouldn't that mean that the house is yours?"

"Not exactly, no. None of this belongs to me. Not the house, or the garden, or the field before us, or even this room. I'm just a guardian of it all."

"Then who *does* it belong to?" I demand.

In spite of my wish for the purple storm to remain at bay, it continues to creep across the field toward us. I can only assume that once it reaches the house, our respite from the chaos will be at an end. As it draws nearer, I swear I can feel small tremors rock through the manor.

"You," Shirun reveals, simply.

This makes even less sense than everything else I've heard so far. Is this really just a dream after all? Everything is so confusing and intense that I'm not sure what this is any longer.

"How is that possible? I've been told I don't even belong here."

"It's true, you were never meant to come here. If not for the foolhardy decisions I made, you'd never have had to see this place. But it does belong to you. The destiny of this household is tethered to your reality or at least reality as it is known to you. I know this is confusing for you, but it is imperative that you believe me, even if you don't yet understand the forces which are at work or the means by which you came to us."

"I'd be far more apt to trust you if you would just give me straight answers." My words may be a little whiny but my voice isn't bitter anymore.

"I'm doing the best that I can with what time I have to work within."

Shirun's tone is hushed. He turns his body toward me and places a hand atop my shoulder. This draws my gaze away from the coming storm. It's not like I could have ever stopped its progress by simply looking at it anyway.

"Perhaps it is better this way," Shirun offers. "The truth is rarely something that can simply be told – often it must be discovered for oneself. If you fight hard enough, Mister Daley, you will undoubtedly uncover the truths which now elude you. Now, we have but a few precious moments left, perhaps enough time for one more question."

"You still haven't told me how any of this is your fault. You locked Sin up, you've been protecting this house, and you tasked Olivia with keeping me out of harm's way. What did you do to make yourself the guilty party in any of this?"

Shirun takes his hand off my shoulder and brings it up to his chin. "I suppose not," he admits. "Sin has always had certain … influences … over the manor, but it was growing in power. I feared that the guests would not be strong enough to keep it at bay – that they would be too ignorant of its power to know what to do. So I cut a deal with it, a wager more like. Gaining control of the manor would give it access to you and therefore access to your world. The more power it has here, the more it will enjoy in your reality. So I agreed to summon you here to fight it head on. If you win, then Sin's power will be diminished irreparably and the household will be safe."

"And if Sin wins?"

"Then all is lost ... for this house ... and for you. I am so sorry to put this on you."

Shirun looks at me long and hard with eyes misted by guilt. It's a rather severe conundrum that I've been pulled into and I should be angry with Shirun for bringing me into it. But I'm not really. It sounds like this would somehow have become my problem eventually though I haven't the faintest idea how my life could possibly be linked to this world. Nor do I see how I could own a property without belonging in it. Before another word can pass between us, lightning cracks through the air and a shockwave rumbles through the manor causing me to fall against the rail. Shirun remains steady on his feet and pulls me up by my wrist.

"It appears that the time for discussion has come to an end then," he observes before turning and entering the bedchamber.

I follow him in to find Olivia and Myles enter from the hall. They look worried, though not entirely taken off guard. I suppose we all expected something to happen eventually.

"What's going on?" Myles asks once we've met in the center of the room.

Initially, Shirun ignores the question as though Myles' earnest look isn't pointed at him. He just reaches into his right pant pocket and withdraws a golden pocket watch with a long chain that somehow didn't show through the fabric – at least not that I noticed. I didn't even realize his pants had pockets. He cups the tiny clock in the palm of his hand and flips open the casing door with his thumb.

"Time is not always our enemy," he says at last, "but on this morn, the hands of time are not on our side."

With that he snaps the watch shut. We look on as Shirun places his other hand over the trinket and slides it along the length of its chain. As he does this, the metal becomes luminescent with a strange radiation of some sort. Did Shirun just enchant it somehow? He uttered no incantation, yet now the object glows with some unknown power. Shirun takes hold of it by the end of the chain, letting the clock fall by his side like a weapon.

"Mister Westerly, please stow your weapon away. It won't be doing us much good in its present state."

"And what? You expect to protect us with just that trinket?" he argues.

"I expect you all to stay close to me and have faith that we will elude our enemy. We head for the observatory and once safely inside, Myles and Olivia, I do solemnly promise that I will imbue you with the means to defend this house."

It's unsettling that he doesn't include me in this promise, but I suppose I've already had my time alone with him. Before any of us can say anything, Shirun moves for the hall. Myles lets out an annoyed growl as he slips his gun into the back of his trousers. We proceed out to the hall in single file. When we emerge, I see the piles of black goo move towards other blobs, creating larger masses of the unholy substance. Shirun slings his watch at a recently formed pile and the attack actually cuts through the slimy substance. The stuff hisses as it evaporates into an onyx steam and disappears completely. Tendrils from a blob stuck to the wall reach out toward me, but Shriun destroys it with a downward lash.

All through the hall, I can hear these piles mushing together. I don't know what sent this vile goo into action, but I'm immensely grateful that we have a way to defend against it. Shirun marches down deeper into the corridor with us close at his heels. He ducks down, swinging his weapon into a pile on the floor. Then he springs back upright and slings it at a blob falling from the ceiling. He strikes another reaching out from a wall beside him before twirling around and smashing one that leaps up from the floor.

"Hurry," he commands as he leads us along with his head on a swivel.

Already, I can see more of the dark matter slithering toward us from down the hall. But I also see a thin, spiraling, metal staircase not so far off from where we are presently. It's a safe bet that the observatory lies at the top of it, but it feels like the darkness bears down on us harder with every passing second. Shirun charges ahead, throwing the pocket watch with deft precision. Looking back, I see more of that ribbon goop slurping along behind us. My heart rate quickens at the thought of it catching up to us and I dare not imagine what will happen if one of those tendrils grabs hold of someone.

Fortunately, Shirun clears the way ahead with ease. He swings his watch so nimbly that it looks like a blur of light slashing through the air. I rush past him and climb up the steps with him right behind me. It feels like we are very nearly in the clear when Myles howls and Olivia lets out a shriek. I stop dead in my tracks and twist around to see one of the blobs perched on the railing, its ribbon-like arms wrapped around Myles' bare forearm. The tendrils constrict around his arm like serpents crushing their prey and a ghastly steam rises from Myles' skin as they do so. Without hesitation, Shirun flips down the steps. He slings the watch up over his head and brings it crashing down into the goop. It evaporates, but I see that it has left Myles with scorch marks across his flesh.

"Keep moving," Shirun urges as he spins back around.

Something golden slipped out of Shirun's jacket when he made his dramatic attack. It's a necklace, a pendent of some sort. Protruding outward is a large, hollowed-out star with a number of filled-in stars around it and a thick, ridged border. Olivia and Myles move past me as I remain frozen against the slender guardrail. Shirun charges back up the stairs and grabs me by the back of my arm. He tears me off the rail, shoving me upward. At the top, I see Olivia fling open a tall door. Bright, white light pours out onto us. It feels warm, like a ray of sunlight, but also conceals what lies behind the doorway. Myles and Olivia seem to not notice it somehow. They don't shield their eyes like I have to. When they step through, they're gone from my sight and I start to fear that I won't be passing through this door.

"This is where we part ways for now," Shirun tells me. "Remain brave, my friend."

I'm pushed up toward the light which I can no longer bear to even peek at. I feel both of Shirun's hands on me and am forced to allow him to usher me along. The light and the warmth start to overwhelm me when I feel myself shoved forward and collapse into it.

# Epilogue

I lurch upright on the sofa. My breathing is heavy and hard. Little specks of darkness disturb my vision but soon clear up. My body doesn't ache, nor does my head throb. My clothes do feel a little damp, but it doesn't help that I fell asleep in my work apparel. I suppose it was a good night in psycho evil mansion world. But did it really go well? As nice as it might be to not wake up feeling like death, there's nothing about this situation that's really going "well." I wasn't supposed to go back there. I relax and I get sweet dreams – that was the deal. But there's a very good chance this isn't a dream at all.

A different reality, another plane of existence, whatever that place actually is or isn't – it's become a big problem for me. But does it actually exist? Do I really believe that I'm the savior of some mystical realm? Can I accept that I'm getting whisked away in my sleep to come and help these people? The toughest part to swallow is that I actually do care. I care about all of it – about all of them. I wish Margaret and Shelly were still alive. I wish I knew if Myles is alright. I wish I could do something about what's happening there. More than anything, I want to know if the others are safe. Like Jack and Jasmine, even William and Joanna. That world has become a part of my reality and it scares me because what if it's not real after all? What if this is one of those stories where someone loses their mind and starts slipping away into a fantasy? Is that me? Am I just falling further down the rabbit hole? A part of me is dying to know, itching to ask for help. But deep down, I know I just need to ride this out – see where it all goes. I need to clear my head and relax. I need to believe that everything will be okay soon.

"*Remain brave, my friend…*" Shriun's words echo in my mind. That's all I can really do right now, isn't it? Stay brave and stay sane. That's not so hard, right? Right?

# Book 4:

# A Deadly Crescendo

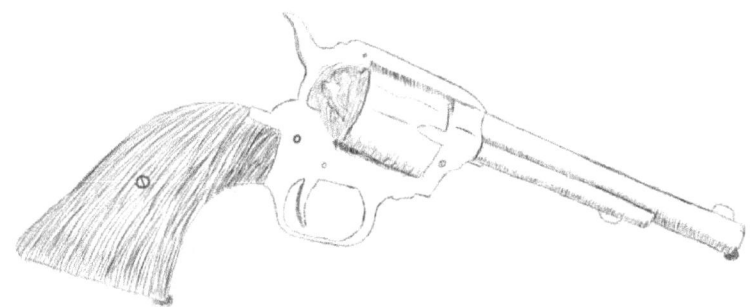

*To those who've found me when I was alone in the dark.*

# Chapter 1

The living room is almost pitch-black. A tiny bit of light from the kitchen appliances reaches me, but I'm otherwise in the dark. I let it stay like that for a little while and hope that I feel tired enough to try going back to sleep. But's been four nights in a row that my dreams have taken me to that place, and if I do fall back asleep now, I'm sure I'll just return there. These are the facts that I have to live with, no matter how crazy they might be. I'd probably never manage to settle down enough to fall asleep anyways. I need some time to process everything that Shirun told me and prepare for the storm that will undoubtedly be wreaking havoc on the manor if I do go back. At least last night's trip there wasn't as traumatic as the one before. I'm still a little on edge, but my body doesn't ache and my head only hurts a little. Picking up my phone off the coffee table, I see that it's 5:45 AM. Ideally, I'd like to have slept in a little later since I have no place to be today, but at least it's around an hour where I can go for a jog and no one will think I'm a total freak for being out and about.

I shut my eyes for a few seconds but find the absolute darkness to be of no comfort so I pop them back open and pull myself upright. My body feels stiff as I rise from the couch. In hindsight, it was probably a strange decision to conk out here rather than in my bed, but it seemed like the best option at the time, so whatever, I guess. I head upstairs into my bedroom where my bed sheets are still messed up from my tossing and turning – and eventual tumble out of bed – the night before. For some reason, I think about the first night I had with Kayla. Maybe it's because I was just thinking about how we met last night. It's weird though, I don't really know if I ever thought back on that moment before. In my memory, it always just kind of happened. I mean we met, we danced, we slept together, it's not like I hadn't had similar encounters with other chicks before. I suppose the main difference with Kayla was that she stuck around – not just for breakfast – she stuck around for good.

~*~

*We woke up together in the dim morning light, but the sight of her smiling at me brightened my whole world. Her sapphire eyes looked every bit as beautiful as Julie's, but they didn't pierce into me like daggers. When Kayla looked at me, I didn't feel so naked, so helplessly exposed to her. I could breathe easy around her and I didn't have to have a firm answer for everything in life. I could be me and she could be her. I think I knew all of this somehow when I woke up with her in my bed. I didn't know how or why, but I pegged her as a keeper right away. I made her scrambled eggs and toast in my kitchen. Normally, I'd just take a girl down the road to Benny's Pancake House. She brewed us a pot of coffee, somehow figuring out where to find my filters and grinds without asking or rifling through my cupboards. I've got no idea what we spent the rest of the morning talking about — I just know that we spent the better part of the day together. She left with my phone number as well as my heart.*

*I took her out a few times after that and she came to party with me on a couple of occasions before we officially became a thing. It's a little hazy to me now, but I can recall how simple it all felt. It was perfect. We were perfect.*

~*~

I wish we could go back to it being easy like that. Now I have all of these frustrations with our relationship that I don't even understand. There's all this anger and disappointment that I can't make go away. I just want that girl in my bed back. I want the person I had breakfast with — the one I could listen to for hours. I wonder if she gets that things feel different now. Does she want things to be like they used to or is the magic still there for her somehow? Does she even give a shit? Sometimes it seems like all she wants is to simply have a relationship, one that can be as exciting or bland as fate decides.

I'd rather not think on this anymore. Checking my phone, I see that it's almost 6:00 AM so I go into my dresser and withdraw a plain, black, long-sleeved shirt, navy basketball shorts, gray compression pants, and some ankle-high black socks. I peel off the work clothes I fell asleep in and change into these then head to my closet for my black and gray running shoes. Dressed like this, I suddenly feel way less sluggish. It's like I've shed all my baggage and can finally just escape from everything. So that's what I'm going to do – run away from it all. Snatching up a set of earbuds and my house key, I trot downstairs, pop my headphones and get some Persephone radio going.

I'm practically already jogging as I leave my apartment and head down the hall. While the elevator brings me down, I'm even bouncing back and forth between feet. I think I can safely say that I've never been this excited to go for a run. Thank God no one is really up and about yet to catch me acting like this. The second the doors slide open, I'm sailing through the lobby and crashing through the revolving front door. At last, I find myself jogging down the sidewalk toward The Commons. Whenever I go for a jog instead of hitting the gym, this is the route I always take. I don't usually go this early though.

As strange as it feels to be exercising at the asscrack of dawn, it's also kind of nice. I'm not in total darkness, but it's also not sunrise just yet. If not for the street lamps, I'd be running mostly in the black. There's something enchanting about running under the fluorescent glow. Every now and then a car comes by – its lights illuminating the block for a short while. I know it's a little strange, but it feels sort of heavenly to have it be just me and the lights. There's a simplicity to it. All I need to think about is one foot in front of the other, one breath in, then out. It's a repetitive pattern that always felt like such a chore to settle into, but now it's inexplicably freeing. The longer I go on like this, the more distant all of my problems seem and the easier it becomes to breathe. The easier it is to breathe, the faster my legs propel me forward. The faster I go, the more distant my problems feel.

Soon, The Commons comes into sight. I break into a near sprint toward it. I don't know why, but I have this thought that if I can just make it into the park, I'll be safe. I've always loved this place, but it's never looked quick so much like paradise as it does right now. Once my sneakers hit the gravel path that surrounds and cuts through the wide field of grass, I slow to an easy trot and let out the deepest of breaths as I take in the scenery. Maybe it's just the dim lighting, but I don't think this place has ever looked as green as it does right now. The white picket fence around it looks positively pristine and the giant white gazebo is equally stunning. I've seen all of this probably a couple hundred times before, yet this time somehow feels like the first. I guess it just goes to show how badly I want a little normalcy back in my life. For now, I'll just take what I can get. The only thing that could make this more perfect is if I had the place entirely to myself. Realistically there are only a couple of other people jogging in the entire park. I guess I'd just love to have absolute solitude. Maybe then I could aimlessly wander around or sprawl out across the grass without anyone judging me.

There's a woman jogging in my direction. She's still a ways off, but she looks like she might be really hot so I try to get my pace back up to a respectable jog. Then I notice that there's something off about her. The closer she gets to me, the more her dark skin tone starts to look familiar. It's unmistakably the same as that ethnically ambiguous bronze that marks Shirun's complexion. But that can't be. I'm just losing it, that's all that's happening. As the distance between us closes, it becomes evident that she is, in fact, very attractive. She's got long, slender legs that are shown off beautifully in her little white running shorts. It would take all of my mental stamina not to stare at them if it weren't for how much more alluring her breasts are. She's remarkably well endowed for a woman with such a petit waist. And all she's wearing is a skin-tight light pink tank top. It's definitely a sort of sport support shirt, but the laws of gravity are rendering it pretty useless right now. I wouldn't say it's exactly nice enough weather to be dressed like this, but you won't hear any complaints from me. It would be great if I was just sitting on a bench, watching her pass by, but she's more than a little distracting while I'm trying to jog. And it's hardly fair that I can't even get a proper look without coming off like a creep.

There's another problem too. Now that we're nearly next to each other, I notice more and more how much she really does resemble Shirun. It's not just the skin, it's everything. It's her impossibly blue eyes, her shapely features that are reminiscent of no particular race, and the thick, black hair that she has tied back into a swinging ponytail. It's a matter of mere seconds that I get to have a good sidelong look at her and then she's behind me. But her face burns itself into my mind. My feet pound onward in a desperate attempt to put some distance between us. She might be knockout gorgeous, but the sight of her is as disturbing as it is thrilling. Am I just letting my imagination get the better of me? I was doing so well. I'd cleared my mind and got my soul at ease. How could this happen? Am I being haunted or am I just officially nuts? A lady Shirun. *Really?*

Whatever's happening to me, I just want to get away from it. I know I can't actually run away from my sleeping problem, but getting away from this lady will certainly make me feel better, so I push myself to make my two laps around The Commons as fast as I can. Fortunately, I don't see her on my second pass around, though I'm not sure if that makes me feel better or worse. On one hand, I don't have to see her again. On the other, I'm left to wonder if she's just a product of my imagination and if she is, then I'm much worse off than I thought. I try not to dwell on it. I'm supposed to be relaxing after all and I can't do that if I keep finding ways to stress myself out. Plus, the sun has come up and it's turning out to be a mild, beautiful day, so I just need to enjoy it the best I can.

I come to the end of my lap and pass through the opening in the park fence. There's a bit more traffic so I have to wait a minute before crossing the street, but once I'm running down the blocks I find little to hinder my progress along the sidewalk. The streetlamps are dark now that the morning sun lights up the street. There's still a soft sort of illumination around me though, one that gleans marvelously off the cars that pass by. I finally feel relaxed again, but that only lasts about a minute or two before I get the chilling feeling that I'm being watched – no, followed. At first, I try to just shake it off. It's only my mind playing tricks on me. I tell myself that the feeling will pass if I can concentrate on my breathing.

But it doesn't work. I still have the urge to turn around and see if I really am being trailed by someone. Eventually, I give in and glance backward over my shoulder. That's when I see her. The lady Shirun, she's the one I sensed behind me. This can't be happening. I know there's no way this is real. I peer back a second time to find that it's definitely her. If the white shorts and long, dark legs aren't a dead giveaway, the breasts definitely are. There's no way I'd just have a random vision of someone who looks that perfect is there? I've never seen anyone like her. She's got the face of a model and the build of one of those comic book heroines. Chicks like that don't just show up and start following you unless something weird is going on. None of it makes any sense, but even if she is just a mirage, I still want to get away from her.

I'm close enough to my apartment building now that I can speed things up a little. Then I glance back and find that she's matching my speed.

"What the hell!" I hiss under my breath.

This needs to stop. There's just one more block now so I break into a full sprint. I don't bother to look back, I don't want to know if she's keeping my pace or not. I don't care what she wants. I don't even want to ever see her again, gorgeous as she might be. It's worth considering that she might just be a regular person who happens to bear a strong resemblance to Shirun — a man who doesn't exist...at least not in this world...

The rotating door to my apartment building is in sight now. I race toward it with all my speed and slow myself just enough to push through it. Once through, I stagger back away from it a few steps to see the woman run right by without so much as peeking in at me. There's an ease in her stride that makes her look rather spritely for the brief moment that I can see her. Maybe this was all a big nothing after all. Twisting toward the elevators, I catch a few other residents giving me raised eyebrows. I pretend not to notice them as I walk past. It's getting to the point in the morning when everyone starts heading out to work so I need to get myself to the privacy of my apartment before I spread my crazy all over this place. It's a long elevator ride up, but at least everyone else is going the opposite way so I get a little time to myself. I get some space to huff and puff like a madman.

Once the doors slide back open, I manage to pull myself together long enough to get into my apartment. I'm sure I still look a bit out of sorts to the people I pass, but hopefully they just think I had a really intense run. I don't get any more funny looks so I think that's a good sign. Once I've unlocked my door and gone inside, I slam it behind me. After locking it back up, I turn around and let myself lean on it. My legs give out beneath me and I slide down to the floor. I probably shouldn't be greasing up the door with my back sweat, but I need a minute to just put my face in my hands and collect myself. I indulge in this for a little while. Is it really so much to ask for this to all just go away?

I'll do whatever it takes. I might still be pissed about this forced time off, but I'm now fully committed to David's orders for me to get some rest. If I just take it one step at a time, maybe I can beat this and get back to normal. I decide the first step will be a long, hot shower. After hearing my stomach growl, it seems like the next one should be getting breakfast at Benny's Pancake House. I'll give myself two more minutes to sit here and then I need to get up and get started. I need to get better.

# Chapter 2

Benny's is about six blocks from where I live. Normally, this is far enough for me to want to take my car, but today I decide to walk. I'm sure I'm fine to drive, but I'd rather not chance it while I still feel a little unsteady, especially while the final wave of morning commuters are on the roads. It's a mild enough day too for this time of year so I just make sure to layer up before going out. A zip-up hoodie, dark blue jeans, a long sleeve shirt and a black jacket keep the chill out alright as I move down the streets. The sun is shining bright and the air is still which makes being outside actually feel pretty good. My legs are mostly mush at this point though so that makes the going tougher than I'd like.

By the time I step through the door of Benny's and hear the bell chime, I feel like I might collapse into a boneless heap. Instead, I set myself onto a barstool and lean forward on the counter. I'm expecting to wait a few minutes before getting service so I just stare upward at the menu. I've barely given it a glance when a chipper middle-aged woman comes up to me.

"How are you doin' this mornin' darlin'?" she greets.

"Good, thanks."

"What can I start ya off with?"

"Large latte and could I get a number three plate?"

"Sure thing, I'll pop in the order and be right out with that latte. You want whipped cream and raspberry sauce with the pancakes?"

I think on this a moment. I'm already here treating myself to a fancy coffee and breakfast junk food, so I might as well top it off.

"Sure," I tell her.

She gives me the kind of smile that does more than hint that she's hoping for a nice tip and then she shuttles off with my order. I let out a deep breath, though nothing so heavy as a sigh. Dropping my head down, I notice that my hands are shaking a little. This isn't normal for me even when I'm really tired, but then what is normal for me this week? I hope it's just the early morning exercise combined with an empty stomach that's doing this to me. Once I've had a chance to eat I guess I'll find out if this is all I'm experiencing, but I'm reasonably afraid that the stress and anxiety from my dreams is manifesting itself into physical symptoms. It was bad enough that my dreams left me with a dizzying headache and sore muscles, but shaking hands and maybe seeing people who aren't there … those are even more serious issues. I need to stop myself from giving into paranoia though. I can't keep finding ways to psych myself out.

Then I suddenly feel two hands clap down on my shoulders. Without hesitation, I pop out of my seat and twist around to face whoever just touched me. I find that it's a man, one that's not particularly assuming and I think he's shrinking away from me now that I'm on my feet. He stands several inches shorter than me and has a lean, but skinny build. I'm not really sure what his deal is. He looks like a wholesome enough person though. He's in nice, faded jeans, leather slip-on sneakers and a movie-star brown leather jacket with a light blue T-shirt underneath. He has shining blue eyes, a square jaw, and shaggy, but well-kept black hair. He seems nice enough, but what the hell does he want?

"Bryan?" he says, tilting his head to the side.

Holy shit, it's Kevin. I just stared him down like some kind of criminal and I'm standing squared off to him with my fists clenched.

"Kevin?" I reply quietly.

"Hey buddy!" A smile breaches his features as he lurches toward me with arms spread wide.

He wraps me into a hug that lasts a little longer than I expect. Even after patting the back of his shoulders, he holds on. He's always been a far more affectionate guy than most, but this seems like a lot of man-love even coming from him. It could also just be me. It's been a while since I've seen or heard from him so maybe I just forgot what his typical hug duration is. Eventually, he does let me go only to then take hold of my shoulders and give me a friendly shake. He's got a beaming grin that instantly fills me with guilt. Anyone looking on definitely thinks that I'm nowhere near as happy to see him as he is to see me. I nearly punched him a moment ago and now the shock of the moment has my expressions frozen so I try and let my face relax into an easy smirk.

"How are you? Everything okay?" He asks.

"Good, yeah, I'm good"

The way his eyebrows briefly pinch together shows me that he's not too convinced.

"Better now that I've run into you, of course," I add while widening my grin in hopes that this can make up for how I've treated him so far.

This brings the sparkle back to his eyes. Then I'm pulled back in for Hug Wars Episode Two: The Hugger Strikes Back. This time, I just let it happen without worrying about it. I embrace him back, even, giving up all attempts at keeping things to a simple bro hug. It's been so long, I guess there's nothing wrong with any of this. It'll just be awkward for anyone who comes in and has to bear witness to two grown-ass men hugging it out in the middle of the diner. Suddenly I sense the presence of someone behind us and begin to feel way more self-conscious than before. I can't see who it is which should make this less awkward, but it's actually worse since I don't know if we're in their way or what their deal is really. It's only when Kevin and I pull apart that I realize that it's Erin. She's standing beside us with a shimmering pair of baby blues that rival her boyfriend's. Now I feel stupid for even wondering who was standing there. It should hardly come as a surprise that where I find one, I find the other. Unlike Kevin though, there's a slight apprehension in the way she stands there. She looks stiff as though she's waiting for me to say or do something.

"Hey there," I say, not really sure what else I can do.

"Hey stranger," she replies softly.

This seems to shatter some of the ice between us because I'm soon wrapped up in another hug. I really don't mind though. Maybe it's because I'm hugging a lady or maybe I'm just getting used to all the unabashed affection. The embrace goes by a little quicker too. By the time I'm released I'm kind of sorry that this business is all done now.

"Feels like it's been forever since I've seen you guys," I offer while gesturing my hands up to both of them. It's a lame segue into conversation, but I'm kind of at a loss for anything of substance.

"It *has* been forever," Erin corrects. I think I hear a little frustration in her normally smooth tone.

"It's really good to see you, man," Kevin adds quickly.

"Nice to see you guys too. What brings you here? It's a long way out for a quick breakfast right? Or have you moved?"

"Nope, same place as when we saw you last." Kevin hesitates for a second before saying, "We're just here to treat ourselves."

"We both took a long weekend," Erin explains. "My parents are having their anniversary tomorrow so my sister and I set up a party for them at the loft in one of their favorite restaurants."

"That's awesome," I pip.

"Yeah it's a fairly small gathering, but it will be nice I think."

"Sure, it's not one of the big ones is it?"

"No," she replies. "No, it's obviously not their 50th or anything. It's their 33rd actually, so not even in the tens, but every year is special, right?"

"Definitely."

I feel like I've been shamed a little. It's not  that I said anything wrong, it's just that my parents' anniversary clearly does not mean as much to me as her parents' does to her.

"What about you?" Kevin asks.

"Oh, I have the day off too, but I'm not travelling anywhere."

They don't seem at all surprised by this news even though they must remember my aversion to taking time off from work. The way each of them nod their heads makes it seem like they almost expected this answer from me somehow.

"Will you join us then?"

"Oh, I –" I hesitate, looking at Kevin, then Erin, then back to Kevin. "I wouldn't want to get in the way of your plans or anything." What I really mean might be closer to, "*I don't want to awkwardly be a third wheel and fumble through small talk.*"

"We've just barely touched our food," Kevin chuckles. "You wouldn't be slowing us down or getting in the way of anything at all. Come on, just for a little while."

It's almost like he's trying to bargain with me. Did I come off a bit strong? It's not like I *don't* want to spend time with them. I just don't want things to be weird, my week's been weird enough already.

"Cinnamon pancakes with raspberry sauce and whipped cream," the waitress calls to me.

I turn around to find my order and my coffee sitting in waiting on the bar top.

"Just bring your food over."

"We'd really like to catch up," Erin states as if to reassure me that the invitation is real.

"Is it alright if I move over to a booth?" I ask, turning back to the waitress behind the counter.

For half a moment, I sort of hope that she'll say no, but she replies, "Sure thing darlin', enjoy now."

I smile and nod her way as I retrieve my plate and cardboard cup. When I turn back, I see Kevin and Erin arranging themselves in their booth. Kevin is sliding his plate over to Erin's end of the table, leaving that second bench all to me. That's great, all eyes will be on yours truly which means I better prepare myself for a whole lot of talking, otherwise there'll be nothing but their baby blues burning into me like laser beams. But I'm in too deep now, so I meander on over to the booth where I take a seat in the now-empty bench. As soon as I do, Erin immediately starts up conversation which saves us from any uncomfortable silence.

"So how have you been? You look well," she starts and I suddenly feel very fortunate that they didn't see me yesterday.

"I'm good... It's been a little hectic lately, but I can't complain." I have, of course, been silently complaining about a lot of things lately, but that's not the best material for a reunion like this. I guess I'm kind of lying to them by saying this, but it's a white lie, right?

"And how's Kayla been?"

Again, I'm going to lie to them. As much as I'd like to have an open and honest conversation, I don't want my first interaction with them in God knows how long to be a sad one.

So I say, "She's good – keeping busy as well. Her agency is finally assigning her to some higher profile listings so she's feeling some pressure, but I think she loves it."

"Yeah that's good. It's nice to be a little challenged."

"Life's more interesting that way," Kevin adds.

I see an opening to switch the focus over to them and ask, "So has work been good for you guys. You're still at ImageInation right?"

"Yes, it's been great there," Erin replies. "We've grown so much since I started, it's unbelievable."

"I saw that you guys moved your office over to Peabody Square," I prompt her to continue as I finally get a bite of my pancakes.

They're as dense and milky as I remember and I'm very happy I opted to go with the toppings. The sauce and the whipped cream are so sweet that I don't even need any maple syrup.

"Oh we actually moved a second time," Erin corrects me. "It was really recent though, about five months ago now, I think."

"I'm pretty sure it's actually been more like seven," Kevin offers.

"What? No..." Erin takes a minute or two to look at the ceiling and let the details work themselves out. "Yeah, you're right. It'll be seven months in a little over a week."

"So it was a crazy move then?" I ask before re-stuffing my face.

"Yes, it wasn't really one we planned for very well so we were actually working out of two offices for a couple of weeks."

I gulp down my food and reply, "Wow, you weren't exaggerating about growing fast then."

"No, it's been pretty insane, honestly. It was slow going for a while, but our marketing guy did a really bangup job at pushing our brand and the work just started flooding us. We had to hire a bunch of new people and move our office just to keep up. Then in less than a year, we realized it wasn't enough so now we've got a whole floor in the Cadwell Building down on 62nd Street."

"That's fantastic," I hum with genuine enthusiasm.

"It's definitely been nice now that things have settled back into a groove. Kevin's had some exciting moves too."

"Oh really, I guess I'm missing all the good stuff on FriendBook then. Where are you at now?"

"Haha right!" Keven chuckles, though it sounds forced. "I got a job as the Manager of Sales for Wilkins Tech a few months back." There's a glimmer of pride in his eyes as he tells me this.

"Nice, what prompted you to leave –" I'm drawing a blank on where Kevin went to work after his Parson days.

"Zerogear Apps…" Kevin finishes for me. His voice is small and his eyelids suddenly look a little heavy. He's hurt and he probably should be, this is the kind of thing a friend would know. "It was just that I felt a little stuck I guess. They're a smaller organization and not really growing so I knew I'd have to do some of the grunt-work, but most of the time I either felt like an overpaid customer service rep or a contract negotiator. Those aren't really things that move me and there was no way to move up so I looked elsewhere."

"And Wilkins has been working out a bit better then?"

"Yes! Much better." His face brightens up, but I still feel guilty for bumming him out in the first place. It's somehow worse that he doesn't call me out for being so out of touch with his life. He's just going to forgive, forget, and move on – he's probably already done so.

"Has life still been treating you well as a Manager?" Erin asks as I shovel down more of my breakfast.

What I want to say is, "*Not as good as how life would be as a Director,*" but instead I go with, "It's definitely a step up from where I was before and it's nice to have new challenges and rewards. It's also nice that I can still climb higher." I try to say this with confidence, but I sound a little pitchy.

They both nod their heads in unison as if they know exactly what I mean. I'm sure they know that David is my boss so maybe they feel bad for bringing this up. I mean, they shouldn't, they were just trying to make conversation. When Kevin's eyes drift down to his plate, mine follow. It's then that I notice that it's completely empty and so is Erin's. From the way leftover maple syrup clings dryly to the plates I'd say that they were done well before I came in here.

"*What the hell!*" I think to myself.

They didn't have to lie to me. Though thinking on how reluctant I was to join them, I'm sure they thought they needed to fib a little to get me to agree to come over here. I'm not really in a place to be mad anyway – I've kind of been lying to them this whole conversation. I'd like to speak truthfully with them, but what is there to say really? It's a shitty time for me and they were just unlucky enough to run into me during it. My brain fishes around for something to say, but I come up with nothing.

"Do you think you'd like to come out with us sometime?" Erin starts back in.

"I know you and Kayla are usually busy on the weekends, but we do stuff on weeknights too from time to time," Kevin adds.

"Right, there's trivia on Wednesdays at a couple of bars in the area," Erin says.

"Tuesdays as well at some other places, I'm pretty sure" Kevin continues.

"Yeah I think that's right," she agrees, "And Thursdays are when a couple places have bingo while others do a karaoke night."

"Now that it's warming up a bit, there will be more stuff going on at The Commons too." Kevin pauses a moment before concluding, "But you know… only if you're able to, of course, I know it can be hard to find time for things nowadays."

*Again, with the tag team negotiation!* I don't understand why they are so convinced that I don't want to see them. Did David say something to them? And what does Kevin mean by "*hard to find time for things nowadays?*" It seems like they're doing just fine making time to go out and have fun. Maybe if I got an invite to this stuff every now and then I'd find *time* for it too. I know I shouldn't express this thought out loud, but the words form a nasty glob in the base of my throat and I want nothing more than to just spit it out.

"I didn't realize all you guys were still so social with each other." My words come quietly, but they also tremble with anger. "If you guys let me know when you're planning on doing this stuff, I'd definitely be happy to join you."

I'm thinking that I managed to sound a little less angry on that last bit, but then I see the frozen expression on their faces. It's a real deer-in-the-headlights moment for them, but I don't think it's guilt that I'm seeing. No from the wide eyes and scrunched brows, I'd say they are genuinely shocked, confused, and maybe even a little hurt. Why? Why would *they* get to be the ones to feel mistreated? Am I not being reasonable? They can't just say that I should spend time with them if they aren't going to invite me to their little gatherings.

"It's usually more of a spur of the moment thing," Kevin explains faintly. "Most times it's just us and Devon and this guy he works with named Erik. We know you normally need a little more notice since Kayla and you usually have plans."

"Where did you guys get that idea? Yeah having notice is nice – it helps, but since when did you guys start thinking I wouldn't make time for you?" I know I sound a little aggressive, but they don't get to just drop bombs on me after all this time and not expect me take exception to it.

"*You* gave us that idea," Erin replies in a stern tone. It kind of sounds like when a parent tries to reason with their kid while trying not to blow their top.

"When?" I croak. "When did this happen."

"Bryan," Kevin cuts in. His tone is soft, but steady. "We didn't mean to make you upset. We're not accusing you of anything, we'd just like to reconnect and we know it's tough when you've got a career and a relationship and you're trying to stay healthy and all that."

"When?" I insist, my eyes locked on his. "Did David say something?"

"No, Bryan, you did," Erin repeats.

"It was our fault too though," Kevin soothes before I can argue. "You weren't with Kayla that long and we should have just given you some space to settle into that relationship – some time to move forward with … things."

"You mean Julie?"

He stutters, unable to form actual words. Erin places her arm around him, pulling him close while staring me down.

"Yes, I was pissed, Kevin. Okay, she dumped my ass, but I didn't need space from you. I needed some support. I needed to feel like you guys had my back."

"Then why did you tell us to leave you alone?" Erin jumps in. Her features look hard, like chiseled stone.

I can't figure out what she's talking about. When and why would I tell them to back off? Was I so busy with Kayla that I stopped having time for them? Then I turn to Kevin and I see the strange, watery look in his eyes. I realize that I've seen that look before and now things start to come back to me.

~*~

*I'd been bombarded with text after text to go out and do this or do that. I felt frustrated. I just wanted things to work with Kayla and she wanted more one-on-one time with me. I figured that wasn't too much to ask considering that none of my friends even liked her. No one would ever admit to it, but I could tell. It was the way they looked at her or didn't look at her — the way they talked or didn't talk to her. The tension was palpable and I had no idea what their problem could possibly be. All I knew was that Kayla made me happy and they were pissing me off. I didn't care that Julie withdrew from the group, I still felt her pulling their strings, trying to sabotage the best thing I had going on.*

*It all came to a head one night. I'd run into Kevin after hitting the gym. Maybe he really did just coincidentally pull into the parking lot as I was leaving. Maybe he waited there for me like a creeper. Whatever the case, I found myself face to face with him. It started with some awkward hellos that I can't remember the details of now.*

*Then he said something along the lines of, "We miss you, you know." Then there was some nonsense thing he wanted me to go to, one where Kayla unsurprisingly remained absent from the invite list.*

*I'd said something like, "Yeah, I'll definitely let you know, but I should be free."*

*"You said something like that last time." This douche had the balls to say that to me … or something like that at least.*

*I'd noticed then how chilly the night breeze felt. It was dark too. Only parking lot lights and the occasional pair of passing headlights illuminated our dismal conversation.*

*"Really? You're going to just corner me like that?" I held nothing back in terms of volume.*

*"I'm sorry, I didn't mean to call you out…" he backpedaled, putting his hands up. But it was far too late for him to try to play innocent — he'd already thrown the first punch.*

*"No, you knew exactly what you were saying," I returned, my voice still raised.*

*"I didn't mean to — we just care about you, that's all…"*

*"If you care so much, then why don't you just fuck off?"*

*My words pierced through the night air and cut into his chest. He staggered back a little and got choked up. His eyes swelled and his shoulders hunched forward.*

*"Okay," he conceded hoarsely. "I'm sorry, we'll try to be a little more considerate to your personal space then. I'll tell the others not to bug you so much."*

*I don't think I said anything back. I knew that what I said was harsh, but I didn't feel bad for saying it. I didn't feel much at all really. Even the chill in my flesh faded to numbness. If anything, I might have actually been satisfied. I felt so justified in my actions — in believing that I only gave Kevin what he deserved.*

*"It — it was good seeing you, Bryan," he stammered while I passed him by. "Take care," he finished, before retreating into the gym.*

~*~

I'm sure I've talked with him between then and now. A couple of texts maybe or at least something on FriendBook. But maybe not. Maybe the last thing I told him was to "fuck off." And if that's the case then why did he go out of his way to say "hi" to me here? Why did they both insist that I sit with them even after they'd already finished eating?

All I can do is slowly dip my head down and wonder, *"What have I become?"*

I stare down at the last remnants of pancake that lay strewn across my plate. It seems like a sad waste to leave it there, but I don't feel much like finishing it. When I finally dare to lift my eyes, I'm met with Erin's unwavering gaze. Now I understand what this hard look is — her hesitation earlier starts to make sense. I hurt her man, now she's worried I'll do that again. Maybe I already have done it again. They've always been funny like that. She can be sensitive too, but he's always been the more vulnerable of the two. He must have taken our last encounter pretty hard which is unfortunate since he certainly didn't deserve to take on the full weight of all my anger towards the lot of them.

"So I think I haven't been doing as well as I'd like to be doing…" It's not really an apology, but I'm still trying to figure out if I really do owe them one and if so, what is it exactly that I need to own up to? Everything is so unclear all of a sudden.

"I know that," Kevin says. "*We* know that," he corrects,

looking to Erin who's still looking stone cold.

"Nothing's been very clear to me lately. I'm tired and confused and angry all the time." Maybe I didn't want to open up to them like this, but I've found myself backed up against a wall here so there isn't much else I can do really.

"Is there anything we can do?" Kevin asks. His cheeks are still puffy, but at least his eyes don't look like they're about to burst.

"I don't think so, but thanks."

"What are you up to after this," Erin asks as though she's trying to get down to business of some kind.

"Probably just going to walk back home and then get some rest," I answer, grateful for the change in subject.

"You walked here?" Kevin asks, his voice piqued.

"Yeah."

"Is something wrong with your car?"

"No, I just didn't want to drive. I mean it's nice, why not walk?"

"Can we give you a ride?" Erin offers.

"No, no, I don't want to hold you guys up or anything. I know you probably want to hit the road soon."

Erin laughs at me like someone might laugh at a child after they've said something ridiculous. "Bryan, you're like a two second drive and we're going by there anyway."

"I –" I'm about to insist I'm fine with *she* strolls in through the door.

She's all dolled up now which somehow makes her look even more like Shirun. Dark makeup makes her crystalline eyes shine even brighter. Her hair falls in long, thick waves over her shoulders and contrasts brilliantly against the soft white of her peacoat. There's a brief moment where my soul is pierced by her stifling gaze then she turns away and takes a seat at the bar. A chill crawls down my spine and I look back to my friends who are a little perplexed by my sudden pause.

"I'd actually appreciate that a lot," I say a bit too quickly.

I don't know why the sight of one woman fills me with so much fear. Maybe it's the bizarre qualities that she possesses, but I think it's more an issue of what she might represent. Is the world of the manor really spilling into my waking reality? Or is this perhaps the first real sign that I'm actually just going insane? Either way, I want to get out of here as fast as I can. I want to hide out in my apartment where she can't find me. I need to escape all of this bullshit, if it's even something that I *can* run away from.

# Chapter 3

I lean my head toward the open car window. A mildly warm current floats around my face and runs through my hair. I'm sure I look ridiculous, probably like a Labrador happily sticking its head into the open air. I don't care though, the sensation is calming and I know it won't last much longer. It's been completely silent between us since we left Benny's. Right now, I'm just sitting in the back seat of Erin's modest sedan. It's a Fonda Destiny, but an older model. Aside from taxis, I can't remember the last time I rode in an honest little car like this. It's still clean and well-kept and all, it's just that it feels so simple compared to a Wercedes. Being in it evokes an odd sort of feeling – one that can only be described as safe. I feel safe – like when I was a child in the back seat of my parents' car. I let my body relax against the soft, felt finish of the seat and try to turn my mind off. The silence is nice too somehow. The radio's not even on. All I can hear are the sounds of passing cars and the wind flooding into the cabin.

All of it is so serene, so secure. I'm grateful to get away from the lady Shirun, thrilled to have a moment of rest, and relieved to be in the care of old friends. They *are* still my friends, I think. If they weren't, I probably wouldn't be in this car right now. My head still spins at knowing that they've been actively avoiding me after my outburst. At least Kevin has. Erin maintained her lunches with David and me, but she must have been furious at me the whole time. How did she manage to stand me after what happened? The guilt at having hurt Kevin begins to sink in. The worst part is that I can't even remember all the details of how I got *that* mad at him. I was probably within my rights to be annoyed or even snippy, but to yell at him like that, there must have been a lot more going through my mind. Or maybe there wasn't enough going on up there. It's no excuse that I can't remember though. There's no good reason for how I treated Kevin so I'll just have to find a way to make it up to him somehow.

Kevin's in front of me seated shotgun. I can see him in the passenger-side mirror since he's leaning out the window a little himself. Unlike me though, he looks worried. His eyes have a distant sort of glaze over them and his brow is pinched. Is it just awkward for him to have me back here? No, I think he might be worried about *me* – worried about my well-being. I may not be as bad as yesterday, but I'm sure I still look like a mess. Plus I also made the mistake of admitting that I'm not doing so well. Looking at the rearview mirror, I can see Erin taking nervous glances at me too. What I've got going on right now really isn't their problem, though. I don't need them worrying about me. I can beat this, whatever it is that's happening to me. I've never faced anything I couldn't overcome. This is just one of life's challenges, that's all. It might be a challenge that bears remarkable resemblance to insanity, but it's a challenge all the same and I've never backed down from one before so I won't now.

"You can just drop me off up front," I tell them as my building comes into view.

"You sure?" Erin questions, turning her head back to me for a second. "We can pull into the garage if you want."

"No, thank you, I've already taken enough time out of your day."

"We're in no real rush," Kevin chips in. He looks at me through the rearview mirror.

"You guys have already done more than I probably deserve. I don't want you to put off your travel plans on my account."

"Oh, no we weren't going to head out right awa–"

"I can hear your bags shifting around in the trunk, Kev. I'm sure you meant to head out right after breakfast and I've probably made you late already. So please, just drop me here and maybe we can catch up more once you're back."

"We'd like that," Erin states as she pulls up along the front of the complex.

"I have all of next week off."

"Yeah, that's great, we'll be in touch then?"

"I'd like that," I answer as I spring out of the back seat and shut the door securely. Coming up to the passenger window, I look in and add, "Thank you both, it was really nice to see you."

Kevin sticks his hand out of the window where I grasp it firmly. He's misty and I hope to God he's not about to have all sorts of man-feelings on me right now.

"I'm glad we ran into you," he says in a wavering tone. My grip on his hand tightens as though that will somehow keep the emotions at bay. "Take care of yourself, okay."

"Sure, yeah, will do." I dodge his eyes as I make this reply. I really can't make any promises so far as this goes, given my current circumstances.

"We'll meet you someplace next week when we're back," he says this more as a statement than a question or an offer.

"Sounds like a plan," I reply without hesitation.

"See you then," Erin says with a quick flicker of a grin.

"Goodbye Bryan," Kevin releases my hand and drapes his forearm back over the window frame.

"See you guys," I say as they roll off.

It's relieving at first to step through the revolving door and into the ivory lobby, but as I make my way to the elevators, there's this feeling of dread that swells up within me. I can't figure out what it is at first, but then as I ascend the floors of the complex, I realize that I'm going to be alone very soon. I'm mostly alone right now. It's a starkly empty building since almost all of the residents are at work and I have nothing to look forward to except for my large, empty apartment. Sure I'll be safe from that woman, but I've also got nowhere to go, nothing to do, and no one to keep me company. I realize that this is the first time in a long time that I've felt this way. Or maybe this is the first time I've had the free time to take notice.

The elevator dings and its doors swing open, giving me a small start. I seem to get stuck in my head a lot while time moves on around me. I step out through the doorway and down the hall. It's dead silent, but not in a peaceful way. The quiet feels uncomfortable, it feels wrong even. So I speed up my pace until I'm basically speed walking to my unit. I jam the key in and toss the door open. Once inside, I double and triple check that I've locked it behind me. Then I wander over to the living room, dumping my keys on the kitchen table as I pass. Sun spills into my living room and shines off of my blue soda with particular brilliance. I come up to it and plop myself down without much grace. I've barely just settled in when my phone rings. Withdrawing the device from my pocket, I see that it's Kayla calling. I'd pretty much forgotten that it's Friday up until this point. The realization fills me with conflicting reactions. One is that I will be able to busy myself with getting ready to go out, but the other is a feeling of dread for heading to the clubs. For once, I don't want to party. I just want company without all the noise. But I can't let this phone ring forever so I tap the answer button and bring it to my ear.

"Hey Kayla," I answer.

"Hey there, babe. Hope you're feeling better." I'm about to answer when she continues with, "Listen, since you've been under the weather, I was thinking you might like another night of staying in. See, Jenny and her bestie Hannah are checking out this new place called The Golden Pearl, it's supposed to be absolutely spectacular. They were thinking of it being more like a girl's night out. But yeah, I figured you wouldn't mind if I just did that and let you rest up."

"Sure," I answer, not knowing whether I should be angry, happy, relieved, disappointed, or what. It sounds like the decision has already been made for me so I just say, "No problem."

"Great! Make sure you're better by tomorrow though, I'm expecting a good night out with you."

"You got it," I assure her without much enthusiasm.

"Super, enjoy your night, Bry."

"Have fun, Kayla."

The line goes dead and I feel a whole new sense of solitude now. I know it's not fair to feel this way. I really don't want to go out tonight, but a part of me wishes I could bring myself to ask Kayla if she'd spend the night with me rather than two people I've never heard of before and maybe never will again. I know that's selfish, but it's what I want. I don't even know if she'd be much help against what I have to deal with. No, it's probably good that I'm facing this alone. It would be pretty awkward to have her in bed with me while I'm going through one of my nighttime fits of madness. On that subject, I don't really want to keep worrying about the manor. It may be afternoon already, but there's a good long while until it's bedtime and I don't want to fret over what the night will bring.

I start by taking my laundry down the hall to the community washroom. Normally I wait to do it during odd hours of the night, but it so happens that it's an odd hour of the day which is just as good as it turns out. It's nice to have the entire place to myself, it's exactly the way I usually like it, but for some reason it feels spooky. I'm conscious of how I'm the only one making any sound in here as I load my lights into one machine and my darks into another. There's no one else around and not one machine is actively in use. After adding detergent, I put the bottle into my basket and grab a seat in one of the chairs that are lined up along the front wall of the room. At least there's a bit of white noise in here now thanks to the washers doing their thing. I ease back in my seat and pull my tablet out of my basket. There's wifi in the room so I could read the news or just aimlessly surf the web a little, but instead I open my Nile Spark app. I don't have many eBooks downloaded on it, but I find that I tend to reread the same books (when I choose to read anything at all) anyway.

I tap on the cover image for my favorite book. It's technically a novel for young adults, but I still like it, even now. It's sad and profound in a lot of ways. The implications of its dystopian world run much deeper than I realized when I first read it as a kid so I think it means something different to me now than it did then. Even though I could probably read this whole thing before bedtime, I find myself skipping to the end as I often do. In the final chapters, the hero realizes that he must work with his mentor to escape from the world he calls home, leave the people he calls family, and even say goodbye to the girl he's smitten with. It's only in leaving that the rest of his people can be freed from the crippling ignorance that enslaves them. My favorite thing about this ending is that he isn't running because he's scared. He's not really running away at all — he's running *to* something. He chases after a new home, a new family, and a new life. In the end, this is what makes everything right.

I switch loads over to the dryers in between chapters. By the time the machines honk at me, I have just a little bit left and it's the best part so I keep reading. I follow the words to their victorious conclusion. It's just as stunning every time I read it and I don't know why, but it always gives me a sense of freedom and hopefulness. I get this idea that nothing is too far out of reach, that somehow anything can be overcome. I hold the tablet over my lap for a couple more minutes to soak in this feeling. Once it's faded off, I lock the device and unload my clothes. Once I'm back in my apartment, I fold everything and iron my work clothes. Next, I find that it's high time I made dinner. In spite of how filling those pancakes were, my stomach growls like a disgruntled beast so I decide to go with the path of least resistance.

Reaching into my freezer, I withdraw a box of frozen macaroni and cheese. I'm sure Kayla would flip if she knew I occasionally ate this crap, but I can't help myself sometimes. I pull out the plastic tray and my mouth is already watering. I know this is the ultimate act of laziness since a box of mac and cheese could literally be cooked in less than fifteen minutes, but I honestly don't care, this is going to be great. Removing the wrapping, I toss the platter into the microwave and wait anxiously as it cooks. After an excruciating two and a half minutes, my dinner is steamy and ready to devour. I slip a napkin under it and pull the indulgence out. With a child-like haste, I snag a fork from my silverware drawer and head over to the couch. Without wasting any more time, a scoopful of the cheesy, creamy noodles is shoved into my mouth. With so much in life that often goes wrong, at least I know that Mama Bovine's Frozen Maccaroni and Cheese will never disappoint.

I interrupt my meal only to click the TV on and flick to a re-run of Superstar in the Rough. I could watch the news, but you don't turn that shit on when your dinner is as happy a course as what I've got tonight. No, tonight, there will be no news – only fun, nice things. After my dinner is polished off, I'm half tempted to lick the cheese sauce out of the tray, but I do have some restraint. I get up and toss the thing into the garbage so it can't tempt me further. Then I pour myself some Merlot and snatch up a can of honey glazed almonds. I just sip and snack while watching talented people compete for a couple of hours. Then my eyes start to feel heavy and I panic for a moment. I can't go to sleep, not now, not when I've had such a relaxing afternoon.

Without giving it much debate, I pop off the couch and go into the kitchen to brew myself a pot of coffee. I'm going to drink all of it if I have to. Anyone watching me right now would definitely think I'm crazy, but I can't afford to spoil things now. Maybe if I just skip a night of sleeping, skip a night of "dreaming," I can break the cycle of these episodes. I know Kayla told me to get some sleep, but screw her. I don't have to face this alone – I don't have to face it at all. I drink mug after mug, trying to space it out so that I'm pouring a new one right as the last has all but worn off. Prime-time TV turns into late-night TV and I'm going pretty strong, but then a weird chill runs across my back. All of my living room lights are on and still bright, but the room feels a few shades darker somehow.

An ominous feeling grips my stomach and refuses to let go. Then a horrible hissing noise whips against my window. This makes me jump a little even though I know it's just the wind. It's really howling though and I swear there wasn't so much as a gust a few seconds ago. As out of the blue as it might be, the wind's nothing to be afraid of. I've almost relaxed again when I see creeping shadows forming in the corners of the room where my walls meet the ceiling. As the screeching of the wind gets louder, the writhing dark spots grow in size. The rest of the room is so well lit though, how can shadows like that even exist? Suddenly, my lights flicker and I leap off the couch with a yelp. Now I'm really freaked out.

For some reason, I look down to where my empty wine glass still sits on the coffee table. I see the distorted reflection of a man in it, but I don't think it's me.

"Leave," a voice rings through my ears. It's strong, but not vicious.

"Shirun?"

"You're not safe there, come back to us."

Before I can protest further, the image is gone from the glass. Without any further thought, I spin on my heels and charge off toward the stairs. Racing up the steps, I see the inexplicable shadows slithering along after me. Somehow whatever's haunting me in the manor can find me here too. I have no choice now. I've got to confront it in my sleep. At least there, I'll have some help. My feet carry me into my bedroom where I slam the door shut, breathing uncontrollably. It looks like I'm safe here … for now. So I strip down to my underwear and leap into bed where I cocoon myself in the blankets. At first my heartrate keeps me awake, but eventually the terror tires me out and I'm able to shut my eyes. The only thing I want less than having another visit to the mansion is facing the darkness alone in my waking hours so I try to relax. Eventually, I feel myself fading. The wind's screams and the creaking I hear around me does make me tremble, but my fatigue takes over. It grabs hold of my mind and drags me down into the realm of unconsciousness.

# Chapter 4

When my eyes snap open, I still hear the howling wind. It's even stronger now and I get a rush of excitement at the fact that I'm waking up in the real world. There will be no crazy-ass adventure tonight. But then my vision clears and I realize that this isn't my bedroom — this isn't my world. My body contracts into a balled position. I'm on a bed, it's just not my bed. The comforter is a thick, silver, down blanket and the tall bedframe is adorned with blue drapes hanging elegantly around it. If these details aren't enough to clue me into the fact that I'm back in the manor, the white collared shirt, beige pants, brown belt, and brown shoes that I'm wearing are a dead giveaway. But this place feels different and it's not just because of the turbulence raging outside. There's a gravity here that's much deeper and darker than I've ever felt before and it makes me want to take shelter under the luxurious sheets. I'd really like nothing more than to just lie my head down, so that's what I do.

The silk-covered down pillows depress invitingly as my head sinks into them. For one glorious moment, my entire body unwinds across the mattress, but then a gust slams against the mansion so hard it feels as though the entire place shakes. My muscles constrict again and I pop up onto my knees. I stay poised like this on top of my refuge for a couple of minutes. Eventually, I accept the fact that I can't stay here. It was never really an option, I'm sure, but if I could just sleep through this storm, I undoubtedly would. Instead, I guess I'll have to take a look around and see what mess I'm facing this time. There's a single window in the back corner of this little room, but my view of it is partially obstructed by the burgundy wardrobe that stands beside it. It would definitely be best to start tonight's festivities by looking outside so I lower myself off of the bed and step cautiously over to the back wall.

The entire house creeks not just beneath my feet, but all around me. It's a chorus of shrieks and groans and when I finally get a good look outside, I see why. It takes me a moment to process, but I'm seeing an abyssal flurry of black and deep purple whisps. The gaseous tumult engulfs everything. I have no idea what side of the house I'm on because I can't see any of the property that lies below me. I leap back when a bit of that ribbon-y black goo flies past my eyes. As it does, a deafening screech blasts my eardrums. I stagger back in pain at the sudden racket and the sight of that stuff which crawled through the house last time. It's flying around the mansion now? What's going on here? What is this stuff and what the hell kind of a storm is this? A bright flash of lightning cracks in the distance, but there's no cloud for such a bolt to shoot from and I can't tell what it's striking. Another bolt flashes then another immediately after.

I can't be sure since there's no thunder to accompany these blasts, but it seems like they're getting closer. The idea that this might be true makes my stomach tighten. What happens if this mystical lightning does strike the building? I'm safe in here for the moment, but for some reason I feel like these walls won't be sheltering me from the storm for much longer. What's worse is that I'm still alone. I thought the whole reason I needed to come here was so I could face this evil with Shirun, Olivia, and Myles by my side. Where are they now? Where is anyone for that matter? I've never woken up alone here before. And at a time like this too. I need someone, anyone, even if it's someone I haven't met yet. Literally anything would be better than being here in this room all by myself as I watch the ultimate storm of wickedness rage. But what if I'm all that's left? What if that thing in the hood and its devilish hound got them all? I need to believe that Shirun is still alive at least. Wasn't it him that called out to me to return here? If so, where the hell is he now? Why bring me here just to abandon me?

I'm certain now that the lightning *is* getting closer. This is shaping up to be my worst visit to the manor yet and now I'm afraid that it might also be my last. I hadn't given it much thought before, but now I'm left to wonder what will happen to me if I do die here. Do I just wake up feeling like a train ran over me or does something worse happen? A heart attack? A coma? Going braindead? Does my body just stay here and go missing from the real world for all eternity? All I know is that I don't want to find out. But I also don't know what to do. I don't want to leave the room and start wandering this place since there's probably more of that evil goop lying around. As the lighting strikes even closer and the shrieking gets louder, my breathing intensifies to the point that I'm nearly wheezing. The flashes creep up toward the house as I remain frozen in place. Time seems to slow to a crawl as a bolt careens toward the window. It's headed straight for me, but all I can do is pinch my eyes shut and let out a small whimper.

The blast tears open a hole in the wall where the window used to sit. I'm knocked onto my back where I lay stunned for a moment. The shrill cries of the storm are no longer muffled by the walls. They now echo through the room and I can feel the icy currents scrape against me. I remain plastered on the floor while chunks of the brick wall are ripped away and torn into the swirling oblivion. A second bolt hits some other part of the house. I don't see the burst, but I can feel its impact. The manor continues to get battered while I'm left feeling utterly helpless against this amorphous force. An explosion tears through the bit of wall that stands behind the wardrobe. Pieces of it fly out into the storm followed by the entire closet. Its doors fling open as it's carried off, causing fine clothes to spill out. It's a horrifying enough scene to behold, but then something flies *into* the room.

It's just a blur at first that shoots in through the now- gaping hole in the wall. It flies over my face and hits the bedside wall behind me. When I twist around, I see that it's some of that demonic sludge. My heart leaps as I see it squirming on the floor – squirming towards me. I don't have any magical pocket watches to fight this thing with so I scramble to my feet and dart for the door. Wasting no time, I throw it open, letting it slam against the wall. The ribbon heap squirms along with horrifying speed as I burst through the doorway and crash against the wall at the other side of the hall. I don't have much time to think about where to go so I just pick a direction and run. The blob of evil is definitely following close behind, but I don't want to look back and see for sure. I just run as fast as my feet will carry me down the dauntingly long hallway.

Then I spot the dark blotches further down the corridor. It's the goop! It's seeping out from beneath the doors of rooms I'm heading towards. By now, I'm sure the place is ravaged with this stuff. Keeping my pace, I continue straight for the blob nearest to me. Somehow it sees me or at least knows that I'm coming its way. It writhes toward me as I rush it. If this goes wrong, I could end up with that thing wrapped around me, burning through my flesh. But I've got no choice, so I keep charging forward. When I'm almost on top of it, the thing springs up into the air straight for my face. It misses me by inches while I dive down to the side and roll into the wall beside me. Springing back up to my feet, I continue my escape without a backward glance. Not that I have to look, the slurping noises these things make when they move is enough to let me know that my pursuers are still hot on my trail.

The next goop-monster that blocks my path leaps up and sticks to the ceiling. It must have seen the stunt I just pulled somehow. That means these things are learning. I keep running, but I'm not really sure how I'm going to get past this one. And the little shit isn't even coming towards me. It just waits there, ready to spring down once I'm close enough. It's like it knows I can't just stop dead in my tracks without having its buddies pounce on me. I'm gearing myself up to just do a quick summersault under it when another blast hits the house. The tremor causes me to trip forward right as the goop launches toward my face. I manage to fall so that it misses me, but one of its ribbon-like tendrils slices through my shirt and sears the surface of my skin. The burning sting elicits a howl from me.

There's no time to nurse the injury so I scramble back up to my feet and keep going. Something's wrong though. The last shadow heap is just sitting in the middle of the floor. It's in the back corner of the house where the huge bay windows are. Behind it, I can see the swirling storm rage. Without warning, two more slabs of dark matter crash in through the window. Glass tumbles onto the floor and a chill floods into the hall. I stop a few feet in front of the blockade before me. There's nothing I can do. There's too many of these things in front of me to try anything cute. Twisting back, I see that turning around isn't an option either. I'm surrounded by these things. At any second, all six of them will be latched onto me and then I'll be finished. I'll probably scream in agony on the floor while they burn me down to my bones.

I feel myself getting choked up as I accept that this is the end of the line. My heart thumps and I get a sick feeling in my stomach. I can't believe that these things are toying with me like this. Maybe they're even enjoying seeing me trapped. I turn toward the window in time to see the blob in the middle of the hoard spring up into the air. I yell as I fall onto my rear and throw my uninjured arm in front of me. Before I can pinch my eyes shut, a streak of bright, golden light sears through my attacker, evaporating it on contact. I twist backward to see the three monsters behind me blasted into a dark, sizzling steam. Two more beams shoot over me and I guess that the last of my enemies are no more.

A man strides toward me. In my shock, he's just a haze of colorful shapes, but I recognize that indomitable gait and I croak, "Myles!"

"Ay there, old chap!" he pips as he comes into focus.

He looks different tonight, more like how Shirun looked last night. He's wearing thick, almost leathery, tan riding trousers tucked into shining, black leather boots that are fastened tight by thick buckles and straps rather than laces. Holding up the pants is a wide set of black suspenders that look a lot more like leather straps. Beneath is a dark blue collared shirt that's buttoned all the way up. It has this weird shimmering effect as though the fabric is laced with steel. It sort of reminds me of some kind of magic mail. He also has his right sleeve rolled up to show the bandages wrapped around his forearm where he must still be wounded. Even this wrapping looks warrior-eque. It's sort of like the way a martial artist might wrap their wrists. It's a ferocious look to be sure and one that puts his intimidating physique on a heightened display. The fit of his trousers in particular makes it clear that he *never* skips leg day – in case I had any doubts before.

"I – I thought I was alone," I sputter as he comes up to where I'm still plastered against the floor.

He throws his arm down to me, his left hand held open and replies, "You're not alone, my boy. Not by a long shot!"

Immediately after taking hold of his hand, I'm hoisted up into the air like a child. It's like my body weight means nothing to this man which is a sensation that I find as disconcerting as it is comforting. Myles gives me a hearty clap on the shoulder once I have my legs underneath me.

"What is all this?" I ask, motioning out the broken window. I know it's the storm I saw off in the distance when I met with Shirun, but that doesn't really explain it exactly.

"Ah yes," Myles bellows. "The Calamity is upon us, old chap. This is the summation of Sin's power. Sin called it here — brought this upon us. I fear this is only the start."

I glance out into the swirling mass of power and grimace. If this is only the start, then how much worse are things going to get? I'm about to pose this question to Myles when the mansion shudders once, twice, and then a third time all in short succession. It takes all of my strength and balance to stay on my feet, but Myles seems to maintain his posture without any trouble at all.

"Shouldn't linger here for much longer," he states evenly. "The Calamity won't dawdle so neither should we." With that, he heads back in the direction that we came from.

I take one last good look out into the storm finding it as beautiful as I do terrifying. More lightning dances off in the distance which might confirm what Myles said about there being more to come. Having seen enough, I peel away from the view and follow Myles down the hall.

"So where is everyone else then?" I ask once I've caught up.

"Well that's our mission, see, we've got to find and save as many as we can."

My eyes drop down to Myles' revolver. It's been changed, just like how Shiun's pocket watch was transfigured. It's golden now and radiates light in a way that feels perhaps a bit too conspicuous. At least it can actually do damage to our enemies now.

"Shouldn't you reload that?"

"Don't reckon I'll need to, my boy. You can probably tell that Shirun changed it and part of that change is that it no longer fires bullets. It just sort of fires, see. Can't quite say what it shoots out, but I suppose it doesn't much matter so long as it gets the job done."

"That's incredible," I say. All I can think of are sci-fi laser pistols, but I feel like we should just go on thinking of this thing as a magic revolver since that's probably closer to the mark.

Without warning, two blobs smash through one of the bedroom doors and stick to the opposing wall. Myles jumps back with a grunt, but wastes no time in blasting the little monstrosities into thin air.

"Indeed it is," Myles agrees as he resumes his march onward. "You've changed a bit yourself unless I'm terribly mistaken."

"What do you mean?" I'm trying desperately to keep my heartrate down, but that's pretty hard to do when a dark creature could leap out at any moment and try to kill you.

"Well, you've got a different air about you for one and I'd daresay you sound a tad different as well."

I don't know what I can say to that really. I think he might be right though. I've been talking more like I do in the real world. Even my thoughts feel a lot more like *my* thoughts. It's like more and more of myself is brought over every time I find myself here. But on the flipside of that, I'm also left to wonder if things from here aren't making their way into my regular life. Is my world actually colliding with this one somehow? Or is this all some kind of demented fantasy that's slowly overtaking my mind?

"It's no matter though, old chap," Myles cuts into my thoughts. "Maybe you're just becoming more like who you really are, closer to who you were meant to be."

These are nice thoughts and all, but I'm not interested in dwelling on them too much. I imagine we're getting closer to wherever it is we're going so I change the subject by saying, "Where are we heading to anyway? Who are we going to save? Where's Shirun?"

"Shirun sent me to find some people who are taking refuge in a billiards room. Hopefully we find them in one piece."

"Where is Shirun now?" I ask again. "Why isn't he helping us?"

"He's watching."

"Watching what exactly?" My tone is incredulous. How could Shirun just be *watching* at a time like this?

"He's got to coordinate our defenses," Myles soothes.

"What about Olivia? Did he send her on a *mission* too?" I know Shirun is trying to protect me, but I'm pissed that he's just deploying us like little minions while he does nothing.

"Don't you worry about her, my boy, she's more than capable of seeing to herself. She's been sent to recruit some new allies to our cause. We'll need quite a bit of help if we're to make it through this."

"Why does anyone need to be recruited? Aren't we all on the same side? Isn't Sin out to destroy all of us?"

Myles twists around and comes to an abrupt stop in front of me. "You're right enough about all of us being equally in danger, but what you've got to understand is that we are *not* all on the same side."

Myles scans the space around us for a moment. It's probably unwise for us to stand here like this, but it seems like what he has to tell me is important enough to take the risk. He reaches into the neck of his shirt and pulls out a gold necklace. It's not the same pendant that I saw on Shirun, though – the chain is thinner and the medallion is far more compact.

"You see this symbol here?" Myles holds up the coin-sized end of the necklace toward me, tapping his finger on the symbol it contains. This particular piece of the necklace is an exact match to the starry pattern on Shirun's medallion. "You see someone wearing this here symbol and that's how you'll know they're with us."

"And what if they're not wearing it?"

Myles grimaces as he turns about and leads us forward. "Right now it's just Olivia, Shirun, and I that's got one of these on their person. Like I said, we're hoping that number will grow. The fact is that if you don't see someone wearing something with the symbol on it then you can't trust them. That doesn't mean you should count them out either though. The tricky thing with Sin is that it won't be content to simply tear us apart, it wants to corrupt everything and everyone first. Our job then is to try and save as many as we can. Trouble is that not everyone is going to want saving."

Myles' pace gradually quickens and I try to match it. I'd guess that we're just about at our destination. I think I remember this strip of the hall. It's not far from where we began our search for Olivia, the search that led us to Sin.

"It sounds like this won't be easy," I comment, hoping for one last bit of Westerly wisdom.

"Indeed, just stay close for now. We're about to get to where we're heading. We've enjoyed as long a respite as we could hope for and while you have many questions left, I'm sure, there simply isn't any more time."

"Won't I need a weapon? You've got your gun, what do I get?"

"Afraid this is all I've got, old chap."

"So what – Shirun couldn't enchant something else to keep me safe?"

"Sorry, supplies are a bit limited at the moment. I get to have this because I already had it in my possession."

"It's a bring-your-own-weapon kind of event then?"

"Don't fret, I've got us covered, just follow my lead now. The more power we gain as a group, the better equipped we'll be in the future."

Before I can put up any kind of argument, Myles stops beside a door that's situated with quite a bit more space between other doors than a bedroom entrance would have. He stands poised in front of me with one hand on the door knob and the other holding his gun tilted slightly forward. There's a tense pause that seems to hang for an extended duration. Anticipation builds to the point where I feel as though I might explode. In a motion so quick I find it jarring, Myles flings open the door and thrusts his gun through the doorway as he bursts into the room. I nearly run into his wide backside as I try to follow him in. He's just standing there, his shoulders hunched forward in a brooding way. I have to side step him to see what's frozen him in his tracks like this.

"What are you all doing?" I hear him rumble as the rest of the room comes into view.

It's a lavishly decorated little social area with light brown hardwood floors, blue walls, and circular gothic windows which give minimal visibility to the storm raging outside. Carolyn Baxter is sipping a red cocktail in the back right corner of the room where a tiny bar counter sits. She's dressed as though this is just another party. She wears a black, floor-length, sleeveless evening gown that is accented by silver hoop earrings, a silver necklace with a crested sapphire center, and thick, jangling silver bracelets. Myles' outburst causes her to twitch a little, but her eyes remain on her drink and her free hand reaches up to pat the side of her hair which she has twisted up into a bun. Jack and Jasmine sit on a black, leather, semi-circular sofa which is placed in the corner opposite the miniature bar. Their blue eyes peel off of one another and point to where Myles and I stand. Two gentlemen whom I don't recognize stand around the billiards table. One is a tall, blond man standing upright with his hands stacked atop the tip of his cue stick. The other has dense, dark hair and freezes mid-shot. It may just be the way he's leaning over the table, but he looks rather dark despite his skin being so pale. A tense silence falls over the room, allowing the hissing turbulence to reach my ears again.

After a moment, the man hunched over the game drops his cue and pulls himself up. Now that he's standing at full height, I notice that he is actually a man of exceptionally short stature. He also has narrow eyes so dark brown that they're nearly solid black. I can't quite tell if he actually has any Asian heritage or if he just exhibits features commonly associated with The East. One thing's for certain though, this man looks pissed. His smooth features can't hide the scrunching in his brow or the trembling muscles in his jaw.

"There a problem Mister Westerly?" he snaps. His gaze feels ice cold.

"There certainly is, Christopher!" Myles barks back, his chest puffed out and a stony firmness consuming his face. "Have none of you bothered to so much as glance at what's going on out there?"

"We have," Christopher replies evenly. He struts over to us with his shoulders pushed back and fists clenched.

"And this is the best you can think to do?" Myles growls with righteous anger. "To hide away in a room and have yourselves a sad little party?"

"Oh please, Mister Westerly, what would *you* have us do?" Carolyn sneers from the back of the room. "What is there for anyone to do? Those ... things ... are indestructible. They'll find us all eventually so why shouldn't we endeavor to soak in what little revelry we have left?"

"Have you so little hope?" Myles asks, looking around the room. "Do you have so little faith?" His voice is low, passive even. "Where is your mettle, your will to live? When did you all become such cowards?"

Jasmine rises from the couch and steps into the middle of

the room as she protests, "There's no need to be cruel, Myles, we're just doing all that we can think to do. If you know of another way, then show it to us." Her tone is sweet and steady — filled with sensitivity and compassion.

"If you have the courage for another way, then follow me. It isn't safe here. You're sitting ducks all gathered into one convenient pond for any hunter who might think to cull you."

"We don't have to go anywhere!" Carolyn rolls her eyes and drains the rest of her concoction.

"I think we should listen to him," the blond man chimes in.

"Oh shut it, Peter!" she retorts. "Get over here and make me another drink. We have no need to be party to this sort of hopeless idiocy."

Peter bows his head and sulks over to the bar. I have no idea why a man like him would stand to be bullied by someone as conniving as Carolyn. What is he, her lover? Or is he actually just that impressionable that he'll obey whoever issues the loudest commands?

"I agree," Christopher hisses.

"Fine," Myles controls his tone, but I can see from the sharp glint in his eyes that this is hurting him.

"*Trouble is that not everyone is going to want saving.*" I guess he wasn't mistaken about that.

"What about you two?" he asks, looking to Jasmine and Jack.

"Of course I'll join you," Jasmine assures him. She sounds downright angelic the way she talks.

"I'm coming too!" Jack chirps as he hops off of the couch.

Both of them head over to us, but Jack stops beside Carolyn. He eyes her with a wide, hopeful glance and then raises his hand toward her. She looks to Peter who takes up a place at the back end of the bar and then turns back to Jack. She shoots him a sideways grin that ripples her face so much that she looks like a savage cat. Without warning, Jack's hand is smacked out of the air by her vicious strike. The poor boy staggers backward and holds the injured hand close to his chest.

"Do what you want, little one," she jeers. "Your power is all but dwindled down anyway. Use the last of it any which way that pleases you, but the rest of us have a good amount of life left in us still if we don't waste it on so foolish an errand as what Myles proposes."

"That's where you're wrong, death is upon us all unless we act," Jack counters. I'm amazed that he doesn't sound angry or even hurt. His is a melancholy tone that makes the words seem to echo through the room.

His misty gaze remains on Carolyn and Peter for a moment longer before he pulls away. As he walks across the room toward me, all I want to do is pull him into a hug. I've got no idea where this bitch gets off treating him like that, but now I'm kind of glad we're leaving her and these other slugs to the evil goop monsters. Before we can go, a loud crack resounds and the manor trembles, disturbing our balance.

"No, no, no, no, NO!" I yell.

A bright flash comes through the port-hole windows and a couple gasps sound off in the room. Then a dark heap crashes through the window on the right. It soars over Carolyn's head and lands on the floor by Christopher's feet. Jasmine screams and stumbles back away from the stuff. Christopher twists around just in time for the little mass of evil to leap up onto his face. He falls back against the ground screaming at the top of his lungs. While he writhes on the ground, a second blob smashes through the window on the left. It lands near where Jasmine stands and its grotesque tendrils immediately start gripping at the bottom of her light blue dress. Myles blasts it out of existence but not before a small portion of her clothing is seared off, marring the lovely white floral pattern on it. She gasps for air as she looks down to where Christopher still screams in pain.

Myles steadies his gun to where Christopher squirms, but before he can fire, a chunk of the back wall is torn off. Then another is taken off at a spot where the wall meets the ceiling. A relentless battery of strikes bear down on our section of the house, ripping off the entire back wall, piece by piece. All of us, even Myles are knocked off our feet by the force of the blasts. We recover in time to see more of the shadow beasts sling into the room. They plop against the floor, smash through mahogany stools, and cling to the crumbling walls and ceiling until there are too many to safely count.

It seems like Sin's been holding out on us, maybe even toying with us until it saw fit to lash out. Now we've really got to get the hell out of here. Myles lights up the room with streaks of golden light. I manage to pull myself to my knees but I'm a little stunned by how quickly the situation has deteriorated.

I'm even more shocked when Christopher contorts into a monkey-like crouch. He's no longer screaming and his skin doesn't smoke anymore. But now his eyes are red – not his irises, the whole eye: irises, pupils, and whites. The goop has fused with him somehow. It covers most of his face, leaving only a little of his right cheek in its normal fleshy color. The rest of it is a smoky gray that looks utterly inhuman. This new skin extends down the left side of his neck and the upper portion of his chest where the dark matter has also melted through his white shirt and blue blazer, leaving them tattered on that shoulder. He's a monstrous sight to behold. His fiery gaze rests on Jasmine who's fleeing the room in our direction. Christopher bars his teeth and lets out a hideous moan as he darts forward. Before I can even yell a word of warning, he tackles her to the floor and his hands find their way around her neck.

"JAAASSSMIINNNNEE!" He sings viciously. "It's not very nice to run away from me, Jasmine. Aren't you supposed to be the sensitive one? Hrm! Aren't you always considerate?"

Her eyes widen as she grasps at his wrists. It's a vain attempt to pry him off of her neck which leaves her gasping for air that won't come. It's strange too because he seems so much stronger now. She might be a small woman, but she should be able to put up more of a fight than this. He's got her completely helpless and there are too many heaps between me and where they are for me to do anything. Maybe the worst part is that Christopher's voice is different. It has a clanging quality to it that sounds metallic. It sounds like Sin's.

"Christopher, get off of her!" I hear Myles yell over the gunshots.

The possessed man ignores the command and continues to squeeze the life out of her. I'm wondering whether or not Myles has it in him to shoot him – or what's left of him – when a beam of light sears through Christopher's skull. Time seems to slow as he tumbles off of Jasmine. Myles unloads more shots at our assailants, Jack tries to weave his way over to us, and Carolyn ushers Peter out from behind his station. I half expect to see Christopher evaporate into the air, but he doesn't. The ribbon-y goo does though. It dematerializes right off of him, leaving exposed bone where it used to be. He's even missing his eyes – there are just singed sockets left in their place. Towards the back of the room, I see one of the piles grab Peter by the back of his ankle. He howls as the thing's tendrils tighten around him. Carolyn yelps when she turns back and sees him fall to his knees, but she keeps moving through the path that Myles' marksmanship has made.

"Carolyn!" Peter cries, reaching a hand out toward her.

All he gets is the burning embrace of another sludge heap around his extended arm. He shrieks in agony while the stuff slithers up his leg and down his forearm.

"Jack," I hear Jasmine cry out.

I twist my head around to see her standing in the doorway behind Myles, clutching the frame. Looking back into the room, I see the monsters converge on Jack who stands completely surrounded. I spring to my feet and charge across the room toward him. I guess the only thing I want less than falling victim to these things is to watch them consume Jack. Myles' shots clear a few of the beasts out of my way toward the billiards table. Once there I snatch up Christopher's abandoned cue just in time to bat an airborne heap out of its course toward me. It's barely smashed against the side wall when another one lurches in my direction. I try swatting at it, but it clings to the end of the cue.

"Shit!" I gasp, flinging the whole pole to the back of the room.

I've managed to draw some of the sludge beasts away from Jack which allows him to move forward a little and not be snatched up by the cretins behind him. *Cretins*, I think that's what I'll call them from here on in. With some now on my tail, I head back to the front of the room. Carolyn and Jasmine stand tensed in the doorway while Myles volleys more beams of that magical energy. Jack and I are nearly in the clear but I hear an animalistic groan behind me followed by a creak, a thud, and what sounds like something pattering above me. I look up to see Peter scuttling across the ceiling like some kind of spider. He plunges down and dropkicks Myles through the doorway before he can react. He's driven back with so much force that he even bowls both of the ladies over – I guess I was right about the cretins giving their victims super strength.

Peter stalks toward me, blocking my path to the door. He's even more terrifying than Christopher was. The cretins have most of his right arm and left leg covered. His clothing is tattered and his eyes are ablaze. Ribbon-like strands of the dark matter cut up the side of his neck and wrap around the right portion of his face.

"Peter wait!" I plead, tossing a hand up.

Jack charges past me as quick as a cheetah. He rushes toward Peter as though to tackle him. I can feel the blood drain from my face – what does he think he's doing?

"Jack!" I shout, but it doesn't slow him.

Peter snarls and lurches forward. I chase after the boy, though I'm afraid he's already a goner. Right as they're about to crash into each other, Jack throws his hands up toward Peter's husk. A bright flash comes from them and somehow Peter is repelled backward against the wall. He recovers almost instantly after he slumps to the floor. I come to a stop beside where Jack stands. Does the kid actually have special powers of some kind? If so, hopefully he has a little extra something for round two. Peter shrieks as he propels toward us. He's stopped short when a golden streak rips through his chest. The gray flesh melts off of him before he can even crumble to the floor. All that's left of his arm and leg are his skeleton and a few strands of burnt muscle holding the bones together.

"Come on," Myles commands before he turns to help the ladies to their feet.

I follow Jack out into the hall where Myles points a finger back in the direction of the bay windows.

"We need to get to the lavatory, Jack you can lead the way."

Jack nods his head confidently and breaks into a sprint down the hall. Jasmine follows close behind him and I behind her. Myles and Carolyn take up the rear. We're like a line of refugees fleeing a catastrophe. I just hope the lavatory isn't too far away. For a second, I think maybe we're almost in the clear, but then the entire manor shudders, nearly knocking me off my feet. Another tremor rocks us, then another. A thick screeching fills the hall as if Sin is shrieking in protest at our escape. The blasts feel close too. No, it's worse – the blasts feel like they're coming from down the hall. Sin's trying to cut us off. The next one trips me up and I face-plant onto the crimson rug. Almost as soon as I hit the ground, Myles reaches down, snatches me up by the armpit, and tugs me to my feet without missing a step. He prods me along with his hand on my back for a few steps.

"No time for falling, old chap!" he says before dashing ahead of me.

The storm continues to batter the manor in a seemingly random cadence of strikes. Further down, I finally see the fruits of its labors. A small chunk of wall is ripped out of place. Whatever room used to be behind it must be completely demolished now. Another blast tears an even greater opening, sending cracks through the stretches of wall left behind. A third blast tears the door out of the wall and now that whole section starts to crumble away on its own. Little bits of plaster fall out of place and are immediately sucked into the storm like dust into a vacuum. Then a small troop of cretins fling into the hall. Up ahead, Jack and Jasmine bring themselves to a stop.

"Get down," Myles bellows.

They scramble to the opposite walls and duck down just in time for Myles to open fire. Suddenly, this whole situation feels even more unfair. A sinking feeling grips my heart as I wonder if we really stand any chance of actually fighting this.

"Go, go, go!" Myles shouts.

Jasmine and Jack immediately obey the command. They're running past the damaged stretch of wall when another blast hits. It tears away what's left of it and sends Jack sailing against the other side of the hall. He crumbles to the ground instantly and for a moment, it looks like he might be dead. Jasmine scoops him up by under the arms and ushers him onward. Even for a woman of her size, the boy seems to weigh almost nothing. Two more cretins fly through the opening, but Myles blasts them out of existence before they can do any harm. He resumes his own escape so Carolyn and I quicken our sprint behind him. Before we can make it past the damaged area, another series of lightning strikes tears apart large sections of the floor and rips the rug to shreds.

"Hurry!" Myles calls from the other side. He has his gun

pointed upward in case any more cretins come through.

I move my legs as fast as they will allow, but my heart races in fear of it not being enough. Another blast takes away even more of the floor, leaving only a thin strip along the undamaged side of the hall. Beneath it, I'd expect to see the room that sits below, but I don't. All I can see is the void which means an entire chunk of the manor is just gone now. Wherever it's getting pulled into, I don't want to get sucked in there myself, so I rush onto what's left of the flooring while it's still intact. Without the rest of the structure to support them, the remaining floorboards feel flimsy beneath me. Some just wiggle, but others bend downward at a slant. For fear of slipping off, I lean one shoulder against the wall for support. This slows me down a little, but rushing across won't do me any good if I slip and fall into the swirling mass that's trying to kill me.

I don't look back to see how Carolyn's doing as I amble along. The terrible thing is that I'm not sure I want to. I know that's awful. She's certainly no Margaret — in fact, she might even be the anti-Margaret, but she's still a person who deserves to live as much as anyone else. When I make it across to where Myles stands, I twist around to see that she's halfway across. Looking in the opposite direction, I see Jack fling open a door and disappear through it with Jasmine on his heels. I guess this must be the lavatory. The good news is that it's close by. The bad news is that we're not safely inside of it yet. A hiss, a crack, and a shriek snap my attention back to Carolyn. A section of the floor behind her is blown away and the adjoining wall is damaged. Carolyn stands with her back plastered against the wall.

"Carolyn, you have to keep moving!" Myles roars.

"I can't" she moans.

I stand frozen in place. I know I should say something, but nothing comes to mind. She's in a rough spot if she stays where she is now. It seems like she's given up hope. Her eyes look into the storm raging beside her as though she's listening to it. Is she just waiting to be pulled into the oblivion? More cretins begin tumbling into the hall. Myles shoots them down with expert aim, but they're starting to overwhelm us.

"Carolyn!" I hear myself yell.

I'm not sure what moves me to call out to her, but it draws

her attention. She looks at me with pale, glazed over eyes and a sullen expression. Bolts of lightning begin tearing into the walls and floor near where Myles and I stand. We're running out of time and already we're forced to slowly retreat from where we stood. Carolyn's running out of time, but she doesn't seem to mind.

She shoots me a Cheshire grin and shouts, "This is far from over, Mister Daley!"

A blot strikes the floor not too far in front of her and she doesn't so much as flinch. What does she mean? What is she doing?

"Carolyn," I shout again.

She retains her feline smile and directs her gaze back to the storm that's about to devour her. The next strike that flashes hits the remaining section of flooring. Carolyn shrieks almost gleefully as she plummets into the swirling void and disappears from sight. As soon as she's gone, lightning dances all around us – ravaging this part of the manor.

"Let's go!" Myles demands as he backpedals down the hall while still firing his revolver.

I turn and run past him right as a series of bolts decimate where I just stood. Once I've passed Myles, he joins me in sprinting to the open lavatory door. The storm beats against the mansion, shredding it to pieces behind us. But we can't fall now, not when we're so close. The open door is just a little ways away, but the floor feels so unsteady and all it will take is one well-placed blast to tear me into the void that's just claimed Carolyn.

"Faster!" Myles demands.

He takes hold of me by the back of my shirt and shoves me along. Once we've made it to the opening, he tosses me through into the room with so much force that I roll over the tile floors a few times. When I straighten myself to face the doorway, I see Myles duck into the lavatory right as a bolt explodes into the floor that held him up only a second before. He slams the door shut behind him and hastily bolts the lock. After that he just stands there, one hand spread against the door while the other maintains a grip on his firearm. It feels like time stands still for a little while. We all remain frozen in place as though we expect something bad to happen at any second. But nothing does happen. I can't even hear the storm's howling anymore. For the moment, at least, we're safe. As impossible as it might be to believe after all of that, the danger has passed.

# Epilogue

When the shock of everything that just happened finally wears off, I take a moment to look around. It's a fairly large space so far as wash rooms go. A toilet sits in one corner while an enormous bath the size of a hot tub is set in the other. Cool, white tile flecked with black squares covers the full breadth of the room. The flooring is accented by green painted walls that have a gravelly sort of texture to them. Thankfully, thick white curtains are pulled over the one, large window in the room. Not being able to see The Calamity outside does wonders for my peace of mind. The relief I feel gives me some sympathy for how Carolyn, Peter, and Christopher wanted to block it all out. I also find the sheer luxury of the lavatory to be rather soothing as well. How many bathrooms have a white marble fountain situated in the middle of them? It's just a little one, the main basin can't be more than a few feet in diameter. On top of its central podium sits a gold sculpture of a cherub holding a water jug. He's bent at the hips with the jug tilted over the front of the pool from which the water trickles out in a constant flow.

The sound of water plip-plopping relaxes me to the point where I sink down on the floor and sprawl out. It might be hard, but right now the tile feels unbelievably comfortable. I could shut my eyes right here and doze off, but maybe then I'd wake up in some other realm entirely. A small hand presses onto the back of my right shoulder blade. I think contact like this would normally make me jump a little, but I'm either so relaxed or trust the people in the room so completely that I don't stir at all.

"Jack?" I ask lazily.

"Are you alright Mister Daley?" His small voice sounds a little breathless.

"Just resting" I tell him.

It occurs to me that I'm being selfish. The people that died back there might not have meant much to me, but I'm sure the others are taking it hard. I pull myself up on my elbows and have a look at my companions. Myles is sitting with his back against the door and his head hung low. Jasmine kneels by the fountain. Her eyes are fixed on the angel and her face is so still that she almost looks like she's a statue herself. Looking at Jack, I see that he looks paler than ever. Even his hair, which is now in wild disarray, has lost some of its reddish luster.

"Are you okay?" I ask softly while I pull myself to a seated position.

"I'm not sure," he answers in a quivering tone. His body is racked with a shiver.

By this point, I'm well aware that Jack isn't some regular teenage boy. But this knowledge seems irrelevant. I still see him as just a boy. So I pull him into my arms and hold him tight. It would be nice if I could think of some way to encourage him. I try to think of something I can say or do to spare him some pain, but I've never been much good at that sort of thing. I don't know why, I guess it's just not who I am. All I know to do is what I'm already doing. I could tell him that it's going to be okay, but I'm just not sure if that's true. It might not be okay at all.

"What happens now?" I ask. The question isn't directed at anyone in particular, I just pitch it to the room.

"Now… we fight back," Myles answers me as he looks up in my direction.

He's a little disheveled himself, but there's a determined glint in his eyes. As much as I hate the idea of facing off against Sin's power again, the sternness in Myles' tone fills me with hope that maybe we do at least have a fighting chance. I suppose we'll find out soon enough…

# Book 5:

# Haunted

*To anyone who stood, stands, or will stand beside me.*

# Chapter 1

"How?" I ask after thinking through our situation. I definitely sound a little combative. "How are we going to fight back; what's the plan here?"

"Easy there, old chap," Myles cautions me. His jaw clenches and he pulls his back away from the wall, but remains seated next to the conservatory door.

Jasmine turns her attention to the fountain and dips her hands into its waters. I can't tell if she's looking for a cooling comfort or just trying to avoid being involved in a confrontation. Jack sits cross-legged beside me with his hands resting in his lap. His eyes stare blankly ahead.

"We all saw what happened back there," I press on, waving a hand at the door. "If that stuff even touches us, we burn. If it manages to get a good grip on us, then we become its puppets. Then there's that dog and Sin itself—both seem completely indestructible. That golden gun is helpful, sure, but will it work on those two? And how are we all supposed to fight if we only have one weapon?" By the end of this rant, I realize I've raised my voice... that's awkward.

Eyes rest on me as I try to catch my breath. I half-expect Myles to leap to his feet and start thrashing me around, but he doesn't. He just sits there with his big, brown eyes fixed on me as I calm down.

"We quite done then?" he asks after he's let a few moments pass.

"Yeah, I'm sorry..."

I feel Jack's hand on my shoulder. "We have more power on our side than you think," he tells me.

I turn to look at him and instantly get a flash of the power he displayed. My mind's eye replays the sight of Jack repulsing Peter with a blast of white light. He looks frail now though. His skin and even his irises look paler somehow. Maybe it's just the sterile brightness of this room creating an effect or perhaps that show of strength drained a bit of the life out of him.

"He's right," Myles chimes in, "There's more hope than you know, but you must remain patient with yourself, with us."

"So, what, we just wait for more power to fight back with?"

Myles shakes his head before replying, "No, my boy, patience should rarely be synonymous with inaction. I don't mean that we ought to wait around at all. Strength does not come to idle hearts. I mean only that we must remain tempered as we build up the strength to defend our home."

I nod in understanding, but find it curious that he refers to this place as "our home." I know I'm linked to it somehow, but this house isn't my home. Is it? Is there something I'm missing or is he just speaking for himself and all of the other "guests" here?

"What do we do then?" I ask, no longer sounding so argumentative.

"We'll need help and lots of it," Myles answers. "We need as many to rally to our cause as we can possibly recruit. Olivia is doing what she can about that now. Jack and Jasmine, we could use you doing the same if you find yourselves up to it."

"You can count on me!" Jack chirps.

"I'll do anything I can," Jasmine promises. She's no longer distracted by the fountain. Instead, all of her focus rests on me as though I'm the one giving out the orders.

"Good, we'll need to meet with Shirun first and get you properly equipped to do the job. The bigger our force gets, the more power we'll have to work with."

"And Sin gets stronger with each guest it kills or corrupts," I conclude.

"Precisely," Myles concurs. "It probably goes without saying that we won't be able to save everyone though."

"But we'll rescue as many as we can." Jack states this more as a demand than a promise or a wishful line of bravado.

"That's right," Jasmine agrees as she pulls herself up to her feet. "Sounds like we have work to do then."

"True enough and it can't get it done here," Myles adds as he stands up and dusts himself off.

"Wait, how can we leave? We can't just go back out there

can we?" My tone trembles a little as I ask this.

"We won't have to." Jack gives my shoulder a light squeeze before he gets to his feet.

"Right enough." Myles hums. "There's another way out of safe rooms like this one."

I watch as he walks to the back of the conservatory and opens what appears to be a closet door. He disappears inside of it and I hear some light shuffling before a click and a swoosh. Of course this place would have secret passages. If this is all some psychotic breakdown, then I'm definitely learning that I played way too much <u>Clue</u> as a kid.

"Come on then," Myles instructs, stepping out of the secret entrance and waving for us to follow.

"Here." Jack offers his hand to me.

I take it, but try not to put too much strain on the boy as he helps me up. Jasmine's the first to step past Myles and enter into the passage. I follow Jack into what really is a regular linen closet with shelves and all and down a set of ivory steps. Myles shuts the door behind us. I'm pleased that the corridor isn't dark at all. In fact, it's very well-lit with wall lamps curling out into the air every few feet. It's quite narrow, but at least the ceiling is tall, a feature that Myles is surely grateful for. We walk for a ways down the mostly straight passage. There's a door at the other end which grows in size as we approach.

"Alright then, time to bid farewell to Mister Daley for now," Myles says as we come to a stop for Jasmine to open the exit.

"What do you mean?" I ask, turning around in a panic. "You're not just going to leave me, are you?"

Myles gestures in front of us so I turn back around to see that the doorway has that same white radiance behind it as the door to the observatory. I realize now that this might mean I'm about to "wake up," but I'm not sure I like the idea of that, not while things are just getting going here.

"Take care," Jasmine tells me with a curtsy.

"You too," I reply as she disappears into the light.

Jack jumps into me, wrapping me up in a desperate hug. I return it with equal enthusiasm, but also take care not to crush him.

"Be safe," he whispers.

"You be safe too," I reply.

I release the embrace and he steps back with a thin smile. "I will," he promises. Then he turns and leaves through the blinding doorway.

"Our turn," Myles prods.

"I don't want to be separated again." I'm put off by how I whimper this out.

I'm being such a pansy, but I really don't want to be left alone here ever again.

Myles' hands clamp down on my shoulders, "Don't be afraid. Wherever you go, one of us will find you. You have my word on that. Just believe in yourself a little more, believe in us—believe in the people that support you. You're never really alone. Say that back to me…"

"I'm never really alone," I repeat.

"That's it, old chap. Now don't you forget it."

Myles lets go of me to give me two encouraging slaps against the back of my shoulders. Then he steps ahead of me and turns with his hand out toward me.

"Come on now, I'll help you through it," he says.

He must see how frozen in place I am. In spite of all the encouragement, I still don't want to step through that light. I forget all of my pride and take hold of his hand. He tugs me forward, leading me along like a child. It's humiliating, but I honestly don't know if I can do this without him pulling me forward. The white light starts to envelop him and I begin to feel the warmth of its radiance. I'm forced to look down away from its intensity as I pass through. For a split second, I fall completely into the light.

# Chapter 2

My eyes snap open with a heavy inhale. I'm home. I'm back in my bedroom with daylight slipping through my shades and a gentle chirping coming from outside. As I sit up I'm grateful to find that I'm not sore or breathless—or sweaty. My heart beats a little fast, but that's not such a horrible thing. I can deal with that. I reach over for my phone, but I don't find it on my end table. In the chaos of last night, I must have forgotten to put it on its charger. I hop out of my bed and take a knee beside the pile of clothes I left beside it. Remembering how scared I was of those shadows really makes me question my mental health. Was it all just some ridiculous drunken mirage? A full-blown psychotic breakdown? Or is there some force that's actually spilling into my world and really is out to get me?

None of those scenarios sound too good, so I turn my attention to my phone to find that Kayla's been trying to get in touch with me all morning. I have three missed calls and a matching number of voice messages along with two texts. A groan slips from me as I imagine how ticked off she probably is by now. Some of these are from pretty early for someone who probably woke up hungover. I open the texts first.

The first one just reads, "HEY, I CALLED YOU, ARE YOU UP YET?"

The second one is a bit more aggressive, "WHERE THE HELL ARE YOU? CALL ME BACK..."

I get a sinking feeling in my stomach that makes me not want to open my voicemail. The first probably won't be that bad, but I'm sure the other two have nice little tongue-lashings for me. I realize I'll only make things worse if I continue to put it off. I could try calling her now, but she always knows if I don't check her messages before returning her call. There'll be some little test to make sure. I also don't want her to call again before I've given them a listen, so I bite the bullet and just hit the play button.

"Hey Bry, it's me. So, The Golden Pearl was a blast and I totally need to go there again tonight. I legit can't even stop thinking about it. Now that you're all better, I know you'll love it too. Call me back ASAP so I can get you **hyped**!"

I scroll to the next voicemail and open it up. The first was every bit as benign as I hoped it would be though I'm annoyed that she assumes I'm "all better" now. I'm guessing that Kayla will be slightly perturbed in this next recording.

"Hi, it's me again. You didn't call back so here's the deal. Annie, Laurie, and Craig will be joining us. Laurie's gonna be everyone's DD which is awesome. I know you're real close, so I was thinking we'd just be by a little after eight-thirty and you can meet us in front of your building. I still want to tell you all about the place though so call be back. Kay, bye!"

I'm relieved that this one is more to-the-point than it is biting. It's interesting that Annie is part of the group since she was a "bitch" just the other night. Kayla's not normally the forgiving type so I'm guessing that she definitely exaggerated about her annoyance level with this woman who I'm still sure I've never met. I honestly have no idea who Laurie or Craig are. I'm fairly certain I've never heard of them before just now. These musings help me delay listening to the final message. I'd much rather continue analyzing Kayla's bizarre social sphere than hit the play button, but I know I can't delay this forever. My thumb tenses over it before I eventually give in to what needs to happen.

"Alright, Bryan, this is the third message I'm leaving you…" Yep she's definitely sour now. "You're either milking your stupid stomach thing or deliberately blowing me off. Either way, I need you to cut it out and call me back. I'm not screwing around, okay."

I'm not really sure when Kayla is ever screwing around, but the warning is duly noted. I know I need to call her back as soon as I can now. Each minute wasted will only up Kayla's annoyance level. If it gets high enough, I know she'll find some not-so-subtle ways to get back at me when we're both drunk. With this in mind, I hop back in bed and give her a call back. The phone rings for a little while. Part of me hopes that she'll miss my call while the other suspects that she might just like to keep me ringing until the last second when she's annoyed with me.

"Hi," she finally answers. Her tone is as flat as a hockey rink.

"Hey babe," I reply, finding it easy to sound tired.

"My God, did you really just get up?"

"Yeah. I read your texts and listened to your messages, but other than that, I just woke up."

"It's like noon, Bryan." she sounds appalled.

"Yep, well that's what people do when they're tired and not feeling well and happen to have the day off," I snap back.

"Okay, wow…" There's a brief but glorious pause on the other end. "I'm just saying, alright. You should be getting stoked to go out and not lounging around in your underwear or whatever it is you do." It annoys me that this happens to be exactly what I am doing right now. "But, whatever, I'm sorry, I didn't realize you were still moody and weird."

"I'm not *moody and weird*," I retort. "And I am excited." Okay, so maybe this last part is a lie.

"Good," she replies, sounding a little softer than before. "I really do think you're gonna love it. They have three amazing bar setups in different parts of the place, a dance floor that lights up, but not like some cheap disco thing, this is more like holographic—"

"Hey, save it on the spoilers, I want to see it for myself." I cut her off jokingly, though, really, I seriously do want her to stop before she gives me a headache. She will literally yammer about this place for hours if I let her.

"Fair enough," she giggles. It's nice to hear her so giddy, it feels like a long time since she's been so girlishly excited for something.

"I can't wait to get there, sounds like it will be a blast." I try to inject a bit more encouragement into my tone, hopefully that will spare me from some of the spite she's harboring.

"Oh it will be. You good with the crew too?"

I hesitate before replying, "Yeah, it seems like a fun enough group to me."

"Do you remember who I said was going?"

There it is. There's the test. What she really wants to know is if I listened—really listened—to her message.

"Well, I guess I was surprised about Annie, I didn't realize you two made up. I definitely don't know who Craig is and I'm pretty sure I don't know who Laurie is either."

"Oh, weird. Laurie's the shit! I have barre class with her. Craig I just met last night, I guess. He's awesome though, I know you'll love him. And yeah, Annie and I are more than fine, not sure where you got the idea that we weren't."

I let this last point go and just say, "Cool, yeah, should be a good time then. Sounds like a fun bunch."

"Definitely!" she sings. "You good with the pickup time?"

"Eight-thirty-ish should be fine," I tell her. I guess I get to have two of her little quizzes today—*that's fun!*

"Great! Rest up, wash up, and do whatever else you need to do to look great for tonight," she instructs.

"Will do."

"See you tonight!"

"See you then…"

With that, the phone hangs up. The sensation is both freeing and lonely. I hook up the phone to its charger and wander around my bedroom. In spite of it being midday, I still feel reluctant to step outside my room. There's a crazy part of me that's afraid of what may still be out there. After a few minutes, the empty pit in my stomach convinces me that it's time to go downstairs. I find a pair of athletic shorts to put on just so I can prove Kayla wrong about me loafing around in my underwear. I also grab one of my belts and wrap it around my knuckles with the buckle facing out as if makeshift brass knuckles will do anything against creepy shadow monsters.

My breathing halts as I fling open my bedroom door. It's a tremendous relief to find exactly nothing waiting for me behind it. I take a moment to laugh at myself before I drop the belt and head down the hall. I descend the steps and soak in the daylight that pours into my living room. The city looks so clean, so pure. I know better, but I can't help but admire the view anyway. I wish things could be this simple, this clean, all the time. When I look down at the traffic below, I get this feeling like I'm privileged to stand up here—free of the hassle—but I also feel left out somehow. It's like the chaos is where I belong, but I'm stuck up here in this calm. These are probably the kinds of thoughts that crazy people have so

I try to abandon them in favor of lunch.

I pour myself a bowl of frosted mini wheats because I'm an adult and I can eat that for lunch if I want to... It's kind of like how some people will do eggs and sausage for lunch but I'm doing cereal and more cereal. I take my time with it, taking care to save the most frosted ones for the end. Once I've finished and cleaned up after myself, I find that I'm at a loss for what to do. I could start getting ready for tonight, but that seems so far away still. As I stand by my windows and look out over the city, there's a part of me that really is excited to go out with people even if I don't know them. The other side of me dreads it. I have this unshakable feeling like I'm not safe out there, no matter how badly I want join the outside world. It may not be safe for me here either after what happened last night, but at least I could hunker down and prepare for whatever might come my way. Out there, I have no idea what to expect. I'd be vulnerable and even in a crowd, I might still be alone.

A sudden knocking makes me jump in place. My heart races as I rack my brain for who could possibly be at my door. I'm not expecting any packages, I didn't order any maintenance, and I'm sure I didn't invite anyone over. As I hear a second round of knocks, all I can think is that it's the lady Shirun. She's found where I live and now she's here for whatever creepy, mysterious reasons she might have. I try not to make any sound as I step over to the door. As much as I'd like to ignore this visitor completely, I need to know who it is. Slowly, I bring my eye up to the peephole and am shocked to see a man. A normal man, no wait, a familiar man.

"Devon," I say as I fling the door open.

His sunny expression drops for a second before he regains his composure and I have the sudden realization that I should have found a shirt. "Hey, buddy, sorry I was just in the neighborhood and wanted to drop by. I didn't mean to catch you at a bad time."

I study him for a second. He's clean-shaven, his hair is combed to the side, and he's wearing a stylish, navy blue jacket with white wool lining. A six-pack of beer hangs from one hand and a full grocery bag from the other. I'm calling BS on this being a casual, unplanned drop by.

"No, please, come in," I reply, awkwardly stepping out of his way and letting him inside. "It's really good to see you," I add while shutting the door. I'm not sure why saying it comes as a second instinct to me—I mean it is good to see him, right?

"It's been too long," he says with a smile as he sets the beer and food down on the island counter. "I uh, brought some things for you to help pardon the intrusion." He shifts uncomfortably by the pile of gifts. "I can put the beer in the fridge for you if you'd like."

It's then that I realize I've been staring blankly at him while I stand frozen beside the door. "Oh, yeah… I'm sorry. It's just been a slow morning for me." I hope that this will somehow excuse how freakishly weird I'm acting.

"Rough night?" He chuckles.

"No. No, I stayed in actually," I answer while I come up to the counter and lean on it for support—feeling a little dizzy all of a sudden.

"Hey, sometimes you need those kinds of nights." He's being uncharacteristically smooth about moving the conversation forward. He's always been thoughtful and understanding, of course, but it's like he came in prepared for be me to act this strangely. He's supposed to be the reserved one, the man of few words. Now here he is offering all the substance to this conversation.

"Hey, actually can you leave a couple of those out. If you've got time to stay a little while maybe we could have one," I say just as he's put the last bottle onto my door's shelf.

"Sure." His relaxed grin indicates that he's either relieved or not at all surprised by this request.

He withdraws two of the beers and places them in between us on the countertop.

"There's an opener in there," I tell him, pointing to a drawer beside my sink.

There are several in there, but he figures it out. He comes back and pops the caps off.

"Trash?"

"Just leave them," I say, taking my beer up.

He raises his and we clink them together before taking a sip—maybe a gulp in my case. He brought me my favorite—or at least my go-to when I don't know what I want to order—Orange Sun, a honey wheat beer that goes down smooth and savory. It's touching, really. Touching that he came by with all this stuff, that he's here in my kitchen, and that he's drinking a beer with me while it's barely past noon. This all while I'm standing here shirtless with my hair disheveled and stubble that's grown long enough to be a little itchy. I probably smell a bit too...

"Why don't you grab a seat in the living room," I suggest. "I'm just going to find a shirt."

"Sure," he replies with enthusiasm.

"Okay." I throw a smile his way and turn for the stairs. I leave my beer at one end of the living room coffee table and then head up.

A casual gait turns into a hasty trot as I get halfway up and leave Devon's sight. I mostly stumble into my bedroom, unsure of basically everything that's going on right now. I'm not sure I've ever been this embarrassed, not even two days ago when I barreled into work like a drunk man only to miss my meeting. I waste no time in retrieving a green tee shirt with the swishy Parson logo on the front. I also take a moment to roll on some deodorant while I'm up here. I could probably do with some cologne too, but that might be weird. A big part of me wants to look myself over in the mirror and maybe just try to comb my hair, but I know that if I see my reflection, it will probably be hours before I've done all the things I want to do before showing my face again. Instead, I just do a finger-comb as I head back down and hope that will make me look like less of a crazy person. I'm sure he's seen me in some pretty rough states back during our Pinnacle days, but I still feel bad about being such a mess.

Devon's seated himself at one end of the couch when I return. He's placed a bag of chips, a wide jar of salsa, a small platter of crackers, cheese, and smoked sausage in the center of the coffee table.

I grab my beer and sit on my end of the sofa. "Thank you, for all of this." I motion stiffly toward the spread.

"Yeah, you're welcome. Like I said, it's the least I could do for barging in on you."

"I'm just glad to see you." I realize that I sound really desperate as I say this.

Feeling kind of awkward, I turn to take a sip of my beer. Devon just watches me. He doesn't show any signs of judgement or concern, but I'm sure he's shocked by the train wreck that is me.

"I'm sorry it took so long for me to reach out." I have a mouthful of beer and can't respond so he continues, "It's just hard, you know. Life gets in the way, work mostly, but other things too. Then you want to be respectful of how much other people have going on. And you know I can be a little shy about bothering people and whatnot. At the end of all that, it's the important stuff that gets forgotten."

I nod along with him as I drain my bottle a little more. "Yeah, I hear that," I say once he's done. "And I—I feel like sometimes that stuff hits you all at once."

It's Devon's turn to nod agreeably. I can tell he's trying to sort out what I mean by that. I'm not even sure what I mean by that, but it definitely sounds a lot like a cry for help. I realize that he hasn't once pried into how I'm doing or what I've been up to at work or even what Kayla's been up to. It's like he already knows and doesn't want to make me answer those questions. Or maybe it's just that obvious that nothing is going well with me right now.

"Do I look okay to you?" I ask. His mouth opens to answer, but then his brow furrows and his jaw hangs open. "Not like that," I self-correct even though I'm not sure what he's thinking I mean. "What I mean is I've been having a rough time and you seem to know that already so I'm wondering how bad I look. Do I look sort of okay or do I look like I'm about to fall over the edge or is it that I look like I've totally lost all my shit?"

Devon's expression lightens and he responds, "I don't think you look like you're even on the edge. I do think you look tired and wired at the same time, but stress will do that to you. It seems to me like you have different sources of stress hitting you all at once and that's probably making you feel a little crazy or at least on edge. But you're neither, you just need some rest—you just need a break from the things keeping you down."

"How much has David told you?" I ask dryly. "Did he send you?"

"What? Why would you ask that?" I can't tell if he's surprised or hurt.

"Please just answer the question," I plead, sounding more accusatory than I mean to.

"We've talked," he admits. "David didn't go into specifics really. He mentioned some stuff at work and that he thought some things might be tough with you personally too. He's worried about you, but I'm not his minion. He didn't dispatch me to come check up on you. I really did just come to catch up."

"What about Kevin and Erin?"

"What about them?" I'm sort of relieved that he sounds genuinely confused.

"They just happened to be at Benny's yesterday when I went which is a little out of their way, plus they were already done when they invited me over so it was like they were waiting for me. Now you're here and I'm supposed to just think that's a coincidence after all this time that I haven't seen or heard from anyone?" I'm not shouting, but I do run out of breath by the end of this rant.

Devon puts a hand up in the air and scoots over to the middle seat. His brow creases, but his eyes stay warm and patient.

"How have you been sleeping?"

"Not well, why?" I growl, annoyed that he's trying to change the subject.

"Well, I think you're probably overtired and that could be making you a little paranoid. Please don't take that the wrong way, I see why you think we might be ganging up on you, but we're not. I didn't know Kevin and Erin saw you. If I had to guess, I'd say they heard about some of your recent stresses from David too so maybe they decided to stop at Benny's in hopes that you would show up there as well. They probably didn't know how else to reach out. It can be hard to do once you lose contact, but we all still care about you."

"I'm sorry." I turn my gaze down to the food.

"You don't have anything to be sorry for, you've just been having a weird time. We all get it, especially David."

I ignore this dismissal. "Problem is, I don't know where to start other than that I'm sorry I don't even know all the things I need to be sorry for."

"Whatever you need to do, take it one step at a time," he consoles me. "Just tell us what we can do to help. Start with me. What do you want from me right now?"

My vision mists over and I feel like words get caught in my

throat as they come up. "I don't know… I want to be alone, but I don't want you to go. I think I'm just all kinds of fucked up and I can't even tell you what I want. It changes every second."

His lips curl inward contemplatively once I'm done and he does his best to make eye contact with me even though I can't look at him. "It sounds like you just want me to be here with you. You don't want any questions and you don't want me to make judgements. You just want my company." I'm not positive that his conclusions are right, but they sound correct enough so I just nod. "I think there's a Vipers game on right now, mind if I get that going?"

"No, please," I tell him, motioning to the remote.

He takes it up and turns on my TV. He navigates to one of my fifty sports channels and there is in fact a broadcast for the baseball game. Devon and I spend the rest of the afternoon watching the game, eating snacks, and drinking beers. We don't compare our lives or ask into each other's problems. We mostly just comment on the players and the game. We chat about stuff we're watching on TV, places we've been to eat, and events we're excited for as the weather heats up. This makes me feel right. This makes me feel human. I get to simply be a guy watching a baseball game with his buddy, drinking beers and shooting the shit. Neither of us are even huge baseball fans, but that doesn't matter. This, right here, is perfect.

When the game finishes, I ask him to stay for dinner. He helps by cooking up some chicken on the stove while I sauté mixed vegetables and make mashed potatoes. As we sit down to eat it, it does occur to me that this is probably the first wholesome, healthy meal I've had in a couple days.

"Let me help with that," he offers as we finish.

"No, don't worry about it, I'm just going to take care of it later," I tell him as he stands, poised to help me clean up.

"Well, thank you for dinner."

"Thank you for everything else." I laugh. "Thanks for just being here."

"I'm always here for you. Try to remember that."

"I will…"

"Give me a call or a text, just to let me know how things are going every now and then. I won't share anything you tell me with the others if you don't want me to. Remember that we're not collectively spying on you. We're maybe hovering a little right now, but that's just because we care. Let me know if you want to do this again sometime. It was nice for me too, so I'd be game for more beers and a ball game."

"I really appreciate that." My tone wavers. I'll be damned if he gets me all choked up now. "I'm not sure I deserve all that, but it's still nice."

"I think you do," Devon admonishes me. "There's been a distance, for sure, but you're still one of us and we're still in your corner. But I should leave you to getting ready for going out now— should be a good distraction for you."

"Thanks, yeah, you're welcome to join you know. Kayla says the place is pretty great."

"Nah, thanks though. You know how I am in unfamiliar crowds. Maybe someday I'll be less picky about that."

"Nothing wrong with sticking to the people who make you feel safe," I tell him, glad to do some understanding for a change. "Kayla and I could probably be more selective about who we go out with sometimes. There's been some interesting nights, I'll tell you." I'm a little surprised that I admit this, not to Devon, but mostly to myself. I suppose I'm not wrong though and I get the sudden fear that tonight will be a weird one—maybe they've all been weird.

"I hope tonight is a fun one then." He chuckles.

"Me too," I agree as I walk him to the door. "It was really good to see you, thanks again," I tell him while I open it up.

"Great to see you too!" He clasps my shoulders as he says this. This simple gesture, this briefest contact, warms me to my core making me feel an even greater spark of humanity. "Take care, Bryan."

"You too, Devon."

With that he turns and walks down the hallway. It's kind of sad to close the door behind him—to close it on the type of day I've had. But I feel lighter on my feet than I have in a long time. It finally feels like I have the strength to face whatever challenge I need to overcome. I feel as though I can take on whatever fight lies ahead of me. For now, I just need to contend with getting myself ready to be seen in public.

# Chapter 3

Now that I'm alone, I go and clean up the dishes. Mostly, I'm procrastinating on the much more daunting task of cleaning myself up. Unfortunately, the chore doesn't take as long as I'd like it to. With no other strategies for delaying the inevitable, I drag myself upstairs and finally face the bathroom mirror. When I look at myself, I realize Devon was generous when he said I looked tired. I look like hell. Stubble covers my face and not in a suave or attractive way. My skin looks a little flushed, my eyes are red, though they're less irritated than this morning, and my hair found a way to transcend bedhead. I look like a tornado ate me, didn't like how I tasted, and spit me back out. I've got my work cut out for me so I start by grabbing my razor and shaving cream.

A shave, a shower, some grooming, some eye drops, and a glass of water later; I look only kind of scary. Feeling like this is as good as it'll get, I go into my room and pick out the rest of my look. I'm pretty sure this club has a more formal dress code so I'll need to break out the best. I find a pair of black slacks that have a glossy finish and a slight stretch. I like the way they fall and how they conform to my legs, but don't hug them too tight. Next I grab a light blue button up. The color stands out, but the fabric isn't shiny so I don't have to worry about it being too much. I finish out the look with a silver watch with a black leather band, a black leather belt with a silver buckle, and black slip-on loafers that have a white rim at the bottom. When I check it all out in the vanity, I'm half shocked to find that I actually look like I'm ready for this.

With a little bit of time on my hands before the others show up, I'm left to pre-game by myself. It's a shame I didn't think this part of the night through. Instead of making this a really sad scene where I play drinking games with myself, I settle for a glass of honey whiskey and some aimless wandering around my apartment. Mostly, I just look out into the city as I sip. I'm eager to join the party of lights that I see before me. I'm dying to feel the night air against my skin. I could just open my window for that, but I want to wait for the real deal—that moment when I'm down there in the thick of it. For now, I just look out and admire the chaotic serenity of it all.

At last, I get a call on my phone from Kayla. "Hey," I answer.

"Bry, we're about ten minutes out from your place."

"Great, I'll head down to the front then."

"See you soon!" she chirps. I can barely hear her over all the other chatter in the car.

The call ends and I stuff my phone back in my pocket. I grab my keys and make sure I have my wallet. I could probably grab a jacket, but it's always a pain to deal with that once you're inside these places and we're not walking much so I skip it. After locking the door, I head for the elevators and happily wait for one to reach me. I'm ready to have a normal night out and leave all my baggage behind. This idea resonates more and more as I hop in and begin my descent. I glance around the elevator, admiring the soft lighting and elegant glow of the gold fixtures. By some stroke of luck, no one else gets on so I enjoy the ride in solitude. The elevator comes to a halt and a ding resounds as I reach the lobby. When I look to the doors there's a split second where I think I see a blurry image of Shirun instead of my own reflection. My limbs freeze as the doors swing open. My heart drops to my stomach and I suddenly get a lot more desperate for this night to go well.

"Shake it off, Bryan," I whisper to myself as I exit the elevator.

I spend a few minutes standing beside the revolving doors before a glittering black sedan rolls up to the front with music blasting so loud I swear I can feel the bass from here. I guess this is it so I head through the doorway, a little bummed that it's such a small car that we'll be crammed into. At least the drive isn't long. One of the back doors pop open and I think I see a short redhead retreat into the middle seat. I hop in with a forced smile.

"Hey," I greet everyone. I expect to see Kayla in the front, but she's not there.

Instead I see a Black guy with a buzz cut and diamond studs in each ear. A woman with close-cropped dusty brown hair sits in the driver seat who must be Laurie. The dude is obviously Craig which leaves the cute little redhead beside me to be Annie. Naming a red headed girl Annie feels a little on the nose, but I guess that's not her fault. Her hair is pulled up into a spiral bun held by a gold clip that matches her gold hoop earrings. Kayla sits on the other side which feels kind of weird, but whatever. We're not kids, we don't have to be glued together all the time. The car takes off almost as soon as I've shut the door so there's no rearranging things even if I wanted to.

"Really good to meet you!" Annie squeaks. She throws her hand out to me.

"Nice to finally meet you Annie," I reply, giving her hand a gentle shake.

I say "finally" even though I'm not sure if I'd ever heard about her until the other night.

"Woof, Kayla! Good job girl!" Craig chimes in, looking around his seat at me.

I shift uncomfortably in my seat and say, "Nice to meet you, man." If he's gay, that's fine, but him staring at me like a piece of meat is not.

"Yes. It. Is." He replies with an eyebrow raised.

Thankfully, he turns back around and starts wiggling his shoulders to the pounding music.

"Thanks for driving us, Laurie." I shout up to her, though I'm not sure she'll be able to hear me.

"Oh, sure thing, honey!" she calls back. "Just found out last week that I'm preggers, so there's no booze for me for a while anyway."

"Wow, congrats," is all I manage to reply back with.

I guess if she still wants to go out and have a good time, then more power to her, though I can't imagine why she'd hang out with a bunch of drunk people while she's stone-cold sober. I do notice that she's wearing a wedding band, but I'm not sure where her better half is tonight. It's not my business, so I decide not to think on it further.

The Golden Pearl can be spotted a couple miles away. The large, white structure is bathed in resplendent royal blue and yellowish-gold spotlights. We pull into a parking garage and walk a couple of blocks to the club. The line to get in moves along quickly so we get out of the cold in almost no time at all. Laurie leads us in and we come to a stop before the main steps. The dance music reverberates against us and a storm of bright colors dance across the walls. The place is already flooded with people hitting up the bars and enjoying the LED dance floors Laurie puts a hand on her hip and twists back to us, the lights catching her rose gold chandelier earrings as they swing around her face.

"Tonight's gonna be our bitch!" she announces with a glowing grin across her face.

"Hell yeah!" I hear Kayla squeal.

"Bar first, people!" Craig demands as he bursts past us.

Annie follows behind on his heels and Laurie trails her. I'm reaching for Kayla's hand when I realize she's already moved past me. My open hand clenches into a fist and if I didn't feel like a stranger in this group before, I certainly do now.

Kayla stops and turns back to me once she realizes I'm not following. "Well, come on," she calls with a wave of her hand.

I follow her to one of the bars, no longer so optimistic that this night is going to feel as liberating as I want it to. At least Kayla is high energy. It's a struggle to even remain remotely by her side with her high-heeled powerwalk that seems to defy what's humanly possible. Girl's gotta get her drink on, I guess. So do I, for that matter. Craig is already chatting up the bartender by the time we get there. The guy comes back with two fruity-looking drinks and a glass of cola. The cola goes into Laurie's hand and one of the fruit cocktails is handed to Annie. I guess I can see why one might want Craig around now. The man makes it rain alcohol.

"Drink up, girls!" he bellows before clinking glasses with each of them.

"I'll grab a strawberry mojito," Kayla says to me as she scoots off toward them. "AHHHH that's what I like to see!" she shrieks with her hands thrown up and her hips wiggling to the rhythm of the pounding music.

"Can I get you anything?" Craig asks her.

"Nah, that's okay, Bry's got me."

"Cool, that's what I figured."

I shake my head as I take up a spot at the bar and give the bartender a two fingered wave. He nods in acknowledgment as he shakes up a drink for someone else. Once he's poured it, he comes over.

"What can I do for you, brother?"

"A whiskey sour and a strawberry mojito, please. And a shot of Jaeger."

"I need to see someone else to give you one of those drinks."

"She's right there," I tell him, pointing to Kayla.

She seems to notice the exchange as she turns to us with a wide smile and waves.

"Kay, you got it then."

Just like that he flies off. Watching him pull together the drinks is kind of relaxing. He's like some kind of drink-making android. He knows where everything is around him and seems to know exactly where the other bartenders are at any given moment. It looks so effortless, like he's not even thinking it through. He just knows what he's got to do so he goes and does it. In almost no time, two glasses and a shot glass sit before me.

"Want to open a tab?"

"Sure, it's Daley," I say, handing him my card.

"You got it." He takes it from me and says, "Have yourself a great time man. Your tab is good at any of the bar stations, just give us the name on it. You'll just have to close it here."

"Perfect," I say before shooting down the Jaeger. I put the shot glass back with an easy grin and take up the drinks.

Craig's clapping in my direction when I walk over. "OOOH boy, starting the night off strong!" The way his voice overpowers the music is as impressive as it is annoying.

"What do you mean?" I hand Kayla her mojito and try to avert his big Bambi eyes.

"We saw you sneak that shot over there! I love it, though. Get shitty. Get weird. Get FUCKED!"

"That's the plan." I force a smirk and turn to tap my glass against Kayla's, but she's already sucking the red nectar down.

"Oh, sorry, babe," she giggles.

Our glasses connect, but it's kind of pointless now. I stand listening to Kayla and Craig try to out-babble each other, but I don't really hear anything. I also don't really taste my drink at all. My eyes point toward the group, but I'm looking off into the distance. For a split second, I see my mysterious stalker woman dancing in the crowd. My heart skips a beat, but then I realize that it's just a buxom Latina woman. Maybe that's all the lady Shirun is anyway—just a trick of the eye, a delusion of the mind. I go to take another sip of my drink but find that there's only ice left. Looking to my side, I see that Kayla's polished off hers as well.

"Want another one?" I offer.

She takes a moment to observe the empty glass before turning and answering, "Yeah, that'd be great."

"Can I get you another soda, Laurie?" I ask. It's kind of the least I can do for her picking me up.

"Oh no, I've got the three of us right now," Craig exclaims with a wave of his arms. "How about it, ladies, we ready for round two?"

"Yeah we are!" Annie yells.

"That. Is. What. I. Like. To. Hear!" He hops in place and gives them each a high-five.

I have no idea what a gay guy gets out of buying drinks for beautiful women. Maybe it's a way to show off wealth, maybe he's actually bisexual, maybe he only seems gay. I have no idea why I'm even analyzing this. Maybe I'm actually that bored right now. I walk up to walk the bar with him, trying not to pay this anymore thought. We put our orders in and I foolishly hope for silence.

"That's one hell of a lady you've got," Craig comments as the bartender puts on his show.

"Thanks, she keeps me on my toes," I reply without looking in his direction.

"I bet." He snickers. "That why you look so bummed out?"

"What?" I snap, turning to face him.

"Brotha, you're either a complete bore or you've got a major case of the angst."

"You don't even know me," I argue.

"I know you're out here at a fancy-ass club with a sexy-ass chick yet somehow you look like you've got nothing to smile about. Ain't this enough for you? Fuck, most guys would kill for all of this."

I delay my reply for the bartender to bring my drinks over. "I'd appreciate it if you didn't talk about her like that," I say once he's left.

"Why not? If someone's fine, they're fine… I think you're sexy too even with this dumb, dark, and brooding thing you have going on."

"Okay, yep, that's great, forget I said anything."

I take my drinks and leave him to wait for his. Apparently this guy is just into being a douche. He's also way too happy-go-lucky to be human. That would make him a bisexual alien, yeah that would make a lot of sense. Of course, maybe I'm just jealous of him somehow. He knows what he likes, what he wants. And he's right. I should be the happiest guy—out in a place like this with a girl like Kayla—but I'm not. I don't know what's wrong with me and I don't know what I want. I don't know shit about anything.

"Good talk," he calls after me. God, he's obnoxious.

Kayla never pauses from her chit-chat when I come over. She just puts her hand out to accept the drink. I contemplate giving her the wrong one just to see if she'll notice but decide against it. I stand idly beside her, sipping from mine and trying to avoid Craig's prying stare. Eventually our second round finishes and Kayla starts making sidelong glances at the dance floor which begins to swell with people.

Suddenly Kayla and Annie give each other a knowing look before simultaneously screeching, "I LOVE THIS SONG!"

"Well, move it, then!" Craig declares.

My hand is snatched up and I'm dragged along through the club. We weave through the sea of people, some dancing with style and flair, some with absolutely no rhythm at all. It's always fun to see the latter since I like to wonder whether or not they're even hearing the same song as me. It's not that I'm all that stellar myself. It's just that some people out there are impressively bad. I wonder how I'll fare in this group. The question hangs for only a moment before we come to a stop and huddle up. Craig's the first to dive in. I'm not sure I'd say he's good, but he's certainly… expressive. His arms toss and stretch about while he throws his waist around in an uncomfortably suggestive manner.

"Uh, work it boy!" Laurie cheers as she starts to shimmy her shoulders around and sway from side to side.

Annie slides back-to-back against her and melds into her groove. I find myself inexplicably frozen. It hits me that I don't feel comfortable around these people. They seem fine enough but they're not my friends. Any sense of safety I may have felt before is quickly obliterated. Then, like an angel sent from God, Kayla steps in front of me with hips swaying and a sly sparkle in her sapphire gaze. She places one hand against my cheek and another over my heart. Her touch sparks an involuntary rocking to the blaring music. I get lost in her eyes and let her rhythm become my own. Is this how it always happens when I'm out with her and her friends? Do I always tense up until she sucks me away into her world?

I guess it doesn't really matter right now. I'm just glad that I'm not still stuck in place. The sight of her calms my mind while her touch electrifies my body, compelling me to move. She slides up and down me and dances all around me. It's like I'm a guest in this dazzling universe—a place that I can't exist in without her. I crave every caress, anticipate each sway, and revel in the sweet release of surrendering myself to the whims of my musical mistress. The songs pass us by in currents of colored light until we break for another couple rounds of drinks. The whole time, I just want to return to the floor. I need to feel that captive freedom again. I need Kayla to look at me that way some more. I need her to want me like she's never wanted anything else. We head back out on our own this time, though I see Laurie and Annie take up a spot not too far away.

"You're really into this tonight," Kayla shouts over the music. Her pearly grin is brighter than all the fluorescent lights in this building.

"It's just a nice break…" I reply as she slides against me, her back on my chest.

She twists her head back toward me and curls an arm around the back of my head. "I love it." She locks us into a long mojito kiss.

When she releases it, the rest of the world looks like it's on fire. Other dancers shift into blurred arcs of color while the spotlights flash and sear down on the crowd. The dancefloor beneath us pulses like an ocean of flames. It's a brilliant orchestra of light and color and I'm in the middle of it along with Kayla who remains boldly in focus. I can't remember the last time both of us were this happy and I never want it to end.

Sadly, it does eventually end when Annie and Laurie come

bursting into our bubble, screaming, "Weee neeed shooottttsss!"

"Well let's go get em!" Kayla wastes no time in replying.

I feel my heart sink at how easily she ends what we have going on right now. Isn't she in this same world of burning luminescence? I follow them out to a bar with a heaviness suddenly returned to me. I don't get why they couldn't just go get shots themselves. I know Laurie's just going to have a virgin one, but still the glasses clink together all the same, don't they? I'm bitter about it all the way up to the bar, so I decide I should remove myself and cool down a little.

"I'm going to head to the bathroom," I say, tapping Kayla's shoulder. "Just put it on my tab."

"What should we get you?" she asks.

I twist back, already walking away. "Just something with whiskey in it," I call back.

I don't wait to see if she acknowledges me in any way. There's this horrible feeling that I have suddenly welling up inside me that makes me pick up the pace. From out of the crowd, I see *her* strut toward me. I try looking away for a moment, hoping I'll see the lady Shirun as a regular person when I turn back to her. But she stays in that same, unnaturally attractive visage. Who the hell is this woman? She's closing in on me fast, but she doesn't seem to notice me at all. Her gaze is fixed beyond me, so maybe this will all go away in a second. I try to pretend that I don't see her, but it's admittedly hard not to look at her what with how bright her blue tube dress is and how her hips rock with each long stride. Her long, thick, raven hair flows like a princess'. Aside from a few sidelong peeks, I really do manage to keep my eyes mostly to myself.

Just as she's passing through, her head twists toward me and she speaks in a reverberating, nectar-sweet voice, "You need to leave, now."

I stop dead in my tracks and spin around to see her maintaining her course away from me. "Hey, wait, what do you mean?"

She twists around on her azure heels and thrusts a pointed finger toward the exit. I turn away for just a second to see it and find her gone once I look back to where she was.

*"This can't be real."* My mind reels at what I think just

happened. I can't actually be making this stuff up right?

My breathing tightens at the idea that I really might be in danger. I stumble along a little ways, realizing for the first time that I'm drunk. I can just get some air and come back in. I don't want Kayla to freak out about it though. Near the tables I see Craig. It's only a little out of my way to see him before heading to the exit so I decide I'll just let him know where I'm going. Him and a thin man with blond hair spiked up in the center stand around one of those tall, circular mingling tables. They're sharing a scorpion bowl and while I second guess my decision to approach this guy, I'm also already here so there's no point in not doing it.

"I mean, I'm just not into labels, you know. I just wanna be whatever I wanna be, whenever I wanna be it," he tells the blond guy.

"That's pretty deep," the blond dude replies as he traces the rim of his side of the bowl with his finger. Now that I'm closer, I see that he's probably a bit younger than Craig, like barely out of college young. The boyish grin he wears only exaggerates this. Though I guess he could be older than he looks or Craig could also just be younger than I think he is. I'm really not sure why this shit matters anyway?

I butt into their conversation with a "Hey"

"Oh, hey, nice to see the party pooper stop pooping on the party," he greets, poking my stomach.

I brush it away and tell him, "I need to go out for some air."

"I bet you do, tiger, you go do that."

"I need you to tell Kayla," I press him.

"Lose your phone?"

"No."

"Then you can just text her, yeah?"

"Right, can you just tell her though… if she asks."

"Sure," he agrees, lazily tossing a hand up in the air.

"Thanks," I slur before stumbling away.

"He's cute," I hear the blond say.

*"The fuck is up with other dudes checking me out tonight?"* I wonder.

"Yeah, a bit of an odd duck I'd say, though."

"I can definitely see that."

Fortunately, their voices drown out after this. I set my

attention toward the exit now. As I get closer, strange shadows in the form of lanky, man-like shapes start to materialize near the wall and beneath the tables. I have a hard time even believing what I'm seeing, but it looks dangerous enough for me to stay the heck away, so I trot forward as fast as I can without falling on my face. My breathing turns into wheezing as the shadows stalk toward me. They have no faces and no eyes, yet they converge on my location. The music seems to fade around me and I'm left with the low growling presumably produced by whatever these things are.

I trip onto my hands and a knee. This show of weakness sends the things into a frenzy. They let out a horrible shriek as they lurch toward me—four of them in total. I roll to the side as the first tries to fall upon me. With surprising agility for a drunk man, I spring to my feet and make a break for the doors. One of the monsters picks up a chair and flings it in my direction. I manage to duck beneath it just in time. As soon as I dodge this attack, one of the shadows makes a demonic leap through the air, landing directly in front of me. It sends the palm of its sharp hand into my chest. The blow shoves me backward until I smash against the cool floor. I lay stunned against it as the entire club seems to become enveloped in a dark fog.

Out of nowhere, my mystery woman comes charging into the scene. She runs up behind the shadow that just got the better of me and leaps toward it with a glowing fist held out. The thing twists around in time for her to clock its featureless face with a superman punch. It crumbles into shadowy ashes on impact. One of its friends comes up to meet her, but she's unmoved by the assault. She just pulls a knee up to her chest and drives her stiletto into its chest. As it staggers backward, she twirls around and pommels it with her golden fist. Now I really need to know who this woman is, what her deal is, and what she wants with me.

A sharp hiss pulls my attention away from her to a creature standing above me. It lets out a blood-curdling whine as it reaches down with its pointy fingers. I try to wiggle away, but it's too late. It picks me up by the scruff of my shirt and hurls me into one of the nearby tables. The blow knocks the air out of me as both my body and the table come crashing down to the floor. The back of my head slams against the corner of something and then my lights go out.

# Chapter 4

In the darkness, I can hear the rattling of chains accompanied by a sharp but muffled voice.

"Your fault!" The words start to take shape in my ear. "This is your fault." It repeats, I think it's a man's voice, but it sounds pretty high-pitched. "Fix this, you stupid twat, this is your fault. YOUR FAULT!" The yelling rips into my skull.

The dark fog clears from my vision revealing a wiry man chained down to the floor. He thrashes against the shackles binding his wrists and ankles. His eyes are wide and bloodshot. Sweat drips down his face and matts his dirty blond hair. Nostrils flare around his pointy nose and he bares his teeth at me like a rabid dog.

"FIX THISSSSS!" he howls so loud his voice cracks.

"Who are you?" I croak as I feel around to get my bearings.

"I'm Ronald Humphrey, you dumb degenerate!"

It seems I'm sitting on the floor, my back against the wall of some hall in the manor. Ronald sits against the wall opposite me, hissing and snarling as though I'm the one that chained him there.

"What happened to you?" I ask, pointing to his bindings.

"AHHHH! You idiot! You imbecile!" His voice barely sounds human. "YOU put me here!"

"I didn't—"

"You put ALL OF US here!" He cuts me off. "This is your fault. None of this would be happening if you and Shirun hadn't fouled up everything. We had such a good thing going…"

He pounds the back of his head against the wall repeatedly. As much as I'd like to just get up and leave this guy to his crazy tantrums, his hot tears keep me planted where I am. I feel like he might have some important information to share too. At the very least, he might be able to tell me how I can fix everything since he seems pretty sure I can or at least should.

"I need you to stay calm," I say as soothingly as I can. "Who really put you here and how can I help? How can I get you out of those?"

Ronald rolls his head against its resting place with eyes upturned. He laughs through sobs. I try to stay patient with him. He's my only companion right now anyway and I'll save him if I can. Looking down, I see that I'm wearing a black collared shirt with a royal blue vest over it along with silver pants, black shoes, and a black belt. While it's certainly nice that I keep waking up here in the fanciest clothes, it would be much nicer to get a weapon. I would literally run around here naked if I could get a golden gun. Hopefully I can find something useful soon.

Finally, Ronald's steamy eyes lock with mine. "There's nothing you can do." He breaks into more hysterical chuckling before adding, "They put me here to get me out of the way. They kept telling me how you don't need me anymore. I'm an offering to the darkness now."

"Who did this? Who told you those things? I've never even met you."

The man before me lifts a hand and points down the hall to my right. "Go on in and ask them yourself. Ask them why they get to have a nice little party at the end of the world while I have to sit here chained up as a sacrificial offering. Go ahead, they're expecting you. You certainly won't be finding the key to these chains out here. No, that thing is long gone by now, so there's no point in sticking around like a sucker is there?"

"I don't understand how they could do this to you, but I'll get you some help," I tell him as I get to my feet.

"No need," he cackles. "Might as well go enjoy yourself while you can. With fresh blood in the water, it won't be long for before the sharks come around. CRUNCH! Ahahaha!"

I don't know what to say to him. I'm so intimidated by his insanity I don't even think to nod. I just keep my gaze on him for a moment and then depart in the direction of this party. I'm forced to remember how badly the last party I stumbled into went. A shiver runs up my spine at the thought that this one might end on an equally disastrous note. I press on until the sounds of Ronald's cry-laughing are drowned out by the merry tunes of a violin and hand drums. Rubble from last night's storm lays all around, but it seems as though this section of the house was only slightly marred. There are bits of fractured plaster laying around, an occasional piece of wood, and some shattered glass. The walls do have some cracks, but there aren't any large chunks taken out. This must mean I'm on the opposite side of the house. Given the somewhat sporadic placement of doors and offshoot hallways that dive into the center of the manor, I'd say I'm on the first floor. The music is loudest from a door down one of the small halls that intersects with this main one. I turn to look back at where Ronald lies curled up on the floor. His captivity makes me wonder what sort of state this place has fallen into. I take a deep breath and turn to face the situation head on.

The door swings open before I can reach out for the knob. A young woman with wavy brown hair stands smiling at me in the doorway. She waves me in without a word and I follow her silent command. The music hits me with far more intensity than I expected. The shrill whine of the violin compels my blood to flow faster while the banging of the drums demand that my heart beat harder. I hear the door close behind me and see my greeter prance by with hands dancing in the air. She wears a shorter dress than I've come to expect from people here. It's layered with several frilly swaths that bounce as she hops around and narrows at the top like a satin corset of sorts. A man with dark skin and a gold suit raises a cocktail glass to her as she twirls around him. Behind them is a stage where I see Natasha standing in a bold red dress and diamond jewelry. A tall slit runs up one side of her garb revealing black heels and stockings beneath it.

"All I know is there's no running from the storm." Her chilling voice fills the air on tempo with the invisible violins and drums. "And I'll need someone to find me in the darkness, someone to take me home."

For a brief moment, her azure gaze meets mine, but flits away before anything of meaning is established. Perhaps seeing me floods her with guilt. I have a hard time imagining her being okay with what happened to Ronald, but I guess I don't really know her. My attention drifts to a woman with long, snow-white hair that falls down to her swaying hips as she holds tight to a silver pole. She wears black calf-high boots with six-inch heels that match her black one-piece lingerie which has flaps of cloth poking out at the hips and thin silk strips falling down the back of her legs like half of a

Roman kilt. Atop her head is an ebony tiara with big, fluffy, white bunny ears attached to it. Her long legs swing up to grab hold of the pole as the drumming intensifies.

"So, call me back!" Natasha's pitch elevates, causing my hairs to stand on end. "Back into the light."

The pole dancer glides around like she's a pixie. She weightlessly ascends up toward the ceiling in a brilliant and admittedly sexy display.

"Because I can't stand alone, I can't be without you in this fight."

Once at the top, the dancer continues to swing around, kicking her legs in delicate arches and extending her arms with regal grace. A sudden clasp on my shoulder sends a jolt through my whole body. I immediately tear myself away and turn to find a narrow-jawed man standing beside me. When I adjust to the sight of his curly brown hair, blue eyes, and pale, slender face, I realize that it's Jeremy. I guess it makes sense he'd be here, him and Natasha are something of a couple, or at least a pair.

"Nice to see you, Bryan, I'm—"

"I know who you are," I cut him off. "What is this and why the hell is there a man chained up down the hall?"

Jeremy raises his hands in the air before me. "Please, try to steel yourself, I'll explain everything best I can."

It's then that I notice he has a golden cufflink on that bears Shirun's symbol. It's elegant sheen contrasts with his navy shirt.

"I'm sorry," I mutter.

"No, that's perfectly alright," he replies with a kind smile. "It can be hard to know who your friends are at a time like this. Here, come and sit with me for a moment."

He leads me over to a cedar bar and has us take a seat on black stools. Platters of different beverages dot the counter top. Judging by the way that they are all full, I can only guess that they are of the variety that restock themselves when no one is looking.

"Things are not as they seem here," he starts. "This is not some aimless party meant to pass the time until we would see our end. Natasha and I decided to host it in hopes of gathering as many as might wander close enough to hear our music."

"To what end?"

If he has the mark of Shirun, then he must have heard how the last gathering ended. I can't imagine why he would think it's a good idea to get a bunch of people gathered up into a small room like that again.

"You might deem it unwise, but we aim to set a trap for our enemy. By hosting a small party and leaving an offering outside, we believe we can draw out some of Sin's forces. They've grown stronger and more coordinated as of late and we need to find out who commands them."

"Wouldn't it just be Sin?"

"I do not believe Sin currently resides in the manor. No, we have reason to believe that there is a lieutenant acting in Sin's stead—one that perhaps once stood in our ranks."

"One of the other guests?" I ask in shock—maybe this shouldn't be surprising given that cretins can possess people but I still hope it's no one I know.

"I'm afraid so, but only time will tell," Jeremy answers.

"So, great, you set a trap for Sin's minions, but by extension you created a honey-trap for these people. They're trusting you to keep them safe!"

"They need to see the true nature of Sin's forces. They've been prowling these walls, infecting our friends, and suckling from their power. Olivia counts on our capture so that we can deliver a blow to our phantom attackers whilst also swaying our new companions to the cause. Regardless of the danger, we will do our best to see them to safety."

"So, what, you let yourself get captured, break free, and then our friends here will be so impressed by our show of force that they'll join our ranks?"

"Something to that effect, yes." He takes a glass filled with golden liquid and sloshes it around a little.

"You realize that there are at least a dozen ways that plan could go wrong right?"

"All I realize is that you would do well to have a little more faith. The risks have been carefully considered."

"And the promised reward is worth it then?"

Jeremy offers no response. Instead, he turns to where Natasha sings upon the stage, her lyrics flowing like a gentle river.

The dancer twirls about on her pole with greater speed as the song nears its final crescendo.

Jeremy gestures his glass toward her and says, "Lily there came to us sobbing because she was all alone. Now she gets to perform for the room and find solace in our company, even if it is for the last time." He then directs my attention to the people dancing in front of the stage. "Kenneth waits here, hoping his beloved Rachel will come. Madeline came because she hopes we'll be stronger and safer together. She dances with such a fervor not because she thinks it is the end, but because she believes we will survive this storm."

I look at the people before us and contemplate what he's telling me. I think the point of it all is that these are people worth saving—people that haven't yet sunk into despair.

"And the man tied up?"

Jeremy winces at this. He turns to where Natasha hits the final notes of her song.

"So fall with me, fall into the deepest dark. Hand in hand, on this journey we'll embark."

Lily's ferocious spinning comes to a dead stop. She turns to the pole in a sort of embrace and elegantly slides down it.

"Thank you, everyone," Natasha says before descending from the stage.

She glides over to us with a model's smile and stops before me. Her eyes lock onto mine as she holds her hand out. I take it up and immediately notice Shirun's mark upon one of her rings. It's a solid gold signet with small diamonds studding a rectangular border around the insignia. I break into a grin and plant a kiss atop her hand.

"A pleasure to finally meet you," I say.

She giggles as though I've said something funny. "The pleasure is mine, Mister Daley. I would ask that you indulge me with a drink, but I'm afraid our time is just about up. We hear a hoarse cry come from down the hall."

"They've found him," Jeremy states the obvious with an unnerving degree of tranquility.

"Well, that's what happens when you leave a sacrificial offering," I hiss. "The monsters eventually find it."

"If you knew what he is, you would also be keen to see him to such an end," Natasha counters.

"I don't think I'd wish such a thing on any man."

She giggles as though I've said something funny again. Is there something big I'm missing here? Natasha then turns to the others who've now huddled in front of the stage.

"It'll be alright," Jeremy says to me in his melodic tone.

He rests a hand briefly on my shoulder before joining Natasha in the center of the room. I hang back at the bar and observe them from here.

"Steady yourselves, friends," she begins, her oration skills rivaling that of a queen. "We do not know what these next moments will bring, but you must believe that we will get through them. We have each other. We also have Bryan. Though some measure of tragedy may befall us, take comfort in knowing that he stands with us against the forces that would infect us and melt us down to naught but ash and bones."

The trio of other guests cast glances in my direction, seeming to take comfort in my being here. The hopefulness doesn't last long though. The door to this room is blown off its hinges in a sudden burst. It slams to the floor, making most of us jump in place a little. Three guests enter, infected by the dark substance that claimed Christopher and Peter. A group of five vaguely human figures follow behind. They're neither distinctly male nor female, but rather lanky and primate-like in form. They're also faceless like the things that attacked me in the club. Their mostly unclothed bodies have that same slimy, black shimmer that the cretins have. *Are* they the cretins? Are they evolving—becoming more like us? I notice that they all wear plated gloves that extend up to their elbows in a sort of modern-medieval style. This must be how they can hold onto Ronald without searing into his skin.

One of the infected guests struts over to us and says, "The offering is appreciated, but unnecessary. We came for a full portion, not one measly taste—especially not one of such a pitifully sour flavor."

"There stands what's left of one named Katelyn Bauer," Jeremy whispers into my ear. "Behind her lurk the revenants of Joseph Black and Michelle Moore."

Katelyn's husk turns her head up to me with a sinister smirk that bars her still-white teeth. "How fortunate that you have brought Mister Daley here for us. We'll have to be sure to put on a good show for him!" She slides her hand down her side and licks her lips as she says this.

I can tell that she was beautiful once. Unlike Michelle, she still has a full head of hair. It falls around her face in spiral, light brown locks. She has the classic hourglass figure and shows it off with a slinky blue cocktail dress. Sin's infection runs up one of her long legs as well as up the side of her arm on the opposite side. It climbs up around one side of her chin and stretches up her cheek, over her nose and around one eye. I can still see the fullness of her lips and appreciate her high cheekbones, but no amount of sumptuousness can hide her monstrosity. She must know this too which makes the flirting that much more sinister.

"It'll be a grand time, Mister Daley," Michelle pipes in with a forced giggle. The whole of her head and arms are covered in the symbiotic goo.

"No, my dear, it'll be the grandest thing Mister Daley ever did see!" Joseph's strong-jawed face has been spared. The infection spreads outward from his bare chest, wrapping around his torso and up his neck. He may not be as big as Myles, but he's still a man of impressive figure made more terrifying by the deadly substance that's overcome him.

"Well let's not keep them waiting in suspense then," Michelle concludes, flitting her hand past her face as though to flip hair that's no longer there.

"No, let's not!" Katelyn agrees in a low, sultry tone. She brings a finger up to her lip and sways from side to side as she eyes me.

"Stay calm everyone," Jeremy orders.

The goo-soldiers march forward, tossing the groveling Ronald down to Katelyn's feet. She strokes his hair while we're rounded up into a single-file line that the minions surround. Katelyn and Michelle each take one of Ronald's now-unshackled arms and pull him to his feet.

"Alright then, off to meet the most glorious doom that can be provided to you!" Joseph exclaims as he spins about and leads us out into the hall. His companions follow with Ronald between them and the rest of us trail behind in one long train of potentially doomed souls.

We're led through the hall until we reach a staircase. The whole time I don't hear anything except for the sound of our footsteps. I keep hoping that a rescue party will spring upon us out of nowhere as we ascend to the second floor, but we have no such luck. Whatever this master plan is, I hope it's executed soon. I don't have a great feeling about where we're going and that sense of dread only grows with each step we take. They bring us to where the house is far more damaged. Bits of rubble lay strewn over the floor and entire chunks of the wall and ceiling have been torn away. I notice that the storm no longer rages, instead the house is surrounded by an endless abyss of dull gray. When we come to an especially large break in the wall, I see a caged-in platform levitating a ways off. A bridge of rubble leads up to it from where we stand. I realize that this is where they're taking us. It's a construct made from parts torn from the manor which makes its existence all the more horrifying. I don't want to die in some magical floating cage and I'm not sure how much faith I can put in this plan once we're locked inside.

Joseph stops us right before the bridge and throws his hands up into the air. "Welcome, everyone! Welcome to the last place you'll ever see and the last soiree you'll ever enjoy."

He lets out a satisfied chuckle before stepping onto the bridge. In spite of the fact that it's made up of clustered bits of wood, brick, and plaster, the cobbled-together surface holds his weight unflinchingly. It supports the rest of us with equal proficiency once we've all stepped onto it. And so we all walk toward the ghastly slaughterhouse that awaits us. I'd love to see the punchline of this brilliant plan any minute now if there still is one. I just hope that something hasn't gone horribly wrong...

# Chapter 5

We're all led through the doorway to the shimmering black chain-link cage. At the other end of this circular prison is a long platform rather like a stage. Upon it stands a hexagonal tent, but there's nothing else. Ronald is dragged up before it and forced to his knees. He squirms as Katelyn and Michelle hold him down. Joseph steps up to the platform and stands over us with a beaming grin. He postures there, silent for a blessed change. The slime people herd us into the center of this arena. We stand gathered as if we're an audience eagerly awaiting some kind of display. I don't even want to guess at the nature of what I'm about to see, I guess that we'll find out soon enough anyway.

For a while nothing happens. We're left to stand here in the dim light and chilly breeze that's perhaps a remnant of the storm last night. Or maybe it's a weakened current and the storm actually still rages somewhere. I do spot a purplish-black mass swirling like a wide, cylindrical tornado in the distance. I have to wonder if Sin and its hound are in there. If so, then what are they doing? Are they taking a break? Are they withdrawn to plan their next move? Are they just stepping back to revel in all the chaos they've caused already—maybe laughing at my group's current plight? Perhaps we're not the audience after all. Maybe that's Sin and its hound while we're the ones on display. If they can see us, I'm sure they're enjoying every moment of it. The thought makes me sick to my stomach and the oppressively gray lighting that surrounds us does very little to help. Gone are the endless fields and never-ending blue horizon. Now only some of the lawn still surrounds the manor and the grass looks like it's dying. I can see how the edges of it crumble away as I look down and over our platform of doom. Turning my sights to the house, I see that it too is falling apart—little by little. It troubles me to see bits of brick, wood, shingle, and glass flake off and take flight in a swirling pattern around what remains of the structure. It seems that even at a distance, the storm's pull can still be felt. At this rate, Sin can just remain there and wait for the unyielding current to slowly eat away at everything until there's eventually nothing left. Somehow, I doubt Sin would have the patience for such a slow form of destruction. I'm sure it's enjoying proving that it can still harm us even while withdrawn. Maybe that entertainment will buy us a little time, not that it'll matter if we can't make it out of this mess.

A grotesque slurping sound pulls me away from the deteriorating manor to the back of the cage. Two more of the humanoid cretins enter with a woman in between them. They each hold an arm with their pointy, gloved hands. I see that the gate sort of melts down, or maybe grows down into itself like gooey vines that lock into place once they touch, closing off our exit. The way it all oozes together reminds me of what our enemies are made of. Is this entire cage one large cretin? If that's what we're stuck in then we're far worse off than I imagined. Only the sight of a familiar face returns hope to my heart. The woman they're bringing in is none other than Olivia. I didn't recognize her until she got closer because of how different she looks now—she's dressed more like Shirun and Myles. She wears a Victorian-style dark blue jacket that falls down the back of her legs like a dress, but leaves the front open. She completes the look with shimmering black slacks tucked into calf-high gray leather boots that have thick, blocky heels propping her up a few inches taller than she'd normally stand. Golden buckles and clasps run up her boots and the front of her jacket, glittering brilliantly despite how dull the light around us is. Set against this dismal gray, her skin appears in the most striking shade of white, her eyes sparkle in the most intense sapphire blaze and her raven, shoulder-length hair flows in thick locks as the chilling breeze passes through it. She's absolutely breathtaking in spite of being literally covered from neck to toe. Her jacket even clamps up to her jawline with white lace poking out and the arms fall in ruffled sleeves pulled close at the wrist by silver bands only to flare outward again over her black, leather gloves.

Once they've brought her into the center with us, she pulls herself out of the grip of her captors one arm at a time. She doesn't even spare them a sidelong glance. Her burning gaze instead looks straight ahead—straight at me. I feel feeble under such a focused stare, but I also find comfort in her indomitable sense of purpose. I suddenly get the feeling that whatever fate brings us next, we can stand against it. I turn forward and wait. As if on cue, Joseph throws his hands out ceremoniously.

"Ladies and gentlemen!" he bellows. "Welcome one, welcome all, on this most auspicious of days, to the most dazzling spectacle you ever will see. And please join me in welcoming our most dignified of ringleaders… CHARLES BAXTER!"

My stomach sinks at hearing Charles' name dropped. He's far from a class act, but to be orchestrating this whole thing... I have only a moment to process this before the man himself pops out of the tent, dressed in attire befitting any good ringmaster. He steps up before us as Joseph slides toward the back of the stage. A Cheshire Cat grin spreads across his half-cretin-infected face and a sickly glint flutters over his blazing eyes. He takes a stately bow, spinning his black top hat in big loops in front of him as he goes down. He even holds a black cane with a gold knob and tip in his other hand. A grotesque expression of pleasure remains etched across his face as he pulls himself upright. I note then how his black, twin-tailed jacket glitters. It's not how a jacket with sequins might sparkle. Really, it's more like how stars shine in the night sky. His hat seems to be made of a matching material though he wears plain white pants and simple, yet shiny, black leather boots.

He snickers a little before addressing us. "Yes, welcome indeed. Welcome to the Circus of Consumption. Prepare to be struck with horror and awe in equal measure. Prepare to meet a new destiny, one unburdened by the frailties of your pitiable existence. Prepare to end life as you know it and start anew in exchange for service to a new master, one who grants you powers beyond your belief. Stand back, gaze upon, and enjoy the wild spectacle that we have arranged for you until you too are consumed by the utter thrill of it all."

He struts back and forth looking down upon us. No one moves or makes a sound. Some of us are frozen in fear while others stand firm in their purpose. I stand waiting to find out exactly how all this ends, hoping I'll awake if I find myself up shit's creek.

"And now…" Charles resumes once he's built up ample anticipation. "I ask my lovely assistants to bring forward our opening act."

Michelle and Katelyn yank Ronald to his feet. Although he's been dead silent for a while, he now resumes his hoarse yelling and cursing. He writhes against the supernatural strength of the ladies' hold on him with no success. They don't even seem to notice the resistance as they drag him in front of Charles and push him down to his knees so that he's facing us.

"Please," he blubbers as tears roll down his face and drip off of his pointy chin.

Charles points to one of the cretin people standing around us and beckons it over to the stage. It obeys without hesitation in spite of the fact that it has no eyes to have seen the gesture.

As we await the thing's presence on the stage, Charles continues his narration. "Tonight, we shall see that our new master embraces even the basest and most lowly of us. All shall be graciously consumed by our god's insurmountable power. All will feel the heat of its insatiable hunger." Placing a gloved hand on Ronald's shoulder, he concludes, "Prepare to join us, dearest Ronald. You, who were never given your proper due, will now be one of the most blessed among us."

He steps to the side and the cretin takes his place behind Ronald who shudders and sobs with greater intensity. My hands clench into fists and I'm about to take a step forward when I feel a light grip on the back of my elbow. I turn to find that Olivia's crept up beside me. She looks to me softly, but also sternly.

"Let him go," she whispers.

"I can't..."

"You must."

The cool and absolute power of her eyes hold me in place. I look back up to the stage to see the cretin remove its gloves and hand them to Katelyn. Then it loses the shape of a person and falls upon Ronald like a demonic blanket. The man howls and writes as the horrible substance burns into him, preparing to claim control of his body. In the commotion, Olivia nudges me. I turn to see her clutching a butcher's knife that glows with Shirun's golden blessing. She keeps it hidden between us, the enchanted blade resting against the side of her leg. I have no idea where she's been hiding it this whole time, but it brings me relief to see that we're not totally defenseless. I suppose herein lies the heart of our trap, but we'd be far better off if that knife were a gun.

"On my signal, get down to your hands and knees, keeping your back straight." Olivia demands as Ronald's shrieking elevates.

I keep my eyes locked on the "spectacle" that wretches upon the stage. The dark sludge envelopes him, constricting his entire frame in its searing embrace. I shudder to think of a fully infected man standing against us. What kind of power will he hold once the bonding completes? Hopefully the knife will cut him all the same. It's sad to think on how I'll never really know the people these infected guests used to be. Maybe one or two of them were alright, but I guess it's possible the whole lot of them were already rotten. Either way, now they're just wicked things that we have to kill if the rest of us intend to survive.

"Now," I hear Olivia suddenly whisper.

I drop down to all fours just like she instructed, assuming my position in time to feel a brief pressure against my back. Looking up, I see Jeremy vaulting off of me and sailing into the air, toward one of the cretin guards. The thing shrieks and I wonder what the hell he's thinking. Then the knife soars over me. He reaches out and the weapon snaps into his hand as though pulled in by a magnet. With it in his possession, he drives the blade straight into the cretin's flat face right before he lands effortlessly on the ground driving the monster down. It falls apart into shadowy ashes that fizzle into thin air once they hit the ground, but also leave a black stain in their wake.

Hardly missing a step, Jeremy spins and hurls the knife back in my direction. I twist my head to see it zip back into Olivia's hand. As if part of a carefully choreographed dance, Natasha bends forward and Olivia rolls over her back. She twirls around and chops straight through a cretin's chest. It howls a sharp, metallic howl before falling apart in a snap and a sizzle, leaving only a burn mark on the ground where it once stood. I get to my feet and watch as Natasha charges toward the back of the cage where one of our guards leaps toward Lily, Kenneth, and Madeline. Olivia flings the knife toward her; Natasha doesn't look as she catches it. She maintains her pace to save our companions—seemingly unfazed by the monster in front of her.

"Get down!" she yells to the three trembling guests.

They drop to their knees as commanded. She leaps up and plants the ball of her foot on Kenneth's shoulder, using it to propel her through the air just in time to slice off the cretin's head as it flies through the air like a hawk about to fall upon mice. Its ashes fall over its would-be victims—I hope those stains aren't permanent...

"Natasha!" Jeremy calls to her as he races past me.

There's a cretin sprinting my way. The knife spins through the air, finding its way into his grip. As the cretin goes to swipe an ungloved hand at him, he falls to his knees. Sliding forward, he chops the monsters legs off from under it. The cretin skids in my direction, stunned at first, but then it looks up and scrambles toward me. It claws at the air and screeches as I back away.

"Bryan!" Jeremy yells. My eyes meet his—they look so serene—they slow my heart and make me feel like there's somehow nothing to worry about. "Be calm," he says as he tosses the weapon to me.

I reach out, terrified that this thing will chop my hand off. Miraculously, the handle slaps into my palm. Energized with it's magic, I plunge the blade into my attacker's skull. It disintegrates at my feet and I feel a sudden rush unlike anything I've ever experienced before.

"Bryan!" I hear Natasha call.

I twist back to see her kick a cretin away with her heel. The way it falls back tells me these things aren't as strong as an infected guest, not yet at least. I try not to think too hard as I whip the knife in her direction, hoping it will reach her. She kicks off her high heels, one of which now melts from its contact with the cretin and reaches up in time to grab the knife. She pirouettes toward the monster who comes at her with renewed aggression, slashing off one of its sweeping arms with an arching slice. It falls to its knees and twists around to slash with its remaining claw. Natasha sidesteps the assault and chops down the offending limb before making crisscrossed strikes through the thing's chest that tear it into abyssal ash.

"Stop them!" I hear Charles growl from upon his stage. I guess the show's not going quite how he expected.

Joseph, Michelle, and Katelyn come to the front and stand

with arms and legs spread like starved werewolves. With hungry snarls, they launch from the platform as a pack with Joseph at the center and the ladies on either side. Katelyn flies in my direction and I look to Natasha for the knife, but she throws it to Olivia instead. I freeze in place, panic gripping my heartbeat. In a split-second act of salvation, Jeremy comes and shoves me aside. As I tumble away from danger, I see him fall to his back, letting Katelyn's torso fall onto the heels of his feet. He lets the momentum roll them backward and then uses his legs to spring her off of him.

I scramble to my feet as Olivia cartwheels through the air away from where Joseph pounces. He immediately lurches forward at her only to receive a deep cut on his forearm. Without hesitating, Olivia sidesteps him and slices through his back. A sickly, steaming black fluid spills out from the lacerations.

Michelle lands a short distance behind where Olivia stands and Joseph crumbles forward. Natasha advances to meet her head on. Without looking, Olivia passes her the weapon to lend aid to the confrontation. Natasha seizes it and holds the blade up as she somersaults beneath Michelle's leaping feline assault—the sliding cut eliciting a pain-filled grunt and knocking Michelle off her course. Natasha twirls around to face the infected woman before she can make another attempt at her. She throws the knife, sticking it into the back of Michelle's head as she skids across the ground.

Jeremy grips me by the arm, his eyes fixed on Katelyn who rises to her feet with a seductive smile. She licks her lips suggestively and slides her hands over her hips.

"Jeremy, baby, why do you always have to play so hard to get?"

He disregards her taunting and turns to me. "Stay close and trust in me to see us to safety."

"Alright," I reply—it's not like I have much else in the way of options.

"AHHHHHG!" Katelyn shrieks. "I don't like to be ignored, you stoic bastard!"

She rushes upon us with hands held out like claws. I look to where the knife is, but realize it's not coming our way. Natasha dashes to Michelle's fallen form and pulls the weapon out of her skull as the black goo evaporates off of her—leaving bone and gore behind. Natasha takes it and runs toward the back of the cage where the last of the cretin guards chase Kenneth, Lily, and Madeline. It seems like Natasha will make it in time to save them—then Lily's legs give out. Her arm reaches out to the others as they flee.

"Help!" she cries to them.

They stop and turn with eyes wide, but there's nothing they can do.

"Get up!" Natasha yells to her.

Jeremy suddenly leaves my side to charge straight for our attacker. My heart drops as he throws himself at Katelyn feet first. When he makes contact, it's like he just drop-kicked a bus. She maintains her forward momentum without flinching as Jeremy flies away from her, landing on his back and rolling over his shoulders onto his feet. He crouches low, seemingly unfazed by his failed offensive. Beside us, Olivia evades Joseph's attacks with a sureness of step and an apparently prophetic set of dodging maneuvers. In the back of the cage Natasha races past Kenneth and Madeline who split apart for her and dash to safety. She's too late, though. Lily twists around on the ground like a classic damsel sprawled out in the face of a monster. She looses a terrified scream into the air, but the cretin is unmoved. It rips off its gloves and bends down— wrapping its hands around her neck.

Jeremy rolls to the side as Katelyn slashes downward with clawed fingers. He ducks down to avoid her spin kick, but is caught off guard when she whirls back around with her fist. It catches his jaw as he comes back up and sends him tumbling over himself down to the ground.

"Gotcha now, baby!" she coos as she bends to grab him by his hair and the scruff of his jacket.

Helpless to do anything else to save him, I yell, "Hey, how about you show me a little attention for a change, you crazy bitch!"

Her head twists toward me with a sinister smile across it. "Oh… how interesting…" she snickers. "Alright, darling, let's have a go of it then!"

She lifts Jeremy up and tosses him aside. The force of the throw sends him skidding across the ground. He howls out in pain as his back connects with our cage. The steam that sizzles off of him proves that this is in fact made of the same stuff as the cretins.

He's able to curl himself away from it, but I don't know if he's in any shape to rejoin the battle. He's lucky he didn't slide straight through it and get chopped up into a bunch of little chunks. Michelle stalks over to me with an oddly sensual glint in her demonic eyes. I look past her to where Natasha falls upon Lily's attacker and lops its head clean off. It falls to ash, but Lily is also no more. I can see from here how its grasp melted her neck down to the spine.

"Natasha!" I scream as Katelyn closes in, glaring at me with those voracious eyes.

The villain's face contorts as she spins to see Natasha throw the weapon to me. Katelyn reaches out a hand to intercept it and my heart pounds at the thought of us losing our one line of defense. Fortunately, it cuts right through her greedy palm and finds its' way safely into my grasp. She turns back to me with barred teeth, holding her split hand together and hissing at me. In a surprise burst of clarity, and purpose, I take a swing at her. The first blow misses— she ducks away with ease. Normally, this is where I'd panic, but somehow I manage to remain focused. With uncharacteristic fluidity of motion, I crouch low and land a sweeping strike against the side of her leg. She attempts to bat me away with her injured hand, but I somehow manage to chop her arm off at the elbow before the blow can connect. She screams and clutches the severed limb against her chest.

Before I can land the killing blow, I hear Olivia grunt. Joseph plants the palm of his hand against the top of her chest. The impact sends her sailing until she crashes against the front of the stage. He lunges forward, aiming to capitalize on her momentary break in defense.

"Olivia," I call, before tossing her the knife.

She receives it in time to roll beneath the weight of Joseph's crashing fist. The blow plunges through the wooden structure until he's elbow-deep. Before he can pull it out, Olivia spins to her feet, places the knife at his neck, and rips it across his throat. He falls into a gurgling heap as the infection melts off of his oozing form. She sends the dagger back my way, somehow clean and free of any stain from her bloody finishing strike. It arrives not a moment too soon. The second I have the weapon in hand, Katelyn clutches my ankle and pulls it out from under me. I lay flat on the ground as she claws over me like a savage beast. Before she can pin me down, the knife finds its way deep into her chest. She whimpers and collapses off of me while the darkness abandons her.

Once I clamber back to my feet, I see that Natasha is tending to Jeremy with Kenneth and Madeline standing close by. Olivia backs away from the stage and I join her in the middle of our field of battle. I realize Ronald's screaming has subsided. He erects himself upon the platform—his body totally encased in black goo and his eyes ablaze with red fire. He remains dead silent as he stands over us. Charles emerges from his tent with a curled up whip. The way it shimmers makes it look slimy, much like Sin's darkness. He exchanges a glance with what remains of Ronald before they look back our way. I realize this is it. This is where we either win or lose— where we live or we die. Ronald and Charles leap up into the air and reach an intimidating height before landing on either side of us. Olivia and I stand firm, our backs pressed against each other.

"Don't lose heart," she tells me.

"I've got this," I assure her, gripping the knife's handle so hard I feel like my fingers might fall off.

Ronald shows me his shark-like teeth. Though I'm not facing Charles, I do hear his whip snap against the ground.

"Go," Olivia commands.

Without giving it a second thought, I charge straight for the naked monstrosity before me. Ronald emits a wolfish howl and bounds toward me like a bear. The cowardly little man is now a formidable beast of the night. He flings himself into the air at me at the last second. Somehow, I manage to slide beneath him—sticking the knife up and slicing open a side of his abdomen. He collapses and rolls uncontrollably as he clutches the deep incision—vainly trying to hold back the flow of steaming, black sludge coming out of him. When I get to my feet, I realize that this dagger might be even more powerful than Myles' revolver. I also realize that Olivia is now in need of it.

Her wrist is caught in Charles' whip. He pulls her to the ground with a vicious tug and strength granted by the disease that empowers him. When she skids to a stop, she rolls into a wide crouch with her free hand planted in front of her and an unmoved spark in her eyes. I toss the knife to her which she uses to chop off the end of the whip. The severed bit evaporates off of her arm, but Charles only chuckles as he curls his weapon up in his hand. I see that the thing starts to grow back like a snake's tail.

"You're not the only one who brought a fun little toy to the party," he sneers. "You really should have just enjoyed the show…"

Ronald groans as he pulls himself up to his hands and knees. He springs forward in Olivia's direction with his hands held out like paws.

"Look out!" I call to her.

She flips through the air over Ronald's tackle, slashing his back before she lands. Twirling around, she cuts into his lower back before he crashes against the ground.

Suddenly, I notice that Charles is charging toward me. I manage to roll away from his weapon as it snaps against the ground. Without the knife, my escape is substantially less graceful and deliberate. I'm also too slow to avoid getting my ankle wrapped up and ripped out from under me. Realizing I'm screwed, I look to Olivia who runs up Ronald's chest and slashes him across his already-ugly face. Before I can call out to her, I'm dragged across the ground to Charles' booted feet. He leers above me and reaches down to grab me by the collar of my shirt. I'm hoisted into the air as if I weigh nothing. For a moment, there's nothing else that exists except for me, this devilish man, and the horrible sensation of helplessness that washes over me. It's a feeling that's cut mercifully short when the butcher's knife spins through the air and slices off the hand that grips me before diving blade-first into the ground. I drop to my feet but don't have time to recover before Charles kicks me. I pop into the air and crash halfway across the cage. My breath leaves me and my vision blurs for a moment.

I lift my head up with a groan to see Charles spinning his whip above him, the wounded, gushing arm held close to his chest. Olivia dives beneath the weapon as he brings it crashing down. She slides over to the knife, pulling it from the ground in time to slice away part of the whip when it flicks down upon her again.

"Come on!" she demands as she advances on Charles while his weapon regenerates.

She bows beneath his arm as he thrusts the butt end of the

whip's handle at her and runs her blade across his chest as she slides by. I leap to my feet and sprint toward them, not having any idea what I'm going to do once I get there. Olivia smirks as she throws me the knife. Charles lunges toward her with his back turned to me so I take the chance to leap up and make diagonal chops across his back. He screams out in agony and curls forward. I return the knife to Olivia's hands when I see Ronald racing toward her. She leaps away from him and hacks at his extended arm, leaving a deep gash in her wake. He tumbles to his side, clutching the wound, but doesn't nurse it for long. He takes another swipe at her which she evades. Instead of retaliating, she flings the weapon over to me. I sprint toward Ronald, meeting the knife halfway and taking the opportunity to cleave into the back of his shoulder while he's still distracted with Olivia. His howl clangs through the air like rusted pipes crashing against each other.

Before I can strike a second time, he reaches back and grabs hold of my arm. He pulls me up and over him—sending me flying. I manage to pass the knife back to Olivia while I'm airborne. She ducks and rolls beneath Ronald's attacks, slicing through his tainted flesh at each opening in his defense. Without warning, Charles' regenerated whip cracks against the back of her shoulders. The force of the blow brings her down to her knees. Scrambling to my feet, I make a break for her, repulsed by the idea of her getting overwhelmed by these freaks. She rolls away when Ronald brings his fists down like an ape. I swear the ground shakes when he pounds the empty ground that Olivia just occupied. She's able to step back from the next snap of Charles' weapon, but she can't keep this up forever. I'm almost by her side again when Charles twists to face me. His whip flies through the air and coils around my neck. I clench at the stinging hot rope, but there's no hope of freeing myself. Charles gives me the lightest of tugs, yet it's still enough to bring me to my knees. I choke on the tightening noose. If he pulls at full force, he could easily snap my neck.

Fortunately, I'm spared from this fate when Olivia comes into view and severs the cord a few feet from where I kneel. The whole thing sizzles off of me, letting me gasp for air.

Charles growls in frustration. "Finish them!" He leaps up onto the stage, presumably to wait for his tool to heal itself.

"Time for the final blow," Olivia encourages me as I continue to gasp for breath.

She directs her attention to Ronald who stumbles around now, black slime pouring out and dripping down his limbs. She takes off and I chase after her. Ronald throws his arm back and swings it down toward her as she advances on him. She tosses the knife to me and flips over the attacking arm. While he's off balance, I sprint around and chop into his side. He screams as I pull the knife out, slide it across the ground to Olivia, and roll backward before Ronald can twist around and bat me away. Olivia scoops up our weapon and rips it across Ronald's other side. She ducks down when he tries to back kick her and seizes the opportunity to hack into his leg. He crumbles to his knees with his head bowed to me.

I get the knife back and immediately drive it into the top of his head. He falls into a messy heap and his abyssal skin begins to crackle off of him. I notice that Olivia steps back a bit and takes a low stance. I don't know what she's planning, but she'll probably need the knife for it so I fling it back. As soon as it hits the air, she bursts forward and snatches it up. She runs up Ronald's hunched back as he's decaying. I twist my head with eyebrows pinched together to see her launching into the air toward where Charles stands on the stage. He snarls and snaps his half-regenerated whip at her, but she chops it down before it can touch her. She lands with her feet planted against his face and sticks the blade into where his neck meets his shoulder. She then backflips off of him and lands in a low crouch where she drives the knife into his calf. He cries out as he grips his neck and falls to a knee.

"Wait!" he begs before Olivia rises and chops off his head.

It bounces and rolls over the stage floor, spitting out black liquid along the way. A deep sigh escapes from me, making me realize that I'd been holding my breath as this last offensive played out. Olivia spins and leaves Charles' mangled form behind her. She steps up to the edge of the stage, hops down, then strolls past me, her eyes fixed on Ronald's charred skeleton. She stops beside it, looking down with an intense glare.

"Goodbye, Ronald, you will not be missed." Her harsh words are coupled with an earnest tone.

She looks up to me with a strange smile that I take for an

expression of relief. She sends a nod my way before snapping her attention to the manor. I follow her to the floating bridge between us and where we need to be. The cretin cage still blocks our path, but the others join behind us, hope burning bright in their eyes. Jeremy is helped along by Natasha and Madeline. He winces in pain, but at least he's alive.

"Time to go home…" Olivia announces.

Before I can ask how we're getting out, she steps forward and makes two vicious cross strikes through the glistening bars. The part she cuts through instantly disintegrates to form a sort of doorway for us. It also starts a chain reaction through the rest of the cage. The whole thing slowly crumbles into dark ashes that flutter down upon us like some kind of evil snow. I let out a chuckle, feeling the sudden rush of what we've just done. This was a big blow to Sin's forces. It feels amazing to kick their asses for a change. The freedom and sense of power this stirs in my soul all but overwhelms me.

Olivia turns back with a smirk. "You did well, Bryan. Remember what we did here and never forget what you can do."

For a moment, I hope that means that I'll get to keep the knife. That hope is quickly dashed when she slides it beneath the train of her jacket and it disappears from sight. She leads the way back to the manor with a confident strut. I know it's not exactly safe there, but somehow it feels good to go back.

# Epilogue

Olivia leads us through the large gap in the wall and back into the warm brown and red halls of the manor. Kenneth and I follow close on her heels while Madeline and Natasha help Jeremy along behind us.

We carry on a little ways before I break in, "So, what happens now?"

Olivia stops and turns to face us. "I need to bring them all to the observatory where Shirun awaits us."

My heart drops that I'm excluded from this group of refugees.

"I'm afraid I can't partake," Kenneth interjects. "I need to find Rachel."

"You need to trust that she will find her way to safety," Olivia responds, slowly turning her head to him.

Kenneth's mouth opens and then quickly snaps shut. "I can't leave her out here..." he finally says.

"And I can't stop you from splitting off from us, but I'm begging you to have some faith in her—some faith in all of us."

"I have to go..." he insists.

"I know..." she sighs. "If I don't see you again, it really has been a pleasure."

She spreads her arms and takes him into a long hug. I didn't picture her as the hugging type, but there she is clinging to him earnestly. Sadness scrunches his face as he steps back from her.

"Be safe," she orders him.

"And a safe passage to you all," he replies. "Pray that you see me again with Rachel beside me."

With that he turns from us and jogs off in the opposite direction. I watch him go with a surprising heaviness considering that I hardly know him. I guess I just find it sad to see how desperately he longs to find someone he may never see again—how he yearns to save someone who may not even need saving or may be beyond saving. A soft touch on my shoulder pulls me back to my present company.

"Let's be off then," Olivia suggests. Her tone is light like a whisper, but also weighed down with preemptive mourning.

"I'll need to patch Jeremy up before we make our way to Shirun. We can hide out in there."

She points to one of the doors ahead of us and ushers us toward it. I get a sudden fear that this is where I'll part ways with them. I'm not ready to go back. I'm not sure who or what I'll wake up to. I'm not even sure where I'll wake up. Before she can open the door, I grab her arm. She stops and turns around to face me, seemingly unsurprised. Her blue eyes peer into me and her face remains still as she waits for me to explain myself.

"Do I get to go with you through that door?" There's a desperation in the way I ask this that catches me off guard.

She tilts her head to the side, inviting the others to hobble past us. She places a hand against the side of my face and stands intimately close to me.

"No," she answers simply. "You'll go to your own place of healing."

"I'm not ready to be alone yet." The words tremble out of my mouth.

"You won't be," she soothes, wiping away a stray tear before it can slide down my cheek.

"Let me come with you," I beg.

"That's not for me to decide. I'll be closer than you think, though, and we'll see each other again before this is all over."

As she makes this promise, I see Natasha throw open the door in question. Behind it lies a blinding light just like I feared. The trio turns to me and all send me encouraging grins.

"Have a little faith," Jeremy reminds me.

"In us as well as yourself," Natasha adds.

With that, they shuffle into the light and leave my sight.

"Just hold on to me," Olivia tells me.

She slides her hand away from my face and turns toward the door. I want to protest, but instead I hold onto her arm and let her lead me through the portal until I fall into the light and out of this world.

# Book 6:

# The Hands of Time

*To the individuals who helped me find peace
within the chaos of this world.*

# Chapter 1

I awake to the sound of beeps and some light buzzing. The space around me is a sterile shade of white. The sharp smell of cleaning products and disinfectants fills my nostrils. I blink a few times and a low groan escapes me.

"About time…" I hear Kayla say—she sounds irritated.

I roll my head to find her sitting in a chair beside me. She has her legs crossed and she's drumming her fingers over her knee. I'm in a bed, but it's not mine. Given the fact that Kayla is still in her club dress, I'm guessing we've been in a hospital this whole time. A pit forms in my stomach. I need to know what happened while I was at the manor. I also get a rush of hope that maybe there's some kind of medical explanation for everything that's happened.

"What's going on?" I ask dryly.

"Don't know, maybe you can tell me," Kayla snarls.

"How did we get here?" I press my head deeper into my pillow as a headache starts to come on.

"We rode here on a unicorn… we came her in an ambulance obviously!" God, her tone is chillier than the Arctic. I'm getting the idea that she might be pissed about me ruining her night.

"I'm sorry something bad happening to me is such an inconvenience for you," I retort with equal venom.

"Nothing *happened* to you, Bryan—you freaked out and then you passed out and hit your head."

"Ya might wanna try softening your tone, honey, or at least lower your volume," an unfamiliar female voice interrupts. I pull my head up to see a heavyset woman typing away at a computer across the room. "He may not be concussed, but he was also unresponsive when the paramedics arrived on scene, so let's not add any potential trauma alright."

"Sure, sorry," Kayla replies sweetly, but she continues to eye me with agitation.

"Did anyone see anything?" I ask after a couple minutes of awkward silence.

"What do you think there was to see? Your drunk ass collapsing and crashing into some empty tables after scurrying around for a bit like a madman? I mean were you sneaking shots the *whole* night or something? I didn't think you had *that* much."

"So, no one saw anything strange?"

"What do you think happened?" Kayla snaps. "Did you have like a whiskey-fueled hallucination or something?"

"No… It's just—" I struggle to explain myself in a way that even remotely makes sense. "There's this woman—I think she might be following me." Even though sharing this will still make me sound paranoid, it's better than telling the whole truth.

"Really?" Kayla yips, lurching forward and slapping my chest. "You're going to blame some mystery chick? What, were you staring at her tits when you tripped over a table? Is that actually what you want to go with as an excuse?" She attacks me with another set of slaps against my chest.

"Ma'am, I'm gonna have to ask that you save whatever this is for later. Long as he's in here, he's my problem so how about we just wait until he's discharged, huh?"

"Sorry," Kayla replies, sinking back into her chair.

I'm left a little stunned by her accusations. How is that the first logical conclusion she came to? I say a woman was bugging me and she immediately assumes I was checking her out.

"Why would you say something like that?" I quietly ask after a while.

"Am I wrong?" she challenges, but she's not even looking at me anymore.

"Yes…" Kayla's been pissing me off lately, but she's never cut me deep like this. "I think she's been stalking me. I saw her on my jog through the park, then at Benny's later on, and then again at the club. She told me to leave, threatened that something bad would happen to me if I didn't. It's like she's maybe trying to help me, but I'm not really sure."

"Makes sense…"

"What does?"

"That she told you to leave. You were probably being a creep."

"In what way?" I demand. I'm getting tired of her taking

potshots at me for no reason.

"Oh, I don't know Bry, maybe the way you stare at other women finally got you a nice little slap on the wrist."

"*What*? I do not *stare* at other women."

"Yes you do! Like all the time!" she hisses, jumping out of her chair and forgetting her promise not to hit me. "I don't give a shit if you want to look or judge, or fantasize, or whatever it is you do, but don't treat me like I don't notice." She slaps my chest again.

"Ma'am," the nurse scolds. This time she spins around in her chair with an eyebrow cocked at us. "Pa-lease just contain yourself for a few more minutes. I'm processing the last of the paperwork now and I can have you lovebirds out right after that. Don't make me file a domestic abuse report to this stack, okay?"

Kayla doesn't respond. She just stands glaring down at me. Tears well up in the corners of her eyes. "It's not like I need your undivided attention all the time, but you'd think that you could at least keep your eyes on me when I'm half naked and shaking my ass around a club... I guess you can't help yourself. You're always looking..."

"That's not true..." I start to get a little choked up myself. As much as I want to reassure her that she's everything I need, I guess that hasn't been true lately.

Kayla gives me no reply. She turns and walks over to the window. Is she right? Am I really always checking other women out? There's no way, right? I would know if I was doing it... wouldn't I?

Time passes in silence until the nurse comes over with some printed forms. "Alright, we're just about good to get you out of here, I'll just need you to sign this."

She hands me a clipboard with the papers on it, but I don't see any mention of what really happened to me. "So, what's actually wrong?" I ask.

"Medically, not a thing. We ran some tests and found nothing for drugs. We also didn't see anything particularly weird in your blood alcohol levels relative to what you were up to last night. Even blood sugar looked fine. Like I said before, there are no signs of concussion, but you can always come in for scans if you have any concerns about head trauma later."

"What happened to me then? Why did I just pass out like

that?"

"Well maybe you did and maybe you didn't, we're not really sure what conked you out like that. You've got a clean bill of health so I would just say you may want more sleep, you might need to eat more before you go out drinking, or maybe you just need to work on keeping your eyes forward while you're walking…" She cocks a judgmental eyebrow at me and saunters back to her computer, sliding the chair up against the desk.

I get why she's being sassy with me. I know I look like an entitled, womanizing prick that can't even handle his liquor, but her answer isn't good enough. There is something else going on with me and I might as well find out while I'm around medical professionals.

"Can I speak with the doctor first?" I ask, holding the pen away from its intended destination.

The nurse looks at me with a blank expression. I can tell she wants to roll her eyes and maybe even sigh, but she doesn't.

"There's nothing he can tell you that she hasn't already," Kayla complains.

"I just need a few minutes…"

"You've had a whole night! I've been here all night, okay. You ruined the good time we were having and embarrassed me in front of my friends. Now, if it's okay with you, I'd like to go home— I'd like to shower—I'd like to not be late for meeting my friend, Margie, for lunch. Then I can finally get some sleep."

I would ask who Margie is, but at this point I truly don't even care. "Fine," I say. "Go then, I'm not trying to get in the way of your plans, I'm just a little worried about my health—no big deal…"

"Oh, you don't think I am too?"

"I don't know *what* you are. Just go, I'll be fine without you begrudgingly waiting up for me."

"Bry—"

"I'll meet you for dinner," I cut her off.

"Alright," For the first time since I met her, she actually sounds defeated. Surprisingly, it's not a sound that fills me with any sense of victory.

She makes her way out of the room wearing nothing but her

clubbing dress. It strikes me that this is like a walk of shame for her. I remain still in the hospital bed until I can no longer hear her high heels clicking against the tile floors. Then I flip off the covers and swing my legs over the side. The nurse isn't shaking her head, but the way she has that one eyebrow raised and is almost biting her lip is enough to tell me how disgusted she is with us—or maybe just with me.

"I'll fetch the doctor," she says once she realizes that I've caught her making this face. "Go ahead and sign that form for him while you wait, he's not going to have much time to spare."

With that, she too heads down the hall, leaving me alone. I sign the release form like she said, then I wait for a while in the nauseatingly clean hospital room. The rational side of me knows the doctor will have nothing helpful to say, but another part of me desperately hopes he'll come to a conclusion he hadn't thought of before. Eventually, I get antsy so I walk over to the doorway and hover at the entrance like an impatient creep. The things Kayla said to me—about how I look at other women—echo through my mind. The more I think about it, the more I wonder if she's right, so I try not to think about it. After lingering here for what feels like forever, a middle-aged man comes up to me and extends his hand.

"Bryan Daley, I'm Doctor William Chang, I oversaw your treatment last night. The nurse told me you wanted to talk to me, but to be blunt, there isn't much to say. You have a clean bill of health and I have to get to someone who doesn't."

I know the nurse said this guy would be in a rush, but this is something else. I guess I'm just a number in this place. "Listen," I entreat him. "I know there's something off with me. Things have been … wrong."

"Wrong how? Are you getting enough restful sleep—having a good dietary balance? Are you experiencing any unusual stresses or pressures at work or in your personal life—trouble with your significant other maybe?"

The barrage of questions leaves me a little stunned at first. I also can't believe the nurse actually told on me to the doctor… although I guess that's part of her job.

After hesitating, I answer, "Work has been stressful and life has sucked lately, but I'm eating plenty and trying to get as much sleep as I can. The real problem might be that I'm not sleeping well."

"Why's that?"

I shuffle my feet bashfully across the tile flooring, but he just looks at me expectantly and I realize he doesn't give a shit if it's something embarrassing.

"I've been having really messed up dreams. It's been every night for almost a week. They're always in the same place with the same people, and things just keep getting weirder and creepier." I can tell he's about to dismiss me so I keep talking before he can. "Sometimes I even wake up with a headache or soreness and one morning I was so dizzy and in so much pain that I could barely move."

He looks to me with what is either mild irritation or saintly patience—or maybe a combination of both. "Unfortunately, that lies a little outside my area of practice, but I do think you should get yourself evaluated by someone in the psychiatric space. I can also prescribe you some sleeping medication, but I would try over-the-counter pills first. Those can help you reach a much deeper sleep than, say, alcohol can. I'd recommend abstaining from caffeine or sugar if possible. Other than that, all I can do for you is have our office refer you to a therapist."

"That's okay, I'll try the sleeping pills, though." I'm not sure why I turn him down, I could clearly use the help.

"Alright, well make sure to grab a card on your way out and give us a call if you change your mind on that. That your release form?"

"Yeah," I say, handing him the clipboard.

He waves me along down the hall and I try to follow his brisk pace. He leads me through the long corridor and by the way the fluorescent lights sear into my skull, I start to realize that I'm at least a little hungover. I try to keep my eyes to the floor and walk in a straight line, but it's a struggle. We round a corner—by the ringing of phones and tapping of keyboards, I know we're getting close to a front office. He leads me down a shorter hall and pushes through swinging double doors.

"Can you take care of him, Darla?" he asks the older lady sitting at the desk.

She's on the phone, but does nod her head and reaches a hand out for the papers.

"Good luck with everything," he says before sailing off.

"Yep, alright, bye now." The receptionist ends her call and turns to me with a kindly grin. "Alright, Mister Daley, I see that your release form is all set and we've already received all your insurance information. Your girlfriend took care of all that for you last night. So, yep, looks like you're all set to go then."

"Thank you," I reply with as much enthusiasm as I can spare.

I move to leave, but then I freeze up when I see *her*. She's right in front of me, but doesn't seem to notice that I'm here. She's dressed in baby blue nurse scrubs and pushing an old man in a wheelchair toward the elevators. She calls it and I want desperately to confront her, but maybe this isn't the place. Yeah, not here, not with so many people around—not when I don't even know if she's real. There's no reason she should be here. I mean what are the chances that she happens to actually just be a nurse that works here? Assuming she's real, then she could have also disguised herself as an employee to continue stalking me. When the elevator doors swing open, I lose my cool and rush over to her. I need to know what happened last night and how she's involved. She wheels the old man in and spins him around. When my eyes meet hers, she shakes her head at me and presses the button for her floor.

I'm left to stand like a scorned child as the doors shut in front of her and she's out of sight again. I really need to know what the hell is going on with all of this. The weight of strangers' eyes falling upon me starts to build up so I call the elevator and ride it down. When I look at my blurry reflection in the doors, I notice that my hair is all over the place. Looking down, I see that my shirt is wrinkled up and I have a shoelace untied. I guess I have a walk of shame of my own to make. The brief flash of hope that I can get a little privacy in here to straighten myself out is quickly dashed when the doors part and a bunch of people invade my elevator car. Although I don't get the ride down to myself, the trip to the main lobby is a short one at least. I use the TrnsPrt app on my phone to call a ride and wander out to the sidewalk.

The fresh morning air hits me like the pleasant rush of diving head-first into a pool. It washes me of the overbearing sterility of the hospital and breathes some new life into my soul. I enjoy this until my ride arrives after a few minutes. I hop into the car, immediately appreciating its non-standard leather seats.

"The Best Aid on fifty-second?" the driver confirms the destination that I provided in the app.

"That's right."

Without another word between us, the car shoots forward. Traffic isn't too bad so we cruise along with relative ease. I try to think on what's happening to me while I have some quiet time as well as take the chance to put myself together as much as I can. There's nothing that can be done about the shirt so I just roll up the sleeves and hope that will make it look more casually messy. I also finger-comb my hair and tie my shoe. I catch the driver giving me a funny look. He's probably trying to guess at what kind of juvenile nonsense I got into. Realistically, this is the second driver this week that's seen me in a train-wrecked state, so, whatever, he can judge. I need to worry about my next step instead of what this guy thinks of me anyway.

By this point, there's a very good chance that I've actually just lost my mind. I'm feeling pretty paranoid these days and I have to wonder if I'm delusional as well. Adding to that is how I'm somehow oblivious to some of my biggest issues. I suppose that last one has nothing to do with insanity, but it's still kind of a bummer to find out I've ignorantly been a dick this whole time. I need to believe that this really does come down to stress causing some extreme sleep deprivation which is then causing a *very* temporary and *very* fixable brand of insanity. I'll give the sleeping pills a shot even though I'm not a huge fan of the concept. If that doesn't work then I guess I really need to seek out some professional help. I don't want it to come down to that especially if some shrink decides I need to end up in a straitjacket and padded room.

As we drive along, I notice a sign for DR. BEN DRAKESON: COUNSELING AND PSYCHOTHERAPY. It's tragically ironic that we pass the building that this office is in, especially since I've never noticed it there before. There's a parking garage nearby so this looks like a convenient enough spot to come if the sleeping pills fail me. It's fairly tucked away too so that should minimize the shame factor of anyone finding out I need that kind of help. The thought of it coming to this awakens a powerful nausea that brings my hand to my abdomen. I try to breathe slow and move my mind away from therapists and loony-bins. All I need is some sleep—good, restful sleep without trips to the manor. Maybe then I'll stop being attacked by evil shadow people that don't seem to bother anyone else.

But what if I'm not crazy or sleep deprived? What if I truly am being transported to some other world every time I think I'm going to sleep? I've known for a while now that these aren't *just* dreams. Even if they're not real, maybe the evil there is. What if it's trying to get into this world, my world? Maybe if I can stop Sin, I can fix things in both of my lives. A part of me almost hopes the sleeping pills won't work. I finally got a taste of victory last night and it was pretty sweet. But this isn't some game that I get to play after hours. This is stuff that's affecting my life and putting me in serious peril.

This is all I have time to think about as the car rolls up to the front of the BestAid.

"Have a nice day," my driver says without looking back.

I have some idea of what he would really like to say to me, but I get that he wants me to give him a good rating.

"Thanks, you too," I reply, trying to sound genuine.

I hop out of the vehicle and look down either end of the sidewalk. Looks like I'm clear of any followers which is good. Maybe I can just get through the rest of today… With this in my heart, I step through the front door and grab a basket at the entryway. I don't want to head straight for the pills though, that would make me look desperate. I'd like to shop around a little first then head over for the medication. That way, it's more of a casual purchase—just something I need to grab rather than my main pickup. I start in the vitamins section since I need a refill of my multivitamins anyway. Next, I head over and grab a couple of smaller bottles of ginger ale for my stomach as well as some saltines and peanut butter. Next, I look for some canned soup and end up picking chicken noodle. Finally, I stroll into the medication isle, grabbing some toothpaste and deodorant before coming up to the overwhelming amount of sleep aid options. Having no idea what to pick, I just grab the one with the nicest looking box as though that's exactly what I came for. I can't have any people-watchers realizing I've never done this before after I put so much effort into making this look like a natural, relaxed thing.

With everything I need in the basket, I turn and take my leave of the aisle. I have to play it cool though. If I race out of there then it'll look like I'm trying not to get caught in this section. I put on a very convincing exit stroll, but stop short as I almost bump into a blond woman walking past.

"Sorry," I say in a suave, but surprised tone.

Then the woman's radiant blue eyes snap to meet mine and I lock up. I probably look ridiculous—like a deer in the headlights.

"Bryan?" she questions, but she knows it's me.

Here I was, afraid of shadow monsters and my mystery stalker and going insane—now I'm standing face to face with someone far more intimidating. One look at Julie and my whole world crumbles around me.

"Hi," I reply quietly. She has me completely disarmed so all I can do is pray that she plays nice.

# Chapter 2

~*~

*The last time I saw Julie, I mean really saw her, I met her for dinner at a nice little Asian Fusion restaurant. It was a pleasant enough meal, but she seemed quieter than usual—a running theme that whole week. It seemed to me that she struggled with something. At first, I liked it. She finally had to struggle to figure out what she wanted. She'd never shown that kind of weakness before and it honestly just made her a little more relatable. Then I realized that I couldn't help her with whatever had her feeling this way and I started to worry that this thing she grappled with might have something to do with me. She didn't drastically change her behavior or anything, but I could notice little things that felt wrong.*

*She'd only half-laugh at my jokes and sometimes I swore she actually spaced out while I talked. We slept together a couple of times that week. Each night, she clung to me like I might somehow fall away from her. We didn't try anything new, but this intensity—this desperation—made me feel like this would be the last time we came together like this. She dismissed comments I made and I felt like she kept picking apart these little things I'd say or do that annoyed her. By the time I met her for this lovely date, I felt like a piece of shit and I couldn't understand what I was doing wrong. I thought we still had a good thing going. I thought we were both happy. Over dinner, I tried to get through to her. I tried to get her to open up about what had her so somber, but she just wanted to talk about more mundane things like how my day went, how the gym went, and where David and I got lunch.*

*After we finished, she led us to the Twilight Gardens, a park of sorts on top of the building where the restaurant is in. She held my hand as we walked along the brick path through the bushes with white string lights wound through them. It's probably one of the most romantic places in the city so coming here filled me with a false hope that things might suddenly get better between us. She took us to a corner of the garden where a bench sits cozily overlooking the city. A grin crossed my face as we stopped beside the seat. The city lights shimmered below us and the stars twinkled above. The darkness of the night hides all of the city's grit—all the imperfections—until all that's left is the stuff that's bright and wonderous.*

*I came back to reality when Julie stepped around to face me. She placed a hand behind my neck and ran her fingers up through my hair. At first, I thought it was just the enchanting glow of the lights that made her eyes glitter, but then I realized that they were slicked with tears she tried to hold back.*

*"I need you to sit down with me now," she said. I'd never heard her voice tremble before so I obeyed her without question.*

*She never lost her grip on my hand and she never looked away from my face. I got the sickening feeling that this would somehow be the last time we got to see each other like this, or maybe at all.*

*"Are you going to tell me what's been going on with you?" I asked even though I felt terrified to find out what the answer to this question held.*

*"I—" she faltered for the first time since I met her. "I need you to know that I thought a lot about this. I just don't want you to think that this is an easy thing for me."*

*"What are you saying?" The mask of composure I wore fell off of my face.*

*Tears spilled out of her eyes before she answered, "I need this to be over… I need us to be over."*

*The words left me winded and a heavy mist washed over my eyes. I opened my mouth to speak, but nothing came out.*

*"I wish I could give you a good, long list of reasons or of things you did wrong. I mean sure there were little things, there are always little things. It's just that… I think we're in different places. We want different things. I've done my best to make it work, because I really do love you, but this isn't something that can be forced. And there's nothing either one of us can do to fix it."*

*Tears fell freely down her face then. As much as I'd like to have comforted her and told her everything was okay, nothing was okay about any of this. This was all wrong and a steady stream began to slide down my cheeks as well.*

*"I don't understand." I barely managed to choke the words out.*

*"I know…" She soothed, brushing my tears away with her thumb, but leaving her own unattended.*

*"That's part of the problem, isn't it?"*

*"Yeah, I guess it is."*

*"I know we can still work this out. I can be better. I can work on whatever's not working." I realized that I was begging at this point, but I didn't care.*

*"I don't think you can and I don't have any right to ask you to change in the way I'd need you to. I'm not sure you could, even if you wanted to. This isn't about you being bad and it's not about me not wanting you in my life anymore. It's about who we are. It's where we are and where we need to go. We'll always hold each other back and I just can't see this being our forever."*

*It hit me that she referred to marriage. I hadn't even considered that yet. I didn't even know her ring size. Is that what this was all about? Or did she just want me to know she didn't think marriage would ever work out between us?*

*"Please just give this some more time," I tried to stall.*

*She shook her head.*

*In spite of it already being over, I made one last plea. "Julie, please don't do this. You're the best thing that ever happened to me. I love you and I need you and… please don't go…"*

*"I'm sorry," she whispered before standing up off the bench and turning to leave.*

*I wanted to scream at the top of my lungs about how much I loved her. I wanted to list off all the reasons why she should stay with me, but my mind couldn't form any kind of sophisticated thoughts. All I could do was cling to her hand.*

*For a moment this stopped her escapee, but then she turned around and said, "Let me go, Bryan."*

*The softness of her words loosened the strength of my grip. Her hand slipped out of mine and I had to just sit there on that bench watching the love of my life—the woman I never deserved—walk away through the magical glow of the garden. When she disappeared from sight, I turned my tear-filled gaze back to the elegant urban vista before me. I felt a strong urge to leap down from this rooftop and join the symphony of city lights below. I didn't, of course. My life certainly felt over at the time, but I never felt tempted to end it short. It's just never quite been the same since that night.*

~*~

I don't know why these memories come back to me so clearly. I've done my best to forget what happened that night or at least block it out. Of all the memories seeing her could have drudged up, of course it would be this one. As all this hurt and heartbreak comes back to me with a vengeance, I now have to somehow make awkward conversation with the woman that can still shatter my world with a single look.

"How are you?" I manage to beat her to the punch.

"I'm doing well, thanks," she replies with an easy grin. "How about you? Good night?" She motions to my basket as she asks this.

My face reddens. I guess that my untidy appearance probably ruins any facade that I'm here on a casual stop.

"Yeah, it was a great time," I remember too late to put some enthusiasm behind my words.

Julie's expression falls, "Sorry, I just assumed with the clothes and the ginger ale and everything that you're coming back from a liquid adventure."

"No, it's fine, you're not wrong..." she has me self-consciously looking down at myself and the odd assortment of things that I'm carrying.

"It just didn't go as planned then?" she pries.

I have no idea why she cares to get into this. I actually don't know why she's trying to make conversation with me at all. A normal ex would be giving an excuse to get away, not drive the dialogue forward.

"Not exactly, no."

"Bummer, I hope everything else is going alright though."

I bring my eyes up to her. As much as I want to fake a smile, my mouth is stuck in a frown.

"Things are going alright, just crazy busy."

"I'm sure, mostly work stuff?"

"Have you talked with David?" I cut off the flow of conversation. I can't believe David would send her like he probably, maybe, sent the others, but am I really supposed to buy that I'm suddenly running into her and she's suddenly interested in reconnecting?

"Well I saw him and a bunch of the old crew the other night at a concert in The Commons. I've been kind of distant from them all which I regret, but lately I've been working on reconnecting with them every now and then. Why do you ask?"

"No reason, just wondering..."

She studies me and I shift uncomfortably as she pins me down beneath her scrutiny.

"They mentioned how much they miss you, you know. Have you talked to them at all lately?"

"Yeah, I've kind of been running into them all week."

"Well, that must be nice."

"Sure, but it's also like I'm Scrooge getting visits from ghosts."

"Do you think David is Jacob Marley then?"

"What?" I chuckle.

"He's the first ghost, then one that explains things to Scrooge and sends the three spirits."

"Oh, maybe." In the midst of everything going on inside of my head and my heart, she actually manages to make me chuckle.

"And am I that third scary-looking ghost?" she pushes the analogy.

"I don't know if you're scary-looking, but I was definitely surprised to randomly bump into you after all this time."

"That's fair enough. It's really good to see you though."

"It's nice to see you too," I say, though I can feel the smile fade from my features.

It finally feels like I'm having a genuine conversation with her, but this is probably the end of our little reunion.

"Were you about to cash out," she catches me as I'm shifting my weight to leave.

"Yes, I was just about to wrap up and head home."

"Great, me too. Care to join me?"

"Sure."

I follow her out of the aisle and down to the registers. We wait for a few minutes in companionable silence. It's the strangest thing for me to stand next to her after all this time. On one hand, it's painful—it drudges up all sorts of hurt and loneliness I didn't know I had. On the other, I have this overwhelming sense of safety. I get to breathe easy even though I'm beside a phantom of my past. Part of me is sad when it's our turn to check out. I'm sure we'll be wordlessly parting ways as I pay for my anti-crazy supplies. When I'm done, I find that she's actually waiting by the exit for me with her bags in hand. She leads us out to the sidewalk and starts to take us to the right, but I stop short.

"You parked in the garage?" she asks, clearly inviting

conversation, but I don't want to make her stand out here holding her shopping bags.

"No, I— I didn't drive. I was just going to catch a cab or call a TransPrt. I can walk a little ways with you if you'd like though."

She shakes her head with a teasing smirk, "Yeah, or, I could just give you a ride home."

My jaw tightens and my eyes widen. "Oh, no, that's okay, you don't need to do that."

"You don't want to catch up a little more?" I see the guilt trip in there and find it funny that she makes no attempt to even be subtle about it. I don't get it though, how could she want to be in the same car as me?

"Yeah, of course, that would be great. I just don't want you to take time out of your day to do that is all."

"This is my only errand today, it's no trouble, I swear. Come on."

"Why are you doing this?"

"It's just a ride," she laughs. "Besides, if I'm your third ghost, then isn't it my job to get you home?"

"Well, when you put it like that…" I chuckle, amazed that this woman always knows just the right thing to say even now.

"Alright then," she concludes with an illuminating grin.

I walk along with her toward the parking garage. The air is still and there isn't much foot traffic on the sidewalk which gives me the feeling that it's just me and her and the light of the afternoon sun. In spite of how surreal this is, I can't help but feel like it's the best thing to happen to me in a long time.

"So, where are you living now anyway?"

"I'm at that big apartment building on Covington Ave, it's right near The Commons."

"Spyre Appartments? Yeah, I know it, one of my friends lives there. She sometimes has me over for drinks and Getflix."

"Oh nice, yeah, I really like it there."

"It's a pretty fancy place. A little rich for me, but it seems worth it."

"It definitely is. They're very spacious and mine has a great view of the city."

"Well, there you go," she comments agreeably.

"What about you?"

"I've got a place down on Amberly. It's nice enough and manageable when splitting the rent, but I've also been looking at condos and even some houses outside of the city."

"Wow, looking to settle down then?"

"At my own pace, but yeah. It's exciting, but I'm not rushing into anything."

"That's great!"

"This one," she directs me as we come up to one of the floors in the garage.

I step through and let her take the lead. She brings us up to a forest green Priat 270, a mini cooper, hybrid car.

"This new?" I ask. It's probably a stupid question given how much time it's been since I saw her previous vehicle.

"Almost a year old now. You can toss those in the back seat if you want." She places her bags behind the driver seat so I open the door on the other side and place mine back there as well.

We hop in and she starts the car up. I'd forgotten how little noise these things make. It kind of throws me off since I'm so used to driving in a Wercedes. I'd almost swear this car wasn't even running as we pull out of the parking spot and roll down to the exit. There's some popular light rock playing on low volume. It's not generally my type of music, but it does put me at ease in this moment. There's something so earnest and honest about Fredryk Shiiren's voice that feels appropriate to the current mood.

"I shouldn't have put you on the spot back in the store," Julie confesses. "How are you, really?"

"I'm fine." I do my best to sound sincere, but I end up sounding resentful instead.

She snorts at the response. "Even if that was at all convincing, I can take one look at you and tell that you've got some stuff going on."

"Would you like to be my therapist now?" I mock her.

"Do you need one?" she responds patiently.

"What would you say if I told you I'm not sure yet."

"I'd say you should give it a try. Make sure you do your research on a good person to go to first, but give it a try. I'd also say that you have a good group of people who care about you and would be happy to help you if they knew you needed it."

I'm grateful that she plays along with my game of hypothetical questions/statements, but I'm not sure I agree with her advice.

"My problems don't need to be other people's problems," I argue.

"It's not about making your problems other people's problems, it's just about being honest with them when you're struggling. Your friends will want to help you if they can. If you never give them the chance then they'll feel shut out and unwanted."

"You know that's not what I'm trying to do to them…"

"I do, but the point stands."

We break from the conversation so that Julie can pay off her ticket at the terminal. The arm swings up and Julie drives forward, rolling up her window.

"I wasn't expecting to get lectured." I mope, looking out the window.

"Well, I wasn't expecting to find you wearing wrinkled up club clothes, smelling like alcohol and sweat, with bloodshot eyes, matted hair, and clammy skin when you don't even seem *that* hungover."

I flip down the sun visor and pull the mirror covering aside. After a few seconds of examining the clearly unwell face staring back at me, I reply, "Fair enough."

"So, what do have going on, then?"

"It's just stress, you know."

As my luck—or lack thereof—would have it, traffic comes to a stop in front of a light. She seizes the opportunity to shoot me a scornful look.

"Things okay at work? With David? I'm sure that relationship has been tough."

"I think I might have been cruel to him ever since he got promoted. He's been a good boss and I realize now that he never stopped being a good friend, but I've been treating him like an enemy."

"Have you told him you're sorry? It sounds like you feel bad about it."

"I'm not sure how to do that in a way that isn't weird."

Julie nods and then turns to face forward as traffic resumes with the changing of the light. "David's a straightforward guy. I'm sure you can just tell him what you told me—get it all off your chest."

"You're probably right."

"He mentioned you guys had a tight deadline to meet when I saw him. Sounds like there was a lot of emergency stuff to do after you guys got your product out there. How are you doing with that?"

"It's been rough," I admit. "David gave me some time off though. It was kind of a forced thing, so I bit his head off for it."

"Sounds like the poor guy is taking a beating." She doesn't sound judgmental or passive aggressive—that's not really her style anyway—but the words still weigh into me.

"Something else to apologize for, I guess."

"How about you and Kayla, I heard you guys were still going strong and all that."

"Going… maybe not so strong, though."

Julie looks at me with a sidelong glance. "I'm sorry to hear that."

I'm not sure, but she sounds genuinely saddened by this which is rather un-ex-like of her, though not so out of character I suppose.

"Yeah, it's just that I'm wondering if maybe it's not right. Maybe I need something different. I mean, I'm not trying to say I'm just bored or that I want something new. I think I just feel like she doesn't care about me like she should. I've got all this stuff going on and I don't think she knows about any of it. I don't know if she cares to know."

Julie remains quiet for an uncomfortably long time. I half expected her to jump right on board with bashing Kayla.

Instead she says, "I obviously don't know Kayla at all. I've heard things from others, but I don't know what the right answer is for you here. At the risk of you getting the wrong idea, I'd just say that if she isn't good for you or she's not supportive of you, then maybe you should consider bringing it up with her and maybe even cut things off if that doesn't get you anywhere. If you don't feel like she wants you to be open with her or it seems like the relationship is always about her, then that's not healthy. Again, I don't know the situation. I can't tell you what the right thing to do is. All I can say is that you deserve someone who will be there for you, especially when things get hard."

I nod slowly and repeatedly. I suppose Julie isn't saying anything I haven't already thought myself. I don't feel like she's being vicious or trying to sabotage my happiness. In fact, it's surprisingly validating to hear her saying these things to me and I'm grateful for her honesty, so I should probably tell her that.

"Thank you," I say at last. "It's been hard for me to sort through what I should do. I guess I'm afraid that I'll miss her and all the good stuff we have, you know?"

"I do and you will. That's what makes this kind of thing so difficult. You'll want to be really sure before you make a call to break things off because you will feel lonely once it's done."

I get a nauseous sensation in my stomach once I realize that she's talking from experience. "Can I ask you a question that's maybe not okay to ask?"

"You want to know how I knew when to break up with you?" Her tone is even, like she expected the question.

"Yeah…" is all I can say in reply. I turn my eyes down to where I have my hands folded over my lap, rubbing the inside of a palm with my thumb.

"I felt like we were stuck for a while. Things felt good for a time, but I was ready for more and the relationship wasn't."

"You mean I wasn't?"

"Not necessarily. Some of it had to do with how comfortable I felt coming to you with the more serious, less fun stuff. Some of it had to do with how I wanted more, but you seemed happy with the status quo."

"But some of it did come down to who I am and what I brought to the relationship?" I know she's trying to shelter me from further mental distress, but what I really need now is the truth, however hurtful it may be.

"Some of it could certainly be attributed to that, yes."

We're getting closer to my street now, so I feel pressured to get some hard answers from her on this.

Cutting to the chase, I ask her, "If you had to sum it all up, what did it ultimately come down to?"

"Bryan, I don't think it's totally necessary for you to hear that. Not right now, at least."

"I really think it would help me, even if it's not super nice."

She takes a deep breath. I can see by the way she's gripping the steering wheel that she's searching for what to say.

"Just phrase it the way it comes to mind. I don't need the sweetened version."

"I guess ... I guess I just got tired of waiting for you to become the man I knew you could be. For all the fun we had, it felt like there would always be something missing and I worried that we'd never mature as a couple."

The words definitely sting, but there's a truth to them that I find reassuring.

She shakily continues, "Maybe I should have had different expectations. It was probably wrong for me to go into a relationship with the hope that you would turn out a certain way."

"Yeah, you were so in the wrong for wanting your boyfriend to be a good man." I tease, though the joke comes out a bit weepy.

"That's not what I was saying. You are a good man."

"I know, I'm not sure where that came from..."

"Well, maybe you've been tearing yourself down without realizing. Just because you weren't right for me doesn't mean you weren't a great guy still. I would never be that harsh on you and you shouldn't think about yourself that way either."

"It's just that lately, I'm realizing that I'm not the person I thought I was."

"I'm not sure what you mean by that," she replies, turning into the garage of my building.

"I never realized I had so much wrong with me before. I didn't know I'd let so many people down."

Julie remains silent until we've pulled into a spot. She turns to regard me with bright eyes and a somber expression.

"Look, I don't know what you've been going through exactly. I also don't know what to say to you to help with whatever's eating away at you. All I know is that we all have our issues, and a lot of the time those can sneak up on us." She pauses to let me think on that as she puts her hand on my shoulder. "It sounds like you're waking up to some things about yourself that you don't like— maybe some things that should be changed. While I get that you're probably overwhelmed by whatever you're discovering, I promise it's not worth hating yourself over it."

"I'm sorry," I say, unable to look at her.

"For what?"

"We haven't talked in years and I made this the most depressing conversation possible. There is no reason that you of all people should have to listen to this."

"What does that mean?" She sounds a little offended.

"Just that we're not together anymore and unless I'm missing something, we're not getting a second chance at things. I'm sure the long list of all your ex's issues is the last thing you wanted to listen to today."

"Just because it's over for us, that doesn't mean I suddenly don't care about you anymore. I think you needed someone to hear you out and give you some advice. I'm happy I found you in time to be there for you."

I can't help but laugh. "You're a much better person than I'll ever be."

"We all have room to grow," she offers.

"How do you always make it look so easy, though?"

"What do I make look easy?" there's a note of amusement in her tone.

"Everything…"

She giggles as though I've said something funny. She does get that I'm dead serious, right?

"Nothing is ever easy," she explains. "That's especially true when it comes to changing something about yourself or how you're living your life. That's the hardest thing in the world. The only thing I can say is that it helps to move forward with as much clarity of purpose as your able to and as few regrets as you can manage."

"Do you have *any* regrets?"

"Yes. I regret that I didn't tell you that I'd always love you the night I broke up with you. I also should have reached out after you blew up at Kevin. I knew you were hurting or at least in a bad place, but you were already dating Kayla and I was afraid you would think I was just coming in to try to ruin that for you."

"In your defense, it sounds like I wasn't the most reasonable person at the time so that seems like a conclusion I'd probably have jumped to."

I finally look up and face her. She's wearing an encouraging smile and there's a kindly softness in the way she looks at me. I don't find her gaze intimidating nor her presence so overwhelming. It's as if I'm somehow seeing her for the first time.

"I'm here for you now, if you ever need anything," she tells me.

"Thank you, I'm glad you found me today at least."

"Me too." She removes her hand from shoulder and wipes a tear that's spilled down the side of my face. It's then that I notice the diamond ring on her finger.

"You're engaged now, huh?"

"Yeah," she replies, pulling her hand back to look upon the ring, "about two weeks ago now."

"That's great," I say with sincere happiness for her. "I hope he's everything you deserve."

"Everything and more," a pride-filled smile stretches across her lips. "I hope you're able to figure everything out that you have going on, just remember that you only have to do it alone if you choose to."

"I'll work on letting people in," I promise. "I think I know what I need to do next now. Maybe we can stay in touch this time?"

"I'd like that."

I start to open the door, then turn back to her and add, "I never stopped loving you either, you know."

"It's really good to hear that." She's choked up along with me now.

"Goodbye, Julie."

"Goodbye, Bryan."

With that, I push the door open and step out of the car and head to the elevator. I wave as Julie pulls out of her spot and starts to drive away. She returns it with a glowing expression. Even when she's gone from sight, I can't help but feel like I've found some long-lost part of myself. Or maybe it's a part of me that's brand new. Either way, it feels good to have it. Before I forget, I pull out my phone and send Kayla a text.

"HEY, CAN U MEET ME @ RYEWAY FOR DINNER?"

After I get into the elevator, I receive, "RYEWAY? THE ONE IN THE MALL?"

"YEAH, DOES 630 WORK?" I return.

I don't receive a reply until I've arrived on my floor. "SURE, IF THAT'S WHAT YOU WANT."

Obviously, that's code for "pick a better, more high-brow place," but I'm not going to play that game.

I send back, "GREAT, SEE YOU THERE!"

This is certainly a dick move, but this needs to happen at a place like RyeWay. Kayla and I need to have a serious talk and some not-snotty witnesses would be good.

# Chapter 3

I spend the rest of the afternoon trying to revitalize myself. This effort starts with a shower and a shave even though I've barley grown any stubble. Once I have the filth of last night cleansed from me, I get dressed in a casual, but classy, dark khaki and collared shirt combo topped off with leather shoes and a watch. I think I'm going to break up with Kayla tonight so maybe how I look is irrelevant, but I'd still like to look nice for her. It's the least I can do if I really do go through with this. With that thought in mind, I style my hair so that it sweeps to one side. I still have bloodshot eyes and a pasty complexion so next I decide to get a protein shake in me and hydrate with water and ginger ale. By the time I have to leave, I look mostly like a normal, functioning human being.

I decide to take the metro to the mall so that I don't have to be alone while I think through what I want to do and how I want to do it. The idea of breaking things off scares the hell out of me. Kayla pulled me out of what could have been a dark place in my life and I'm grateful for that. Things have been good too. It's just that when I'm with Kayla, I don't feel supported. At best, I'm distracted. The more I think about what Julie said to me, the more I realize that I can't picture us getting married, buying a home, having a kid. The part that tears me up is that plenty of couples still find happiness without some or even all of that. I'm not sure I really need a house or a kid. Maybe I could be perfectly happy with her in a nice apartment with a pet chinchilla or something. These thoughts start to make me sweat so I take a break to observe the people around me. There's an adorable, elderly Asian couple sitting across from me, reading a newspaper together. Down the car is a younger guy standing with his bike, but he's dressed nicely and I think I can smell his cologne from here so I'm guessing he's got a hot date or some sweet party across town. He'll learn to take it easy on the smells eventually. A middle-aged Black woman with a very large tote slung over her shoulder sits to my left while a couple Latino kids are bickering about which of them is better at some video game to my right.

I look down at my hands and realize that we're all here with our own stories—our own destinations. At some point, we all need to step off of this train. Some of us will get off together, others will step off on their own. I'll never know how cologne dude's night goes or which friend will best the other at their game. They'll be out of my life forever and that's fine, I don't really know them after all. I just can't decide if I'm ready to get off at a different stop from Kayla. Am I really ready for her story to separate from mine? Maybe I don't have to follow through with this, at least not tonight. Julie said I should be sure of myself, but I have no idea how I could possibly be sure about something like this. Maybe I don't need to go in with any kind of special plan or objective. I'll see how things go once I'm there. If my gut tells me to follow through with the breakup, then I'll do that. If I'm not ready, then I'll step back and give it some more thought. In spite of this resolution, my stomach is still all twisted up when my time comes to get off the train and start walking to the mall.

It's six thirty by the time I enter into the sparkling white interior of the building. By the time I've ascended the elevator and crossed the skybridge over to one of the eight food courts, it's closer to six-forty. I find Kayla at one of the tables. She's busying herself with her phone, but also tapping her foot in the air. She uncrosses her legs and puts her phone against the table once she sees me coming up to her.

"It's about—" She blinks for a second before exclaiming, "Wow, you look good."

"Thanks," I reply, feeling my cheeks redden at the compliment. I can't remember the last time she said that to me—or *if* she's ever really said that to me.

"Right, well you're also late to the ball, Prince Charming, so I grabbed us a table. How about you go up and order us something."

"Do you know what you want?"

"Just their Greek Salad is fine."

"You sure? Those are pre-packaged, they make the sandwiches fresh."

She makes a scrunched-up face before replying, "That's fine, babe. Honestly, I'm thinking we just get something quick so we can do something after."

"Alright…"

I leave her to get in line. When I look back, she's happily tapping away at her phone. I get that this isn't really her spot of choice, but she could still be a little happier to be here. So far as she knows, this is still a date. I feel like half of me is looking for reasons to end it all here, but the other obviously wants excuses not to. It's all very confusing and my mind reels with both until I make it to the front of the line where I order a Turkey Havarti along with her salad and two waters. It's hard for me to go back to the table. My feet get heavier with each step. Kayla is still typing when I sit down and place our food between us. Since I'm hungry, I start without her. I know it's rude, but so is being absorbed in your phone while people are trying to share a meal with you.

"Everything okay there?" I ask after a few minutes.

"Oh, yeah, sorry, Bry," she replies, putting her phone down and popping the plastic top off of her salad bowl. "Craig was just telling me about where he ended up last night. That guy is crazy, I love it!"

"He's definitely something else," I agree, hoping we can move onto another topic.

"Annie and Laurie told me about a bunch of other crazy stuff that happened after we left. Apparently this one guy tried to hit on them by showing them magic tricks, but he was either so drunk or so bad, he botched every single one. He also had a weird name, something Biblical like Job, maybe.

"Is that your way of reminding me I should feel bad for what happened?"

She hesitates. I've probably never called her out like this before. But really, why else would she be bringing this crap up, it's not like the story of Job, the terrible magician is all that funny on its own. Sounds like a "you had to be there" kind of a joke and we weren't there so…

"No, I'm just saying…" Nice recovery, Kayla, real nice.

"Right, well again, I guess I'm sorry my distress ruined your fun…" I return to my sandwich even though I'm starting to lose my appetite.

"Yep, here we go again, like do you even hear yourself.

Don't you think you're being just a little bit dramatic?" She plunges her fork into the salad and cocks an eyebrow at me.

"What I think is that you could have started the conversation by asking me how it went with the doctor rather than telling me all about the great fun everyone had after I left in an ambulance."

"I don't need to ask because I know how it went. You're fine, I asked him three times while we were there and he told me the same thing all three times."

"Am I though?" I don't snap or take a bitter tone with her. My question is asked in earnest. I really do want to know if she truly thinks I'm alright.

"I guess I'm confused now…" she admits. "Yeah, you've been weird and grumpy. I mean are you stressed? Are you still feeling sick? I really don't know. You were normal one day and then all angsty and disagreeable the next."

"Maybe I've been going through some stuff and maybe you haven't exactly been there for me through it."

"Is that what this is all about? You can talk to me about anything."

"I didn't think you wanted to hear it," I tell her.

This could be it. This could be where we come to an understanding. I feel so much lighter to just say this stuff out loud.

"Well I mean no one *wants* to hear about stuff that's got other people down, obviously, but we're together so I'll obviously listen if there's something you want to tell me."

My heart sinks at her response. Julie's words rattle through my brain, *"Your friends will want to help if they can."* It sounds like Kayla doesn't *want* to do that at all. She will listen and possibly help out of a sense of relationship-duty, but that's not what I want from her. She shouldn't feel obligated to support me, she should want to do it, otherwise, what the hell is the point of this? Maybe this sums up everything that's wrong with us. It's easy to have fun with someone, it's hard to share in their hurt. That takes effort. Or maybe that takes a special kind of desire, one that needs to be real.

"Is there something you want to tell me about then?" she interrupts my thoughts and takes a bite of her salad.

"I'd like to ride the Ferris wheel after this."

"What?" she gasps with her mouth full.

"You know, the one in the middle of this place."

"Yeah, I know what you're talking about, but there's no way I'm getting on that with you. That's for kids and teenagers trying to find a spot to make out for the first time."

"It's also a good place to talk, privately."

"Alright, that's weird. Whatever you want to say, just say it. It's so loud in here, like no one is gonna hear you."

Here she is even ruining my breakup plan. I guess it's clear to me that I have to do this after all. I half-expected her to shut me down, that's why I picked this place. It's public enough where I hope she won't blow her top, but also has a random enough crowd that neither of us will be too embarrassed if she does freak out.

"Fine, this isn't working," I blurt out.

"*What's* not working?" Kayla gives me a narrow, measured look as though to warn me to choose my next words with care.

"We're not working," I counter, keeping my voice steady and my gaze firmly set.

I can see her face darken almost instantly. "Don't you dare do this…" she hisses. "If you do this now, you'll regret it forever."

"If not now, then when? How far do you see this going?"

"I don't know." She puts both hands on the little round table between us and leans in. "All I know is that I never saw it ending."

The way her eyes mist over makes me wonder if she's going to cry. I really don't want her to cry, but I also can't blame her if she does. This is clearly something she wasn't expecting.

"We're stuck," I try to explain. "We're not there for each other in the right ways, I don't think we really even have any idea what's going on in each other's lives. While we've never been disloyal to each other, I don't feel like there's any sense of commitment either. I mean were we ever going to move in together or were we just keep doing our own thing?"

"Really?" Kayla leans back in her seat with eyebrows raised and eyes widened. "You're gonna bitch at me about commitment? Did you ever give me a key to your place? No. Did you put a ring on my finger? No. Hell, did you even Ogle engagement rings? I'm guessing not."

"Kayla—" I try to interject.

"Uh-uh!" she stops me with a finger held up. "Now, I've

301

been fine like this, okay. I could probably grow old with you like this. For some reason, you've suddenly decided that everything we have isn't enough. *You* are the one that needs things to change."

"I know," I say softly.

Just this morning I re-lived this happening to me, I get her anger and she's not wrong about any of it. Suddenly I'm scared I've already ruined this. I'm not Julie, I can't just say all the right things, in the right way, at the right time. What if I hurt Kayla more than I have to?

"I also get that this seems sudden, but it's not. I think it's been a long time coming, I just didn't know how to reach out—or *if* I should reach out. I still don't see how it can be fixed."

"*What* needs to be fixed?" Kayla raises her voice a little and smacks a hand down against the table. I think that draws some eyes and ears, but I try to ignore that.

"We're not good for each other..."

"Look, there is nothing wrong with us and there is nothing wrong with what we have."

Kayla's eyes swell up, but she manages to keep them from bursting. Her voice softens into a pleading tone—she's probably figured out that the more aggressive approach isn't going to sway me.

"Did you know David is my boss now?"

She freezes up, "No, is that why you've been so messed up all week?"

"That happened six months ago, so no. This week has been... other stuff."

"Well, why didn't you tell me?" Her lips quiver and I get chills at seeing things finally click for her.

I'd like to stop now, but I feel the need to finish it. "Why don't you ever ask about my work? I hear about yours all the time, but I really don't know that you've ever shown an interest in mine."

"I thought you liked to leave work at work, I mean you never really *tried* to bring it up."

"You might be right so some extent about that, but maybe it's more about you caring to ask than me actually talking about it."

"This is such bullshit..." Moisture begins to trickle down from her eyes. "You think I don't care?"

"I guess I've never really been sure. It's always about the next dinner, or the club of the weekend, or this show, or that friend I swear I've never heard of before. I'm not actually trying to put this all on you though. We've both got a lot of issues and I think that we might be feeding into each other's faults because that feels better than dealing with them. At best, we're holding each other back from growing. At worst, we're dragging each other down."

"What am I even supposed to say to this?" Kayla's eyes are fire and water all at once. "I think you're just bitching because your bored with me and you've come up with a hundred excuses to make it seem like something else so you can pretend that you aren't like every other guy who's made a girl fall in love with him only to fly away when you're done with her like some sick, sexual Peter Pan."

"That's *not* what this is."

If we've reached a point where she's throwing words like daggers, then I don't think there's much longer that she can remain calm or even remotely reasonable. I need to wrap things up before one of us has an outburst.

"I'm sorry," I say, nearly shuddering under her burning hot glare. "I need to move on. I need to move forward. In some ways, I guess I need to move backwards too."

"Don't you dare leave me, Bryan Daley!" Her volume is definitely audible to those around us now. "Not like this. If you do this, I will never take you back. You'll beg me for a second chance, but I'll make you live in regret for the rest of your life."

I rise up from my seat, almost crying, but I force myself to maintain my eye contact with her. "I'm sorry I hurt you, Kayla. In my head, I did this differently—I did it better. *That* is what I'll always regret. I don't think we'll ever talk again so I wish you nothing but the best."

"The fuck you do! Sit down!"

"Goodbye, Kayla, I really do love you, I think I always will, that's why I'm so sorry." With that, I turn and walk away, trying to keep a steady pace rather than bolt even though there's a solid chance she'll pounce on me.

"Get back here you fucking asshole!" she calls after me, I think she stands up since I hear a chair slide backward. "Bryan!"

I stay in stride until I'm out of the food court and walking along one of the main strips. I dry my eyes with the cuffs of my shirt, but I don't look back and I don't second guess myself. I only hope this decision pays off the way I hope it will. I come up near the skybridge and merge into the flow of people marching across it. For one blessed moment, I can feel this sense of peace and purpose wash over me. It's so intense I even take one extra-long blink to soak it all in. Once I open my eyes though, I see a weird shimmering in the glass wall that's rushing toward me. At first, it just looks like a ripple of color reflecting off the surface, but it takes shape as it closes in. I think it's Shirun. He walks past me, looking me dead in the eye with those unnaturally blue irises. It's like he's looking into my world from one behind the glass.

Our paths cross for only a moment, but that gives him enough time to say, "Run, it isn't safe here."

I stop short and twist around, but he's gone when I look back. Instead, all I see are the annoyed faces of people who need to swerve around me. When I face forward again, I see bulky shadow figures that should cause a mall-wide panic. They're lurking on the other side of the skybridge, waiting for me to wander into their clutches. *Not this again!* Someone walking in the opposite direction grabs me by the arm and tears me along with them. When I look to my right, I see that it's my mystery stalker woman that's clutching me by the bicep with surprising force.

"What are you doing here?" I demand under my breath.

She shoots me a defiant glare and replies, "I'm saving your dumb ass, what does it look like?"

I have nothing to say back to that. After all the mystery and suspense surrounding this woman, I guess I never expected her to say something so crass. She also looks way more normal tonight, at least so far as her dress goes. She's in jeans and a white designer sweater with her thick hair swinging in a ponytail. I feel helpless to resist her as she pulls me forward to an unknown destination. I do mean literally helpless too—I barely even imbalance her when I try to pull my arm free. She doesn't even bother to tell me to cooperate with her, she just ushers me along with unyielding conviction. She starts to push through the people walking in front of us too. I find some relief in all the nasty looks people give her as we part through the traffic stream. At least they can see her. At least I have some indication that I'm maybe not crazy.

"Where are you taking me?"

"Out of here, obviously," she retorts.

We're almost back on the other side of the sky bridge when I see more of the shadowy people come into focus amid the mass of people who don't even notice them. The whole mall dims down oppressively like it's trying to close down on us—on me.

"What are those? What's going on?" I try to keep my voice down, but it's hard to control.

"They're darkness." She gets us off the bridge and curls away from where our hunters lurk. "They're here for you."

All around us, new shadow people appear and start to chase us as we quicken our pace.

"I shouldn't fight them here, we need to move."

She shoves me forward into an empty elevator shaped like a glass tube. We ride it down to the main floor of the mall as light fades and there somehow seems to be less people walking around below. In their absence, more of the shadows stalk the ground floor. They're all looking up at us, stalking toward where we'll be coming out.

"How are we supposed to get out of here with all of them down there?"

"You need to trust me..." There's a blue flame behind her eyes as she looks at me. She finally releases my arm and adds, "I will keep them distracted, you just need to get outside."

"Who are you?" I know this is a dumb time to ask something like this, but how can I trust her if I don't even know who she is?

"I'm your fairy godmother—the fuck does it matter? Just listen to what I'm telling you."

"I know you helped me at the club, but do you expect me to trust you without knowing who you are or what you really want?"

"I expect you to get your ass out of here. Think you can handle that—actually don't answer, just get ready. Lord, why are men such basic creatures?"

Right as she's finished her huffing and puffing, the elevator door opens with a swoosh. She puts a hand on my back and pushes me out. We break into a full sprint for the door, but our attackers screech and rush to cut us off. My mystery protector suddenly flips over my head and brings a glowing fist down into one of the creatures. It barely falls into black steam before she snatches another one up by the throat and squeezes it to ash. She spins about and back kicks a third through the air. It doesn't melt apart, but it does crash into one of the monsters blocking my path.

"I'll find you outside," she calls once I'm past her. "Just get into the open and you'll be alri—" her words fall off as the distance between us grows and the screeching of our shadow hunters intensifies.

I think I see a weapon of some sort start to materialize in her hand as I turn my attention to the exit. I wonder if there are still any people around to watch this happen or if the whole place has somehow been transfigured into some kind of nightmare mall. The main entrance is within reach now so I put all of my energy into one last burst toward the door. I barrel through it, getting some funny looks once I'm on the sidewalk. A teenage couple shoot me a particularly scornful glance as they head in. I want to tell them not to go in there, but when I look through the door, the mall is bright and safe and filled with non-monstrous people again. Was that a full-blown hallucination back there or did something weird really just happen? Either way, I need to leave and I'm not going to wait for my mystery woman with an attitude. For all I know, trouble may just be following her. There's a cab available right in front of me so I take advantage of that rare convenience and hop in.

"Spyre Apartments, Covington Avenue, please," I tell the driver, finding that I'm out of breath.

Fortunately, this driver doesn't seem interested in judging me. He just says, "Sure," keeping his eyes forward and wasting no time to get moving.

Looking out the side window, I see my alleged protector pop out of the mall entrance and look around for me. Her eyes snap onto my cab and she yells after me with her arms thrown in the air—I think that makes two women in one night that I've left like that. I do feel sort of bad for ditching her, but I'm trying to leave crazy behind, not bring it home with me. My heart races the whole ride home. I almost forget to pay after the cab pulls up to my building. Fortunately, the driver still takes no interest in my ridiculous behavior.

Once out, I make a beeline for my apartment, trying not to look at anyone and waste any time with getting home and hidden from whatever's out to get me. After I explode through my door and lock it up tight, I pull the sleeping pills out of the BestAid bag I left on my table. I find a glass and get myself some water to swallow the pills down with. With that done, I head straight upstairs. These pills are my last hope at solving this through ordinary means. I don't want to think about what I need to do if these don't work, I really hope that they do. Although, I'm also getting myself psyched up for another night in the manor regardless of how much I'd like to cut that narrative short. As I undress and crawl into bed, I figure that whatever comes will come. I've done my job, here's hoping the pills do the rest. The effects aren't instant, but before I know it, I do feel myself falling into sleep's embrace. It's a steady, sinking feeling that lulls me down until I'm plunged into the black.

# Chapter 4

I come into consciousness with a groan. When my eyes pop open, I find that I'm lying on my stomach against a wooden floor. I curl my back up and try to slide my legs beneath me, but I feel so sluggish that I sort of get stuck with my ass up in the air. After a couple of blinks, the sheen of the flooring and the soft white cuffs of my shirt tell me that I made it to the manor after all. I growl in defeat at this revelation, but then a firm hand on my back makes me go dead silent. I flop down to my stomach and roll to the corner of the wall away from whoever just touched me.

"Be quiet," a man with dark skin hisses. My mind is groggy, but I realize it's Kenneth.

"Sorry…" I sound like someone who rolled out of bed way too early.

"They're everywhere," he whispers as he strides over and gives me a hand up.

He's not as strong as Myles. It takes some effort for him to lift me to my feet, but to be fair, my muscles are mush so I'm practically dead weight for him. There's still a certain vigor to how he helps me out, something that breathes a little bit of strength back into me. It's not the same as how I feel around Myles or Olivia, but it's better than being a heap on the floor.

"Come on, we need to find her." He hastens forward, forcing me to trot after him.

"Who?"

"Rachel."

"Oh, that's right, you still haven't found her?" I really do remember now as my mind clears up, but I try to cover up my lapse in memory and kind of sound like an ass in the process. "Sorry, I didn't mean it like that," I try to recover.

"No, it's alright. I'm starting to wonder if I'll ever find her. I've been searching everywhere, but what if I'm too late?" He stops by a corner and peeks around it. After he's sure it's clear, he continues, keeping his voice low. "I can't give up though, if she's still out there, I've got to get to her."

"Olivia seemed to think she could handle herself, so I'm sure she's alright. I'd say she's as good a judge of who can make it out here as one could find."

"Right you are," Kenneth agrees, the briefest grin breaking through. "But you haven't seen how they've taken this place over. Sin's minions are everywhere and I think they're rounding people up."

"Maybe they're putting together another one of those freak shows."

"Oh, I'm sure…"

"Maybe we should get caught then. We might find Rachel that way."

"Or we could discover an untimely end to our existence," he retorts.

"Well, I can't do nothing. I need to get back into the action so we can end this."

I'm not really trying to sound heroic even though this statement sounds like cheesy bravado. I need this to end so I can get my life back.

"At the very least, we should find Shirun and the other survivors, maybe they have a plan," I suggest. "Maybe Olivia's right and Rachel's been there this whole time."

Kenneth steps ahead of me and spins around to block my way. "You listen to me now. You don't need to get back into anything. You're nothing without Myles or Olivia beside you. Do you understand me? You and I can't fight anything, so let's stick to hiding and seeking instead."

Kenneth's words slam into me. I don't think he means to be cruel, but they cut deep all the same. I suppose he's not wrong. I get this sudden sensation of nakedness. It's just me and Kenneth. We don't have powers, we're not carrying weapons, and we're not wearing any armor. If anything happens, we're completely screwed. It's then that I hear a faint howling.

"Is that the storm?"

"Indeed, the calamity draws near again," he answers, but he's still sternly locked onto me.

"I get it," I break, putting my hands up. "No fighting then, let's find Shirun."

"I'm not going to Shirun." Kenneth's tone is completely flat. I think I'm only making him more distressed.

"She could be there…" I try to remind him.

"She could be anywhere."

"Fine, if she's not, then you can just go and look somewhere else."

"What do you think Mister Shirun is running up in that Observatory? I can tell you, it's not some refugee camp where you can come and go as you please. He's building an army for the end of this ordeal."

"Isn't that smart?" If Shirun really is training a small force, that makes his absence in all this a lot more forgivable.

"Perhaps, but I've got other objectives in mind."

"Point me in the right direction, then," I snap. I'm not sure if Kenneth is a coward or if he's just so selfishly obsessed with finding this Rachel that he can't see sense, but I think I'm done with him either way.

He lifts his head and snorts at me. "They'll be watching the stairs."

"I'll be alright." I'm not sure if I even believe that.

Kenneth narrows his eyes, but steps aside. He lifts a hand up in the air and opens his mouth to speak, but then something stops him cold. "Did you hear that?" he asks through a breath.

I listen for a moment and do hear a soft thud like a boot hitting the floor. A nod lets him know I hear it too. He grabs me by the shoulder and ushers me forward with him.

"Stairs it is then," he sighs.

"What if it's a friend?" I suggest, keeping my volume to a whisper.

"It's not. I didn't make it this far without learning the sound of their footsteps."

We rush down the hall with Kenneth slightly ahead of me. I'd like to trust that he'll lead us to safety, but I'm not really sure where he's taking us or if he even knows what he's looking for right now. The footsteps behind us intensify so he breaks into a light jog and I do the same, doing my best to keep each step soft. I turn my head back to see shadow people following us in a full sprint. They look a lot more like deformed people than gangly, androgynous, bipeds. They're still a shiny black silhouette of a figure with no face or identifying features to speak of—they're just either distinctly masculine or feminine in shape now. Their attire hasn't changed at all, they're still only wearing those armored gloves and boots.

"We're made, let's make haste!" Kenneth commands right before he bolts off.

I chase after him, realizing he's panicked. I don't know what else I can do, so I follow him anyway. We fly down the corridor and burst out into a foyer where more of the cretin men and women wait, crouched low like predatory cats. We sling around and clamber up a staircase to our right. I whip around the open-style railing and charge up after my companion, but he stops and I crash into him. When I look around his broad shoulders, my blood turns to ice. The hellhound from my second and third visits—the beast that had Shelly's throat for dinner and tore Margaret to shreds right in front of me—saunters down the steps in front of us. Its red eyes blaze out in apparent pleasure at our peril. We find ourselves caught between it and the cretin people who now ascend behind us at a casual pace. My eyes remain locked onto the beast. At any second, it could pounce and devour us, but it seems content to just wait there and block our escape. It watches as the dark soldiers come up and take hold of our arms. I think I even see it smile before they twist us around and lead us back down the stairs.

They drag Kenneth along in front of me into a narrow corridor. It's horrifying to think that their grip would melt our arms if not for the gloves they wear. The fact that their bodies are this volatile makes it pretty discouraging to try to struggle against their hold on us. One false thrash or pull and I could melt half of myself or at least get absorbed and have what's left of my body hijacked. I'm really not sure which would hurt more or if there's even any difference between those scenarios. We're led along in complete silence with no choice but to willingly walk to whatever fateful destination they have in mind for us this time. I expect some surreal floating fortress of death. Instead, we're just brought into a large room within the manor—a familiar room, even. The tall windows, the sparkling chandeliers, that wide stage... this is the ballroom I awoke in on my second visit. This is where it all started to go wrong.

A sick feeling forms in my stomach like a hard pit I can't digest. It thickens when I notice what's different about it. There are ten smaller platforms forming a wide semicircle around the back of the room. They're like single-person, cylindrical stages and all but two of them are occupied. The people on them are all guests. They stand tensed, staring forward to the empty main stage.

"What the devil is this?" Kenneth gasps as he starts to lightly struggle against his captors.

"Try to stay calm," I urge him right before they pull him up onto one of the empty platforms.

"What are you doing?" he groans as they arrange him there like a mannequin in a department store. "Hey, have you seen Rachel?" I hear him ask the people on either side of him, but I'm moved along before I can hear if he gets any answer, all I know is that she must not be in this room if he's asking around.

They put me onto a platform of my own. I feel like a little figurine put out on display and my sense of emotional nakedness comes back with a vengeance. Once I'm in position, my onyx captors step back behind my field of vision so I can only assume they are standing guard behind me. As much as I'd like to turn and step right off of this platform, there's a crippling dread that keeps me locked down right where I am. I can turn my head to look at the people around me, but that's the most I can manage. I don't know most of the people in this room. Even Kenneth is someone I'd hesitate to count among people in my circle of trust. He's not wearing Shirun's symbol anyway which means I can't be sure I can rely on him to have my back. He does seem more interested in finding this Rachel person than actually confronting the threat facing this place. No, there's really only one friendly face in this whole room and my heart sinks when I see him here. He looks so little standing on his platform and I imagine that he must be terrified. But it's not fear I see when Jack's eyes meet mine. There's a sadness there as vast and lonely as an utterly still sea. It's a look I don't really understand. It's not one of total defeat, but there's also not a ton of optimism there. It's like he somehow has a sense of what horrors we're about to face.

I need to get to him somehow. I need to save him from whatever's about to happen. As much as I want to move, I remain stuck here against my will. All I can do is look at him. I'm just a helpless spectator. He suddenly averts his gaze and looks to the stage. I turn there as well to see the velvet curtains part. The room somehow falls into an even deeper silence as a hooded figure steps forward from the darkness. I instantly recognize that animalistic gait—it's Sin. My blood curdles at the sight of whatever this thing is. Apparently, its dog won't be needed for whatever it has planned for us, but somehow that's of no comfort to me at all. What could be worse than that beast? Sin loosens the strings around the neck of its robe and then pulls it apart. The garment drops to the floor and Sin steps out of it without missing a stride.

What moves into the light of the stage is by far the strangest thing I've seen in here yet. Sin is entirely naked though it seems to have no genitals. Its skin is smooth and looks damp like clay. It has a relatively flat face almost like one of those Japanese cartoon characters—narrow chin and all. It comes to a point in the middle at its foxlike nose. It has big, round, yellow eyes with slitted snake pupils and large, round, cat ears. Its shoulders and chest are broad like a man, but it has a feminine waist with wide hips. Its thighs are thick like tree trunks that narrow down to a double joint around the knee and fall to wiry, claw-like toes. It also has a large, lizard tail that swishes slowly from side to side as it walks. It raises its spindly, branch-like arms and pointy, spider-leg fingers into the air once it's at the front of the stairs. Its chin tilts upward and its fierce eyes seem to flash with excitement.

"I'm so glad you could all make it," Sin bellows. Its metallic voice carries through the room even though there's no microphone. "I'm especially glad you could be here with us, Mister Daley!"

"What do you want, Sin?" I yell back without thinking.

I'm panicking and I need to stop doing that. But it's hard when this creepy, man/woman/beast/reptile/bug/bird/machine/mud monster has such an inexplicable hard on for me and my destruction.

"Sin?" it sneers. "Oh, you poor, poor child! Who encouraged you to such ignorance? Was it that vile Shirun? Did he put you up to calling me by such a base approximation of my nature? If you must call me anything at all, call me by something far more profound, something magnificent... something like

313

'Despair!'"

His incredulity catches me off-guard. A creature as powerful and bizarre as this thing actually cares about what I call it? I'm moments away from some kind of doom and this is really what Sin wants to harp on?

"Why are we here?" I repeat, deciding I give exactly zero shits about this thing's naming preferences.

"My, well that is a rather complicated question, dear Mister Daley. The answer is a bit different for each of you."

There's a silence that hangs. I roll my eyes wondering if this is all I get. I expected a supervillain-like monologue about his masterplan to kill us all in some horrifying way. I mean that's clearly what we've been rounded up for.

At last, Sin points to a man at the corner of the ballroom nearest the door. "Indigo Parsons is here because he didn't believe he could make it to Shirun's little safe haven. He skulked and hid, trusting no one he saw move by him. I, of course, knew where he was the whole time and so I had my soldiers go and snatch him up when I tired of his antics."

I look to where the man shivers and shrinks into himself on the platform. Shaggy hair falls over his face and I think he's crying.

Pointing to the next person in line, Sin bellows, "Skye Adams, what a lazy girl you are! Hoped you could just wait around for someone to save you like a damsel in distress, did you? Well look at how splendidly that worked out! Prince Charming only exists in children's tales, my dear!"

The lady starts to sob and I realize I've just made things worse for everyone. "Stop it," I yell, "That's not what I meant."

"Oh, hush now, it was an excellent question, one I am happy to answer to the fullest. Let me finish," Sin hisses.

Next up is Kenneth who's just looking at his feet now.

"Kenneth Green here simply could not stop searching for his sweet Rachel, comforting Rachel, beautiful Rachel, the woman he hopelessly pines after. That refusal to stop mindlessly searching like a nose-blind dog is what got you here."

Sin cackles sharply. The sound is enough to make my hairs stand on end. My heart aches for prompting this kind of humiliation. It's bad enough these people have all been herded up to die, now they're going to have their deepest flaws and poorest decisions picked apart and exposed for all to hear first.

"Richard Keys, yours is the dullest tale of all. You were so careless that you ran right into us—no effort even required on our part. You on the other hand, Mister Evan Bourne, you weren't hasty at all. No, you did your best to elude me with careful sneaking and well-timed moves from one hiding spot to another. You probably had no idea I was stalking you personally the whole time—giving you just enough hope to think you could actually get to safety. Bravo on your unyielding perseverance though, it was really quite impressive. If it were only my minions hunting you, I'm sure your caution would have paid off, but I couldn't let that happen, dear boy. You should feel honored that I needed to intervene in your capture."

"Please don't do this!" the next man shouts. His dress is nice, but not posh, and his hair is combed, but not styled with any product.

"My, my, Samuel Dashner, what do you have to fear? You're one of the least shameful people here, after all. You can always be counted on for an honest word or two. That's why I must tell you in all sincerity that I very much look forward to your last moments. Hopefully there will be some good, earnest begging, or screaming, or at least a solid whimper. You are here with us merely due to an unfortunate stroke of luck—wrong place at the wrong time and all that."

I cringe when Sin finally turns to me. Nothing is said. It just eyes me up and down. A smile cracks through its features, revealing sharp piranha teeth.

"Mister Daley, I look forward to seeing you come out of this alive, yet ruined. I've enjoyed this systemic destruction of everything you are—both good and bad. There's so much more fun we can have together, so don't let one of these blokes best you, alright? I have more ideas to taunt, tantalize, and torment you that I'd like to explore. I hope you do not deny me the chance."

I shiver at the thought that this is all some big, sadistic game for Sin to get off to. Screw this monster, screw it's messed up plans, and screw whatever agenda it has for us. I'm not dying here, but what did it mean by saying it hoped I'd be the one to come out of this alive? For me to live, everyone else needs to die? Is this some kind of battle royale?

Sin laughs as he turns to the two people on my left between me and Jack. "Oh my, what an utter embarrassment you two are! Leif Wekstrom, a man so fixated on always getting gratification no matter what the form and Christina George, never before have I seen so much contempt held in one's heart. What a humiliating scene it was too when we captured you!"

I realize now that neither are properly dressed. Leif stands barefoot on his platform wearing only trousers held up by crooked suspenders. Christina is in a frilly corset with lace panties and a garter to hold up her nylon stockings. She keeps her arms crossed and scowls severely.

"Poor Leif looking for comfort in all the wrong places. If Katelyn were still around, I'm sure you and she would have had a grand time. Instead you were left with this little wench who never liked you by the way. She lured you into that intimate scene only so that she could deny you that which you so pathetically sought after. In the moment of this cruelty and disappointment, we came for you. Oh, what a delicious time to spring a trap!"

We're all looking at these two as they cower from everyone's gaze, but have nowhere to hide. I'm sure being mostly undressed is bad enough, now they'll probably die in utter humiliation.

"And at last you, little Jack Flemming. You are here so I can snuff out whatever is left of your irritating light. I cannot wait to see you fizzle out and die. It'd be lovely if you could scream a little for me while you do." Jack seems unaffected by Sin's sneering, but I shiver at the thought of him getting brutally murdered.

Sin scans the room in quiet contemplation. I guess I got what I asked for. Now I even know the names and stories of people I might have to fight to the death here, so, that's great. Sin waves a hand toward the middle of the room. At this command, a number of the shadow guards step past us, each carrying armfuls of swords, knives, bows, arrows, spears, clubs, and other deadly weapons. They drop them in piles around the room's center and I suddenly see the ballroom as a gladiator arena. Everyone looks around in fear as the guards return to their posts behind us.

"In a moment, I will allow you to step off of where you now

stand," Sin explains. "When I do, you will all run for these weapons I have provided and you will kill each other until there is but one still standing. Whoever should succeed will become an honored pet of mine and be spared some of the torments of the days to come. If you should refuse to partake in this sport of blood, then you will be cut down by one of my servants. So, you see, there is really no need for scruples. Just be smart and do what you must to have a tomorrow. The odds are in no one's favor this night. Be a murderer or be dead, either way, I leave you to it, but do not fret, I shall still be watching... I am always watching."

With that, Sin turns its back to us and saunters off the stage. It snaps its fingers just as it re-enters the darkness it came from and then it disappears from our sight. I suddenly realize that I'm no longer tied down to this platform by whatever force held me here. The others discover this as well and start to step off, making a mad dash for the different weapon deposits. When I look to my side, I see that Jack steps down, but he's not even trying to get to the weapons. I sprint toward him instead of joining the frenzy. Tears well up in his eyes as he sees me coming—I hope he doesn't think I'm going to hurt him.

"Jack, I need to get you out of here," I huff as I twist around in front of him, grabbing his shoulders.

I see then that his blue vest—which almost looks like it's made of cloth chainmail—has Shirun's symbol embroidered on its right chest pocket. The sight of this symbol fills me with hope that there might actually be a way out of this. Sure enough, he reaches into his pant pocket and withdraws something with a golden glow.

"Shirun says that tonight, the hands of time are on our side." He offers me the trinket with a sparkle in his gaze.

My brow furrows as I receive the same pocket watch that Shirun used on my fourth visit here. "No, Jack what are we supposed to do with this? We're not fighting goo monsters, we're fighting..." I look back to see everyone else fumbling to snatch up a weapon. "...each other."

Skye takes up a loaded crossbow and aims it at Kenneth as he grabs a curved sword. He barely looks her way when the bolt plunges through his chest. He drops to the floor before I can even shout anything. Indigo arrives late to the pile that Richard draws a rapier from. Trying to seize the advantage, he leaps toward Indigo who barely picks up a short sword in time to deflect the blow. The clang of steel and whooshing of arrows fills the room.

"You need to set them free!" Jack yells, grabbing the collar of my shirt. "The hands of time are on our side, but you have to set them free…"

I tear away, horror gripping at my heart. "What does that mean?" I scream at the watch, cupping it in the palm of my hand.

Richard leaps forward for another blow, but Indigo falls onto his back. He at least has the sense to keep his sword held up. The blade pierces Richard's torso as he falls upon the tawny man. I know I have to stop this, but I don't know how. I can't clear my head and although I know Jack is talking to me, I can't make out his words. When I look back at the watch, I think I see the vague reflection of a woman's face in the polish of the watch's casing.

"Smash it, you idiot!" The words echo through my head and then the reflection disappears.

"Set them free," I repeat.

I put an arm out to push Jack back and then wind up. I whip the timepiece down with as much force as I can. On impact, it shatters like glass into tiny pieces. Rays of light shoot out from the wreckage followed by golden pins, plates, and cogs that pour out in far greater size than what could have possibly fit inside such a small device. They burst and fizzle out like fireworks in the air above us as two black, sword-like objects fling up in front of me. I reach out and grab them by the only section that could pass for handles. I suppose these are the hands of time—a bit more literal than I anticipated, but still cool. Tonight, they are our secret weapon.

I look around the room to see that's it's bathed in a heavenly light. Better yet, everyone except Jack and I are frozen in place. People stand mind-swig, mid-aim, or mid-escape. I can see now how close I stood to failing.

"The hands of time are fickle," Jack warns me. Gripping my arm, he adds, "We have to hurry."

I'm about to ask why when I realize the storm still rages outside. A sharp snarling resounds from behind us. We turn to see ten guards bending low, ready to charge upon us. I take one peek behind me to find the remains of the pocket watch are still glowing in a bright orb of white light. That same ivory radiance shines off of my ebony blades suggesting they will be enough to win this fight.

"Time to work," I agree, handing Jack the hour hand.

He swings the blade with an alarmingly confident grin. "One last time together then, old friend of mine," he whispers to it.

Without any more posturing, Jack sprints straight to where our enemies stand. I chase after him, but he moves so fast. With little effort demonstrated, he dips down and launches into the air. He sails across the room as though he's as light as a feather. A trail of light drags behind his sword as he slashes down a cretin warrior that leaps up to meet him. He lands as easily as he leapt, twirls away from a guard that tries to tackle him, and slashes another nearby soldier down before it can even react to his assault.

Two of the monsters vault toward me. I fall to my knee, skidding across the floor beneath the grabbing fingers of one of my assailants. I sweep my weapon up and cut off the thing's legs above his knees. He tumbles down and gropes around in a vain attempt to get away before I rush over and drive the minute hand through his back. My second attacker takes a leap away from me and I realize that I wasn't his target. He's going after the weapons! Looking up, I see the other five guards soaring over my head. It appears as though Jack managed to finish off that one that tried to tackle him at least. He lands beside me with his blade held aloft.

"Good work, keep it up," He encourages me.

"Yeah… You too," I tell him though he probably deserves a bit more praise than that since he's taken down three times as many of these guys as I have.

It's strange how much he seems to enjoy this. I want to ask who or what he really is, but I guess now's not really the time for that.

His eyes widen at me in sympathy. "Here, this will help you for a bit…" he says with a hand on his chest.

A white sparkle surrounds his index and middle fingers. He pulls it away from his heart and places it against mine. There's a spark and then a sudden lightness that comes over me. The sensation made me feel rejuvenated, maybe even revitalized.

"That's incredible," I gasp, as though re-learning how to breathe.

"I'm pretty underrated," Jack replies in a much slyer tone than I imagined him capable of. "Time to finish up," he announces before taking off again.

I chase after him, able to more closely follow his pace this time. It's like I'm somehow a hundred pounds lighter, yet no less strong. I can barely feel my feet connect with the ground as I step. It's a good thing, too, because the six cretin people are all holding weapons now and some of them are eyeing the frozen guests. One armed with a bow and arrow aims to pick off Jack. She looses her shot, but Jack takes to the air as whimsically as Peter Pan might. The arrow whizzes beneath him and sears past me. Jack lands with one foot on Samuel's shoulder. He pushes off with basically nothing but his toes and returns to the air in time to evade another projectile. This time, he somersaults through the air and cleaves the bow in two as his attacker raises it in defense. I see him land, spin around, and run the she-cretin through out of the corner of my eye as I set my sights on a target of my own.

Up ahead there's a guard about to take a swing at Evan who's stuck standing wide with his spear pointing forward. It's time to put Jack's gift to the test so I dip down and leap forward, praying I won't fall on my face. Fortunately, I rocket through the air. It's a little dizzying at first, but I soon steady myself and hold the minute hand out to the side. The monster never even looks my way as I sail up and lop his head off before he can land a blow against Evan. I even manage to stick a graceful landing that somehow doesn't blow out my knees. A nearby cretin takes notice of my newfound agility and turns away from Leif to confront me.

She bounds forward, holding and impressively large bastard sword above her head. I guess I'll find out just how durable this hand of time is. The guard swings her weapon down on me with all the brutality of a Viking warrior. I chop upward to meet the strike and my eyes widen as it shatters that massive blade as though it were made of glass. I sidestep my enemy as she stumbles forward and then twist my weapon in my grip so that it points backwards. I don't even look when I drive it behind me, but I do feel the hand sink into its target.

When I look to the side, I see Jack decimate a guard's pike as it's thrust at him. He backflips away as a second cretin smashes his spiked club against where the boy just stood. Filled with the thrilling knowledge that we've almost won this impossible fight, I dart toward the conflict and take a spritely leap up through the air. I arrive right behind Jack and stand back to back with him.

"Take us home, Jack," I huff although I'm not really feeling all that winded—just amped up.

I can hear him giggling boyishly behind me as the two cretins come forward for a second round. Jack vaults over my head as the one with a club attempts its attack a second time. Maybe Jack is worried about getting hit with a stray spike or maybe he's just messing with this guy. The former spear wielder picks up one of those weapons that's like a sword on a stick—I can never remember what they're called. It takes a nice stab at me which I expertly curl around. I chop the sword part off of the stick part before he can pull it back. Jack steps out from beneath my armpit and rushes forward, kicking the remains of the cretin's weapon as he holds it up in front of him like a staff. The stick breaks in two, its splintered middle sections driving into the shadow man's abdomen. It lets out a pain-filled shriek that chills me to my bones, but doesn't slow Jack down. He leaps up and over the cretin with the club as I step away from its swing. Our attacker whips around in an attempt to whack Jack, but the boy flicks the hour hand up in front of him with a carefree precision. The cretin's club arm falls to the floor and fizzles apart. As he twists to the ground with a reverberating hiss, I waste no time in plunging my blade down into his chest. Jack front flips, over me and drives his blade into the back of the cretin's skull that he just impaled with the stick. It dissolves into that grotesque ash and I crack a smile. We really did it.

"Get behind me," Jack commands.

I do as he says but ask, "What now?"

"The hands are nearly done with our cause."

Looking over, I see that the glowing residue where I broke the watch has shrunk to a flickering bulb of bubbling light. Jack's body seems to take on a luminance of his own as he holds out his downward-pointing clock hand and sets his jaw. He plunges it to the floor, causing a ripple of ivory power to roll across the room like foamy ocean waves. It incinerates every weapon that it smashes into until the whole place is free of all these murder-y instruments.

Looking over Jack's shoulder, I can see the hour hand burst into hundreds, maybe thousands, of little, black, iridescent particles and float off into nothing. Not a moment later, the minute hand I hold breaks up just the same and seemingly vanishes from existence.

"Jack…"

"It was just a thing," he calms me—really—he's consoling me! Who's the adult here again?

The angelic light bathing the room phases out and time releases its grip on the warring guests. They fumble around in understandable disorientation—frantically searching for answers. Jack marches up into the middle and I follow close by his side. Whatever power he lent me is gone now, I'm normal again, but that was exhilarating while it lasted.

"It's over," he tells the group. "Mister Daley and I took care of everything. Now it's time to go." His voice is soft, but his words still carry a certain sense of command.

"This can't be real…" Indigo whines. He checks around the room as if to make sure that the weapons are really all gone.

"Sin and its forces are still nearby. We need to get to safety at once. If we can, we should go to the Observatory."

"No, I can't go with you. You all saw what I did to Richard!" Indigo's complexion is pale and he wheezes with each breath.

"It's not too late for you," Jack pleads, "Besides, you were only defending yourself."

"I can't…" With that, Indigo turns his back to us and trots off for the door.

"Have faith in us!" Jack calls after him.

Skye starts to back away from the group herself, tears dribbling down her eyes

"No, don't…" Jack begs. He takes a step toward her with a hand outstretched.

"I'm sorry, I can't face Shirun. I won't face the rest of you. This is over for me," she sobs. Before anyone can stop her, she also flees for the door.

Leif eyes us contemptuously before announcing, "I'm grateful for the rescue, but I won't be party to Shirun's thankless war. If I die, I want to do so knowing I enjoyed every last moment of my existence. You would all do well to consider the same for yourselves."

Jack doesn't even argue this time. He just watches with puffy eyes as Leif makes a sad attempt at straightening his suspenders over his bare chest. He turns about and strides off without another word.

"I'll go with you to Shirun," Samuel says, as he comes up and puts a hand on Jack's shoulder. "You know I'll always stand with you."

This brightens the heavy expression on Jack's face. He looks up to the man with renewed hope twinkling in his gaze.

"We should be careful, but I agree that there isn't much time to waste," Evan offers.

Jack nods in assent.

"Christina?" Jack questions as he turns to her. All of us follow his gaze.

She rolls her eyes. "I never much liked any of you, you know." Her expression is stony at first, but it soon breaks into a grin. "Desperate times though, am I right? Perhaps it's time for a change of pace anyway and you wouldn't make for the worst company."

"Great!" Jack beams.

With his band of committed refugees together, he leads us out of the ballroom and down the hall. We march along, trying not to make too much noise as we go. In the relative silence, I feel as though the howling outside is intensifying. When we walk past a spot where there's a hole in the wall, I can see that the thick purple energy swirls all around the manor. Its chill pours through the opening, giving us all cause to shiver. Once we're further down the corridor, a sharp crack echoes all around us and the building shakes, knocking some of us off balance.

"You!" someone howls—it's a deep, throaty sort of robotic shriek.

The noxious sound comes from seemingly nowhere until Sin rounds the corner of a small offshoot hall perpendicular to ours.

"Run!" Jack yips.

We break into a far less cautious pace down the hallway. A large blast of dark energy pounds through the wall behind where we just were.

"Get to the stairs and get to safety," Jack orders as we run.

I get flashes of how Margaret offered herself up to that horrific fate when she tried to defend us.

"I'm not leaving you," I protest as I run beside him.

"Just make sure you're behind me then," he replies, seemingly unconcerned.

It brings me some relief that he has no intention of dying here, but I still wonder what his plan is exactly. We're nearly to the foyer where we can climb upstairs when he abruptly halts his flight. I skid to a stop behind him and my chest tightens as Sin's hulking form skulks around into sight.

"You ruin everything!" it hisses. "Why can't you just die out already? Be a good boy and do it for me now, Jack. You know your time's almost up anyway. He doesn't need you anymore."

I have no idea what Sin's going on about, but it's hard not to admire how Jack stands firm against this thing that's literally the stuff of nightmares.

"He may not need me anymore than he needs you, but he'll always cherish me, even when I'm gone," Jack returns. "You, on the other hand are more like a collection of cheap fads he's better off without, a thing easily forgotten."

Sin screeches with its mouth wide open and its eyes ablaze. It lowers at the knees and pulls its hands back to its side. A purplish-black fog travels down its arms and pools into a ball between its curled fingers. Sin hurls the dark magic toward us at blinding speed. My heart skips a beat, but before the blast can hit us, Jack steps forward with his hands held up—fingers spread wide. A semi-opaque white forcefield snaps into existence in front of us. Sin's magic slams into it and bursts apart over it like water smashing against a window. Once the projectile dissipates, Jack turns sideways, takes a wide step, and shoves his arm forward like some kind of Kung Fu master. The white force field shoots down toward Sin who cackles before Jack's protective barrier smashes into it and sends our enemy crashing through the wall behind it.

The forcefield turns to a cloud-like dust, clearing in time for me to see Sin fly out into the storm and get sucked into the swirling vortex. Just like that, we're suddenly safe from whatever that monster had in mind for us. I'm about to come up and pat Jack on the back when he stumbles around to face me. He holds a hand up to his nose and I realize that blood is dripping from it. I rush forward as he falls to a knee and catch him by the shoulders before he can hit the ground. There's a vacant look in his eyes and a pale clammy-ness in his face.

"Jack?"

His head drops to his chest and his body goes limp against me.

"Jack!"

There's no way we can go through all of that just for him to die on me now. I try to stay calm in spite of how my heart thumps in my chest. He's still breathing so that's a good sign. He must have just passed out. I remember how he looked weakened after he defended us that night in the Billiards Room. Maybe he overdid it this time.

"Alright, Jack," I soothe as I shift him around in my arms so that I have him cradled. "I've got you, we're gonna be alright."

I hoist him up into the air, finding him strangely weightless. It's a good thing though given how vulnerable we are out here. I need to get him to safety and I need to do it fast.

# Epilogue

The storm flares up as I make it to the top of the steps with Jack. I do my best not to get tripped up by the quaking of the house, but it's like Sin is throwing a temper tantrum in the form of a magical disaster. I just need to go up this second set of stairs and get to the Observatory now. So far things are clear, but that could change at any moment. I've barely started my ascent to the third floor when two cretin guards step down toward me, blocking my path.

"Dammit!" I hiss as I turn and head back down.

Heading to the first floor isn't a great option so I head down the storm-weathered hallway of this second floor. I try to keep Jack steady, but I don't really have time to be delicate so I start a brisk jog toward the next corner of the manor where I hope that staircase will be open. We've gone from an unstoppable force to an utterly helpless mess and my heart races at the idea of failing now. We're closing the gap between us and where we need to get to, but the guards chasing us aren't in any particular hurry to catch up. They're sort of just trotting behind us at a leisurely speed. They're toying with us. They know there are more of them waiting at the end of this hall and they know we can't turn back with them barring the way. I pick up the pace, but I may only be hastening our doom.

"Leave me the boy and I'll let you walk free for now," Sin's voice echoes around me—or maybe inside of me.

"Fuck you!" I yell at the top of my lungs.

I enjoy the moment of bravado while it lasts. When I notice a break in the corner of where the wall meets the ceiling about three fourths of the way to where I'm headed, I realize I'm definitely screwed. Sure enough, two of the cretin people shoot out from the storm and smash through this hole. They crash down to the floor in shower of rubble and set a wide base as they hold out their hands. These two aren't wearing boots or gloves. All they have to do touch us and we're done. I come to a stop in between each pair of my would-be killers. All optimism leaves me, but I wonder how this can actually be the end.

Then I see a figure come into view as it descends the stairs to the third floor. He's big and wears tan pants with a blue jacket from what I can see. He marches toward us with something golden held out in front of him.

"Myles?"

Two blasts of gold light sear through the cretins in front of me in answer and a relieved smile comes to my face.

"Get down!" he shouts as he closes in on our position much faster than his heavy stride would suggest.

I fall to a knee and hold Jack close to my chest. Two more bolts tear through the air followed by the brief sound of cretins fizzling into ashen waste. With our enemies gone, I rise to my feet and turn to our rescuer.

"We've got to stop meeting like this," I joke. My voice is far from steady, but I hope I sound grateful.

He grins. "Mmm, quite. Let me take him from here then, old chap."

He slides his revolver into a leather holster strapped to his thigh that I don't remember being there before. It's a good sign that Shirun's forces are getting little upgrades as this ordeal drags out. I place Jack into his outstretched arms, grateful to see someone more competent take him off my hands.

"Jack, old boy, you've got to be careful. Not much more voltage in the bulb these days. Too much of this and you'll burn yourself right out." Myles whispers this to the boy as he leads us toward the staircase.

There's a deep tenderness that Myles has for Jack that I don't have the full context for. I guess Jack is an easy enough boy for anyone to love, but there's a history between these two that I'll probably never understand—a history they shared with Margaret who I'll never see again.

"Do you know what happened to Samuel, Evan, and Christina?" I ask as we begin to step up to the third floor. "They were with us until Sin attacked…"

"Olivia and a team were sent for them, they'll be alright."

"Do you know what became of Indigo, Skye, or Leif?"

"Sorry, old chap, if they've gone off, they've gone off—

nothing we can do for them now."

"No, I understand, I was just wondering."

"It's like I said before, of course, not everyone wants saving, but you did well, old chap. You've got a lot of folks where they need to be and we're almost at the end here. Just a little longer to go."

He stops in front of a door. We're still a ways off from the Observatory which weighs my heart down.

"This is where we'll have to part ways for now, I'm afraid," he explains. "I'll be seeing you soon, yeah?"

"I hope so…"

"That's my boy! Stay brave now, there's a helping hand waiting on the other side of this door."

On cue, it swings open on its hinges. That overwhelming white light lies behind the entryway, but it's a little less blinding this time.

"Got to run, you take care now."

"You too," I tell him.

"Always!" Myles gives me a wink before turning and taking off with Jack.

There's nothing left for me now, but to walk through this door. I know I'll just be waking up in my apartment, but the idea of there being some help waiting there gives me some hope. I do wonder what form it will take, but I guess I just have to step through and find out. Eager for a change of scenery, I enter into the light and prepare to embrace whatever lies beyond it.

# Book 7:

# Memory's Graveyard

*To any that have helped me face the parts of
myself that I don't like.*

# Chapter 1

When I open my eyes, I expect to see my bedroom. Instead, what I get is an endless swirling field of nothing but white. I'm rolling through it like I'm weightless in space. Or maybe it's more like I'm sinking in a vast ivory sea. I can't tell which way is up or which is down and I can't stop myself from gradually tumbling down into the nothing. I'm also completely naked. Why the hell am I just casually naked? Where are all those nice, fancy dream clothes? I am still dreaming after all right? Or am I dead—is this Hell? Constantly rolling downward over myself all by myself in nothing but my birthday suit sure feels pretty hellish. If this is Heaven, then lots of lovely people clearly got screwed. I curl up into a ball to conceal my junk even though no one is around to see it. I just have this odd feeling that I'm still being watched somehow.

There's something completely unnatural about this place. It's neither warm nor cold, bright, nor dull. There's no sense of direction and nothing seems to even be here except for me. It's like one of those art pieces that's just a random black dot on a white canvas—where I'm the dot, I guess. I suddenly get a feeling that washes over me. It's less like something brushing against me and more like a pair of eyes setting upon me. It doesn't feel like a malevolent stare, but it does make me feel exposed and vulnerable. Whatever it is, it draws closer, almost as if to envelop me. My heart starts to pound at wondering what this thing wants. I wish for it to keep away with every fiber of my being. I don't actually yell, but my soul screams out for the presence to leave me alone—to stay away from me. I'm surprised and relieved when whatever this thing is not only halts its advance, but also retreats into some corner of this abyss where I can't feel it any more.

It's almost sad when I'm alone again though. How long will I be trapped like this? I try closing my eyes and seeing if they open to more worldly surroundings. It doesn't work, of course, but I decide to try again—if at first you don't succeed and all that. After seeing if the third time really is the charm, I do spot something different on the horizon. It's not much—just a speck I see in the distance right before I tumble through the ocean of white. Each time I do one of my lazy flips, the speck gets a little bigger until I can vaguely make out the shape of a person. I wonder if it's someone stuck out here like me, but I hope that it's somebody coming to save me from whatever this is. The person draws a little nearer and I can tell that it's a man with bronze skin and white clothes. Why does he get clothes while I'm stuck being butt-ass naked? In spite of how dizzy I am from all this spinning, I think I recognize this guy—I'm pretty sure it's Shirun.

"Shirun!" I call out to him, but my voice is muddled as though I'm speaking underwater, or maybe just through really thick glass.

"I'm here." The words ring out clear as day, somehow managing to echo off of our endless bounds.

He floats up beside me, seemingly in perfect control of himself. He places a hand on my shoulder and one on my back. It's an uncomfortably tender sort of touch, but at least it steadies me. He holds me in place and smiles—it's a sad smile, but a smile all the same.

"It's okay," he reassures me.

Keeping his eyes on me, he reaches down and unties the sash holding his thick white tunic together. I start to squirm in place, I mean what the hell is even happening? If this is my mind doing this, then it needs to stop it. Right now. Shirun slowly slips out of the shirt, keeping a hand as well as his gaze on me the whole time and making no acknowledgement of how awkward this is.

"Here," he offers, pushing the shirt toward me.

He's holding it out so that the sleeve is wide open for me. I slip my arm through it feeling awful about being nervous about him pulling some funny business while he was literally just trying to give me the shirt off his back. Once my arm is in, Shirun glides around me, draping the tunic over the back of my shoulders and holding the second sleeve open for me. He grips me by the shoulders once I'm fully into it and lets me handle pulling the front of it together. I tie it tight with the sash around my waist and am overjoyed to find that the shirt hangs almost down to my knees—allowing me to finally stretch out a bit.

"Where are we?" There's pressure around my head when I speak, like the place is trying to stuff the words back into my mouth.

"We're both nowhere and everywhere. It's not really a place in the sense that you'd understand."

I turn my head back to him with eyebrows raised—exhausted with all the riddles.

He seems to get this since he sighs and continues, "I'm sorry, I never imagined speaking to you would be so hard. The truth is that complex questions rarely have the answers your kind craves. I suppose you can call this place The Void. It's like a world between worlds. Perhaps more accurately, it's the fiber that connects them all. It's a place where only beings like me are meant to walk. You are only here because I managed to catch you before you could reach the world you call your reality. I've broken many rules by doing this..."

He suddenly lets go and swings weightlessly around to the front of me. Before I can start tumbling through The Void again, he catches me by the arms. He looks at me in a manner that I can't discern. Perhaps it's a look of uncertainty. His dark skin seems to glow golden against the soft white luminescence that surrounds us. I notice too that although his hair is neat, it sways up in the air a little as though it's underwater. I roll my eyes up to see that mine is doing the same.

"If this is a world between worlds, then why is it empty? How is it a void?" As unpleasant as talking is, it's more unpleasant to let all the questions I have burn inside me.

Shriun's face scrunches. "Oh...no, it's not that kind of void. I suppose you can't see any of it can you?"

"See what?" What could he possibly be seeing?

"Everything..." Shirun pauses to look up and around at all of our supposed surroundings. "There are pasts and presents and things that could come to pass as well as outcomes that can never be. People who used to live and those yet to exist walk here. Prayers, hopes, dreams, and everything in between are all here as well. Then there are those who may walk The Void as they please like myself. Those who are more of The Void than they are any world it connects to."

"How is any of that even possible for you to see? Why can't I?"

"Time, space, it's all irrelevant here. There is only one thing that matters in the whole of it all. As for why you can't see any of it as I do, I suppose it's mostly because you couldn't possibly comprehend any of it. You only see me because I have made it so that you can."

"How's that?"

"I have shifted my form to something more recognizable, though I know you still think I look strange."

"Not in a bad way," I protest, afraid he can see lies too.

"No, not in a bad way. I don't think of this as a mask though, it's me, the true me, I was never made to be confined to a singular shape."

"That must be nice," I'm not really sure what else I can say to that.

"It's just how I am, we all must change our state in different ways."

"Can you describe what you see to me? I'm feeling pretty left out at this point..."

Shirun's gaze continues to wander the depths as he releases one of my arms and hovers around to my side. He drags me along with him though I still can't tell if we're looking laterally or vertically or if those are even concepts that matter here. I'm more fascinated by Shirun. I can't help but study him as he basks in all the beauty I can't perceive.

"It's difficult to explain it."

"Just do your best," I tell him. "Pretend I'm a blind man who's never seen anything."

"Compared to me, you are a blind man who's never seen anything."

"Right...so just be my eyes then."

Shirun sets his jaw and squints his eyes for a moment. It's clear that he's never had to do this for anyone before.

"It's color mostly, not like any colors you've ever seen though. Imagine all the most striking, vibrant colors in the spectrum. Imagine they're all swirling together in streams of light, billowing out like puffy clouds, and pulsing outward in lovely fractal patterns. Amid all that, there are these flashes of people and events from the past, present, and all possible futures, only you don't see them as flesh and blood. Instead, you see all the warped and wonderful hues of their souls. Then there are all the words ever spoken, all the things that could have been said—perhaps many things that still ought to be discussed. They're joined by every thought and fantasy. Together they reverberate throughout everything at frequencies that are more like temperatures."

"Why is it all like that? How can you even process any of that?"

Shirun chuckles, patting my arm with his free hand. "You are a linear creature so you don't yet understand. Things are this way because that's how they are. They're truths that light our way."

"I felt something here earlier, before you came."

"I was always here…"

"Before you were **with** me."

"I was always … oh I see what you mean now."

I eye him for a second, not sure how he can perceive all this crap that's invisible to me yet not grasp simple concepts.

"I felt like it was coming after me. Do you know what it was?"

"Of course," he replies with some hesitance.

I get the distinct sense that he either doesn't want to or isn't permitted to discuss the nature of whatever presence I felt was so I just ask, "Do you know what it wants?"

Shirun gives me a light shrug, "Just to be with you?"

"Then why did it leave?"

"You made it clear that you didn't want Their company."

I pause to consider that I thought some extradimensional cuddle monster was attacking me. "Is it mad at me?"

"No, just sad, mostly. Also, They're not an 'it.'"

"Oh…" I guess I can be an insensitive douchebag even out in some weird void where there's basically no one to even be a douchebag to—no one I can see at least.

"Don't fret. Forgiveness is in Their nature," he tells me as if sensing my thoughts.

"Who are they?"

"I warned you about complicated questions…" he dismisses

me.

"Right–no simple answers. Can you tell me why I'm here then? Why didn't you just let me awake in my bed?"

"You need rest," he circles back around to face me. "This is the only way I can guarantee your safety. I can protect you here, shelter you from all the Powers that would do you harm. I can help you find rest, even if it is only temporary.

With that, he tugs me toward him, rotating me around so that I have my back against his torso. He reaches around, grabbing both my wrists and crossing them over my chest. I really don't think I love any of this, but I try to trust him. He's right that I need a good rest with everything going on. Suddenly, this incredible warmth washes over me. I'm pretty sure it's coming from Shirun—almost like he's a man-shaped fire and I'm sitting at just the perfect distance away.

"What is this?" I'm so relaxed I think the words slur out a little.

I hear him chuckle behind me. "Try to be at peace, it's just another of my forms."

I try to peer back and see said form, but all that I see is a hazy white radiance that obstructs my vision.

I'm so blissfully sleepy at this point that I just whisper, "Okay…"

"One more thing, Bryan. When you go back out there, I ask that you do your best to trust the woman that you keep encountering. She's coarse and she may seem scary, but she will protect you while I cannot."

I'm not able to make a reply of any kind—finding myself consumed by the comforting warmth that cocoons me. The world of white dims until I've sunk down into the veiled universe of sleep.

# Chapter 2

My eyes open and I finally find myself back in my bedroom. My head is a little fuzzy as I sit up but I feel great otherwise. My heart isn't racing, I'm not damp with sweat, and there's this amazing lack of tension throughout my entire body. Whatever I experienced in that void with Shirun seems to have really given me some much-needed rest. I pop out from under the sheets and march into my bathroom, excited to see how much better I look. I find that a little color has returned to my face and a spark is back in my eyes. There's still a hollow, almost gaunt, look that mars my features and keeps me from feeling totally cured. This is probably a good time for me to get myself together and get some help. Better to seek it out while I'm a little more collected. A buzz from my phone pulls me out of the bathroom and back to where my phone sits on my end table.

It's a text from Kayla that reads, "PLEASE LETS JUST TALK!"

Upon checking my other notifications, it looks like I have three more texts, two missed calls, and a voice message all from her. I don't really want to deal with the voice message right now, but I do glance at the texts.

"HEY THIS ISNT OVER ASSHOLE!!!" I guess she sent this one shortly after I left her at RhyeWay.

"LOOK LET'S JUST TALK THINGS THROUGH. I STILL WANT THIS. I STILL WANT US." She sent that one late last night.

In the wee hours of this morning, I received, "YOU'RE MAKING A HUGE MISTAKE. PLEASE DON'T THOW THIS AWAY!"

I hope my poorly delivered breakup didn't drive her to some sleepless drunken night, but that's kind of what it's looking like. Scanning through these is like seeing her go through the different stages of grief which is heartbreaking. Is she just trying to manipulate me or does this actually have her in this much pain? I can't judge, I'm sure I sent one or two or twenty of these messages to Julie after she dumped me. As much as I want to check in on her, I also feel like I've said all I can. If I even attempt to make contact at this point, I'll probably make things sloppier than they already are so I close out of the texting application and switch my focus to looking up therapists in my area. I find plenty of seemingly good options with well-reviewed specialists, but for some reason, that sign for Dr. Ben Drakeson keeps flashing in my mind. I'm not sure if I get good or bad feelings from it, but given the office's location, it would definitely allow me to explore the idea of talking to someone without being too conspicuous about it. I'm about to look up their number when a different idea crosses my mind. I could just drive to that garage that's nearby, walk over, schedule something in person, and take care of some errands while I'm out. That way I can scope the place out. If I schedule an appointment now, then I'm kind of committed, plus they'll probably need a bunch of forms filled out before they can see me anyway so I can just take care of that too. I mull it over for a moment before placing my phone on the nightstand and nodding to myself in agreement with what I've decided.

About an hour later, I'm showered, changed, and in my Wercedes driving along toward my destination. It's the middle of the workday so the roads are conveniently clear. I'll definitely be less self-conscious about this adventure with less people around too. I've dressed down a little so I'm even less noticeable—keeping the attire to jeans, a blue and white tee, a silver zip-up hoodie, and black sneakers. I caved and put on one of my leather watches—my wrist felt naked without it. I try to just relax now. I've planned it all out in the smartest way I can. All that's left is to just follow through with what I've set out to do.

Doubt creeps in the second I'm parked in the garage. I feel like this may not be such a good idea after all. Now that I'm close, I'm just getting all sorts of bad vibes. Maybe I should do a couple of errands first and then swing by to set up an appointment. I consider this, but I know full well that if I don't do this right now, it won't get done at all. Locking my car, I decide to stop being such a child. I mean it's not like you tell one shrink that you're having bad dreams and suddenly they toss you into a looney bin. It's all supposed stay confidential too so it probably wouldn't work like that anyway. By the time I've hit the sidewalk, I've finished second guessing myself. I'm still so nervous that I feel queasy, but this needs to happen.

The building is one of those humble brick mini-towers that's probably as old as the city itself. All of the structures around it are newer and taller, but I guess this one just never got torn down and rebuilt. There's not a lot in here either. A couple spaces are up for rent amid an electronics repair shop, a hardware store, a bicycle shop, a dry cleaner, and Ben Drakeson's office. The metal and glass exterior door creaks wearily as it opens and there's an interesting musk that fills the air. I take the stairs since I'm not sure I want to trust the elevator. It's a bit of a climb up to the eighth floor, but I'm also in no huge rush. I could probably use the exercise anyway—my gym routine has been a little lacking these past few days. I'm greeted by a little wooden door set in a faded crimson wall. There's no fancy glass sign-window, but the name of the office is written out in shiny black metal letters drilled into the door, though the alignment looks crooked. The door knob is a little wobbly too, but at least that funky smell doesn't seem to linger up here. Instead, it just kind of smells like nothing at all.

The office is small in a cramped—not cozy—sort of way. There are two rows of three cushioned chairs sitting on opposite sides of a long table covered in magazines. They look old though— I can't imagine Patty Kerri has appeared on any covers of <u>Elegance</u> recently. To the right are some wall-mounted coat hangers and a tiny restroom. In front of me is a modest wooden desk where an older woman sits. She makes a sudden swivel in her chair once she sees me enter.

"Hello, there," she greets, leaning forward with her elbows on the desk and hands folded under her round chin.

"Hi," I reply, suddenly realizing I need to explain why I'm here. "I don't have an appointment... I was just in the neighborhood and I wanted to check you guys out, maybe set one up." I want to facepalm—I couldn't have failed more miserably at playing cool with this.

"Sure thing! We always welcome new appointments."

There's something unnerving about the way this lady smiles.

Maybe it's too girlish for her age. Maybe it's a little too eager—like she was somehow expecting me. Maybe it's just the lighting in here—of which there actually is none. There's natural light coming in from the two windows, but the only lamp in the room is missing a bulb, which seems like a bizarre expense to skimp out on.

"So, you guys have plenty of openings then? I'm really just looking to try this kind of thing out."

"That's no problem, we can take you right now!"

I can feel my eyebrows shoot up and my jaw start to drop. I guess I don't see anyone else in here after all, but I have to wonder if I've made a horrible mistake.

"Um, okay, I mean I didn't really come prepared with anything for today... I wasn't expecting to be able to go right in."

The lady, whose name is Marilou per her brass name plate, leans back in her chair and giggles as she twirls an auburn curl. "Therapy doesn't work that way, silly. No one's ever prepared for it. But don't worry, we're prepared for you!"

I don't know if I find that last sentence at all comforting. Honestly, I think I grimace the second it comes out of her mouth.

"So, is there some kind of paperwork I need to fill out then?"

"No need for that. Your first session with us is completely free and we don't make you fill out anything with us. No fee, no commitment, no judgement." She tattles this off like a slogan I should have seen on a subway ad or something.

"Well, that's pretty low pressure then, huh?" It's also kind of desperate-seeming, but that wouldn't be very polite to comment on.

I guess I've got nothing to lose then, chances are this guy's a total quack, but even if that's the case, at least it will only cost my time.

Marilou rises from her seat and practically skips over to the door beside her desk. "Come on in!"

She's beaming from ear to ear in a way that makes me wonder if she's just really stoned. I follow her over in spite of how my better judgement says I should probably just get out of here. It's all just so awkward that I'm not really sure what else I can do.

"Doctor, we have a patient!" she coos as she flings open the door.

"Good, good, please do come in," a thin, wry voice replies.

The room I enter is darker than the waiting room in spite of the presence of a shaded lamp turned on atop an end table. The doctor rises from behind a tiny writing desk in the corner where an old computer is crammed onto, though it doesn't appear to be powered on. What kind of practice is this anyway? Do these guys just twiddle their thumbs all day? If so, how can they afford to stay in business. As Doctor Drakeson steps past the table lamp, I get a quick glimpse of his light frame, narrow face, and short, but disorderly blond hair.

"Pleased to meet you, I'm Doctor Benjamin Drakeson. You're here for a consultation visit, is that right?"

He leans in to shake my hand. Shadows partially obscure his face, but this guy looks pretty young. Maybe he's just starting out and having a rough go of it —that would explain a lot.

"There's no need to share your full name for your first time if you're at all uncomfortable," he offers as we pull back from the handshake. "A first name or even an alias will do so I can call you by something. If you decide to stay with us, I'll of course be needing your legal name."

I flush with embarrassment. I'm not scared of this guy knowing my name, it's his bizarre office that has me tongue-tied.

"I'm Bryan," I decide to just go with the first name for now.

"It's nice to meet you, Bryan." I guess no one at shrink school ever taught him that it's customary to pair this kind of statement with a smile. "That will be all, Marilou." He turns his back to both of us as he dismisses her.

"Sure thing, Doctor Drakeson, I'll be right outside." Her words hang longingly in the air right before she pulls the door shut behind her.

Does she have a crush on this guy? I shudder to think that that they might get freaky on the therapy couch off-hours. Ben takes a seat in a chair opposite the sofa. His movements are slow and stiff. It also occurs to me then that I am not even clear on if he is technically a therapist or a psychiatrist anymore.

"Have a seat," he invites, motioning his hand to the couch that may or may not double as a place of scandalous love-making.

I could still try to get myself out of here, but at this point I guess I should see this thing through to its weird and wild conclusion. I walk over and take a seat, careful not to touch it with my hands. Ben adjusts his thin, silver glasses. I expected him to take notes or record our session or something, but I guess this first one really is on the more casual side.

"So, Bryan..." He begins—his tone sounds more like a lawyer's than a therapist's. "What brings you here today?"

The end table where the single lamp sits is right next to me so every fidget and micro expression is easily readable. In spite of the sunlight coming in from the window in the back of the room, Ben sits in relative darkness.

"I'm not sure I even know where to start without sounding nuts."

Ben tilts his head back a little and maybe smirks. "I don't think you're crazy, Bryan. A crazy person wouldn't be sitting where you are now. I think there are things that are troubling you—things that you can't share with anyone else. That puts a great deal of stress on the mind and that stress can really mess with how we think and how we perceive the world around us."

I nod agreeably. It sounds pretty reasonable to me. I mean my visits to the manor are the very definition of stressful.

"Just tell me your story," Ben prods. "You can start at the beginning of when things started to go badly in your mind or you can just tell me about yourself. This session is your time to discuss whatever you'd like."

I shift uncomfortably. Do I jump right into talking about my dreams? Do I mention my distant friendship with David or recently broken relationship with Kayla? The more I think on it, the more I realize how many stresses I've been dealing with.

"It'll take some time to get through everything—that's precisely why our first session is free." He chuckles, but it sounds kind of sinister. "Just pick one thing—whatever's top of mind—and we'll go from there."

This guy's pretty good. Weird and nerdy-looking as he may be, he's a borderline mind-reader with this stuff.

"I— I guess I'd like to start with some stuff that's actually not even going on in my life. See, when I go to sleep, I keep going back to this mansion where things are falling apart, people are dying, and an evil creature is taking over."

Ben leans forward and clasps his hands in front of him. Now that his face is a little closer to the light, I realize that his eyes are an unusual color. They're either very light brown or some sickly greyish green. This could just be a trick of the dreary atmosphere, but they're sort of hard to look at.

"It's intriguing that you didn't explicitly describe these episodes as 'dreams.'"

"Well I guess they just feel like more than that," I get defensive even though I don't think Doctor Drakeson is accusing me of anything.

"Describe them to me." His tone inflects almost a little too much interest.

I take a moment to collect myself, then reply, "It started last week when I had a dream that I was at a mansion for a fancy dinner party. The next night I was back there with the same people, but in a different room and at a different party. Things got spookier and someone was killed near the end of it. Things only got darker and more violent each time I went back. It turned out that there's this horrible creature trying to destroy the mansion and everyone inside of it. It commands a hellish dog, a big purple storm, and an army shadow monsters that can latch onto someone's body and take them over."

"Interesting..." Ben hums as he leans back and places his hands on the chair's armrests. "These episodes sound intense and while I'd love to hear about each in full detail, it'd probably be better for now if I just ask you how you feel during them."

"I mean, it's all so vivid and time seems to flow logically and while there is no shortage of oddities, I also feel like there are no glaring inconsistencies either. Things don't randomly shift around, timelines don't get jumbled, and the rules don't seem to change like they might in a normal dream."

"So, you're saying that these experiences feel real?"

"I know it sounds crazy, but yeah, they really do and now I think I'm seeing things while I'm awake and I even passed out in public once."

"I see how that would be concerning, but neither the

343

realness of the dreams nor the possible hallucinations during your waking hours are necessarily strong indications of any kind of mental illness. You may know that dreaming helps the mind process what's going on in our lives…"

Ben glances at the window momentarily and seems to consider his next words.

After an uncomfortably long pause that makes me wonder if he isn't looking for answers out that window, he continues, "I couldn't help you interpret the meaning behind any of it without at least a couple more sessions, but it's clear to me that your mind has put a great deal of detail and energy into this nighttime narrative of yours. You've been maintaining this whole little world of your own imagination which, while fascinating, can't possibly result in peaceful slumber."

"I can definitely confirm that my sleep has not been especially restful most nights. Last night was better than the others, at least the end of it was, so I'm feeling like I'm having an uncharacteristically good day."

The room somehow manages to get a tad darker. It's way too early for sunset, so I guess a cloud just rolled by.

"I'm not surprised," Ben comments. "The fact that you feel like the experience is real is also not shocking. You probably feel attached to the characters and events in your dreams in much the same way that you connect with a television show or a novel. With this, you are superimposed into the center of it all as a sort of main character which makes the points of connection that much stronger. Any delusions you're experiencing are likely a result of sleep deprivation, or rather, a deficiency in restful sleep."

"You're saying this is all normal?" I challenge, noting that the cloud still hasn't passed yet.

"I'm saying that there's a causality to it all that I think we can work through if you are interested and willing. I truly do believe that you've made the right choice to seek out therapy and my hope for this meeting is that you realize things are not as dire as they may feel—your problems are quite fixable."

What little light is in the room fades even more which obscures Ben from my vision.

"I'm sorry, is there a storm rolling in?"

"That's not the cleverest way to change the subject that I've ever heard." I can't tell from his tone whether he's teasing or scolding me.

"I'm serious, it's getting hard to see in here."

"Are you afraid of the darkness?" There's something unsettling in how he asks this—something that chills me.

"I mean, it's kind of weird to have a therapeutic conversation in the dark, isn't it?"

"There are those who find it uncomfortable to discuss things in the light," he retorts.

How did he suddenly become so nonsensical? What does that even mean? Short of vampires, I can't think of anyone who wouldn't want to speak under a sufficient amount of light. I get up off the sofa and walk over to the window. I can't see anything out of it though. There are no storm clouds and night hasn't fallen. It's like the world outside this office is simply swallowed up by darkness in the form of an ebony haze. Suddenly my heart skips a beat. This is like the club and the mall. Whatever's hunting me knows I'm here and it's probably closing in on me.

"Doctor, I might be hallucinating again, but all I can see out there is darkness. Please, what is this?"

I can hear him arise from his chair before he replies, "Oh, Mister Daley, this shade is your past, your present, and that which will likely consume your future."

I spin around. "Wait, I never told you my—"

The words catch in my throat when I see that Doctor Drakeson's teeth as well as the whites of his eyes are glowing. The solitary lamp flickers as Ben removes his glasses and flings them across the room.

"Your last name?" Ben finishes my thought with a toothy grin that makes me shiver. "We know all about you, Bryan, and we're so happy you came to us. Just stay a little longer and we can make all of your problems disappear." He makes a little fluttering gesture with his fingers as he says this.

What the hell is going on? What am I seeing now? Is any of this even real? I guess it doesn't matter, I just need to get out of here now. I lurch to my right, but Ben's darkened figure sidesteps to position himself right in my way.

"Please don't go. I think we were making really good progress." A long snicker escapes his bioluminescent mouth.

"Get out of my way!" I yell back.

"Just let me help you…" he pleads mockingly.

He drops down to all fours and looses and animalistic growl. I step back from him, realizing how screwed I might be. He screams and pounces into the air like a jaguar. Without even thinking, I fall onto my back with the heels of my feet sticking into the air. I roll back as I catch him by his chest and propel him up and over me. By some stroke of luck, the maneuver sends him crashing through the window and out into the dark haze. I hear him shrieking as he falls—hopefully to his death—but I don't stop to look out and see how he fares. Instead, I get to my feet and rush to the door.

Marilou's head twists toward me as I burst into the lobby. The room flickers between light and dark even though there are no lights to be flickered. Every time it falls to darkness, Marilou's eyes and teeth glow just like Ben's. She pounces up onto her meager desk with a cat-like hiss.

"Did you enjoy your session, Mister Daley?" she cackles.

The whole office starts to quake and I know I need to get out of here, but I need to be careful too. I lurch forward, faking an escape attempt and Marilou falls for the bait. She leaps forward to cut me off with her hands spread in front of her. I take off the second she hits the floor—almost tripping on a rug thanks to the unreliable lighting. I rip open the door and race to the stairs. I don't look back—I don't need to. Marilou's screeching follows close behind as I descend the steps. I wonder if this is like the mall where I just need to get outside.

With that thought in mind, I set my sights on a fire escape. There's an emergency exit onto the fire escape ramp just one floor down. At the sound of Marilou stumbling around at my heels, I rocket forward toward my only hope of salvation—skipping steps as much as I can without tripping. The fire alarm sounds when I fling open the exit. Figures that that's the one thing that makes sense in this whole situation. Unfortunately, the dark haze around me doesn't fade once I'm outside. It just lightens to a smoky grey. I make my way down the fire escape to find myself in the middle of a dingy alleyway hoping this isn't where I meet some untimely end.

I can hear my pursuer scuttling down behind me. How can I shake her if she can come outside? Can I somehow break through this fog?

I hardly have time to contemplate it when I reach the bottom of the escape. The bottommost ladder doesn't budge when I try to kick it from its upright position. I make two more attempts and even throw a shoulder at it, but its hinges are too rusted. What kind of building manager lets that happen? Marilou lands on the platform above me so time's up. Without thinking, I climb over the railing and drop down to dangle on the platform's railing. I'm hanging in the air when Marilou pops into view. Her face is charred and now and she's completely covered in a dark slime. I let go of the escape ramp before she can snatch my wrists and try to land like one of those parkour people, but just kind of end up landing too hard on my feet and then rolling clumsily over the back of my head before ending up sprawled out over the cracked pavement.

I struggle to get to my feet and stagger forward, wincing and gritting my teeth the whole way. I know that was just a one-story drop but it still hurt **a lot**. I can hear Marilou cackling hysterically from her perch, but she doesn't seem to want to chase me so maybe I actually have a shot at getting out of here in one piece. The thought barely crosses my mind when Ben limps out from behind a dumpster sitting at the corner of the building. I stop in my tracks and my heart sinks at realizing this might just be another trap. Sure enough, as soon as I turn and run the other way, Marilou plunges down, blocking my escape on the other side. I'm trapped, just like when the cretins cornered me in front of the bay windows. Maybe this confirms that the same evil haunting the manor is hunting me here. I look back and forth between my hunters, noticing that their eye-whites and teeth are both glowing yellow now like a pair of ravenous hyenas. Their slimy coating and mangled faces make me wonder what they hell these two even are. They don't look like anything I've encountered in the mansion.

Then I think I can see something shining through the thick smoke. It's faint at first, but intensifies at a rapid pace as though trying to come toward us. Next, I notice the silhouette of a person— a woman—sprinting toward us at a ferocious speed. It's my mystery woman that finally bursts through behind Marilou who pivots and

347

screeches at the lady Shirun. Lady Shirun holds an ornate sword with a golden glow at her side. It's strangely medieval in design, yet modern in its shape and that luminescence is inescapably similar to the power Shirun can bestow upon objects. The weapon suddenly turns to a blur of light as my savior/stalker swings it in front of her. She slashes at Marilou who leaps and spins over the attack and claws at the lady Shirun's face as she's landing. My rescuer twirls away, using the opening to thrust her blade through Marilou's chest. The ghastly woman howls out as the slimy texture over her dries up and breaks apart like cracked charcoal.

An angered cry pulls my attention back to Ben who's bounding toward me like a crazed chimpanzee. While not the bravest thing I've done all day, I dart toward the mystery woman as she tears her weapon out of Marilou's disintegrating corpse. My best chances are with her anyway. I can hear Ben gaining on me, grunts and huffs escaping him as he gives chase. Fortunately, lady Shirun starts running to intercept him. She runs at impossible speed before vaulting high into the air above me. I stop and look back to see her spin-flip before crashing down and lopping Ben's head off. She lands crouching low with a knee to the ground, her open light brown leather jacket swinging forward and her long, dark locks pouring over her shoulders. She erects herself tall above Doctor Drakeson's crumbling remains.

The fog around us breaks apart too, allowing daylight to break through, though it seems that we're just about into the evening somehow. The woman's sword explodes into shimmering triangles and disappears into thin air. She turns to me, her deep-water eyes sparkling in the light and her thick hair gently swaying in the breeze. It's a ridiculously perfect image of a ridiculously perfect-looking woman—so ridiculous that I still have to call her reality into question even though she just saved me. Am I just going from dream-dreams to daydreams now? She strides over to me before I can dwell on this question, stopping in front of me and eyeing me with an unreadable expression. She stands a little taller than me—probably at around the same height as Shirun. I shift uncomfortably under her gaze, wondering if she's going to say anything. It takes everything I have not to look down at her distractingly large breasts which are tightly held by a light blue V-neck tee shirt.

"You're an idiot..." she says at last, as though it's a decision she's arrived at from simply studying me.

"What?" I take a half-step back and raise my eyebrows at the random insult.

"You're an absolute fucking moron, a monumental pain in my ass, and an exemplary microcosm of everything wrong with both your species and your gender." Her words are sharp, but her tone is as relaxing as a wave rolling up onto a lonely shore.

I remain frozen in shock at everything that just came out of her mouth. She rolls her eyes and grabs me by the scruff of my sweatshirt.

"Come on, we need to leave before the Fire Department gets here."

She jerks me forward with a surprising and unnecessary amount of force. I guess her and Shirun are super strong? I let her drag me out of the alley and out of sight from the few people pooling together at the front of the building, probably wondering what triggered the alarm that's still sounding. Once we're onto the main sidewalk, I try to tear away from her grip.

"Alright, enough, I'm not going anywhere else with you, not until I know who you are and what you really want from me."

Much to my embarrassment, I'm not able to break myself free. I don't even manage to loosen her grasp. She does come to a stop, but just looks back at me with scornful pity written into her creased brow.

"Who I am is someone who's saved your dumb ass not once, not twice, but three fucking times, you filthy little ingrate." Again, her voice is as soft as satin. "What I want is to save my brother and unfortunately, I need you alive to do that... for the moment, at least."

"Shirun's your brother?"

My chest tightens, hoping she won't look at me like a crazy man. I guess she's already called me worse things so maybe I shouldn't stress over it.

"Correct, at least that is the closest word for him that your people possess."

"So, what do I have to do with that?"

Her eyes lock onto me and her eyebrows rise ever so slightly.

She considers me as if to question whether I'm serious.

"Do you truly not know what he is by now?"

I shake my head and toss my hands out to the side. Am I supposed to understand what any of this is? If she is just a figment of my imagination then she's oddly condescending.

"He's, well he's… I suppose there is no word in your tongue to fully describe his relation to you. The key thing to note is that his destiny is bound to yours in the most powerful manner imaginable."

"So, he dies if I die?"

She snorts as though this is some preposterous conclusion. "No, not really. He doesn't exist as you do. It's not his life that's in peril, it's his hue."

"His color? Are you guys racist or som—"

"Okay, I'm done, I can't discuss mature things with an infant. The point is that Shirun resides within your soul. He's serves as a sort of guardian over it."

"Wait…" My stomach drops. "You're saying there's what, a little man inside me?"

"Don't be a dumbass, your soul isn't a fucking body part…" She gives me an annoyed shake. "He's not **in** you. There's nothing but guts and bone and assorted anatomy within you. I'm talking about the essence of what you are—a thing which can't be contained by a mere three dimensions."

"My soul is an extradimensional entity?"

"Close enough…"

"And Shirun is within it? Is my soul the manor?"

"The manor?" she questions.

Now it's my turn to be surprised by something **she** doesn't know anything about. I figured she'd have all the answers. Plus, if I'm imagining her, then she should already know all about the manor.

"The place where I see Shirun and all the guests." I explain. "Where Sin has invaded and is trying to kill all of us."

Her eyes widen. "Oh… I see. I suppose that must be how it has manifested itself to you. That explains the backdrop I saw when I reached you through the hands of time's shell, but your soul is no more a place than it is an organ. In order for you to have direct contact with it, I suppose it needed to confine itself to terms you'd find suitable. While fascinating, it's useless to dwell on this detail."

"No, wait a sec." I try to pull free from her, but I'm not going anywhere. "This seems like way more than a **detail**. You're telling me that every night I've gone to that manor, I'm really just exploring my own soul? What does that make all of those people: Myles, Olivia, Jack? They're not like Shirun, so what are they?"

The woman tilts her head up and stares at the sky. She doesn't grumble or sigh, but her aggravation is unmistakable.

When she finally turns back to me, she explains, "I don't know who those people are, but they are definitely not of the Shiran. If I had to guess, I'd say they are fragments of yourself presented as individual personas. I have never heard of anything like this before, but if I'm right then they are like the manor in that they are some kind of facade or metaphor to help you understand what you are actually interacting with."

Without warning, she releases my shirt only to grab me by the arm and start dragging me along again. I'm so shocked by the abruptness, that I don't even think to resist at first.

"We're back to bullying me, then?" I instigate.

"We're back to saving your ignorant ass. I can walk and talk at the same time, I believe your species also has this capability." This time there is a distinct mockery in her tone.

I decide to ignore it for now and persist in my questioning. "What were those things? Are they the same as what attacked me in the club and what you saved me from in the mall? Do they work for Sin? How do they keep finding me?"

She looks to me with no amusement in her eyes. "The creatures that tried to claim you in the club and the mall are splinters of your own darkness. In a way, they do serve the entity who hangs to your soul like a leech, but they don't belong to it—they are yours and yours alone. That is how they find you. They're never far away, they simply choose the right moments to strike and they are getting stronger. Soon they will be upon us in droves."

My feet stop working and I fall to my knees. A couple of people pass by and give me funny looks, but I'm more worried about how hard it is to breathe. How can those shadow monsters be a part of me? They're out to destroy me! The woman lets go of my arm and scoops me up by my armpits.

"Perhaps I have oversimplified that… There is an entity that's bonded to your soul. It's made the darkness within you stronger which has in turn made the thing you call Sin stronger. Together, they are spreading their corruption through your soul like a virus inside of one's body."

"Why is this happening?" The words can barely escape my throat.

I feel the woman press her hand against my back, gently shoving me forward. "You have more questions than you do time to ask them," she dismisses me. "Judging by your hues, I'd say that this must all come to an end tonight, otherwise you're most assuredly fucked."

"Where are we going then?"

At this point, I think I'm just going to go with the flow. Whether this is truly a spiritual encounter, an elaborately constructed delusion, or one big, really bad dream, at least it can finally come to an end. I just hope there isn't something more horrible waiting on the other side of this.

"First, we're going to your apartment," she informs me.

"You want me to let you into my home? I'm pretty sure you could have broken in at any point, you at least know what building I live in."

"That's not entirely true, my kind is not supposed to just let ourselves in. We must be invited in some way—even engaging you out in the open like this is bending the rules. But I'm not trying to get into your apartment, I want to gain access to your soul."

"So you can save Shirun?"

"I'll save you too… That's sort of my line of work I guess." She removes her hand from my back and strides ahead of me.

I have to question why she showed up to save me wearing faded, form-fitting jeans and calf-high leather boots. The leather jacket is cool, but she looks like a chick from some just-very-okay action movie.

"If you keep staring at my ass, I might fucking kill you myself…" she threatens.

"I'm trying to figure out what you are exactly."

"I just am what I am," she retorts flatly.

"Are you some kind of angel? I mean what should I even

call you?"

"I'm nobody's angel, so definitely don't call me that if you value your life. There are lots of words in your world that have been used to name us, though none have ever captured our true nature. The oldest among them is Shiran, but that is a word long forgotten to time. As for what to call me specifically, I can be Sheera to you. Both my nature and my existence are beyond your ability to comprehend, so please don't make any attempt to do so, much wiser people have already tried."

"Noted…"

"What I need from you is your trust in my ability to see you through this tribulation. If you can manage that, I think we can all make it through to the light that lies just out of reach."

We arrive at the entrance to the parking garage I left my car in. I'm hardly surprised she knows where I parked. She holds the door open for me and scans around us for signs of danger.

"What happens if we lose?" I ask as I pass through the door.

She follows me up the stairs and answers flatly, "Then all will be lost. What's been released within you will become all-consuming. There will be no more hope for you."

It takes me a minute to process this news. "So, it's up to us to save the world?" Maybe this is all some ego-driven fantasy after all—one in which my personal failure results in the end of everything.

She passes me once we've reached the correct floor. Looking back to me, she replies, "No, not this world, just yours." There's a somber glint in her eyes and a hollowness in her tone that brings me great unease.

The only thing that vexes me more is when she makes a beeline for my Wercedes and stands at the driver-side door. She looks at me expectantly and puts her palm out in the air.

"No, no way you're driving us." I'm determined to put my foot down here.

"Why? Because I'm a woman?"

I stand dumfounded in front of her with my keys clutched in my fist. Did she really just pull that?

"That's not the reason, no," I stammer. "I don't know what you are exactly other than that you're not human and your existence is beyond my comprehension, but that could also just be mumbo jumbo to cover up the fact that you're just a figment of my imagination."

Her eyebrows pinch together. "You think you're just imagining all of this?"

"I think it's a possibility…"

"You've got to be the dumbest piece of shit I've ever encountered…" She crosses her arms and shifts her weight to one side.

"Yeah, well you tell me what's more likely: I'm having a psychotic breakdown or I'm arguing with a foulmouthed yet somehow still angelic lady. I need to be open to all the possibilities, you know?"

She grins, "Well I wouldn't feel the need to swear so much if your fucking species weren't so fucking infuriating."

"Well, Shirun doesn't swear," I egg her on—mostly to see where this will go.

"Your Shirun has clearly found different ways to deal with his prior experiences… Come on, you're wasting time." She puts a hand out and curls her fingers in the air, demanding the keys.

I shake my head, keeping us at an impasse.

"This is the first step," she reasons. "If you can't trust me to drive you home, then how are you going to grant me access to your soul? You need to know that I can guide you through this."

"I guess that makes sense…" My grip on the keys loosens but I don't hand them over yet.

"If I was just part of your imagination, would I even be able to start the car?"

"Maybe." I shrug—I don't know how psycho stuff works.

"Fine, whatever. We're not leaving until you hand over a little of your precious control to me and trust me, we really need to leave right now."

I don't reply other than to step forward, drop the keys in her hand, and walk around to hop into the passenger seat. She takes the wheel and adjusts the mirrors as she starts the vehicle. An angel in a Wercedes, what a picture. Well, I guess it's time to ride this crazy train to the end of the line and see where I end up. Shirun asked me to trust this Sheera, so that's what I'll do from here on in. It does feel kind of nice to just sit here while she backs us out of the parking spot and rolls us out of the garage.

# Chapter 3

As Sheera drives us through the city streets, the sky darkens above. Regular pedestrians seem grow fewer in number—shadowy figures creeping out from behind buildings to fill their absence. They start to climb up streetlights, get on top of parked cars, and watch us pass from the edges of the sidewalks. Their slimy forms leave little traces of black sludge behind them. Shivers run down my back and the palms of my hands get clammy. I look at Sheera who keeps her eyes fixed on the road ahead of us.

"You didn't answer my question before…" I really need something to keep my mind off these things closing in on us.

Her gaze remains forward-facing and her jaw tightens. If she thought this was going to be a silent ride then she's going to be sorely disappointed. I plan to make the most of us being in a confined space.

"Which question?" She sounds unenthused or maybe she's actually nervous to touch upon the subject.

"Why is this happening to me?"

"We talked about this already." This time, she does shoot me a sympathetic, sideways glance.

"No, we talked about how there are forces in my soul sowing darkness. That's the **what,** I'm asking, **why?** Why me? Why now? Why hasn't something like this ever happened to anyone else?" I'm trying not to accuse her of anything, but I really do need some answers, especially if I'm supposed to somehow trust her enough to let her into my soul/mind/delusion.

She lets the question hang in the air. Her nose scrunches up a little and the corners of her lips dip down. Is this one of those "*complicated questions*" Shirun warned me about? She turns on my headlights now that the sun has all but exited center stage. The shadow people line the streets in greater numbers, shielding their eyes from the car's lights. It's like the world around me suddenly turns into some kind of post-apocalyptic Halloweentown. Street lamps and even entire buildings flicker against this oppressive force.

"How much has Shirun told you," she questions.

Is she that nervous about driving us safely home or is there something she's genuinely afraid to tell me?

"He told me that he noticed Sin's influence over the manor getting stronger. He feared for the future so he decided to unleash Sin by opening the door to the room he'd trapped it in. Other than that, he was pretty vague. At the time it sounded like the manor was inexplicably linked to this world—linked to me. He never said it **was** me."

"And after everything I've told you, what can you infer from Shirun's explanation?" Her grip tightens on the steering wheel and her vocals are getting audibly tighter.

I ponder the question, but in my heart of hearts, I know what the answer is—it's just not what I'm looking for.

At last, I conclude, "Sin has always been a part of me, but Shirun did his best to keep it contained. He saw that Sin began to gain influence over me and he saw where that would lead, so he set it free and somehow some other darkness found its way in. Now I'm forced to fight it by night and am haunted by it during the day."

"Correct, he broke a lot of rules in doing that."

"Why would he make a choice like that?"

"I don't know..." There's pain laced through her words. "Perhaps it was an act of vanity—not common for our kind. It could also be desperation driving his actions—a fear of what you would have become had he not intervened. Maybe he simply couldn't bear the possibility of losing you. It's also possible that he truly sees something in you that I'm missing. Something worth risking it all for."

I swallow hard, trying to imagine how my future could have possibly been so bleak as to instigate an extreme act like this. We're in nearly complete darkness now making all the shining eyes and teeth gleaming at us that much spookier. What does all of this mean—I mean, really mean?

"What is Sin?"

It's hard to tell in this ghoulish rendition of the city, but I think we're just about at my apartment building.

"It's everything and nothing." She pauses. "It's things you

do and things you don't." It's the words spoken and those withheld. It's all your weaknesses, all your wickedness, and all your capacity for evil. It's everything that prevents you from becoming the best version of yourself. More importantly, it's an empty chasm desperate to be filed, making it a force with the singular desire to devour everything you are, were, and could be."

"I see," is all I can say to that.

Turning into my building's parking garage brings this conversation to a close. Sheera pulls the car into my spot—I guess she'd just know where that is for no apparent reason. She looks over at me once the car is off and puts a hand on my shoulder.

"We need to hurry. Stay close and do your best to trust me at every turn."

She hops out of the car and I follow her lead as she charges toward the elevator—her head on a swivel. The garage is entirely empty, but there's an unmistakable feeling that we're being watched. It persists even after we've stepped into the elevator and the doors close around us. It only gets more pervasive the higher up we get. My blood is thoroughly chilled by the time we're at the lobby. The doors part, unveiling the ivory space. Dark, steamy figures stalk its pristine floors. Their iridescent eyes glare at us as we step out. The entrance is well lit but somehow there's an unbearable darkness and sense of dread that shatters the warm, safe vibes it's always given off.

"Sheera..." I murmur.

She reaches behind her, palm outstretched toward me in reply. I take her hand and match her measured trot through the monsters that lurk around us. The golden sword she used earlier materializes in her free hand.

"What do we do?"

"We haul ass..." Without warning, she bursts forward, tugging me sharply behind her. "Claim him if you dare!" she challenges our enemies.

I'm not convinced this is such a smart move, but it does compel the shadows blocking our path to part, clearing way for us to reach the main elevators. Sheera releases my hand to slap the button to hail the elevator and twists around with her weapon held up. The shadows slowly converge upon us like zombies about to fall upon their dinner. I watch them with uneasy breath. There's an acrid, smoky smell in the air that stings my lungs and dries out my throat.

"Step back," Sheera orders as the elevator dings.

I sidestep the entrance in time to see her launch into the car. She slashes down the monsters hiding within—splattering black muck all over the shiny gold and warm auburn interior. I scramble in behind her and furiously punch buttons to close the doors and get us going up to my floor. The ghoulish apparitions screech and reach for us, but none manage to get to us before the doors close. In their golden sheen, I see the blurred reflection of a man with dark hair and a blue jacket.

"Just a little longer to go," a muffled voice fills my ears.

"I did what you said," I reply to the reflection, who I assume is Shirun.

He nods back to me before fizzling out, leaving my and Sheera's reflections behind.

"He'd be here with you if he could," she tells me. There's a somber expression on her face.

"Why can't he?" I'm not sure if this is question is entirely tasteful or not.

"I believe that when he released Sin within your soul he also trapped himself there in that plane of existence. Not that our kind ever ventures far from our charges, it's just that he should be able to move about freely and manifest himself to you as more than just a reflection."

"If that's true, then how did he take me to The Void?"

"He did what?" she exclaims in genuine shock. The elevator doors whoosh open, eliciting a grumble from her. "He's broken so many fucking rules…"

She keeps her sword aloft as she leads us down my hall. There aren't any creatures of darkness out at the moment, but chilling wails seem to resound from every part of the building and a horrifying black mold spreads rapidly over the walls and doors.

"Come on." She rushes ahead, her step seemingly in sync with the flickering of the lights.

I sprint behind her, having trouble keeping up. I fumble with getting my keys out of my pocket once we've skidded to a stop in front of my apartment. The abyssal infection crawls in at harrowing speed, but Sheera marches up to meet it. She drives her sword into the wall as I manage to stick my key into the lock and fling the door open. As I shuffle into my apartment, I get a sidelong glance at the line of light that stretches from ceiling to floor where Sheera's sword impales the wall. It seems to act as a barrier holding back the parasitic mold from advancing. I step back from the entrance, as I see it spreading from the other side of the hall. Sheera pops around the corner with her sword in-hand so I suppose she's given up on her attempts to hold back my darkness. She slams the door shut, but doesn't bother to lock it. Instead, she rotates her grip on her weapon so that the tip points downward and presses it against the door. The weapon seems to burn its way into it, causing a flurry of vine-like symbols to shoot out from the t-shaped hilt and across the walls. The white glow that emits off of these magic glyphs warms the whole apartment.

"That won't protect us indefinitely," she cautions, turning to face me. "I'm not equipped to protect you from the evil within, I can only help you face it." She steps past me and opens up one of my kitchen cabinets.

"Why has Shirun broken so many rules for me? I know he thought it would save me, but why go so far and why take me into The Void if he wasn't supposed to?"

She shakes her head slowly. "This kind of hubris has never been attempted before. Shirun defied the most important rule set for our kind—to preserve the sanctity of free will. We watch and we protect our charges, but forcing them into battle with their inner demons is nothing short of fucking blasphemy. As for his motivation to disavow what we hold most sacred, all I can offer is that we have a love for charges, the depths of which you may never understand. Our capacity to love is our most treasured blessing, but also the most dubious curse." She pulls a stemless wine glass out of my cupboard and eyes me in a way that suggests she's measuring my worth.

The stare is uncomfortable, but so is hearing that Shirun's got some incomprehensible thing for me. That completely makes our time in the Void a whole lot more awkward.

"So, is he **in** love with me then?" I shift from side to side as

I ask this.

Her composure breaks into surprised laughter. "Not, it's not like that at all, dumbass!"

"Well what is it like then? Does he feel some kind of kinship to me?"

She snorts as she goes to open my refrigerator door. "Kinship...to you...pa-lease!" She ducks into the appliance and I hear a mild shuffling of its contents.

I'm about to drop the subject when she starts to give me a real answer. "It's like knowing someone for as long as you've existed. It's growing with them, living every second of their life with them. It's sharing in the glory of their joy and helping bear the burden of their pains. It's being able to pan back to each moment of their past in vivid detail, seeing the colors of their present that they can't even perceive, and knowing all their possible futures—knowing all their potential as well as all the ways they can fall short."

She emerges from the refrigerator with a pitcher of filtered water. I come and take a seat on a stool in front of the island countertop as she pours water into the glass.

"It's the duty of the Shiran to do everything in our power to protect someone. We have so much power and yet, we have no ability to control our charges in any way—no means of stopping them even if we know they are headed straight into danger or outright ruin. All we can do is hold them tight and hope they don't shake us off. We can whisper in their ear, but it's seldom that we're heard. In the end, it's holding their hand when it's time for them to ascend or watching from afar as they drown in all the things that have damned them."

She puts the pitcher down and places her hand over the rim, holding it close to her chest. There's a glimmer in her eyes and her lips are pressed tightly together.

"Is that what happened to you?" I'm afraid of provoking her, but I'd like to understand who she is and where she's coming from. "Did you lose someone you loved—someone that shook you off, that wouldn't listen, and that you had to watch sink from a distance?"

Her eyes well up. "Yes, on all accounts, except one. My love for this person isn't in the past tense. It will last forever and I'm afraid the heartbreak will as well. The process is supposed to begin anew for me, as it has before, but I won't be allowed to have another charge until I've forgiven myself. Saving you won't bring them back, it won't change a fucking thing, but I also can't stand by and let this atrocity persist. Perhaps a happy conclusion will even allow me to finally reconcile with my past failures." Tears dribble out the corners of her eyes. "Ugh, I forgot this form weeps, it's disgusting!"

I hold back a chuckle at her disdain for crying. I suddenly see how much pain she's in, it was written across her face this whole time, but I only just now notice it.

"That's a lot of pressure to put on yourself," I offer.

"Perhaps," she admits, drying her eyes.

"So, you mean to tell me that isn't your natural form?" I try to be funny or at least change the subject.

"No, of course not!" I manage to make her laugh, so that's good. "You would not be able to perceive me in my truest form, but there are plenty I can take which are more perceptible to you, none of which are disingenuous to who I am."

"What made you go with that one?" My eyes widen as soon as I ask this—I really don't mean that as an insult—I'm actually just curious.

She smirks, seeming to know the full effect of my internal panic. "I went with a form that you would be most likely to trust."

"A beautiful woman?" I question, hoping flattery will get me some brownie points back.

"An impossibly beautiful woman..." she corrects me, waving a hand mockingly over her body. "You're not a man of exceptionally refined or mature taste."

"Oh, well, thanks for that..."

She shrugs in reply and hands me the glass. I'm not sure what the deal is with this—I mean why all this ceremony over a glass of water? She cocks an eyebrow at me, so I take a sip without verbally questioning her. The water tastes oddly sweet, almost like it's been mixed with honey or some kind of nectar.

"What is this?"

"Refreshment," she replies as though it's a dumb question. "Finish it and meet me in here," she instructs, walking over to my living room.

I consume the rest of this sweet water, finding it aptly refreshing. I'm not sure if this is some trust game we're playing now or if whatever she turned the water into will actually help me with what I have to do tonight. It's probably the most pleasant thing I've experienced all day so really, it's pointless to think too hard about what it actually is. I've drained the glass when I get a text from David.

"HI BRYAN, HOW HAS YOUR WEEK BEEN?"

For the first time in what's probably been a long time, I don't feel instant rage at David reaching out. It's a welcome light as the darkness—my darkness—closes in upon me. I'm not sure what I should say back. *"Please save me from the forces of evil"* hardly feels like a fair ask. Instead, I type, "CAN WE GET DINNER TOMORROW NIGHT AT THE PENINSULA?" I'm about to send this when I add, "MAYBE LET ME GET THIS ONE."

I know I owe him a lot more than dinner, but it's a good start at least. I go ahead and send this.

"THAT WOULD BE AWESOME!" he messages right back.

Now I have to prevent Sin from eating me alive so I can make good on these plans. I guess things are down to the wire now. With nothing left to do, I walk over to where Sheera sits on the couch waiting for me. Her legs are crossed and she looks at her nails which are manicured and painted white at the tips.

"He's a nice guy," she comments—it takes me a second to figure out that there's no snark in her tone.

"He's been pretty patient with me, he's a good friend." This might be the first time in a long time that I admit that out loud.

"Yes, well I've been pretty patient with you too, it's time for our moment of truth though. I need to reiterate that I can make no guarantees about what happens next. Your futures are buried and blurred by a murk I have never encountered before."

"You can see them right now? You don't need to be in The Void for that?"

"Wait, you saw futures there?" her gaze snaps onto me.

"Well, no, but Shirun described what he sees there to me." I shrink back a little, I should probably stop accidentally ratting the poor guy out, he's trying to save my soul after all.

"Right..." she groans. "The Void is everywhere and

nowhere so I'm there now just as much as I am here. That's why Shirun was able to be there even though he's confined to your soul."

"That's amazing!"

"Not really…"

I know for her, this is just part of existence, but she could at least humor me a little. She rises up from her seat and motions for me to take one. I stare at her questioningly. If her master plan is to get me to go to sleep, I can do that in bed just as easily.

"Lay down," she orders like I'm some little kid rebelling against bed time.

I do as she says, sprawling out on my back. "So, uh, are you just going to watch me while I sleep then?"

"Normally that would be my duty, yes, but I will need to be fused with you in order to help you in the soulscape."

I pull myself up, "Wait are you saying you need to have sex for this to work? I mean, no offense, but if you've got all these different forms, are you even actually a woman?"

She gives me a horrified, angled look as she shoves me down and straddles me. "For one second, could you not be a fucking moron! Our offspring would be monstrous creatures with nothing good to offer the world. I don't have a mammalian sex, but my kind also doesn't need one, we're transcendent of your fleshy reproductive needs. Not that it concerns you, but you **can** consider me female, that's how I manifest whenever I take a physical form.

"Okay, that's neat…" I really don't know what else to say.

Apparently neither does she since she forgoes words for an eye roll. She takes hold of my wrists and moves my hands—which I didn't realize I held up defensively—to the sides. Her eyes soften at me, maybe she's got some sense of how strange this actually is.

"Your body is a physical anchor to your soul. Since it's currently engulfed by The Calamity, I cannot reach it directly. That makes physical contact with you the easiest way to establish a connection. This contact will **not** be sexual … in any way.

"Okay. It's just that the way you're on top of me right now is a little suggestive."

She rolls her eyes again. "Perhaps if you just let your barriers down, this would feel less uncomfortable for you. I need you to trust me, wholly and completely, especially when it feels strange to do so. I'm not your most avid fan, but I'll do everything I can to keep you safe."

I hear banging outside my door. If Sheera hadn't warded it, I'm sure I'd be knee-deep in darkness right now. I guess I just need to listen to her and hope for the best.

"Alright," I tell her.

She grins lightly. "Okay."

With that, she spreads out over me as though to shield me from an explosion. I tense up beneath her, unsure of what to make of all of this. I really hope this is all real, because I'm one seriously screwed up dude if this is all in my head.

"Just breath." Her voice is even more soothing than before.

I follow her instructions, finding the pattern of my breathing quickly in sync with hers.

"That's it. Now, close your eyes and relax your muscles. Let me watch over you. Let me lend you my strength."

I try to do as she says, shutting my eyes and allowing myself to unwind. Somehow, I no longer feel the weight of her on top of me, only her warmth. This heat wraps itself around me and permeates through to my core. It's such a glorious sensation that I manage to enjoy it for only a moment before I slip away into unconsciousness.

# Chapter 4

A sharp chill reawakens my senses. My eyes open to an expanse of swirling black and midnight purple broken up by the occasional flash of thunder-less lightning. I groan and prop myself up at an angle, finding the surface beneath me soft, yet somehow crunchy as well. I look down to see that I'm on grass, but it's all matted and blackened. So, this is what became of the once-flawless lawn. Seeing it in this state is certainly troubling—especially if it is any reflection of the state of my mind/soul. What I see when I look to the side makes me spring up to my hands and knees. I scramble away from the line of graves that share the ground with me. There are twelve total and in front of each is a translucent figure. The one closest to me is Shelly Simmons. I get to my feet and walk over to her.

"Shelly?" I question, but there's no reply.

She's just a phantom reflection standing perfectly still, so still that not even her dress or hair sways against the harsh currents that dominate the atmosphere. She has both hands over her heart and stares tenderly, but also blankly, into the distance. I follow her line of sight to what's left of the manor. To say it has crumbled would not do it justice. The building is shattered to the point that it looks like some kind of surrealist art piece. Some portions of it are just floating independent of the rest, most of the roof and much of the walls are torn off, and lighting continues to blow off small chunks of what's left at an irregular cadence. Debris as large as part of a wall swirls around this decimated structure. Even the lawn rotates around the house in fractured swaths of earth like some kind of puzzle. The bit that I stand on now is in the process of circling around what I think is the rear of the manor—it's pretty hard to tell at this point.

"Welcome back, Mister Daley," Sin's voice crackles inside my mind. "I hope you'll enjoy the theatrics I've prepared for you this evening."

I start spinning around, looking for Sin even though I'm pretty sure he's not anywhere around here.

"While it's adorable that you thought it appropriate to bring a plus-one to our little soiree, I simply could not abide by such an imposition."

"What did you do with her?"

"Oh, she's quite alright for the time-being, but I'm doing my best to keep her out of our affairs. You see, I hoped this would be an evening of intimacy between you and I. If you would be so kind, I'd love it if you could turn your attention back to the short trip down nightmare lane that I've so painstakingly prepared for you."

Sin cackles. I shiver to think of what lies ahead of me. Coming back here was a scary enough proposition to begin with, but I feel even worse knowing Sin's made preparations to pack even more terror into this house of horrors.

"No need to rush; you really should indulge in the opportunity to look into the eyes of all you've lost along the way..."

When Sin's taunting fades, I turn back to the graves. Shelly's visage remains unmoved so I proceed to Margaret's. Her apparition stands tall with her hands cupped in front of her. I'm relieved to see her whole again, even if this is just an echo of her former self. She even bears that kindly smile I've come to associate with her. If Sheera's right and these guests are all just aspects of myself then I wonder what Margaret stood for—I don't recognize any piece or part of me that's nearly as good as she is. Maybe that's why she didn't last very long... Next in line is Christopher who just scowls with his hands dug deep into his pant pockets. I never got to know him as anything other than an angry little man who got angrier after a cretin possessed him. I didn't know Peter either though his time-shadow is much more pleasant to look at. He has his arms crossed and his shoulders hunched forward. His eyes are wide and stare off into the horizon with what I read as uncertainty. He looks like a blank slate—someone who could be anyone. It's hard to imagine him becoming an infected, evil, murder-monster, but those are the most prominent memories I have of him.

The next bunch of memorials harbor images of even more unsavory individuals. Ronald's the first I step over to. He's crouched, curled into a little ball with his head turned to look over his shoulder. Beads of sweat are stuck from falling down his face and his eyes are glossy from tears that will never form. Such a scared little man. Katelyn, Lily, Joseph, Michelle, and Charles all succeed him in line. It's hard to feel sorry for any of them besides Lily who's still in that ridiculous playboy-ballerina getup she wore when she died inside the cretin cage. She's frozen mid-pirouette with her hair and ribbons tossed wildly about. She looks pleadingly outward as if to see if anyone notices her dancing. I have a hard time pulling away from her, but I know I need to move on. Kenneth and Richard are last in this line of deceased personas. Kenneth stands with his hands at his sides. His head is turned as if mid-swivel and there's a searching look in his eyes. Whatever longing drove him will never be fulfilled now, but I'm not sure if that's good or bad for me. I knew next to nothing about Richard, but he tried to kill Indigo so it's hard to feel sympathy for him getting killed instead. Now that I've come to the end, I shudder to think about how many more graves might be here before the night is up.

"See, that was nice, wasn't it?" Sin taunts.

"You're a sick piece of shit!" I yell back.

Sin snickers, "I'm as much a part of you as they are, Mister Daley."

"Even if that's true, I'm going to put you down and I'm going to do it tonight."

"We shall see, little one..." There's amusement in Sin's tone. "For now, be a good boy and play along. Your nostalgia-laden adventure isn't over yet."

The sections of withered lawn swirling between me and the manor speed up before coming to a gradual stop. There are a number of smaller patches that line up in a sort of stepping stone pattern to allow me passage across the abyss. Behind these is the back of the rose garden. A gap of charred bushes leaves an opening for me from this side. I take a farewell glance at the graves for all the dead parts of myself. With them accounting for twelve of the thirty guests, does their destruction mean that I'm basically half of what I once was? Maybe that isn't important, maybe I just have to save what's left. With that in mind, I turn and jog over to edge of my plot of corrupted lawn and hop across the swaths lined up before me. A part of me does fear that Sin could just suddenly send these into motion again, though I feel like that would be far too unceremonious an end for me after all the planning and plotting he's conducted.

Fortunately, I leap into the rose garden without any trickery or foul play. Now that I'm here, I'd hardly describe this as safety. The leaves on the bushes are dried and shriveled. Some peel off and flutter down to the dusty cobblestone path. The roses look deadened, too, but their black petals aren't dehydrated—instead they're gushing with some foul, dark goo that drips off of them and sticks to the ground like blood. Most of the maze is untouched by the lightning strike, but somehow this feels like a much more sinister form of destruction. There's a pungent smell in the air, something that smells like vomit, or maybe just rotting vegetation.

"Welcome back to where the festivities really kicked off. Tell me, do you know what this place is to you?"

I look around, but don't have any guesses. "Whatever it was before, I'd say you've pretty sufficiently destroyed it."

"Now, now, you barely even thought on it. Let's not be so hasty, hmmm?"

A sudden jerk almost throws me off my feet. Once I regain my balance, I look back to see that all the bits of the lawn are back in motion. I guess that means going back isn't an option.

"What you must understand is that every piece and part of you has the capacity to be the exact opposite of what it is. Take this rose garden, for example. In its heyday, it was the representation of every good deed you ever did. Sure, you've done bad as well—and plenty of it, at that—but those branches were pruned and hidden in the shed. I've pulled them all out and replanted them for you."

"What happened to the good ones, then?"

"Oh, don't worry, I have someone to tend to those troublesome little things."

"Did you bring me here just so I could smell the nasty roses you planted?"

I start to wander along the path even though I feel like something spooky could leap out at any point.

"**You** grew them, Mister Daley, I'm merely making sure we have them put out on display. The place has been in desperate need of redecorating for some time, after all."

"Fine, whatever, is there some point you'd like to make or can we get on with this?"

"Such haste!" Sin's mocking tone rattles the towering bushes around me. "I'm afraid there is far more for you to see here before I can permit you to move onward. The roses are not the only thing that I have seen fit to bring to light—I'd like you to encounter all the other things you've been pretending aren't there."

"Why don't you just come out and face me?" I yell, looking up to The Calamity.

"I'm not in any rush... We do have all night after all! I'll have plenty of time to enjoy the dark, defeated version of you later. For now, I plan to savor how your light desperately flickers against the shadows I cast. So, please, step along and prepare to suffer. The rose garden has grown a bit more labyrinthian since you last visited, but don't worry I've sent along a guide—you can thank me later..."

I round a corner and find myself at a dead end. Twisting back, I see a tawny man with shaggy hair and a scraggly beard scuttle on his hands and knees out from one bush and into another. Then the ground beneath me suddenly rotates around at one hundred and eighty degrees until I'm facing a brand-new path. Apparently, Sin can even shape my route through this maze. That's great...

I've only just taken a couple of steps down this walkway when a girlish voice fills my ears, "Fancy seeing you here!"

Before I can turn around, a spritely girl with a sideways blond ponytail skips in front of me. She's outfitted in a black, sequined dress that cuts off mid-thigh and has flaring princess sleeves. Petal-like shapes formed from fuzzy ebony wiring are sewn along the seams of her low-cut neckline and across her back. The way they shoot up whimsically makes her look like a dark pixie.

"You've come a long way since that first night in the billiards room, haven't you?" she tilts her head as she asks this, causing her ponytail to swing around.

"Jasmine?" I gasp, squinting my eyes.

It really is her! But she's also not Jasmine. Her skin is alabaster and her eyes are such a deep shade of blue that they don't look like eyes at all—more like frozen pebbles.

"Bingo!" she chirps as she bends forward and reaches out to poke my chin.

Her touch is freezing, causing me to jolt back with a low yip. She giggles playfully and scampers around.

"Gotcha!"

"That hurt," I complain, rubbing my frost-bitten face.

"Well it didn't hurt me at all sooo..." She eyes me for a moment and pauses as though recalling my initial reaction and then breaks into even more maniacal laughter.

"What happened to you? Did Sin's cretins get you? Are you even real? You can't be real, can you?"

"No! Bad!" she scolds, marching back over to me with a finger held up—which I back slowly away from. "You need to be very careful with that word. Everything is **real** here. Forget your facts and your logic and all the rest. The only thing that matters here is the truth. The truth is that I **am** real and I **am** Jasmine—just not the Jasmine you've been getting to know. I'm her opposite, her reflection. We stand feet to feet and at any moment, she can become me and I her, but you'll rarely have us both at the same time."

So, there are good and bad versions of at least some of the guests. I doubt there's a worse version of characters like Charles or Ronald, but I do have to wonder if this whole yin-yang thing is just an indication that I'm secretly bipolar.

"What do you want, then?" I ask her.

"Wow, so down to business," she groans, putting her hands on her hips and leaning forward. "I'm your guide through this place. Not because I particularly care much about whether or not you make it through, Sin just told me to do it because I'm the only one who has my wits about me..."

She titters and spins around with her hands in the air. When she's done, she shoots me a smirk.

Refraining from any kind of reaction, I just ask, "So, you listen to Sin, then? You're on his side?"

She squares off to me with a dead serious look in her hard eyes. "Of course, Sin's the only one around here that makes any sense."

If she truly believes that, then she's a much darker creature than I initially took her for.

"Alright, well, let the guiding begin then, Queen of the witless." I give her a mock bow as I say this.

She squeals, "I love that!" She prances around humming, "Jasmine, Queen of the Witless Whelps in the Garden of Misdeeds." Once her glee subsides, she turns around and says, "Well, come on then."

I follow her along the stone path. It's nearly silent for a time as we navigate the maze. All I can hear is the patter of our footsteps and the sickly dripping sound of whatever oozes off of these dark roses. Eventually, I begin to hear the light din of voices in the distance. Even as we draw closer, it's still hard to make out who they belong to or what they're saying. Dark Jasmine scampers ahead. As she approaches the bush wall, the ground beneath it rotates, positioning the rose bushes so that the paths to our left and right are blocked off, but we now have access to a new one in the center.

"Stop, you're making it worse!" I hear a man's voice declare.

I pick up my pace to meet Dark Jasmine at the entrance to a little courtyard in what must be the garden's center. I get there in time to see two long, skinny legs disappear into a bush. Could that be the bearded guy from before?

"Here, I can fix this! Oh boy, I hope I can fix this!"

"P-p-please just l-l-let me do it..." a woman replies.

I don't immediately recognize the two people in the middle of the square. The woman sits hunched on a circular bench. There's a lot wrong with her—visually at least. She looks like a doll, or rather, a culmination of different types of dolls. Her egg-white face has cracks across the cheeks like damaged porcelain. White hair fails in long, ragged locks over bony shoulders where plastic, socketed arms attach like an action figure. One of her hands seems to have come off as it just lays over her lap. She's also missing what looks like a glass eye. A leg has been torn off at the top of the shin. It's all tattered like cloth and stuffing sometimes falls out from what's left of the limb. The man next to her pats frantically at the grass.

"I'm sure I can find it...gah, it's got to be here somewhere!"

"P-p-please s-stop. It's f-f-fine."

"No, no, no, I can fix this, just give me a moment."

"You can't even see, you idiot," Dark Jasmine mocks him as he scrambles around on his hands and knees.

The man's head shoots up in shock and I finally realize that this is Dark Jeremy. I also notice that his eyes are, indeed a solid milky white with red scars crossing over the skin around them. Does that mean that this creature beside him is Dark Natasha? She turns and regards me with her one, glassy eye. It takes careful examination, but I eventually discern from the shape of her marred face that this shambling figure is indeed Natasha's dark reflection. Looking back at Dark Jeremy, I observe that he's also a complete mess. He has little black veins nearly bursting through the skin of his hands and neck. Sweat beads up over his face and his curly hair tangles outward in half a dozen different directions. Although he's dressed head to toe in formal attire, everything is unbuttoned, untucked, and wrinkled to oblivion. Natasha's in a strapless sundress that seems largely in order except that its color has faded to a dull grey and it's frayed at the edges. My heart breaks to see them like this. Is this what they'll be like permanently if I lose? I step forward, moved by their distress, but Dark Jasmine puts an arm out to block me.

"Ut-tut-tut, hero!" she scolds.

"We should help them."

"Why?" she asks wide-eyed. "It's so much funnier to watch them struggle." She turns away from me and skips around the horrors before us. "Silly little dolly who can't keep herself together and her spastic, blind fool. What a pair you two make!"

"Wait!" Dark Jeremy gasps. "Did you remember to close the door?"

Dark Jasmine snickers, "No, does that make you nervous?"

"Close it, hurry!" Jeremy wheezes.

"P-p-please," Dark Natasha agrees, with fervor.

"What are you two ducks so worried about?" Dark Jasmine goads them, leaning forward with her hands folded over the small of her back, her ponytail seemingly always in motion.

"Olivia's in here, you know that! Just go, leave us be."

Dark Jasmine steps back and crosses her arms. "Well, alright then, fine!" She sticks her tongue out at them before prancing past me and into the maze. "Come along then, this part of the tour is officially over!"

I look to the sad, morbid pair before me. "I will save you," I promise them.

Natasha looks remorsefully at me, "N-n-no you won't…"

Her words make my stomach drop. What does she know that I don't? I try to smile reassuringly, but nothing can hide the concern that creases my brow. With nothing left to say, I turn away from them, hoping I'll see the normal versions of them again. The maze shifts around once I've left the courtyard—closing off access to Dark Jeremy and Dark Natasha, but opening a new route to the side.

"Don't mind them," Dark Jasmine says as she hops along, though I don't think her tone is all that comforting. "The dark side of things is easier for most of us which means it'll be easier for you too."

"You think I want to turn into a monster?" I challenge.

"Well, I never said you'd enjoy it, just that it's easier. You'll find out soon enough I think…"

"So, who's next?" I sigh, pinching the bridge of my nose.

She stops dead in her tracks and swings around to face me. "No! Bad! No spoilers, that'll ruin the fun."

"Well, I'm not having any fun…"

"Didn't say **you** were…" She sticks out her tongue at me and then spins back around to lead me onward.

The path ahead of us shifts around until a shed is revealed. I'm pretty sure this is the same one that Olivia ambushed me from during my second night here. Is this where Dark Olivia is hanging out? I'm terrified to find out what this other version is like. What we find instead is a scrawny boy with shaggy ebony hair falling over his smoky grey face. He stumbles over to the open door of the shed where a massive pile of red roses spills out onto the cobblestone. He falls to his knees in front of it, heedless of the impact of the stones against his tiny kneecaps. As he falls, the hair over his face briefly sways up and away, revealing distinctive freckles over his cheeks and button nose.

"Jack?" I manage to croak even though I'm left breathless that there's a Dark version of him.

He doesn't even look at me, instead, he reaches down to grab a rose from the pile with his elongated fingers. He regards it like some kind of treasure as he holds it up. His sharp, black fingernails form points around the soft, moist petals. I only get a pitiless shrug from Dark Jasmine when I turn to her. Without warning, Jack shoves the fully bloomed flower into his mouth. He squishes it around a little before gulping it down. I can see the outline of it travel down his skeletal throat.

"Ahhh..." he moans as he pulls himself to his feet.

"What are you doing?"

My voice seems to catch his attention this time. His head twists to me, revealing solid black eyes broken up by pale red irises for a brief moment before his hair falls over them again. I rush over and grab him by the shoulders. He's not cold, but he does smell of rot.

"Oh, hello there..." he says sluggishly.

His head lolls around as if he's high on something.

"I don't understand," my voice wavers. "What is this version of you?"

"Who, me?" he giggles, showing his pointy teeth as his darkened lips part. "You don't need to worry about me, I promise I won't be a bother. I just want to eat, really."

His head rolls to a sideward angle, causing his hair to fall to one side. His one uncovered eye peers up at me and I suddenly realize that his irises swirl with different shades of red.

"Eat my good deeds?" I clarify.

"It's the only thing I've got to eat here." His face suddenly contorts. "Excuse me," he whispers.

He somehow manages to slip out of my grasp as though he's a phantom—maybe that's what he actually is. I watch as he stumbles over to a woven basket filled with those drippy, dark roses. He crouches over it, clutching its handles. His breathing is heavy for a couple moments before it becomes sharp as though he's in pain. Then he heaves and vomits up the flower he swallowed. It falls into the basket followed by a stream of thick, black goo. He's making more of those disgusting, bleeding roses!

"Jack!" I shout more in horror than anger. "What the hell are you doing?"

"Oooh..." Dark Jack groans. He sways away from the basket and falls to a seated position.

"Oh, baby! Tell me that wasn't the sexiest thing you've ever seen!" Dark Jasmine cheers behind me with genuine enthusiasm.

"That hurt," Dark Jack complains.

"Oh, be a man!" she scolds. "You know you liked it… You know you'll want to do it again—you can't help yourself."

"That's true…" Dark Jack agrees, rolling onto his back and putting a hand on his stomach as he attempts to wipe the dark sludge away from his lips—only managing to smear it around.

I'm as moved as I am disgusted by all of this. This is still Jack, right? A really fucked up version for sure, but I still feel just as drawn to him. I walk over and take a knee beside where he lies. The odors coming off of him make my stomach turn a bit.

"What can I do for you?" I ask, placing a hand over his stomach in hopes that will help steady it.

His nose scrunches at the question. All of his hair is spread back over the ground. With it out of the way, he almost resembles Jack, even with the dark eyes and grey complexion.

"I just want to eat…" he says softly—eyes fixed upon the swirling storm above us. "I'm so hungry." Rolling onto his side, he adds, "Maybe if I just have another one…"

"Don't'!" I beg him, grabbing him by his bony wrists as he reaches for another red rose.

"Please!"

He struggles against me, somehow managing to slip right out from my grip again.

Dark Jasmine squeals. "You can't stop him, not really at least. The way he's been gorging himself lately, you'd think he'd be full by now!"

"Can he keep any of it down?" I'm not sure why I ask this, even Dark Jasmine looks at me like I'm out of my mind.

Jack rummages through a small stack that must be of his own making and devours another rose.

"Of course not!" Jasmine informs me. "But it's just delicious to see him regurgitate those dull things into something glorious. Let's have one for the road. What do you say Jack, baby?"

Jack stops spinning like a drunk ballerina to look at her. His head drops to the side and he gives her a wide, pointy grin. Then his expression drops and he trips over to the basket. I look away, but I can still hear him vomit his ruined flower out. He flops down beside the collected byproducts of whatever dark power he possesses.

"Yes! That's the stuff!" Dark Jasmine swoons in borderline ecstasy.

"I'm sorry, Jack," I say loud enough for him to hear me.

"Oh, that's alright. The other me probably won't even get his last supper."

I don't want to know what he means by that so I turn away and follow my guide down a path that's just opened up for us.

"Ohhh, the way that boy works..." Dark Jasmine moans as she twirls along.

"When does this trip through the haunted garden end?" I grumble behind her.

"When you're done seeing everything you need to see," she answers coolly.

I suppose that's the best I'll be getting from her. The garden starts to shift around us more and more, making it kind of dizzying to traverse through it.

"Stay close now," she instructs. "I think I spot someone else that you really ought to meet."

The walls of rose bushes rotate and shuffle until another small clearing opens up. At the center of this clearing is a bed of grass under much shorter rose bush stands covered in unopened white bulbs. A man's feet stick out from under it, one on top of the other as though he's wrapped himself around the trunk of the plant.

"What's that supposed to be?" I ask my tour guide, motioning to the bush.

"Those would be all the deeds you could have done, but chose not to, both good and bad."

We move a little closer to it and I'm about to comment on how there are not that many of those buds, at least. Then I realize that what I initially took for a bed of grass is actually a squished layer of fallen rose buds that have grayed and frayed apart. I also note how the bush is overflowing with these little colorless buds. They're popping right off at irregular intervals and whoever the man underneath is has been squishing them down into a nest of sorts. Who is this mystery napper? I realize I'm about to get my answer when Dark Jasmine saunters over and reaches down to grab the man by his ankle. He howls as she drags him out from his hiding place and slides him in front of me.

"GAHHH! Why did you do that," he stammers as he clutches his ankle and frantically examines his surroundings.

His eyes go wide as they fall upon me. Dark Jasmine giggles so uncontrollably that she actually falls into the bush. I examine the tall, gangly heap of a man before me. His unruly hair and scraggly beard remind me of a cave man and his tattered clothing only reinforces that image. Who could this possibly be though? Is he the Dark version of someone I don't really know? There are a few people in the manor I haven't officially met yet, but I don't think any of them looked at all like this.

"No, no… why did you bring him here?" His voice is vaguely familiar, but it sounds wrong, maybe higher pitched?

He scrambles around like a dog chasing its tail. In a sudden moment of clarity, he scurries over to hide behind the bush—which Jasmine is just now extricating herself from.

"Who is this?" I ask her. "Is it a taller, even more afraid version of Ronald?"

"I'm not Ronald," he snarls, briefly popping his head out from his hiding spot. "Maybe we're a little similar, but not the same…"

"Why don't you tell him your name then, baby?"

Jasmine leans around the bush. I don't see what she's doing, but a sharp yelp comes from the odd man hiding from me.

"Ouch! I'm Myles, okay!"

My heart must have stopped beating for a second as all the air leaves my lungs. **This** is Myles? I wander around the plant to find him cowering in a little ball. He yips and scrambles around, out of sight once he realizes I can see him.

"Don't look at me!"

"Pull your shit together, man, I need you right now…"

Dark Jasmine snickers, her icy eyes meeting mine.

"What is this abomination?"

She smirks, twirling around aimlessly. "I dunno, Bry-Bry. I think you're just having a hard time accepting us. I mean we've been here the whole time, you've just refused to notice. Now Sin has set us free and it's time to smell the roses." She falls to her knees and clutches her stomach as she laughs hysterically. "Get it… cause we're in a rose garden…" She cackles even harder and I think I'm really starting to hate this little imp. "I couldn't resist..." she finally gasps breathlessly.

"Quiet!" Myles suddenly screams.

I snap my attention to where he grovels over the bed of fallen rose buds, then I notice that there's a distant rustling that gets louder with each passing moment.

"What is—"

Before I can finish the question, Dark Myles scuttles over and grabs me by the ankles.

"She's coming!" he wheezes, looking up to me with tear-filled eyes. "Please don't let her hurt me!"

"Aren't you supposed to be the one protecting me?" I challenge, hoping to awaken some shadow of the real Myles in this pathetic reflection.

"No, no, no..." he quivers and looks to the side in fearful anticipation of what's coming our way.

Dark Jasmine walks past us and leans forward with her hands on her hips. "We're gonna have to make moves pretty soon here, Bry-Bry. You're supposed to see this first, though."

The rustling turns to thrashing. My guess is that I'm about to meet Dark Olivia. I'm admittedly pretty terrified to see what her demonic reflection will be. Apparently Dark Myles has no intention of sticking around for the big reveal. He releases my ankles and crawls off into one of the hedge walls, disappearing from this place. I stand beside Dark Jasmine and square off to where the noises are coming from. The wall of roses before us shakes, quakes, and bursts apart—sending tainted petals, leaves, and twigs crashing through the air. They hang there, falling ever so slowly, as if caught in a gravitational field.

A woman stands in the wake of this destruction, her dark hair blowing up in the air like a tongue of flame. Her skin is a fiery shade of red and her eyes are solid black. She's stark naked. She has the torso and face of a shapely woman, but her hands and feet are large and clawed like a beast. She tilts her head back and lets out a sharp noise that's something between a banshee's scream and a wolf's howl.

"Well, that's that, then," Dark Jasmine states, unconcerned by the monster that's ready to pounce on us. "There's no talking to or reasoning with this one so let's skedaddle!"

She turns and flees at this suggestion and I follow close behind. The bush wall blocking our escape deforms just in time for us to pass through. The entire garden starts to twist around us as we run, clearing a straight path for us, but making it very difficult for me to maintain a sense of equilibrium. I try to keep myself steady in the ever-twisting surroundings, knowing I can't really afford to get tripped up. I can hear Olivia tearing through the bush walls as they attempt to close on her. The screeches that she looses into the air are hard to interpret, but I don't think her intentions are any more complex than a desire to rip us apart. Dark Jasmine stops and turns once we've reached the end of the garden's ruins.

"The end of the road's just a hop, skip, and a jump away, Bry-Bry," she pants as she marches back toward where we just came from.

I look off to where some plots of solid ground orbit the manor. They're not within reach yet, but moving in my direction at least. I glance back to my companion and find her blowing kisses into the path before her. Each kiss fills the air with a steamy chill that slowly crusts into some kind of magical ice wall. When she's finished with this barrier she spins around and leans forward, giving me a wave.

"It's been a blast, baby! Move along now, don't want to miss your ride outta here!"

Dark Olivia smashes into the frozen barricade, sending small cracks through it. She bounces back, stunned at first, but starts smashing into with her fists.

"Yeah, well what are you going to do about it, you crazy bitch?" Dark Jasmine taunts as she prances up to her wall.

I turn away and walk up to the edge of this cobblestone path. I definitely don't want to miss my ride out of here. A slab of grass with dirt crumbling away on an upside-down hill arcs toward me from my left. I guess this is my "hop." I do so as it passes and stumble to my knees as I attempt to gain my footing. Once I'm sorted, I see my "skip" coming up in the opposite direction.

"How does it feel to meet the darkest sides of your soul, Mister Daley?" Sin's voice scratches in my ear.

"These freaks have nothing to do with me!"

"Oh, make no mistake, Mister Daley, these figures **are** a part of you. They have been overshadowed by their duller counterparts up until now, but soon they will roam free in this place and you will be far better off for it."

I shake my head even though I'm not sure whether Sin can actually see me. "Stop trying to get in my head!"

A sharp chuckle rattles my eardrums. "I don't need to be in your head, I'm already wrapped around your heart. I just need to squeeze a little more before it becomes putty in my grasp."

"Shut up!" my voice cracks as I yell.

"Well, there's no need to shout now, is there? Let's just breathe a moment and be sure to watch your step."

I realize that a stretch of what must be the main driveway swings around from my right. I take a deep breath and skip onto it. The pavement is lined with Victorian-style street lamps that flicker intermittently.

"Think about it this way," Sin rambles on as I walk down toward the manor. "During a lunar eclipse, the sun covers the moon, but that certainly doesn't mean it's no longer there, does it? Those poor people you just met live in perpetual eclipse, desperate to poke out from where they remain blissfully out of your sight—out of your mind. They want nothing more than to trade places with the light that blocks them. I'd like to see their dream come to fruition."

"Those monsters will never see the light of day!"

"Your self-loathing has always been so delicious!"

**"Fuck off!"**

My juvenile response elicits a sickening cackle from Sin. "Run along now, there's one more special someone I think you need to meet..."

There's someone else? What other horrible version of one of my allies could Sin have drudged up? I guess I'll find out momentarily if this upcoming "jump" doesn't kill me. The stretch of crumbling driveway I'm on floats around toward the manor's front entrance: a ring of stone tiling with a set of wide, granite steps leading up to twin mahogany doors. The gap between the edge of this thing and where I need to go is large enough to cause some stress. My walk turns into a dash and my heart races at the dumb action hero stunt that I'm trying to pull. I try to push aside all my doubt as I near the end of this roadway. With a deep exhale, I spring into the air and time feels as though it slows while I sail with arms and legs gracelessly flailing.

A lump forms in my throat as I realize I'm going to come up short. My waist crashes against the corner of the stone ring—knocking the air from my lungs. I grasp for something to stop me from slipping, but there's nothing to hold onto. I slide right off of the only solid ground I have, but two hands snap around my wrists before I can plummet to my doom. It takes some effort, but I am hoisted up to safety. I'm about to thank my saviors when I see that there're two cretin people standing in front of me. I fall back onto the ground, confused and terrified of why they would help me. Maybe Sin is really just that serious about making me suffer before going in for the kill. The cretins are different now. They're not wearing armored gauntlets, yet their touch didn't sear through my skin. They also look more like actual people now. They're still faceless, but their jaws are shaped more like how a real person's might look. Their hair flutters about like seaweed at the bottom of an ocean. They stand more upright and maintain a posture befitting a proper lady and gentleman. The man wears a shimmering black suit and the lady, a long evening gown. Thin, ebony smoke seems to radiate off of their bodies, but neither of them appear to notice—I guess they don't have eyes or noses, so how could they? They're like dark, demonic mannequins.

"Oh, no you don't…" Sin goads. "We're not done with you yet…"

I guess Sin's determined to ensure I experience his haunted trail to its completion after all. Sin's minions motion for me to follow them. I stay down for a moment, watching their languid forms ascend the front steps. They pull open both the front doors once I'm back on my feet. I keep an eye on them as I step up and enter the manor. They remain solemn and still. I have to wonder what this could possibly be building up to. What's the endgame? What's the point of me going through all of this? The sound of the front doors shutting startles me from my thoughts. I'm not really sure if the cretins lock it shut, but I know there's no going back anyway. At least the main foyer is mostly intact, giving me some welcome shelter from The Calamity. Glass from the windows that surrounded the front doors crunches beneath my shoes. A couple of lamps are also knocked over, but the rest of the room looks undisturbed. Two cretin women come out from a hallway entrance carrying a tall, black mirror between them. Thy set it down before me and sail away, the trains of their dresses slithering like snakes.

I step cautiously up to the dark vanity, but don't see my reflection in it. Instead, I see the visage of a woman in a black and deep purple Victorian dress. She's walking up to meet me as though she's in some other place that exists behind the glass. A sea of grey fog surrounds her, but the rest of the backdrop is just pitch black. My heart leaps when she gets close enough for me to see her face. I guess I knew all along that it would be her. She looks like some kind of fairy tale villain with the flaring collar of her gown, a bulbous updo, crimson lipstick, dark blue eye shadow, and ebony nails. Her skin is alabaster and her eyes are a neon green color that looks radioactive.

"Margaret?" I exhale in hushed astonishment.

# Chapter 5

Dark Margaret's stony gaze falls to a frightening scowl as her threatening eyes crash onto me. Without warning, she steps out of the mirror. I stumble back, wondering if this thing is a mirror at all or just a doorway to some unholy place. She struts toward me as I try to keep my distance from her. The sharp clicking that resounds with each step tells me that she must be wearing a mighty pair of stilettos. The jewelry adorning her is far more lavish than the Margaret I know would ever deign to wear. Gold and ruby rings all but cover her fingers and a pair of diamond encrusted earrings with black pearls on the bottom dangle from her ears. All the frills of her attire leave little room for a necklace but every button and buckle are golden and engraved with fanciful patterns. I'm so busy taking this figure in that I obliviously back into the wall beside the front doors.

One side of the Dark Margaret's mouth curls upward ever so slightly. She brings a hand up below my chin and holds it in her long finger nails. I shiver at how they pinch into my skin and I have a hard time making eye contact with her.

"Is that really all you have to say to me?" Her voice is similar to Margaret's, but it has a sharp edge to it. "You know full well who I am, yet all you can think to do is question my identity … you're a damned fool!"

I realize too late just how much trouble I'm in as Margaret releases my chin only to pull her hand aloft and backhand me across my face. The blow knocks me to my hands and knees.

"You imbecile!" she hisses as she kicks me in the stomach.

The impact causes me to crumble all the way down to the floor. She grabs me by the hair and pulls my head back as she bends menacingly above me.

"I'm queen of this house, you little ingrate! For too long have I been living as one of The Eclipsed. Now I can claim my rightful throne here in the new world order. I think my first act shall be to beat you till you're nothing but a shaking, sobbing puppy in my lap."

"That's quite enough, Margaret..." another woman's voice cuts in.

It draws Dark Margaret's attention, compelling her to let go of my hair and even take a few steps away from me. I look up to see her squaring off to three hooded figures in silver robes.

"What do you want, you harpy?"

"We have our own plans for our dear Mister Daley—plans that I'm sure he'll find far more amenable than what you design." I know I know that voice from somewhere.

"What makes you so sure I'll acquiesce to the likes of you?"

The woman—who is the tallest figure in the middle of the group of mystery people—chuckles before replying, "You know who we are. You are royalty here, yes, but our combined strength has always been the source of your own. You cannot fight us, so please do be a dear and step aside."

Dark Margaret growls at these figures. Turning to me, she snarls, "I'm fairly certain we'll get the chance to continue this later..."

With that, she shoves her way through the group and marches out into one of the halls that branch out from this foyer. The question now is whether I'm in better hands with these guys. The two shorter people come over, one definitely a woman and the other probably a man. I'm about to try to squirm away when they pull back their hoods. My mouth hangs open when William and Joanna reveal themselves—not Dark/Eclipsed versions—the actual William and Joanna. They may not be my favorite people in the manor, but at least they're not some twisted version of somebody I hold dear. They reach down and help me to my feet, holding me steady for a moment before their leader turns her back to us.

"Come along, the third floor awaits us," she commands.

My heart leaps at this—she must mean we're going to see Shirun. William and Joanna guide me along behind our mysterious leader. It's somewhat unnerving that she won't reveal herself, but at least I'm otherwise surrounded by familiar and not entirely unfriendly faces. We head into a narrow hall and all my suspicion turns to shock when I see that it leads into a gaping chasm within the manor. I step up to the fractured edge and get an up-close look at all of the ruined pieces of the manor floating in place. I shiver at the sight and turn breathlessly back to my companions.

"How are we supposed to get anywhere?" I ask.

I hear our hooded leader snicker under her breath before she replies, "The landscape has changed since you were last here, Mister Daley. It is in ruins, yet not entirely impossible to traverse."

She opens what must be a closet door, but behind it is a wall of baby blue light that ripples and shimmers like a pool of broken glass.

"The routes through this place are no less winding and obtuse than before, but we will find our way to our destination," she explains.

With that, William struts through and is slurped up by the magical portal. Joanna follows him, leaving me alone with the woman in charge.

"Go along, then," she encourages me, though I'd describe her voice as neither gentle nor kind.

"Who are you?"

"You'll see soon enough. For now, try to trust me."

This can't be Sheera can it? No, she's all wrong to be Sheera. This must be one of the guests, but why won't she just come out and reveal herself? I guess I'll just give her my cautious trust. There's not really anywhere else I can go or anything else that I can do so I turn and step through the portal. It's weird because I don't really feel anything as I push through the shiny blue film that lines the doorway. One second I'm in the hallway and the next I'm stepping into a cozy library with towering shelves. The place is a mess, though. Books are scattered across the room, their pages rustled by the sharp currents pouring in from the back wall that's been completely torn off. One of the shelves has even fallen over, propped up by the wall it crashed into. I spot William and Joanna beneath it, kicking books off the floor and into The Calamity so that they can open a door.

I walk over to the fireplace which seems to have been put out mid-burn as charred chunks of wood and stray ash are scattered around it. Reaching down, I take hold of the poker that's also laying strewn out of its place. The hooded woman shakes her head slowly as she makes for where Joanna opens our next door. The ladies step through it but William waits for me.

"You won't need that where we're going," he says with his hand held out.

He gives me what looks like a condescending grin when I hold tight to the implement. He probably meant it as a reassuring expression though, maybe his face is just weird. Either way, I hand the poker over since it probably wouldn't do much against any of Sins' forces anyway. William tosses it aside and leads me through the passage into what looks like a stretch of narrow hallway on the first floor. We proceed along until we come upon a doorway, except we find another blue portal on the other side when our leader pulls open the door.

"What happened to what used to be there?" I inquire.

"Gone," Joanna states simply as she leads the way through.

We all file in after her, ending up in a storage room. Wooden boxes are stacked up all around us. I walk up to a smaller stack where the top box is open. Inside are dozens of picture frames in different colors. I pick up one framed in gold. It's of me and my childhood friend, Adrien, when we were little. The image is moving as if I'm looking at a home video of a moment I don't think was ever captured on camera. But there it is now in vivid detail, I even feel the lightness of it, the pure joy of playing soccer with someone I care about. We were so close until he moved away.

I pick up two more, one framed in vibrant royal azure and the other a faded cerulean. The first plays out a scene of me on my first real date with a girl named Jessica. I relive the excitement and nervousness I felt at The Feta Grove with her as we ate dinner. The other frame encases me stifling tears as I'm reading her breakup text to me—something about my bad attitude which was bullshit because the truth was her dad just didn't like me. As I put down the frame, the adolescent anger lifts off of me and I wonder if it actually was just my bad attitude...

"There isn't time to dawdle," our leader snaps as I'm reaching for another frame.

I look up to see the trio waiting for me by the open door and reluctantly pull myself away from these magical little mementos. Even with my whole world on the brink of collapse, I could probably spend forever looking through everything stored in this room. It's with a heavy heart that I step through the portal, leaving it all behind.

We arrive in a hallway that's been pretty badly beaten. All the destruction makes it hard to tell, but this looks like the second floor based off the spacing of the remaining doors lining it. If that's the case, then it feels like we're weirdly hopping between all three floors to get to where we're going. As we move along, I begin to hear some kind of muffled chanting. The louder it gets, the more it actually sounds like pots and pans clanging against each other. Finally, we come to a spot a whole section of the wall to our right is missing and I suddenly realize where I am. I peek around the corner to see that dark platform where I fought Charles and the others levitating out there in The Calamity. There's a black and silver bonfire in the middle and dark figures dancing like apes around it. I stumble back and look wide eyed at my guides. This isn't where they're taking me is it?

Our leader turns to me. "They're pre-emptively celebrating the end of this house," she explains, "We should keep moving."

I exhale deeply when I hear her say this and try not to look back at whatever this disturbed ritual is. The woman still wearing her cloak pulls open another door with a portal behind it and we all go through. This time, I know exactly where we are. We're just outside of Shirun's chamber. Its twin doors stand warm and welcoming and I crack a smile at knowing the observatory is just down the hall. I start to head that way when our leader catches me by the arm, her grip surprisingly firm.

"In here, Mister Daley."

I'm alarmed to find William and Joanna at the doors, ceremoniously pushing them open.

"Shouldn't we get to Shirun?" my voice is tight.

"This is the way we must go…" is all she says.

Why would Shirun change bases? He didn't seem to think this room was safe before. The vague familiarity in this woman's voice continues to be of little comfort. There's something about her grasp that's equally unnerving. She guides me into the room and almost shoves me in. Instantly, I realize that something's horribly wrong here. Three more figures in silver cloaks stand scattered around the room's center. All of their shadowy faces turn to me at once. I see that they've done some redecorating in here too. The warm burgundies and soft whites still dominate the room's color scheme, but now dark chains and black apparatuses line the walls. Even the bed has been remade with silky ebony betting and silver drapes.

"What is this?" I demand, suddenly starting to sweat.

I twist around when I hear the doors shut. William and Joanna secure them with a chain and a padlock.

"Tut, tut, Mister Daley, there's really no need to get yourself all worked up," the woman holding me says in a patronizing tone.

William and Joanna come up on either side of her and begin to unfasten the necks of their robes. The garments fall from their wiry bodies to reveal strange, fetishy outfits. Joanna's wearing a shiny black bra beneath a transparent mesh cardigan that hangs open around her narrow, but defined abdomen. She's also wearing a black lace thong, open-toe stilettos, frilly thigh elastics, and leather wrist cuffs that seem locked in place with miniature silver padlocks. William is in a black thong that's so shiny it looks like it's wet and a pair of knee-high superhero boots. Gold rings adorn his skinny fingers and a gold chain clamped by a large golden lock is around his long neck. He also wears wrist cuffs, locked in place like Joanna's.

"What the hell's going on here?" my voice cracks when I yell.

"We're sorry we tricked you, Mister Daley," Joanna soothes, though her own voice is piqued.

"We're going to take very good care of you, though," William promises, though it's hard to trust a man who sounds like a weasel.

"Very good care," a man's voice behind me agrees.

I twist back around to see that the three people waiting for us are Indigo Parsons, Skye Adams, and Leif Wekstrom. But I helped save them just the other night! How could they be part of this trap for me? In unison, they step out of their robes, wearing leather-like undergarments. The robes evaporate into crystal specs that flutter into nothing.

"I wasn't sure about it either at first, but this feels right,"

Indigo adds. For some reason he's the only one in the room wearing an onyx and stardust masquerade mask.

"Sure about what?" I snap. "What are you going to do to me?"

The mysterious ringleader speaks up, bringing my attention back to the front of the room. "We're going to ease your pain, spare you further suffering, and usher you through the darkness into an uncertain future."

She lets go of my arm, but makes a small hand gesture to the people behind me. Both my arms are seized from behind before I can react. I thrash against Indigo and Leif, but it's no use and I start to breath heavily in a panic.

"Hush now, my little crumpet," the hooded woman mocks me as she undoes her robe.

In one fluid movement, she throws back her hood and lets her clothing fall to the floor. I notice her midnight hair, her purple, Cheshire grin, and that insincere glint in her eyes.

"Carolyn?" I nearly suffocate on her name.

How could she be here? How didn't I recognize her? Didn't I pass by her grave? I honestly can't remember now—maybe I didn't... Could this just be a dark version of her? She was already pretty dark, but she does have grey skin, a hollow voice, and solid black eyes with little white dots where the pupils should be.

"I thought we lost you," I whimper.

She snickers, "I suppose you did. You knew me as a dim shade of the spectrum that I could be. But I've passed through The Calamity and all this conflict, all this chaos, has remade me into something far more glorious. When I finally made it back to this side, I knew what I needed to do."

"What, start a sex dungeon?" I sneer.

Her grin angles to one side and she tilts her head diagonally. Her pin-straight ponytail sways behind her. It's pulled back so tight it almost hides her wrinkles.

"Lie to yourself if you must, but I know what you need." Her tone is almost motherly, but the way she's eyeing me definitely is not.

"Please, just let me go! I need to get to Shirun. I need to end this madness."

She snorts and shakes her head. "Shirun will build you up and lead you into a battle that's already lost. I'll not let you have any part in that fool's errand. Tonight is the end of an era and we must celebrate it. We deserve to revel in pleasure up until this house finally crumbles to ash, not to die in fear and agony."

Her face suddenly softens as she steps up next to me and places a hand over my cheek. My lips quiver at her touch, but my heart races at the delightful heat it offers me. I notice how scantily clad she is and how strangely alluring her body is for an older woman. A silver swimsuit-like lingerie hugs her full breasts and wide hips—the top and bottom connected by wide strips of cloth that wind and crisscross around her stomach. Thin, shiny, steel-colored piping covers the garment like vines stretching over a truss. Transparent, white fabric is wreathed over her shoulders and around her waist. She's also wearing calf-high heeled boots that look like they're made of velvet and are tied off by big silky bows at the top.

"Let me be your angel, sweetheart," she whispers, her chestnut breath warm on my face.

She pops a couple of the top buttons of my shirt open before snickering and stepping back. She raises her hand up in front of my nose and snaps her fingers. At this, I see my fine clothes start to burn up. It doesn't hurt, but the thin lines of molten cloth rush across my body, disintegrating all my modesty. I look down panicked that I'll be suddenly naked. Thankfully, I'm not quite exposed—the essentials are covered by a pair of itty-bitty red briefs that have a plastic-y sheen and are adorned by black seams around the top of my thighs and up the sides of my crotch. I also notice that my ankles and wrists are covered in locked leather cuffs.

"What did you do to me?" I ask breathlessly.

"I only uncovered what was already there, it's no great magic."

"Bullshit! I think I would have noticed if I was wearing these the whole time." I kick my feet in her direction to emphasize the cuffs.

"You might be surprised by how comfortably one can wear their shackles, Mister Daley. Sin showed me and we should be grateful for that. I know how to take care of you now." She tosses both her hands in front of her with a low nod.

On cue, Indigo and Leif rotate me around and drag me over to an "X" shaped black wooden structure situated right in front of the balcony door. Skye is draped against it, wearing a lazy smirk. She slides out of the way once I'm brought over and takes up one of the chains attached to the structure. Indigo offers her my left wrist for her to clip a loop in my cuff onto the chain. They fasten my right wrist to the other side so that my back is pressed up against the apparatus. They also hook up my ankle restraints to chains coming out of the bottom legs of this thing. Once they've finished, they step back to admire their work. I've officially found myself in Fifty Shades of Messed Up... How could my own mind or soul be doing this to me? We could all die if I don't get out of here. Where the hell is Sheera? She's welcome to swoop in at any time... What if she can't find me?

"Stop it!" My tone has lost any note of masculinity or bravado—I just sound like a terrified little boy. "Let me go!"

"Ohhh, hush, bunny," Carolyn cocks her head and purses her lips.

"Please!" I search desperately around the room for a sympathetic eye, but my captors just close in around me like starved crows.

"Just give into usss.... We know whatss bessst..." Her speech suddenly takes on a hazy quality that I find disorienting—maybe even hypnotic.

Carolyn struts past her minions and stands with the tip of her nose almost touching mine.

Her breath slides over my face as she places a hand on my chest. I'm so freaked out, I can barely move, but my body tenses instantly when her free hand comes up to cup my genitals. Her touch is so pleasingly warm, I don't even want to fight it. It also gives me an inexplicable feeling of power and control in spite of how helpless I am. All I can do is gasp for air as she slowly fondles my manhood, occasionally sliding her hand up and down it.

"Jussst relax darling... It'll allllll be alright..."

With that, she slowly withdraws and motions her dark harem toward me. Skye slinks around the back of the apparatus I'm stuck to. She drapes her arms over my shoulders and wraps them around my neck as she plants long, lazy kisses on my cheeks. Her grasp instantly gives me a sensation of heaviness that almost crushes my will to escape—or do anything at all. Leif comes up to my side with a crooked grin.

"Don't..." I plead, even though I've got no idea what he's about to do.

He grabs one side of my ass, squeezing it possessively as he rubs his other hand over my abs. I get flashes of some of the most gratifying moments of my life from every athletic triumph to my academic achievements to nights spent with women I've dated, and all the promotions I've received in my career. Indigo comes up in front of me and looks down at my body with some hesitation before reaching out to rub, pinch, and twist my left nipple. At his touch, I am filled with this overwhelming doubt about everything. William steps up beside him and starts rubbing the other side of my chest. With his other hand he grabs me by the crotch and starts to massage my junk. For some reason, I feel a sudden sense of pride at having such a fancy home to live in, such an expensive car to drive, and so many nice clothes to put on my gym-hardened body. Joanna comes up behind Indigo, faintly pushing him down by his shoulders until he's kneeling in between her legs. She resumes his work on my helpless nipple while also leaning up to lock her lips with mine. Her kiss makes me shiver as I suddenly become keenly aware of how average my height is, how my midsection isn't quite as firm as it could be, how I'd like my chest, arms, and legs to be bigger, and how much I wish I hadn't fallen behind David on the corporate ladder.

Joanna sticks her tongue into my mouth, making it hard to breath and impossible to make any noise in protest of what's happening to me. Indigo meanwhile, lifts one of my feet up by the heel and proceeds to suck on my toes. I stiffen at all the unsolicited attention, knowing how wrong it all is, but somehow still liking it, maybe even craving more. I become lightheaded, or maybe intoxicated from all these different feelings and sensations assaulting me, and lose all hope of getting out of here in time. I guess there are worse ways to go, but I don't want it to end like this. I don't want it to end at all—I was supposed to make my final stand against Sin and win my life back. I think I'm about to pass out when

Joanna finally releases me from her suffocating kiss.

My eyes lock with William's as I gasp for air. He looks stranger than ever. There's a darkness around his eyes and an unnaturally rosy glow in his cheeks. His hair is somehow even more sharply parted into spikey locks arranged over his brow. But under that, there's something else—something behind his eyes. It's not sinister or hungry. It's like this little light that's trying to shine through. Carolyn got darker when she plunged into The Calamity, so maybe there's a way for this guy to change too. Maybe I can save him somehow and then he can save me. He tilts his chin up and brings his open mouth close to mine with a cocky smirk.

"My turn…" he taunts.

"William, wait…" I whisper. He pauses his advance, his breathing hot on my lips. "What if you didn't have to be what you are. What if you could be something different—something more?"

He looks intently into my eyes, "What if I like what I am?"

A tear falls from the corner of my eye. "What you are is keeping me trapped here when I should be fighting for a brighter tomorrow. Please, I need you…" I have no idea where this entreaty comes from, but it feels like the realest thing I've ever said. "I need us to change, I need us to be better."

William's gaze remains fixated on me, but all the confidence falls from his face—replaced by a sober frown. Just when I think I've broken through to him, his face dives down to my chest and he starts to suck on my nipple. My heart sinks, but is instantly lifted when I feel my wrist cuff unhooked from its chain. William moves the chain away slowly, careful not to let it swing or clang. His kisses start to trail down my torso and he removes his hand from my crotch to reach up and catch Joanna's hand as she strokes my diaphragm. Her glance catches his for only a second before he lets go, but there is some sort of silent understanding that passes between them.

He turns his attention back to me, planting soft kisses all over my thigh. He reaches for the cuff around my ankle, but also slides his other hand up beneath my butt. I mean he doesn't have to make it **that** convincing, does he? He keeps this routine going, moving his hand around my calf after he's unchained the cuff. Now I have to wonder if he isn't just messing with me. Joanna hasn't helped my cause, though I guess Leif and Skye would notice if she tried to free my other wrist. She steps over Indigo and twists around, getting his attention, she slides down to a seated position against my leg. He finally withdraws from his slimy assault on my poor toes to straddle Joanna's lap and stuff his face into her bosom. She strokes the back of his neck and undoes the chain on my still-restrained ankle all while looking up to my crotch and planting big, sloppy kisses beneath it. I try to clear my mind as I prepare to make my move. This is it. This is the one chance I get so I can't mess it up. Carolyn watches me hungrily with a finger massaging her lips.

Suddenly, the twin doors to this twisted chamber kick open, letting a small amount of warm light flood in. Sheera marches through—the sight of her filling me with renewed hope. Carolyn smirks and casually spins around to face her.

"What do you want, failed protectress?" Carolyn jeers.

Sheera squares off to her, letting the blows roll off her shoulder, "I'm here for a soul not yet lost and a brother not yet beyond saving."

"You know you cannot raise a hand against us. He's not going anywhere, so why don't you just leave us to our revelry?"

Sheera's eyes briefly connect with mine before she looks back to my dark mistress. "Are you sure about that?" She smiles wide.

Joanna uses the commotion to slap Indigo across the face and wriggle herself free from him. I follow up her attack by driving my heel into his nose once she's moved safely aside. He reels back from me with blood dripping out of his nostrils. I start to feel Skye's arms constrict around my neck when William grabs her by the throat and shoves her into the back wall. Leif releases my ass and retreats, winding up for a punch. I swing my free arm around in time to catch his fist. I'm surprised at how easy it is to stop him from hurting me and I'm even more astonished when yanking him to the side sends him tumbling across the floor. I hear the balcony doors open behind me while I undo my remaining restraint. I guess Skye has had enough fun…

Carolyn turns back to us with a snicker. "Well, what's this little diversion, then? Don't you worry, sweetie, we'll have you back in the delightful safety of your bonds in no time." Her eyes flicker between William and Joanna. "I am so terribly disappointed in the two of you. We have no use for anyone trying to act as something they are not."

"Anytime you want to step in would be great," I breathlessly call to Sheera.

A golden sword materializes in her hand. This one is different from the one she had at my apartment. It's more a like a katana with a shorter blade and elongated guard. "I can't do them any harm—though their nature is amiss, they are a thing of you not of Sin..." she informs me. "... but I may give you the means to cut them down yourself."

With that, she heaves the blade my way. The hilt snaps into my palm and I can feel the sudden rush of its power coursing through me.

"Depart from your folly or be culled by he who is your source," Sheera announces to the room.

"Put that down, darling," Carolyn pleads. "We're only looking out for you. This siren doesn't know what's best for you, she invites you down a path of suffering."

Leif staggers to his feet while Indigo wipes the blood from his upper lip. Both eye me with furious desire and I decide that neither can be saved.

"Get down!" I yell to Joanna as Indigo charges forward.

She drops to the floor with her hands above her head. I skip over her and drive the blade through Indigo's chest. His eyes go cold, his face falls flat, and his body slides limply to the floor as I pull my weapon out of him. I turn in time to see William take a swing at Leif, but Leif ducks away, steps up behind William and throws him into a choke hold. William grunts and thrashes against his captor, but his eyes are wet with despair when he looks at me.

"I can snap his neck right now!" Leif threatens. "This little twit never held a candle to me!"

William's face starts to turn blue. "He's not stronger than you," I tell him, though I'm not sure if that's true or not.

This seems to light a fire in William that brightens his whole complexion. In one decisive move, he shifts his weight and drives an elbow into Leif's side. The blow loosens Leif's hold on him long enough for him to fall away. I use the opening to rush over and drive the short sword up through his gut.

"No," he exhales before he goes white and slumps to the floor.

Carolyn eyes the broken bodies as blood spreads out beneath them. "You've destroyed your best chance at seizing happiness." Her tone is bitter, but also mournful. "I won't abandon you though, no, I can still help you, even if you can't see that I know what's best for you."

William and Joanna step up in front of me awkwardly, like they have no real clue what they're doing. At the snap of Carolyn's fingers, heavy chains suddenly spring from the floor to clamp onto their wrists and drag them down to their knees.

"You're both still **my** disciples!" she hisses at them. Her gaze is full of brimstone when she faces me, "Time to tuck you in, dearest!"

Thin, silver chains suddenly start slithering down and around her arms. She grips them like weapons as they drape down toward the floor.

"You can overcome her," Sheera encourages me—she better be right about that.

Carolyn growls as she lunges forward, swinging a chain straight at me. I lean to the side, but her weapon grazes my cheek and draws blood on contact. She lashes with her other chain as she draws the first back. This time, I'm able to get Sheera's sword in front of it. The shiny links wrap around the blade. She uses my inability to pull it away as an opportunity to crack her free chain-whip into my bare ribs. I yelp out as the sting shoots up my side and blood trickles down to my waist. She's relentless in her follow up as she flicks her weapon over my shins. I collapse to my knees the second the skin breaks and look up in terror.

"Help me!" I call to Sheera.

"You need to do this for yourself," she replies—her arms crossed and brow creased.

I manage to roll away before Carolyn can land another blow. At this angle, I manage to slide my sword out from the chain tethering it. Pain sears up my legs from the lacerations as I get to my feet and I know I need to start defending myself better. Carolyn swings at me viciously, but I'm able to bat the attack away this time and I bring my blade up just in time to swat down her next strike. On instinct, I spin about on the balls of my feet, twirling my sword in the air and straight through Carolyn's neck. Blood oozes and splashes out from it—some splattering on my face. Her expression falls and suddenly I see how very old she is. Then her head slides off her neck and crashes to the floor with the rest of her body.

I look up breathlessly to Sheera who still stands tensed as though it's not quite over yet. I scan the room, but I don't see any remaining threats. William and Joanna are still chained to the floor. Both of them give me that same tentative, but expectant, look that Sheera wears. The balcony door suddenly slams against the wall, causing me to jump and remember that Skye's still around. I look to Sheera wide-eyed. Why do we have to worry about her? She's no threat to us, is she? Unfortunately, Sheera stands resolute before me so I turn and amble toward the back of the room. Icy currents pour into the chamber, causing the door to swing and the entry curtain to flap. I step through to a borderline beautiful view of The Calamity twisting and crackling all around us—it's dark purple hues violently broken up by flashes of lighting. Skye is draped over the balcony railing, looking out into the horizon. Her hair swishes to the whims of the unforgiving winds that rock what's left of this place. I come up behind her, grab her by the shoulder, and twist her around to face me.

She laughs through the tears—her back slumped against the bannister. "We could still have fun, you know…" Strands of hair get stuck against her damp cheeks.

"You can come with us," I offer. "It doesn't have to end like this. We can all stop trying to ignore the problems in front of us by indulging ourselves."

She titters, rolling her head from side to side. "I don't want any part of that. No, sir, you have a grand old time facing down all your demons. I'll stay right here, thank you."

"I can't leave you," I try to reason with her. "I really don't feel like killing you too."

"I know." She gives me a crooked smile and pulls away from the railing to lean in close. "Don't do it, you don't have to do anything you don't want to…" Her hands drift up to the base of my neck. "Just stay here with me, we can go lay down—we can go relax, enjoy what comforts we still have…"

She lets loose a little gasp when my blade pierces through her torso. She slowly looks up to me with dumbfounded eyes and an agape mouth before I pull it out of her. She stumbles back against the railing and gently crumbles into a lifeless heap. As awful as this all is, I get an amazing rush of liberation—of peace and optimism—of stripping off a weight I never knew I carried. I don't understand it, but I imagine it's a sign that I can go now.

William and Joanna's chains disintegrate when I return to the room. Lighting begins to strike at the balcony, tearing it from the side of this fragment of the manor.

"It's time we leave," Sheera announces—I guess that's her version of, *"Oh hey, Bryan, nice work, buddy!"*

Without question, we hasten after her out the doors and into the hall.

"To the Observatory?" I confirm, loathe to think about making any more surprise pit stops.

"To the end of this struggle," she corrects. "We're about to find out if we can save you after all—we're about to find out how this all ends."

Her sword dematerializes from me hand as we follow her lead down the hall. I'm definitely ready for all this madness to come to an end.

# Epilogue

We come up to the observatory's spiraling staircase. Sheera begins to ascend it and I follow close behind, but I hear William and Joanna's footsteps suddenly stop behind me. I grip the railing and twist around to see what's wrong. They're just standing like frightened children at the base of the staircase. I can't read the sullen expressions on their faces so I come down to them, relieved that there's no immediate danger.

"We can't go in there," Joanna explains.

"We'd never be accepted, certainly not like this," William agrees.

I look the three of us over. We're all still in our freaky little outfits and leather cuffs.

"They kind of have a point," I say, turning back to where Sheera stands above us waiting. "Can't we at least find something decent to change into first? I don't really want to march in there almost naked." I look down at myself again and add, "Not to mention bleeding all over the place."

Sheera shakes her head solemnly. "It will be hard, I know, but you need to enter in as you are. You need to be seen like this by everyone that's left—no more compartmentalizing who you are. Only then can you change in a way that matters."

"I can't…" Joanna whimpers.

I catch her hand as she tries to step back. "Yes, you can … we've come too far to stop now." It's then that I catch a beautiful spark behind her watery gaze.

Sheera descends to us, her steps nearly soundless. "I think I can see it now…"

"See what?" I question.

She takes William's hands in hers and eyes him carefully. "That you have a chance at making it through this, I'm sure of it now, but you need these two to stand with you."

"You see," I look between William and Joanna. "We've got

this, just a little farther to go."

Sheera releases one of William's hands and leads him over to me. "Come on then, I'll help you all as you pass through."

William extends his hand to me and I grasp it firmly. Sheera leads us up the steps, all of us linked like a train. She opens the door to the observatory, but there's not blinding light behind it this time. I guess that means I'll finally get to go inside. I'll find out who else is left and I'll see how all of this insanity comes to a close ... one way or another ...

DEREK BAILEY

# *Book 8:*

# The Fate of a Soul

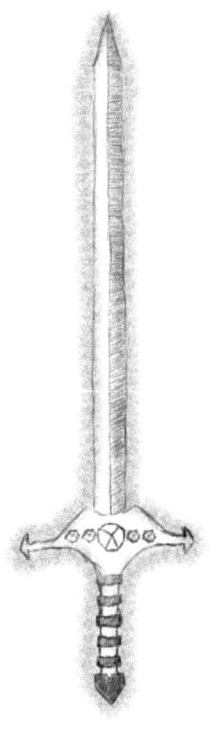

*To those I'm blessed to call family, both in blood and in spirit.*

# Chapter 1

The observatory's even bigger than I imagined. The top of the glass dome towers above us and sparkles despite the darkness lying beyond the panes. Golden supports curl up to the peak where a great, golden telescope is held in place, pointed straight up into where the swirling storm rages. Lightning flashes tear angrily through The Calamity, but this room is so well lit that they don't cause too much of a stir. Our entrance is another story. We freeze in front of the doorway, barely even clothed. We're disheveled after our escape from Carolyn's sex dungeon and the wounds from my fight with her still bleed.

The other bodies in the room gather around us. I think there are twelve of them in all, some of the faces look familiar, others not as much. Shirun suddenly breaks through the small crowd and his visage comes into focus. I hear the door shut securely behind us as he comes up with a smile—he holds his hands out wide.

"You made it," he beams.

"Could have used a hand," I jab.

"And you had one." His eyes drift up over my shoulder. "Sister, it's good to see you. I'm grateful you came."

"I'm here to bring you back to The Light," Sheera states as she steps past me.

"You know I have to see this through first."

She eyes the army of refugees for a moment. "It's quite the mess you've made here. I'll do what I can to help you clean it, but if this child falls to darkness, I'm pulling you out."

"I...understand," he concedes.

I'm not sure if I like the sound of that any more than Shirun does, but I get that he's her top priority. I guess I'm glad they'll do what they can to stop it from coming to that. Shirun's sad gaze falls on me as Sheera wanders the room, examining our soldiers. I notice that they're all dressed like Shirun now in fierce, but formal, attire.

"So, this is everyone that's left?" I address him.

"Yes, and I'm glad you could gather up William and Joanna."

I look to where they stand on either side of me with a grin, "I don't think I'd be here without them."

"No, I'm sure you wouldn't," Shirun replies without hesitation—his tone both genuine and ironic. "We did well, Bryan, but as you've probably guessed, there's a lot more to be done."

"Could we start by finding us something to wear, please," I chuckle nervously looking down at my leather cuffs and bright red fetish gear.

Shirun shows no signs of amusement. "I'll be sure you're all armed for the final struggle, but you must make peace with all that you're ashamed of. Plus, there are some who are dying to greet you."

He steps aside where a little line forms. Myles stands at its helm, a sideways smile stretched across his face. He comes up and clasps me by the shoulders.

"Hey there, old chap!"

"Mister Westerly," I reply with a formal nod before breaking into a grin. My awkwardness suddenly leaves me.

As soon as he's released me, Olivia steps forward and plants a fervent kiss on my cheek—the one that's not still oozing blood. One look into her azure eyes and I get this unshakable need to kick Sin's ass. She moves away just in time for Jack to dive into my arms.

"I'm so glad you're alright!" he exhales, his forehead pressed against my chest.

"It's good to see you on your feet again," I tell him. "I was pretty worried about you the last time I saw you."

I see how gaunt he is when he looks up at me.

"I'll do my best to hang on for you," he promises.

I pat him on the head as he moves to my side, "I know you will…"

Jeremy and Natasha stand behind him. They're wearing frilly white shirts beneath thick, forest green jackets with gold buckles running up the front. They also wear silver leggings and brown clog shoes. I'm greeted with a ballerina bow by the both of them as they hold hands—hair falling around their faces. Jasmine steps out from behind them and walks up to me. She's in a snow-white jacket that hugs her slender torso like a Valkyrie's breastplate, baby blue slacks tucked into white, leather battle boots, and a silver chain around her neck encrusted with a large sea-green gemstone. Her hair is braided up and around her head elegantly. She places one hand on my arm and another over the necklace.

"To make sure Margaret can be here with us too." She explains motioning at the gem—her words as soft as flower petals falling into a pond.

A tear slips from my eyes, "I wish she didn't have to die..."

"We can give her new life if we can defeat Sin," she promises. "Until then, the rest of us are here to stand by you."

I look around to see that William, Joanna, and I are surrounded by what must be the best parts of myself.

"It's good to have you all here," I tell them. *Especially* **this** *version of them.*

Jasmine's expression dips as she seems to pick up on my remembrance of all those dark and twisted versions of my friends here.

"You've seen The Eclipsed, haven't you?" her voice is hushed.

"They were like all of you, except that they weren't you at all."

"No, they're not," Olivia steps in. "I suppose it was only a matter of time before they'd get involved, but their presence changes nothing."

"Speaking of change," Shirun reenters the group with Sheera beside him, "are you ready for a new look."

I nod vigorously and follow them across the room. The rest of our forces drift behind. I'm led up to an ivory pool set into the floor that's filled with crystalline blue water. Everyone forms a circle around it, leaving William, Joanna and I by the steps on one end. Fountains shaped like angels line each corner, gently trickling water into it from the large pitchers that they hold.

"It's time to wash off everything that weighs you down," Shirun declares, looking at me from across the pool like he looked at me from across the table on my first night of this ordeal. "Let the water take your guilt, your regret, your shame, your uncertainty. Come out clean—a new man with a new future—a new pair of eyes to see through, a new heart to move you, and a new coat of arms to protect you."

Having all these eyes on me makes me nervous. Looking

back to William and Joanna, I see that they're jaws are tight and their eyes wide. Their unease is somehow reassuring.

"Strip off what you've come here with," Sheera instructs from our side.

I notice that the locks on our leather cuffs are gone, maybe they have been for a while. We remove those first, then I gulp and pull down the red briefs as I stumble into the pool. If these guests are all a part of me, then I shouldn't really be embarrassed to be naked in front of them, but I kind of am. The water is refreshing, but not cold. I walk forward until the water is over my head—my wounds healing instantly as I submerge them. Somehow, my feet stay on the smooth tile lining as though I'm not under water at all. I look up—my vision clear—and see a chorus of brilliant colors dancing above me. A comforting warmth wraps around my body, scrubbing me clean at some subdermal layer. Suddenly, the top of my head breaks through to the air above me. I slowly come up from under the surface—the beads of water combing my hair up into a frontal sweep and forming a coronet helmet around my forehead and down my cheeks. Matching gold and blue armor crusts around me as water slides down my neck, chest, and arms. By the time I've stepped out, my body is covered in a suit of armor fit for a superhero. Shirun waits for me with a long, gold sword held out in his hands. I take hold of the ribbed handle, admiring the snowy gemstones encrusting its hilt. In spite of its size, the weapon is shockingly weightless. It has a soft haze around it as though the blade is made entirely of solidified light.

I turn my attention away from the sword to see William and Joanna exit the pool. They both look so different now. They're wearing uniform black coats that fall mid-thigh and have silver shoulder tassels, trim, and front buckles. Their faces also look changed—cleaner somehow. Joanna has only the smallest amount of lip gloss and maybe eye liner on. Her short hair is partially pulled back into a half-ponytail. William's hair is neat, but less stringently arranged, more like he just finger-combed it over his brow. There's also an easiness to his features. His eyebrows aren't so sharp, his eyes aren't so dark, and his mouth rests in an upward curve. The three of us have definitely come out of that pool brand new.

"Incredible," Sheera comments, seemingly surprised to see

us look this good—*thanks for the confidence!*

"Indeed," Shirun agrees, though with far less astonishment. "Well, now that we're all dressed for the occasion, it's time to make sure Mister Daley meets the rest of our forces. Then we can review the plan."

I'm just relieved to know that there **is** a plan. Six of the guests circle around us. Shirun walks up to one end of the arch and places a hand on a young woman's shoulder.

"Do you remember Madeline Rose?" he asks.

She's the girl who wore a frilly skirt during the party where we sprung a trap for Sin's forces—where Olivia led us to victory against Charles and his freakshow.

"Yes," I reply simply.

Her lips part wide and there's a light in her eyes—one that makes me feel optimistic. She still wears a frilly skirt, but she has black, metallic leggings on underneath with gray ankle-high boots, and a chainmail cardigan over a black satin blouse. Her wavy brown hair falls freely.

Shirun walks around behind her, "Samuel, Evan, and Christina you saved from that mess in the ballroom."

"I remember."

Evan and Samuel both still wear pleasant smiles. They've also been outfitted with thick, brown leather jackets and military boots. Christina catches my eye though. She seems so much warmer now. Her hair is braided over her shoulder and she looks formidable in her blazing white trench coat.

Shirun comes up behind two newer faces and places a hand on each of their shoulders. "Bryan, this is Rachel Sampson and Kyle Westbrooke. I don't believe you've been formally introduced. Last time you even saw them would have been at Shelly's funeral."

"It's nice to finally meet you," I have a hard time looking Rachel in the eyes since this must be the same Rachel that Kenneth died searching for.

She seems to notice though as she steps up and slides her hands up my armored arms. "It's okay," she entreats me. "I know what happened to poor Kenneth. There's always a chance for rebirth when the morning comes, perhaps a new Kenneth would even be freed from his prior burdens."

I smile appreciatively as she falls back into the line.

"We all know how hard it is to change one's nature," Kyle adds. His voice has the grit of wisdom and his eyes emit a fatherly warmth although his face is so young. "We stand with you, from now till the end, proud to join you in this fight."

"Thank you," I reply soggily.

Shirun comes to the end of the group and loops back to me. "Stay strong with us now, then."

I set my jaw and nod the affirmative.

"Let's take a look at what we're up against," Shirun commands.

He leads us all over to a large ovular table which we surround. It's indented and filled with blue particles, making it seem much more akin to a child's sand table than a war table despite its rich burgundy stain. Shirun waves a hand over it, summoning the grains up into the air. They swirl around until they've formed a sculpture of the fractured manor.

"We're obviously in the observatory," he begins, gesturing to domed replica of this part of the building. "When we leave, we'll be taking a left and heading through this door." Shirun flips his hand up and the observatory lifts up like a building block, revealing the hall he's referring to. "I've been stitching our fractured home together with gateways to allow us to move between sections, though the path forward is neither straight nor easy."

"We will meet some token resistance in the hall below, but the real fight is going to start once we're through that first portal," Sheera adds.

"Yes, from there, things are going to get a little chaotic and probably confusing, so I'll keep the rest of this plan brief since you'll all want to just try to follow Sheera and I from battle to battle. Essentially, we'll be coming out here in this hall on the first floor, exiting through this door, rounding the bay windows on the second floor here, and coming out into what's left of this corridor where we must reach the exit at the other end."

Shirun waves his hands over the projected sculpture of the manor and points to the different doors we'll be using—the grains of each piece lightly separating and condensing to highlight the areas he's gesturing to. I note that this last stretch goes by where we defeated Charles—where I saw that fiendish bonfire tonight.

"Our final charge to the dining hall will be through the parlor," Sheera picks up.

"Where we mourned Shelly," Myles says under his breath.

"This place is full of painful memories as of late, though it is easy to see that Sin intends a path for us full of intent and light on coincidence," Shirun offers. "That is assuredly why we must eventually confront him in the dining room."

"Where do you think The Eclipsed will factor in?" I ask.

"I don't know..." Shirun admits. "We should remain vigilant, but it will be difficult for them to confront us out in the open, even with Sin giving them freedom to haunt these halls. They cannot occupy the same space as those who mirror them so they cannot emerge as long as you are all still standing."

Myles, Jasmine, Jack, Jeremy, and Natasha all reply with solemn nods.

"What are they, really, though?" I question.

"Every light casts a shadow," Olivia states firmly, "they are our shadows."

"I see..."

I suppose that's about as clear an answer as I'll be getting. They're bad news and I guess that's all I need to know.

"Since Margaret is fallen, I imagine her eclipsed counterpart could show at any time," Shirun reminds us. "She may even devise some way to force a confrontation with the others somehow, but it is hard to say."

"And remember that Shirun and I cannot defend you against them," Sheera adds.

"Because they are of me?" I clarify.

"That's right," Shirun confirms.

"You should all arm yourselves now," Sheera suggests. "More importantly, steel your hearts, this is going to be a clusterfuck."

On her word, the guests all depart from the table. Myles gives me a pat on the back of my shoulder before leaving my side. Shirun and Sheera come up to me with cautious hope twinkling in their impossibly blue eyes.

"You ready?" Sheera asks.

"He's ready," Shirun answers for me.

"We can do this, right?" I feel like victory is within reach, but I need to hear them say it.

"It will all come down to how hard you can fight," Sheera replies.

"You have everything you need—everything we may provide. And we'll be right there with you ... even if it all falls apart." He gives Sheera a measured glance that she tries to ignore.

"Your house is a fucking disaster, but I really do think that you can purge the darkness from here. From the ashes that remain, I'm sure something beautiful can rise," she reassures me.

"Thank you, both of you," I reply.

Myles approaches and I notice he now has two golden revolvers holstered against his legs. "We're ready," he informs us.

We follow him over to the door where everyone stands with a golden weapon in hand. Olivia's traded her butcher knife out for a large sickle. Jeremy and Natasha hold long javelins while Jack is armed with a shield that has a sharp blade jutting out from one half of it. Jasmine is armed with what looks like an automatic crossbow. Kyle and Samuel each wield staffs tipped with spikey mace-like balls on each end. Evan stands holding a bow with a quiver strapped across his back that's filled with luminous arrows. Christina has her hand over a rapier sheathed at her waist. Rachel holds a heavy-looking battle axe and Madeline's got some kind of bladed glaive that she holds around her waist like a hula hoop. William and Joanna bring up the rear with short swords in one hand and curved daggers in the other.

Sheera opens the door for us, but Shirun stops us at the exit. He eyes us all, seeming to push back a mist that wants to form in his eyes.

"I want you to know how sorry I am that we find ourselves in this situation." He takes a pause to collect himself. "I have always loved this house and I'm so proud to see so many of you standing ready to fight for it. I believe that we can see it through to a new tomorrow. I believe with all my heart that the dark infestation can be cleansed." His gaze suddenly locks onto mine. "I believe in you."

All around me cheers resound and before I know it, we're rushing out into battle—Katana-like blades materializing in Sheera's hands and a pointed blade attached to a chain sling forming in Shirun's.

# Chapter 2

The cretin ladies and gentlemen stand waiting for us in the hall below. They're making screeching noises as they charge toward us with shadowy swords and smoky whips held up in the air.

Sheera and Shirun are the first to leap into the fray like airborne Seraphim. They cut down cretin people as they land and immediately bound onward for another assault. Jeremy and Natasha follow their trail. They plant their javelins into the floor and vault up off of them, soaring forward. Their hair almost scrapes the tall ceiling before they arch downward, poking their spears through cretins that leap up to meet them. They land on their toes and pull their spears out from their cretin kababs just in time to pirouette and thrust their weapons past each other into cretins about to strike at them. Myles marches forward, beams of light streaming from both pistols. Evan and Jasmine keep close to his sides. They take their time to aim their shots with care and manage to mop up some of the stragglers. It's not long before the hall is cleared.

"We've got this, Mister Daley!" Jack pips as he jogs past me.

As promised, Shirun and Sheera locate our exit and open the door. They pause only to look up and acknowledge the group before they disappear into the portal. Jeremy and Natasha follow them through before the rest of us catch up and enter into its glassy surface. We come out in that wide hall on the first floor that Shirun pointed out before. The group has already dispersed, taking out cretin ladies and gentlemen as they round corners and pop out of doorways like an undead hoard. Myles plants himself in the middle. He maintains a wide stance as he picks off cretins at either end of the hall. Olivia steps around him, defending his flanks and cutting down enemies that get too close.

Sheera and Shirun are off a ways, moving as though of one mind and purpose. They bound away from each other to protect different guests as they start to become overwhelmed, come back together, and repeat. Their luminescent blades leave streaks behind them as they go about their routine.

Jeremy and Natasha cover our rear. They dance about with wide, high strides and plunge their weapons through cretins before they can even get close enough to strike. It's a good thing they're such efficient killers too, this place is flooding with cretins. I guess the last hall was just a warmup round. It's not going take long before I'll have to use my weapon—I just hope that I'm everything I'll need to be. My moment of truth arises when I see Evan and Jasmine start to become overwhelmed. They're not too far off—each of them carefully picking off our enemies. Rachel runs by them, swinging her axe at an incoming cretin gentleman who blocks her attack with his shield. While she's busy with him, a few more manage to slip by. Kyle takes notice and breaks off from where he and Samuel twirl their spikey staffs through the air.

"Hang on!" he shouts to Jasmine and Evan as he charges to their rescue.

I look back to Jack who immediately gets low. "I'm on it," he pips as he springs forward.

I rush after him, mindful to keep my sword held out to the side as I run. Kyle bats one cretin's saber to the side, pivots, drives the other end of his staff into a lady cretin's gut, then spins again to bring the other end down into her head. Out of the corner of my eye, I see a cretin wind up with a spear behind where Madeline rushes to Samuel's aid. It's aiming the projectile at where Kyle fights and no one notices.

"Look out!" I yell right as I lift my sword up to deflect a cretin's tomahawk swing.

I push his blade to the side with surprising ease and then continue to impress myself with how gracefully I leap forward and drive my sword into his chest as he stumbles backward. Jack sails past my head just as the spear screams by Jasmine and Evan—flying straight for Kyle. Jack bashes away a jagged blade, lands in a low crouch, and spins on his heels, using his shield to cut through a cretin's legs. He pops up and slices off the creature's head before it can so much as screech.

"Kyle!" I yell again, afraid we're too late.

He bashes a cretin man down and turns, but only just in time for the spear to sink into his chest. His eyes go wide as he falls to his knees and spits up blood. Jasmine takes down one of the cretins ahead of me. I somersault forward beneath a swinging mace and come up with my sword through the wielder's torso. I catch Kyle as he falls to his side and set him down gently.

"It's okay," he whispers even though he's crying. "I was never all that strong…" He stops to cough up more blood before finishing, "…maybe if you win, there'll be another me, a stronger me…"

With that, the light in his eyes goes out and even though I interacted with him for all of like five seconds, I feel an intense hollowness inside me at this loss. Jack leaps over where I'm kneeling like a gazelle, bringing his shield down on a cretin charging at me.

"We have to keep fighting, Mister Daley," he urges.

"I know," I reply softly as I rise up and bring my sword in front of me.

The cretin hoard is thinning, but it's probably not good that we've lost one of ours so soon into the fight. Rachel and Christina come up behind us, joining in our forward march. Shirun and Sheera stay low to the ground up ahead. They duck, dodge, and wait for just the right moment to sink their blades into our enemies. Jasmine and Evan rush ahead to pick off their scraps while Rachel and Christina cut down the remaining forces as we make our way to the door that Shirun opens. He disappears into it, but Shera remains behind this time to stand guard as we all funnel through.

"This part will be much trickier," she warns me as I pass.

I come out in the back section of the second floor to see that she's right. Cretins flood the space—shattered glass from the ruined bay windows crunching beneath their feet. Shirun has already charged into the mass, slinging his chain blade above him. He swings his weapon aside and whips it down around him, cutting a couple cretins down and dispersing the others near him. With a jerk, he sends the blade out in front of him, skewering a couple more of the dark creatures. Myles trots behind, lighting up the hall with golden streaks. Olivia rushes past him, flipping through the air and bringing her sickle down upon a pair of lady cretins.

I dash toward them, passing William and Joanna who run, bent at the waist, along either side of the hall. Jack is beside me. I feel like he's gotten even paler as the fight goes on. Some of the cretins who ran away from Shirun and slipped past Myles and Olivia now charge toward us. I lunge at one, stabbing my sword forward. He manages to block my strike, but falls to the side. Before he can recover, I shift my grip and drive the blade down into him. Jack pounces past me, swatting away a spear thrust up at him, twisting through the air, and falling with the blade of his shield driven into his attacker. He rolls forward once his opponent is reduced to ash, arching his shield to cut through the next cretin's abdomen when she swings wide with her sword. I rush up and lop off her head as Jack pivots to block an axe from cleaving into him. He shoves the blow aside then ducks down for me to hop over him and run my sword through the cretin's chest.

More cretins creep around our flanks, but William and Joanna sneak forward, stabbing and evading to thin them out. Even their efforts aren't enough though. Enemies crawl up through the frayed openings in the walls and pour out from each corner. As I fight to stand my ground, I see Jeremy and Natasha sprinting to us. They run up the sides of what's left of the walls and spring off of them like booby traps with their weapons held out. Each of them manages to skewer two enemies on their drive and somehow even land gracefully on a hand and two feet. They arise shoulder to shoulder, ducking down and splitting apart when more danger approaches. They skip aside, putting distance between them and their attackers—just enough for them to safely thrust their javelins into the monsters.

Things start to look clearer as Evan and Jasmine step forward, picking our enemies off from afar. Rachel and Christina keep them better guarded this time. No cretins can even get close before Christina's rapier guts them or Rachel's axe cleaves through their oily forms. The path ahead remains too blocked off though. We've managed to edge our way up around to the corner in front of the ruined bay windows, but we need to get down the hall at the other end to escape this section. We're too exposed like this, especially as lightning starts to poke at this part of the building, breaking it apart even more.

Sheera gets low and shoots forward like a laser beam. She spins and slashes at our enemies as the momentum carries her up to where Shirun fights. Madeline charges forward too with Samuel behind her. She twirls her giant glaive around her body, making her untouchable as she cuts her way to us. Samuel dashes from side to side tossing around his spiked staff to clean up any cretins swift enough to avoid her. With the pressure alleviated from us, Jack and I sprint into a more offensive set of maneuvers. I fall to a knee and thrust my blade out with one hand—sinking it into a cretin gentleman's abdomen—while Jack flips over me and swings his shield at a cretin who's about to club me. William and Joanna dart along our sides. They fling their knives into cretins and run past us to retrieve them as the fiends crumble apart. Then they get low to block incoming strikes and drive the knives into the enemies whose swords are locked with their own.

We finally start to make good progress. Sheera and Shirun round the corner with Myles and Olivia not far behind. Jack leads us onward with a spritely lightness as he leaps off the wall of fallen and crooked paintings. He lands behind a cretin trying to cut him in half with a great sword. Jack's shield rips through her back then he spins around falling to his knees and tripping a cretin in front of him with the blunt part of his shield. While the villain falls, Jack arcs the shield up, over, and down into the cretin gentleman's chest—slicing into him and pounding his body into a pile of ash. Before I can even help, Jack does a backflip over the lady cretin with the great sword as she makes a second attempt on his life. He lands safely on the other side, driving the bladed end of his shield down into where her shoulder and neck meet. I finally catch up in time to clash swords with a new attacker coming for him while William and Joanna pounce upon targets of their own.

We're nearly around the corner when lighting strikes down on our location with greater intensity. The hall shakes under the impact, but we all remain steady. We've thinned out the cretin hoard and I can see Sheera opening our doorway out of here down the hall.

"Hurry," she calls to us.

Sin's voice suddenly booms into my eardrums as I rip my sword out of a cretin, "Oh, not so fast now…"

Jack twists through the air, cutting an enemy across his chest in a downward spiral. Pivoting around, he looks past me wide-eyed. I look to see Christina stab her rapier through a lady cretin while Evan shoots the one behind her. Behind them, I can see the dark purple swirls of The Calamity form into a condensed knot.

"Run!" Jack suddenly shouts as he darts off toward them.

With the hall cleared, they take one look at what's brewing beside them and make a break for it.

"Jack!" I call, horrified.

The gathering darkness discharges a flurry of large lightning bolts. They tear into what's left of the walls supporting the bay windows, obliterating them on contact. They pepper the floor like machine gun fire trailing after our friends. Evan, Christina, Jasmine, and Rachel run for their lives while Jack and I head straight for the danger for some reason. I can only hope the kid knows what he's doing.

"Jack, Bryan!" I hear Myles yelling after us.

I guess he's only just now seeing us charging at the explosive lightning. We're nearly to our friends though as the hall crumbles around behind them. Jack bounds forward like a reindeer. He pulls his shield back behind him as he soars up to where the ceiling should be. Before he can land, a bolt smashes into the floor right at Christina's heel. The blast trips her up and she falls to her stomach. She only has time to look up to me with remorse stretched across her face before another strike cracks down and devours her. This impact causes Evan and Rachel to crash to their knees while Jack sails over Jasmine's head. She and I stop and grab hold of each other when we meet. Chilly sweat slides down my face as Jack lands in between Evan and Rachel, slamming his shield down against the edge of the floor. An arc of white light suddenly materializes into a half dome that stretches above us. The lightning batters it mercilessly and Jack bows his head at the weight of these blows. I have to wonder how much abuse the poor little guy can actually handle—will his protective barrier be enough to save us?

Myles comes up beside me with a creased expression. Evan and Rachel get to their feet and move for the door. I look back to see that everyone has passed through the exit, except Shirun, who waits and holds it open. I turn to Jack again, seeing him quake under the stress of protecting us. He looks so small hunched over like that too… so much power coming from someone so frail-looking.

"Oh, Jack, old boy," Myles laments.

Finally, the lightning ceases. I look up to see that the knot of dark spirals has lightened, but it starts to thicken again almost immediately. Jack's forcefield fizzles out, but he doesn't get up. He kneels over to his side after a moment and coughs up blood. On instinct, Myles shoves his revolvers into their holsters and rushes over to the boy. I stay at his heels, afraid that we've dodged one catastrophe just to suffer another. Jack is practically limp when Myles takes him up in his arms, but he seems to be conscious. I pick up his dropped shield, but get the sickening idea that Jack may not need it anymore. This is reaffirmed when I see how his face isn't just pale anymore, it's literally radiant white. Little grey lines stretch across it more like cracks than veins and luminescent flakes float up from him.

"We've got to move," Myles tells us as he marches by.

Jasmine leads me into a jog as we see Rachel and Evan slip through the exit. Jasmine dashes ahead, her crossbow held out as she exits this section. I take up the rear with Myles as Shirun waits.

"Mister Daley..." Jack wheezes faintly as his head bobs against Myles' shoulder.

"It's okay, Jack, you're gonna be alright," I tell him though panic has a vice grip on my voice.

Jack pinches his eyes closed. It's barely perceptible, but I think he shakes his head.

"Should we really be bringing him through?" I question.

"We can't linger here," Shirun replies, tilting his chin at the new cluster of darkness that's ready to unload on us. "There's nowhere else to go but forward."

Accepting that it's not safe to stay here, I step through the portal with the rest of them behind me. I come out to the other section of the second floor where the abyssal bonfire still rages. There are far fewer cretins here than we faced in the last area, but there are still enough to keep our forces busy. I should charge off to join them, but instead I turn back to Jack as Myles sets him down on the floor.

"I'm sorry." He sobs as I take a knee beside him.

"Don't be sorry, old friend," Myles soothes.

"It's fine, you're fine," I blurt out. "There's nothing to be sorry for..."

Myles looks to me with a furrowed brow. The glowing white

flakes peel off of Jack at a faster rate and his skin becomes increasingly transparent.

"I really wanted to be with you until the end…" Jack's voice is so faint I have to strain to hear it over the clash of blades. "I wanted to see you through to the other side of this, make sure you get a happy ending to all this."

"You kept on as long as you could, yeah?" Myles strokes the back of the boy's neck as though doing so can somehow revive him.

My heart throbs as I start to get that this really is the end for him. "What can we do?" I croak.

"The other me…" Jack is practically disintegrating into magic dust before us now. "… when you find him, you have to kill him. He's got my face, but he's everything I'm not and nothing that I am. Promise me you'll stop him."

"I promise." A tear escapes my eye and slides down to my jaw.

Jack looks up to the ceiling with a distant twinkle in his eyes. "Thank you. Thank you for holding onto me for as long as you could."

"Goodbye, Jack." Even Myles' somber whisper has a booming quality to it.

"I'll miss you…" I manage to get in before Jack bursts into a cloud of sparkling particles that flutter upward before fizzling out.

I think I catch a slight smile on his face before he's gone, but maybe I imagine it.

"Come on then," Myles exhales, "Got to be on with it, that's what he'd want."

He rises up and reaches down to yank me up by my armpits as he marches by. He prods me forward to where Sheera, Shriun, and the surviving guests finish clearing out this hall. Sheera slashes through a cretin lady's throat with both her katanas and then sends me a shockingly sympathetic glance. I never imagined her hard, sapphire eyes could go so soft. Shirun slings his blade into an enemy's chest before he turns to face me with an equally somber expression. Once the room is cretin-free, Jeremy, Natasha, Olivia, Jasmine, Samuel, William, Joanna, Evan, Rachel, and Madeline all look my way as I approach them with heavy feet. No one says anything. There's probably nothing to say, but the silence isn't uncomfortable. In fact, it feels right. After a moment, Shirun pivots and heads for the door.

Something catches my eye as he opens it. I look off to the floating platform where we defeated Charles and his circus of freaks to find that the black bonfire isn't burning there anymore. This is doubly strange since an arid smoky scent still fills the air.

"Run!" I hear Myles bellow beside me.

It takes a second to see that the whole bonfire is snaking across the chasm like a dragon coming to feast on us. Myles grips my arm and propels me forward as we all dash for our exit. Sheera, Shirun, and Madeline have already passed through—the bonfire must have sprung to life after they entered into the portal. William and Joanna catch a wide-eyed glimpse of it before they rush out from this zone. Samuel, Evan, and Rachel all manage to follow them through, but the flames crash down in front of Jeremy and Natasha, forming a fiery wall barring their escape. Myles and I skid to a stop behind them with Olivia and Jasmine coming up beside us.

"Tut, tut, little ones," Sin's ominous sneers fill the air. "I have a few friends who would be just delighted to rip you to pieces."

As Sin cackles, the flame wall suddenly contorts around us, boxing us in like a band of trapped rats. We huddle together, watching each other's backs as the space around us goes dark. The fire caging us crusts into a hard, shiny surface that's somehow even covered the floor beneath our feet. There's a blurry quality to the otherwise pristine obsidian color of our cell. Actually, I now see that it's more like there's a dark gray, but slightly luminous fog behind these dark panels.

"Shit," I hiss, realizing this looks just like the mirror that Dark Margaret stepped out of.

"What is this?" Myles whispers.

"They're here!" I yelp. "They're in here with us!"

"The Eclipsed…" Jasmine exhales.

"Damn it all, there's no time for this!" Myles groans. "Where are they, how can they be here? I don't see anyone but us."

I squint and search around for an answer, then I wonder if this isn't some kind of actual mirror. Sure enough, when I look to Myles' boots, I see a pair of bare, hairy feet standing bottom to bottom with his as though on the other side of the floor hanging upside down like a bat.

"It's a mirror, they're on the other side!" I blurt out.

Before anyone else can react, a pair of long, gangly hands rise up through the fog beneath Myles. They burst through the black flooring and latch onto his ankles, yanking them forward. Myles falls onto his back with a grunt, losing a grip on his guns as Dark Myles leaps up from the floor and lands on our Myles' stomach.

"What the hell are you?" Myles growls.

Jasmine shoots a bolt at the scrawny, snarling reflection of our brawny protector, but the little fiend rolls off to the side before it can hit. Jasmine repoints her crossbow, but Dark Jasmine falls face first through the ceiling and twists her body around to kick our Jasmine's weapon away. Dark Jasmine lands and backhands our Jasmine across the face.

"Miss me, Bry-Bry?," she regards me with a crooked grin and a wave.

I'm about to help our Jasmine when Dark Jeremy sails sideways out from a wall and shrieks like a madman as he latches onto Jeremy, tackling him to the floor. Olivia suddenly runs into me—pushing me down before a fiery red claw pops up from the floor and nearly slashes my face off.

Olivia reels back and swings her sickle down at her monstrous reflection. Dark Olivia catches the blade in her claws, leans in and roars. She rips the weapon away and bashes the blunt end into Olivia's forehead. Olivia's demonic reflection rotates up through the floor like something from an exorcism movie and stomps towards her dazed opponent. I get to my feet and slash at her back. She roars, barring her teeth at me. I'm about to take another cut at her when she drops the sickle and dives back into the floor, vanishing into a grey tuft.

Dark Jasmine has our Jasmine by the neck. She pushes her up against a wall and shoves her through it into the shadows beyond.

"Jasmine!" I yell, horrified.

Natasha thrusts her javelin at the Dark Jasmine, but she just cartwheels over the attack with impish agility. Myles scrambles to his revolvers, but Dark Myles climbs onto his back and wraps his sickly arms around our Myles' neck. Dark Jeremy manages to pull himself free of Jeremy. He stands, looking down at Jeremy before lifting a knee and stomping him through the floor. Olivia tries to pick up her sickle when Dark Olivia springs out from beneath her. She tackles Olivia upwards, sending them tumbling through the ceiling and into the darkness together. Myles grabs his shabby reflection by his unkept hair and rips the whelp off his back. Dark Myles crashes to the floor, splayed out and dazed. Our Myles takes the opportunity to pick up one of his guns and splatter his Eclipsed counterpart's brains down into the grey mists.

"Remember that they're not us, old chap!" Myles yells to me.

I chop at Dark Jeremy who somehow manages to duck away despite his utter lack of coordination. Dark Jasmine leaps over Natasha's head, twisting away as her javelin shoves up to impale the dark pixie girl. She charges toward me, leaping around my sword as I swing it at her and using this break in my defenses to drop-kick me onto my back.

"I thought we were besties," she taunts, looming over me with her sideways ponytail swinging wildly. "I mean we had such a splendid time together, didn't' we?"

Dark Jasmine falls prone as golden streaks cut through the air. Still low to the ground, she blows a frozen kiss into her hand, rolls it up in her fingers and flings it like a dart. It sinks straight into Myles' forearm causing his next shots to fire wide as he drops his revolver with a pained growl. While Myles is clutching his arm, Dark Jeremy flails forward and drop-kicks Myles in the chest with such a lack of finesse that the move looks accidental. The blow doesn't knock Myles over, but it causes him to stagger back and drop to a knee. Natasha charges at Dark Jeremy, but a hand suddenly pierces the floor and grabs her by the ankle, tripping her up. Still on my back, I point my sword up to Dark Jasmine who just stares me down with a smirk. I see Natasha yank herself free in my peripheral vision—or rather that she actually just tears the hand holding her free from its wrist. Dark Natasha rises up in front of where Natasha's down with her feet in the air until she eventually settles on the top of her porcelain head. Cracks form on her face from the strain before her spine contorts so that her feet reach the ground and she's able to pull herself upright like a human slinky. I'm able to squirm to my feet, but I'm not totally sure what I should do.

There's something about Dark Jasmine that makes it hard for me to try running her through, maybe it's just how young she looks.

Fortunately, our Jasmine comes bursting through the wall beside me. I guess she's alright after all. She ducks beneath her dark doppelganger's cartwheel kick, spins on her toes and back-kicks the little ice princess onto her ass.

"Bryan!" she calls to me with her hand held out.

I toss her my sword hoping that this will work like the knife did. To my relief, the hilt snaps right into her palm. As soon as it does, she rears back with a determined frown.

"Wait," Dark Jasmine shrieks as Jasmine drives my sword into her chest.

Myles gets to his feet and Spartan-kicks Dark Jeremy onto his back and neck as he frantically tries to pounce on Myles. While the evil spaz is sprawled out with his hair strewn all over his face, a pair of arms suddenly wrap around his neck. Before he can squirm out, a pair of legs clamp down around Dark Jeremy's waist. The body around him rolls him over onto his stomach, revealing our Jeremy as the one who was underneath. He gets up, straddling his paler and darker copy and gives him a hard shove on the back through the floor until he's fallen from sight. Jasmine tosses my sword back to me as I charge at Dark Natasha. She's just staring at her handless wrist which has stuffing rather than blood dribbling out of it. She turns to me with a dead look in her one glassy eye as I step up and lop off her head. It tumbles off her neck and shatters over the floor. I turn my attention to Natasha, who's picking herself up, when Dark Natasha's headless body spins at the waist and bats me across the face with her handless forearm. I drop my weapon as I crash on my side. Still dazed, I stay there while the headless doll-lady scuttles over, plants a foot on my chest and grips my throat with her remaining hand. I thrash around, hoping this hand can be torn off as easily as the other, but it seems to have already been reattached with staples so I'm not having much luck ripping myself free.

I'm almost out of air when a javelin shoves through this monster's chest. Natasha twists the body off of me, but even this wound doesn't stop it. I scramble to my sword while what's left of Dark Jasmine pulls herself free from the polearm. Fortunately,

Myles retrieves both his pistols so he steps up and peppers this revenant form with beams of gold. Stuffing, pins, cogs, bits of plastic, and fabric scatter into the air until the body is so tattered, it flops into a heap of damaged parts.

Jeremy retrieves his weapon and stands tensed with its tip pointed downward. We fan out around him with our arms trained on the cloudy haze beneath us. Nothing happens right away and the cramped space falls into eerie silence. Something catches my eye. I realize the reflection of Jeremy's shoes are wrong. He's wearing clogs but the reflection has dark riding boots. They got us again with that trick.

"Beneath you!" I stammer.

Without flinching, Jeremy leaps up with a knee to his chest. Dark Jeremy propels up after him with wild eyes, an open mouth, and his fingers spread wide. Jeremy plunges his javelin down into his ghoulish twin like a fish. The villain instantly goes limp and crashes to the ground when Jeremy flings him aside. I watch as Jeremy lands unaffected, but my relief is cut short when I remember both the Olivias are still out there somewhere. I look up when I see Jasmine aim her crossbow at the ceiling. At first, I don't notice anything, but then I see a red flicker that breaks through the unholy mist. We all retreat to the corners as two bodies crash through.

Our Olivia is tossed aside, but she manages to roll backward and enter a wide crouch. There's a gash across her forehead that some of her raven locks are matted against. The demonic visage of Dark Olivia lands heavily in the center of the room, snarling and foaming at the mouth. She contorts viciously when a few golden streaks tear through her. She bounds toward Myles, taking his fire as though she's numb to the pain, and hops up like a kangaroo to kick his abdomen with both feet. He slams against a wall and remains hunched in half-consciousness against it. Jeremy and Natasha dash at her from both sides. They skip up in unison and drive the tips of their javelins into her sides. She howls at the impalement and at how they drive their weapons deeper once they've landed around her. In spite of the agony, she manages to yank her body around, hurling each of them away—sending them skidding across the floor.

Dark Olivia's fiery red body is now slicked with crimson as

contempt burns behind her eyes. I charge forward as Jasmine fires bolts into Dark Olivia's arms and breasts. I fall to my knees, dodging a swipe of her clawed hands and slicing into her thigh. She falls to a two-jointed knee, somehow catching a bolt in her hand before it can drive into her neck. Olivia's retrieved her sickle now so I decide that I should try to distract this beastly creature. I stand and let a battle cry out, drawing her attention as I drive my sword downward. She twists to me and catches my blade in her forearm while howling into my face. Her breath smells like burnt cake—which I decide it the saddest scent in existence. Before she can mount a full retaliation, Olivia comes up from behind. She swings her golden sickle through Dark Olivia's waist.

The creature's wild eyes go dim and her flame-like hair falls flat around her face as the blade cuts her in two. Then she topples over, blood spilling out from both halves. We surround her with our weapons held tight, but she doesn't come back for an encore rampage.

"Everyone alright?" I check.

"Some of us are a little banged up, but we're still standing, old chap," Myles responds hoarsely.

"That probably went as well as it possibly could," Olivia agrees.

She marches over to Myles and grabs him by the wrist Dark Jasmine impaled. She examines the wound, drops her sickle and then yanks the frozen spike out of his forearm, eliciting a pained groan from our big companion. She pulls out bandages from some fold in her jacket and wraps up his injury before he can ooze blood all over the place.

"And what about you, then?" Myles asks, gesturing to the gash on her head.

She reaches up and touches it, seemingly surprised by the blood that sticks to her fingers. Without saying anything, she just pulls out a tube of some kind and hands it to him. Holstering both his weapons, he spreads a bit of it over her forehead. It doesn't magically heal the cut, but it does seem to stop the bleeding. He gives it back to her in exchange for a gauze pad that he cleans her up with.

As he tosses the bloodied cloth to the floor, he says, "Now

we just need to figure out how we get out of here."

"Where are we exactly and how is it possible that those monsters were able to fight us?" I ask.

"It must be these dark mirrors," Jeremy offers.

"This place is like a bridge between us and the darkness that The Eclipsed reside in," Natasha adds.

"Someone orchestrated this," Olivia states.

"Clearly Sin was hoping our darker selves would take us off the board," Myles says.

"I'm just glad they're gone," Jasmine sighs.

"You've never seen them before, have you?" I ask the group.

They all shake their heads solemnly.

"No, we we've always been aware of their existence, even felt their presence at times, but to see them up close was something else entirely," Olivia replies.

"Not sure quite what I expected," Myles says.

"I suppose they truly were our direct opposites, not just some twisted mirror images," Jeremy muses.

"There's still two more of them out there," Natasha reminds me.

Our boxed-in space suddenly shatters into sharp obsidian shards. We plunge into the darkness and I lose sight of everyone in the smoky haze as I freefall. A chill begins to consume me as I plummet further into this nothing. Suddenly a surface comes up to meet me. My heart leaps, but I manage to land solidly on my feet with a slight bend in my knees and my sword held out to the side. I notice that it glows rather brightly down here in the near pitch-black. There's just one dim light source around so I turn to face it.

"Hello there, darling," Dark Margaret's venomous tone greets me.

She's sitting on a spikey throne of luminescent silver ice crystals. Dark Jack is curled up on her lap, clutching his stomach and resting his head over her bosom.

"I wasn't terribly sure I'd ever get the chance to see you again—at least not in your present state—but here we are on this joyous occasion."

"Get out of my way," I warn them.

"Come now, you wouldn't want to see us die twice, would

you?" she taunts.

"Please don't hurt us…" Dark Jack adds.

In some ways he sounds just like Jack, but there's this foreign, less-than-genuine quality in his voice.

"You're not the ones I've lost. You're everything they never would be," I retort.

Dark Margaret nudges Dark Jack off of her and then rises from her throne with the gravitas of a queen. "I understand that you like them better, I really do. Why wouldn't you? They're from up there. There're squeaky clean and all full of smiles and other lovely, benevolent things. All the while, we've been down here, hardened by the darkness and the cold. For that, we are the stronger, the better, the more deserving of your admiration…"

She's not kidding about the cold, even in this body armor, I might literally be freezing my tits off.

She continues her supervillain monologue with, "What you should know is that we are not some castaway creatures banished to this hell. No, we're the realest parts of you in this whole damned place. We are more integral to who you are than anyone else! Without us, you would not be where you are today, you would not be what you are today. You **need** us, Bryan Daley."

"Not anymore, I don't," I snarl. "You're standing between me and my freedom so I will cut you down no matter what you think you are or who you share a face with."

"Bumbling fool, we **are** freedom!"

Without further discussion, I rush forward, gripping my sword with both hands. Margaret shrieks so loud I think I might go deaf. Then she corkscrews into the air to meet me. I'm about to chop her down as she descends, but then a foot suddenly connects with my gut. I stumble back, winded, realizing Dark Jack snuck up and kicked me while I focused on the queen of darkness. He scuttles back as she lands in front of me, ripping a crushing backhand across my jaw. The blow spins me through the air, but I manage to keep hold of my weapon when I crash to the slick black surface beneath us. Dark Jack comes from out of nowhere and steps on my blade, pining it down. The sound of Dark Margaret's clicking heels draws ominously closer. My heart thumps furiously. Getting bitch-slapped to death is really not the way I'd like to go out. With surprising dexterity, I twist up into a crooked handstand and drive my boot into Dark Jack's stomach.

He crashes into a ball and coughs up some of that black vomit he likes to cover my roses in. I get to my feet in time to raise my sword at Dark Margaret's chest. She halts but shoots me an unconcerned grin. I thrust the tip of the blade forward, but she folds back at the knees and snaps upright again once I've pulled my weapon back to my side. She steps aside nimbly as I take another desperate stab at her and snatches my wrist with one hand. She drives the other into my chest. I sail back and the wind is fully knocked out of me when I land on my ass. I'm still holding onto my sword, but I don't know how I'm supposed to win this anymore.

"Myles! Olivia!" I shout, hoping any of them might be out there somewhere.

Dark Margaret saunters over as I struggle to get back off the ground. "Dearest, did you really think you could overpower me?" she asks as she places her fingertips on her chest. "You know I'm stronger than you, swifter than you, so much more resolute than you. You cannot beat me and none of your bright little buffoons are coming to save you from me…"

Dark Jack snickers. I snap my head to the side and see that he's crouched low next to me like some kind of impish frog. I feel my world closing in, but this can't be where it ends, can it? Not down here in the dark with them. Every unkind thing I ever said or did suddenly flashes before me like a sepia film reel. Every time I talked back to my parents, the people I talked down to as a kid to feel cool, the tricks I'd play on Adrien, that time I shoved him on the ground in front of everyone just because he made me angry, the times I cheated in school or bitched about my teachers, and every girl I ever pissed off in college when I never texted or called them after I talked them up and got them to sleep with me.

I see some of my more recent transgressions too: the cold shoulder I've been giving David—how I cut him off as a friend, when I yelled 'fuck off' to Kevin in the rain, my sloppy breakup with Kayla, and all the times I could have been real with her, but wasn't. It all hits me like a bag of bricks, but there's also something in that pain that returns the air to my lungs.

I look up defiantly at Dark Margaret and say, "You're wrong.

You're not stronger than me, you never really were. Your power comes from lies, you win because I'm weak, not because of any strength that lives within you. I think it's time for you to know what it's like to lose…"

I kick up to my feet and side-kick Dark Jack away as he tries to pounce on me. Dark Margaret dodges my attacks just as easily as before when I slash at her, but this time, I follow it up by falling into a crouch, spinning on the balls of my feet, and driving a heel into her shins. She collapses, her arms spread out to catch herself. I spring up, changing the grip on my sword and driving it down into her back before she can get back up. She moans as I pull it out from her and falls into a pool of her own blood. Dark Jack flings himself onto me, clawing at my face and pulling at my hair. I fall to one knee and use the momentum to rip him off of me.

"No, please," he pleads as he wriggles away from me. "You can't kill me…"

"Why not?" I keep my blade pointed at his face, following him as he thrashes on the ground.

"I'm not like him. I don't just fizzle away into sparkly dust. I don't diminish once I'm here. You're stuck with me." He titters.

"I bet I can still cut you down, make you a fraction of what you are now. I bet it would hurt." In spite of my tough talk and the promise I made to Jack, I'm admittedly having a hard time ending this little fucker.

"Please don't…" he whimpers. "You're right, it'll hurt so bad…"

"I can't have you running around in here," I say in half-apology.

"You think I'm bad, but I'm not, I swear it! I make you more interesting, I let you have more fun. You'll be sad without me!"

"I made your reflection a promise…"

"No!" he screams as I stab my weapon down through his heart.

For a second, he looks so much like Jack, but then he melts into that same black sludge that he vomits up. It oozes across the ground, shriveling and evaporating a bit until it's so thinly spread that I can't see it against the already-slimy ground anymore. The space around me starts to sizzle and fizzle out like a dying flame.

The darkness gives way to the hallway that it took me from.

"I'm impressed, Mister Daley!" Sin's voice clangs. "I truly did not know whether our battle would be over at this point or not. I mean, there have been several opportunities for our struggle to end prematurely, but I'm just delighted that you've made it through all those little pickles. And not a moment too soon, either! Your allies are all in a rather precarious situation presently."

"I'm coming for them and then we're all coming for you, Sin."

"I do very much look forward to it," Sin answers with a chuckle. "Oh, and do be a dear and try not to fall along the way. You've come this far, so it'd be a shame for me to be robbed of the chance to end you by my own hands."

I'm by myself so I have to trust that Myles, Olivia, and the others already made it through this doorway. I take a second to collect myself. This is the final charge before the final battle. I hope that I can actually win—it'd be a shame to get to the end only for Sin to destroy me. Before doubt can creep in again, I push on through the portal, determined not to fall, and anxious to discover how this will finally end.

# Chapter 3

I come out of the portal to the sound of blades clanging and cretins screeching as a fight rages in the parlor. Sheera and Shirun plow their way through the room's center where tables and high chairs lay strewn across the floor. Shirun dashes into a swarm of cretins, dropping to his knees, spinning and sliding as he whips his chain blade around above his head. It guts any cretins in its way before he skids to a stop and cracks it down on a couple of swordsmen in front of him. Sheera covers his rear, leaping into a cretin lady with both her swords and then rebounding off the monster's chest to sink her blades into a cretin gentleman coming from the other side.

I rush into the fray, cutting down a villain that manages to duck beneath Olivia's sickle as she chops through a group of them. Jasmine backs up to my side and takes a knee. She looses a bolt across the room into a cretin who's winding up to throw a spear at Olivia. With that handled, I head over to where William and Joanna start to get overrun. William rolls toward me and away from an axe that almost reams into him. I leap sideways as the cretin lady swings again—trying to chop my legs off this time. I slice through her neck, land on my feet, spin on my heels, and drive my sword up through a cretin's back who's locked blades with Joanna. She takes this opening to backflip over another enemy before he can step up to run her through. Landing behind him, Joanna tosses her blades up to catch them in a downward grip and drives them into the cretin man's neck. William runs past me to trip up a cretin charging us with a downward sweep kick. I step up to skewer the cretin while he's down so William and Joanna can rush on and tag team a cretin holding a long pitchfork. William draws the cretin gentleman's focus away with a feint advance while Joanna goes in for the kill. I can't get over how much these two have changed and I wonder if that means that I'm also very different now. There isn't much time to contemplate this as we advance to join the others.

I break off from them to cut down a cretin coming for

Myles' back. William and Joanna meet up with Samuel to help him fend off enemies trying to reach Evan who's dropping targets near where Sheera and Shirun fight. Jasmine comes up to help, taking shelter in the protective circle forming around Evan. I duck under Myles' arm to stab into a cretin coming at him head on while his aim is set to the sides. I somehow know when he's about to shift his positioning so I bend at the waist as his arm swings over me—a maneuver made much easier by the fact that my head only comes up to his armpit anyway. While he blasts away out in front of us, I defend his flank from an enemy pikeman. My sword cleaves the pole in two and I cut the cretin down while he's disarmed. Then I swing around behind Myles as we march onward. He stops to kick a cretin with twin daggers that he can't be bothered to shoot. I get down and come up in front of him to finish the job while Myles pivots so that we're back to back. He blasts enemies down either side then switches back around, placing his revolvers around my head and dropping cretins who are about to fire arrows at us.

I see that Sheera already made it to the other end of the room with Madeline, Jeremy, and Natasha around her. Sheera rockets into a group guarding our exit, holding her swords out to slice through a couple cretins while she's airborne. She lands by tackling a cretin with both swords through his chest. Jeremy and Natasha vault over overturned tables and skewer enemies as they come back down. Madeline follows behind, spinning her giant glaive above and around her as she twirls and skips. She joins them in defending Sheera as she kicks down the final door. Jeremy and Natasha stab their weapons into a couple straggling enemies before following Sheera and Madeline through.

There are still a number of cretins around, but their ranks are thin enough for us to rush for the portal. We've only just begun our charge when the room is suddenly rocked, nearly knocking some of us off our feet.

"Very good, little ones!" Sin taunts. "How about one last challenge to see if you are worthy of our final entanglement…"

The impacts pick up in tempo and I look up to see portions of the broken ceiling ripped away by lightning strikes.

"Let's move," Samuel orders as he bats down a cretin.

William, Joanna, Jasmine, and Evan all break for the door.

I'm impressed by how quickly Jasmine and Evan learned to pick off enemies while on the move. William and Joanna pounce on any that get too close to them. They're through to the other side when the ceiling has completely been torn off and the storm now rips into the walls and floor. Myles, Olivia, and I race across the room when we see a blotch of dark spots plummeting out of the torn sky. Shirun looks up from where he's come back to help Rachel and Samuel cut down the last cluster of cretins. His eyes widen at the projectiles as they grow in size.

"Move," he commands us.

We quicken our pace, but we're still a ways behind. It turns out those growing dark spots are cretins plummeting down to ambush us. As the lightning tears up the room around and behind us, they bounce off the floor before us and barrel back into the air like rubber. Shirun launches into them, spinning his weapon in front of him like a deadly fan blade. Me mows down a respectable number, but there are plenty that get by him. Myles takes it upon himself to thin out the ranks as Rachel and Samuel tear into them. The lightning starts to make the ruins of this room a whole lot narrower. Debris shoots up only to get sucked into the vortex. Shirun swings back around to lash at the enemy soldiers, but they've already ganged up on Samuel and Rachel. She does her best to chop down the cretins two at a time, but the slow, heavy arc of her axe proves to be her undoing as a cretin with a spear hops free of her chop and pokes his weapon through her heart. She drops to the floor at Samuel's feet eliciting a pale look of horror from him as he bats down an enemy.

Myles comes to a stop, blasting away into the horde like a turret. Olivia leaps in with a big swing of her sickle, but I stay behind to guard Myles as some enemies try to close in on his location. Samuel goes to block a strike from a war hammer, but the blow is too powerful. It knocks him onto his back and sends his staff skidding across the tile floor. Fortunately, Shirun arrives in a downward spiral, slashing apart the monsters hoping to finish Samuel off. I spin around to slice a cretin down and through it's back. When I face forward again, Olivia's joined them. She catches several enemies in her curved blade before bending down to lift Samuel up. He reclaims his staff, but the floor beneath us—what's left of it anyway—feels far more unsteady. Shirun tosses his blade through a string of cretins, clearing the way to the door. I pivot and clash blades with a cretin man when the remains of this room suddenly jolt downward at an angle. The shift throws my enemy off balance, allowing me to slide his weapon aside and run him through. Olivia and Samuel skid a little as they rush into the doorway.

"Come on, old chap," Myles urges me as the floor continues to dip with a groan.

I sprint forward, using the new incline to extend my leap toward a cretin that I plunge my sword into before he can raise his axe to properly defend himself. Myles bounds past me, doing his best to tear through the enemies before us. Even he's having some trouble keeping his footing as the slant steepens. Shirun whips his weapon through any enemy around him as he slides to the door and leans up against its frame. Lightning rains down with greater intensity. The force of the blows rattles our already unstable surroundings. One bolt even shoots straight down at Shirun, but he's able to deflect it with a swing of his chain blade. There's a sudden rumble followed by a series of cracks and snaps, then the ruined room enters into a full free fall as it continues to roll over itself. Myles and I find ourselves suspended in the air a moment before our feet reconnect with the floor. Figures that the laws of gravity pick **now** of all times to show up.

The angle becomes too hard to run on anymore. Myles pulls his knees up to his chest and falls like a cannonball while he fires his revolvers on either side of his legs. I collapse into a one-legged slide, grateful not to feel any friction in this armor. I lightly spring off of the surface and pencil dive down to the door, hoping I have the right trajectory to plunge through it. Shirun perches himself on the door frame, deflecting lightning and dicing up falling cretins. A number of them leap up to meet us though. Myles guns most of them down, but a couple do get past him. I shift my weight to fall into one with my sword, then push off of him to propel myself up and away from his friend who almost catches me with her lance. My feet connect with the floor briefly, allowing me to take a couple of steps and launch myself downward. I bat her spear away before she can repoint it and catch her by the wrist of her free hand as she tries to punch me. I twist my body and toss her into the storm where the debris from a lightning strike slams her into the dark vortex.

Myles soars through the portal, but I start to fear that I may not make it. I think my angle is wrong and I have no way to correct it. The door is starting to twist down under me such that I'll overshoot the top of the frame. I see a shattered wine cellar come into view. I think we're about to crash into it. I twist so that I'm feet down and my body is straightened with my weapon held over my chest. Now I can see for sure that I'm going to miss the door. Shirun's eyes narrow after he shields our exit from another lightning attack. He flings his weapon over his shoulder and wraps it diagonally across his body, then leaps up. He catches me by the shoulders and nudges us back on course. Our feet drop into the glassy exit and I see the last portion of the parlor start to explode into the wine cellar right before my head dips down to safety.

Shirun and I fling out through the other side and torque our bodies so that we can land on our feet – drawing our weapons out to the side as we plant ourselves. Sheera and the others stand encircled around us, but they part for us to see that the dining hall is remarkably untouched. There's even ominous drum music coming from the empty stage. I'd expected it to be crawling with cretins, but instead we're left standing awkwardly in front of the door while Sin is seated at one head of the table for thirty-two with fifteen cretins lining each side of it. Its sharp chin points up in the air as its glowing yellow snake eyes glare at me and its round cat ears twitch with anticipation.

"So glad you could join us, Mister Daley. Bit of a close call getting here, wasn't it?" Sin chuckles, tapping its spider-leg-like fingers on the table. "Looks like your merry band is a little smaller too—not as small as I'd have liked, but we can remedy that shortly." Sin sends me a wide, toothy smile that gleams sickeningly even across the distance between us.

"Well, here I am—here we all are—so let's finish this!" I yell across the room.

"Oh, Mister Daley… while I am more than happy to rip each and every one of your little friends apart and break you down to nothing, I'd like to first offer you a less painful way. Come here and take this seat across from me that we've saved for you—the very seat in which you sat that first night you arrived here. Sup with us and I may just let you keep a couple of your dear ones. I can't have them running about, of course, but just as The Eclipsed had their pit of misty darkness, your more luminous companions may live out their days trapped in a plane of sterile light. Come now, let us end the story right where it began."

"Don't falter now," Sheera growls.

"He knows what needs to be done," Shirun assures her.

"Don't think on it too long, Mister Daley, it's not all too complicated," Sin urges. "You submit to me now and I will show some measure of mercy. Enter into battle when you are already weary and I swear to you that you will suffer dearly whilst losing it all regardless of how hard you make me work."

"If you didn't think I had a good chance of beating you, then you wouldn't be offering me this parlay," I challenge. "You're on your last legs, Sin, so how about you get off your sick, twisted ass and face us like a good little monster."

I'm not sure how bright it is to taunt this creature, but it's played enough mind games with me, time to rattle **it** for a change.

Sin chuckles low, "Very well, little Bryan. One way or another, we will sup tonight. Regardless of what you chose, you were always going to be the main course. I'll just have to make you pay for making me toil for my dinner…"

I suppose that makes sense given the distinct lack of food on the table. I have no intention of being anyone's dinner though. Sin arises, but the cretins remain seated, their attention fixed on the center of the table. Sin waves it's arms out, making strange finger gestures. A red symbol suddenly burns into the white table cloth— that same glyph we saw when we first met Sin. The inner triangle singes up through the tablecloth first, then out to where the spikey circles form the outer square. Then the different parts spin in opposite directions.

"Shit," I huff.

"Steady everyone," Shirun calms us. "We knew this beast would be back for the final battle."

"So right you are, my dear Shirun! Got to pull out all the stops for our grand finale, don't we?" Sin replies.

The unholy shapes spin so fast that they're no longer especially discernable. The murderous mutt pops out of the symbol-portal and crashes down onto the table. The whole thing collapses under the hound's weight, knocking all of the cretins back in their chairs in a surge of smokey, crimson vapor. The seats break apart on impact and the cretins lock up with their hips thrust into the air as if suffering from some kind of tetanus. They cry out in unison with a horrible squealing noise as their fingers elongate into sharp points, their backs stretch and arch, their ears fold into twisted horns, and they form snout-like mouths filled with razor-sharp teeth. Even the wolfman would be disturbed by the thirty monstrosities that slowly pull themselves up and stand with glowing red eyes matching the hellhound's. Speaking of the hound, I'm almost positive that it's gotten bigger and I don't mean since the last time I ran into it—I mean literally since the last time I looked at it. It might be as much as twice the size as what it was when it popped through that glyph.

Sin struts around the table and squares off with us. "Alright my ravenous little morsels, dinner is served!"

With this announcement, the cretins scramble forward, chomping their teeth and making perverse noises. I step up to the front of our group and stare Sin down as it waits back with its dog.

"Let's finish this," I yell back to my forces.

As we run to meet our enemies, it occurs to me how lame of a battle cry this is. At least I didn't say something completely awful like *"Charge!"* or *"To victory!"* As we draw close to the mutated cretins, it literally looks like we're charging the forces of Hell. Jeremy and Natasha suddenly fly by me like arrows. They take two of the cretins down right away and then twist around just in time to drive their spearheads through the sharp, wide hands of cretins trying to claw their faces off. I sidestep a claw coming for my own head and chop it off as it reaches past me. The cretin lady-beast-thing pulls her knee up and kicks me right in the ribs before I can take another swing at her. The blow sends me skidding backward so far that Myles and Olivia have to hop over me as they enter the fray. Myles guns down the cretin that just kicked me while Olivia takes a wide swing at several others. While she does manage to cut one open, these evolved cretins seem more agile—a couple of them manage to leap clear of her blade with ease. As I get up, I realize that they're also much sturdier. Myles has to rip a dozen or so holes into the cretin that kicked me, including a couple shots to the head, before she goes down.

Fortunately, Madeline is having a little more success. The cretins are still nimble enough to not get mowed down, but the way she spins her glaive around her also keeps them from being able to get close without losing an appendage. Samuel is having a much tougher time of it. The cretins evade his staff with ease and whack him with their claws. His armored clothing holds up, but he's still getting thrashed around. Sheera and Shirin see this too so they leap to his location and plunge into the enemies surrounding him. Sheera lops off a cretin's legs and drives her swords up through his jaw when he falls. Shirun whips his weapon through a cretin's chest, then swings it up and back around into the top of his head as the monster staggers back. He manages to surprise a cretin behind him by rotating and flinging his blade straight through her throat and then spinning himself so that the blade slices out and swings back around to fully decapitate her. Samuel regains a bit of momentum with these two fighting beside him and bats down a cretin dodging an assault from Sheera.

I get back into the fight, defending against a strike from a cretin trying to attack Myles. I chop off the forearm, but the creature gets his good claw wrapped around my neck. Myles pivots and fires into the cretin's bicep until the whole arm falls apart and then charges up to pistol whip him across the face. He follows this up by blasting a series of holes through his chest until he drops. Myles gives me a nod before stepping away and unloading into an enemy going after Olivia while she's busy chopping through one leaping at her from the front. As I charge in to aid her, I notice how well William and Joanna fare—leaping off the heads and shoulders of cretins like monkeys flying between trees. They slash and stab at each of the enemies they land on, slowly weakening their ranks. Jasmine and Evan do their part too—sending arrows and bolts into the battlefield. We're making some good ground between all of this. I turn to cut down a cretin oozing from quick stabs and projectile wounds. I find it much easier to catch him with my blade now that he's been broken down a bit.

In the face of this promising opening, my heart drops when I see a big, smoky, black shape bounding around the battlefield and leaping off a wall. Sin's dog is heading straight for Jasmine and Evan. They don't see it though because they're firing at a cretin who's slipped out of the battle and making some kind of kamikaze run at them.

"Look out!" I yell after slicing an attacking claw away.

Evan looks to the side once they've dropped the stray cretin. Sin's hound is already leaping at them with its mouth open wide. Jasmine spins around with her crossbow pointed up, but Evan shoves her aside as the beast falls onto him with its oversized paw. She rolls to her feet and fires a few bolts into it, but that doesn't seem to do much. Sheera and Shirun leap away to help—arriving too late to prevent a giant bite from being taken out of Evan's chest. Undeterred, Sheera flies over the hound, slicing into its back with both her blades. Shirun cuts into one of its hind legs as it bounds away, trampling Evan's torn corpse in the process. I make a leaping stab into a cretin's face when all of the sudden the dining hall starts to shake from the impact of lightning strikes.

I look aside past where Madeline saws through an enemy to see Sin sauntering our way with hands spread out to the side as if running its fingers through the electricity in the air. Its tail flicks from side to side and it wears a hauntingly wide smile. The ceiling starts to get torn up and the room rattles with each impact.

"That was a fun little warm up, now wasn't it? You really didn't expect it to be so easy, did you?" Sin clangs as it locks eyes with me from across the room.

I do my best to remember Sin's just trying to get in our heads. It's not that big a deal that it is entering the fight. This is what we came for, this is what we're ready to face. I do feel fear's chill when I see the hound turn and barrel towards us. Sheera and Shirun rush back with Jasmine, but they won't be back in time to stop it. Myles kicks a wounded cretin and blasts him apart while he's down. Olivia cuts the claws off of one attacking her and then rushes to meet the hellhound. Myles bumps me away and steps in front of where I stumble aside. He unleashes a barrage of light into the beast. While his shots at least seem to tear through its flesh, unlike our first encounter, they don't do much to slow its course. Olivia drops to a slide, running her sickle across its belly as she skids beneath it. Dark steam spews out from the laceration, but that doesn't seem to faze it either. It just heads straight for where I'm pulling my sword from a cretin I just evaded and stabbed. Myles rushes past me to intercept its path, continuing to fire at it.

When it's clear that the beast isn't stopping and he's about to be overcome, Myles turns to me with a warm smirk and a glint in his eyes. "You've got it from here, yeah?"

Without another word, he tosses one of his revolvers to me, turns, and rushes to meet the hound. He leaps up and fires into the beast's mouth before it clamps down on him. I bend as it leaps over me with Myles' limp form hanging from its mouth—his blood dripping from its jaw.

"No!" I croak, feeling as though my chest has suddenly been hollowed out.

The sensation paralyzes me. I just watch as Myles' killer gets away, dropping the body and crawling up onto the stage to lick its wounds. Samuel rushes over and deflects a cretin's attack on me. He steps back, spinning and swinging a spiked end into the cretin's skull. Olivia returns to my side as well, appearing unaffected by what we just lost save for a tear running down her cheek.

"This doesn't change a thing," she tells me. "You hold some of his power now, make good use of it and we might still win."

Sin steps through the battle. It ducks down and flicks William away with its tail as he's attempting an airborne assault. Joanna leaps off one cretin's shoulders and sinks her blades into another's neck. She rides it down to the floor and rolls off as it collapses into ash. Before she can pounce on Sin, it traps her in one of its cylindrical, onyx forcefields with a toss of its hand. Jeremy and Natasha drive their javelins up into a cretin and hurl his body at Sin who just backhands it away like a bug. Madeline comes at Sin with her glaive, but Sin catches it before her attack can land. Inky blood drops out from its hands, but Sin has little trouble tearing the weapon away and flinging it aside.

"Madeline!" I cry, feeling dread at the thought of losing her even though I barely know her.

Time seems to slow as I look back, finding that Sheera, Shirun, and Jasmine are confronted by four cretins. Olivia, Samuel, and I aren't close enough to help yet, and William is just getting back up to his feet. Sin kicks Madeline's legs out from under her and bends back at the knees as Jeremy and Natasha fly straight over it—their weapons not so much as landing a scratch. With no one to intervene, Sin reaches down to grab Madeline by the throat. She's lifted off her knees, into the air, and then repeatedly slammed against the floor in rhythm with the lighting strikes cracking into the walls and the still-beating, invisible drums. By the time we get there, Sin is already chucking her broken body out of the way.

Olivia and I chop down cretins blocking our path and square off to this creature. Looking back, I see Shirun catch two cretins, Sheera cross-chop a third, and Jasmine put down the fourth by sending two bolts through the cretin's eyes. Sin's snake eyes gleam as it raises a hand. With a snap of its fingers, the last of the tattered, bloody cretins collapse into sludge and worm their way into Sin's hands there they harden into an ornate great sword with what looks like an eye engraved into the pommel.

"Let's see this to the end, shall we?" Sin sneers.

The Calamity has worn the walls around us down to almost nothing, exposing us all to its chilly and unforgiving currents. Samuel's attack is deflected by Sin's massive weapon, but the offensive gives William the chance to slide his knife across Sin's torso. It shoves Samuel backward and shifts its weight to side kick William. The blow sends William sliding across the room with so much force that he has to drive his blades into the floor to stop himself from going over the ledge. Olivia and I advance—me firing Myles' revolver—when the forcefield containing Joanna bursts. We find ourselves flying backward until we crash onto our backs. Sheera and Shirun stop us from skidding too far with a foot tilted up to catch us. They step over us with Jasmine close behind, firing bolts. While Sin is slicing the projectiles out of the air, Jeremy and Natasha flip over it, sinking their weapons into its shoulders and drawing a pained growl. They land in front of Sin, offering a distraction for Joanna to slide past and stab into its leg.

Sin howls, favoring the hurt leg a little as it takes a wide swing at Jeremy and Natasha. They get their javelins up in time to stop the blade from cleaving into them, but the blow knocks them both aside and splits the shafts of their weapons. A few of Jasmine's bolts stick into Sin while Joanna leaps up onto its back, stuffing her blades down deep. A deafening screech rocks us before Sin reaches back. Joanna slips off of Sin before it can grab her. She ducks beneath its featureless crotch, slicing its inner thighs as she runs between them.

Back on our feet, Olivia and I resume our charge. I note how Sin's not really bleeding. I also don't spot any muscle or bone through its wounds. Sin seems to just be made of chunky, deep purple goo on the inside that seeps out of the cuts into its body. Joanna flips over Sin's weapon as it tries to cleave her in two. With a flick of Sin's wrist, William finds himself caught in a forcefield cage as he's trying to rejoin the fight. It launches a ball of black flame at Sheera and Shirun as they launch forward. They chop through the projectile together, but Sin manages to get its great sword up in time to guard against their attack. They stumble to the side as Olivia and I charge past Jasmine. Olivia leaps high while I slide low and Sin's weapon cuts through the air between us. When Olivia lands beside me, I stab my sword into Sin's belly while she slips her golden butchers knife out of some mysterious fold in her coat and into her hand. She flings it across the room to where Jeremy catches it as he and Natasha rush toward Sin with the top halves of their javelins held out like knives.

Samuel makes another attempt at Sin, but his staff is knocked away when it clashes with Sin's sword. Sin ducks away and thrusts a foot up to the side, kicking Joanna in the waist as she's flying at it. She manages just to slice its shin before she's knocked from her trajectory. Sin shifts its weight onto its other foot and levels Samuel with a vicious downward spin kick. Sin stomps the flattened man in his gut and punts him away in time to swing its blade aside to block Shirun's strike and side step Sheera as she chops down with both her swords. Jeremy and Natasha flip overhead, tossing what's left of their javelins down into either side of Sin's neck, hitting the same holes that they've already poked into him. Between those and all the bolts Jasmine's been firing into it, Sin is starting to resemble a pin cushion.

"I will not be subdued!" Sin growls.

With a couple of flicks of the wrist, William's cage explodes around him and Jasmine finds herself trapped his stead. Olivia and I are knocked aside when we clash blades with Sin. While I'm down, I notice Samuel writhing away. The crunching noises his body made while Sin kicked him around made me think he might be dead so it's good to know he's still with us even if only just barely. I see Sheera and Shirun have a little more success when I get to my feet. Sheera locks swords with Sin, giving Shirun the opening to step around and sink his weapon into the monster's side. Sin takes a hand off of its hilt and back slaps Shirun. His chain blade slides out from Sin as he crashes away, but with only one hand holding its sword now, Sheera is able to shove Sin's weapon aside and swing round to lop off Sin's whole arm at the shoulder. Sin cries out breathlessly, gripping at where goop sputters out from the stump.

A ferocious roar startles us all. We look to where Sin's dog ambles over the stage and hops down. It hobbles in our direction with its teeth barred.

"Your master is almost finished and so are you," I taunt even though I'm not sure that's such a smart idea.

My stomach drops and my blood freezes when the beast opens its mouth and laughs. My horror only grows when it actually speaks.

"Fool, did you think I was Sin's pet this whole time? Of course you did, what more can be expected of one someone so small? Mark me, whelp, Sin is **my** bitch and this is hardly over."

"Stay back," Shirun orders as he and Sheera march past me.

They square off to the hound as lightning pokes away at the edges of this arena.

The beast laughs again, "I must admit, I did not expect your interference." Its gaze is fixated on Sheera. "Quite the arsenal you have contributed, too."

"This atrocity will not be tolerated," she snarls at it.

"Yes, well, what do you hope to do to me, Shiran, peddlers of hope, creatures of love?"

"Your kind all too often forgets the true value of hope. You also know nothing of love or how fierce ours can be." Shirun levels with this thing, his head held high.

With that, a glowing white aura envelops him and Sheera. Their bodies seem to morph, getting taller and skinnier. The backs of their heads elongate to a point and their hair sways like blades of grass against the wind. Fiery crystalline energy shoots out of their backs like wings and their weapons ripple in white flame. The hound undergoes a transformation of its own. It stands high on its hind legs as its body singes in smoldering crimson smoke. It transforms into an anthropomorphic creature with a tooth-lined snout, horn-high ears, double jointed legs, and skeletal bat wings sprouting from its shoulder blades. It's eyes still burn like a raging fire.

Sheera turns back to me, her voice full like a strong current, "You must finish off Sin. We will not be able to fully expel The Hound until you do, but we can keep it busy for as long as you need."

Red-hot chain-maces form in the demon-man-dog-bat's hands. All three of them dip down and launch up into the air where they fly about, clashing weapons as if in some supernatural joust. I turn back to Sin as it snaps its fingers. Sin's great sword melts down into black goo that slithers to Sin's feet, coils up its body, and morphs into a tentacle where Sin's missing arm used to be. It sharpens into a fin-like blade at the end. We all encircle Sin, weapons held out. Olivia and I are the first to rush forward. Sin deflects my swing with its tentacle, but Olivia manages to slice across its back before she's sent flying by a swift rear kick. Jeremy and Natasha follow up our attack. He side flips over a swing of Sin's fin blade and tosses the knife to Natasha who sinks it into Sin's thigh before spiraling away to safety. I make a deep cut into Sin's forearm during the distraction. William leaps onto Sin's chest, driving his blades into it and then pushing off to backflip away. Joanna leaps up behind him, propelling herself off his shoulders and up over Sin's head. She lands and thrusts her weapons into its lower back— eliciting a sharp growl. Sin leaps back, flattening Joanna beneath it.

"Joanna!" William screams as Sin rolls off of her and deflects a downward chop of my sword.

She's still breathing, but she's out cold. Sin shoves me away to block Olivia's next attack and then kicks her shins out from under her. Jeremy runs along the villain's side, catching the knife over his shoulder and making a good hack into Sin's ribs. After skipping aside, he tosses it back to Natasha who ducks beneath Sin's tentacle and lands a weighty chop into it from below. Sin pivots around, bashing Natasha away with its forearm. In the commotion, William leaps up for an aerial attack, but Sin catches him by the throat before his blades can connect. Long, pointy fingers clamp down around

William's neck, causing him to drop his sword and grasp at the hand holding him. He repeatedly stabs into Sin's arm with his knife, but the monster just laughs at the gooey wounds.

"Valliant effort, little one, but your reinvention of yourself doesn't impress me. Now you're simply more enjoyable to snuff out..." Sin jeers.

Olivia and I halt our advances. "Sin, wait, I plead."

"Oh, don't worry, Mister Daley, I'm saving the best for last."

William looks to me with teary eyes. "I'm sor–" is all he can get out before his head snaps to the side and Sin tosses his limp form away.

"No!" I cry out, feeling an agony in my chest.

I start firing the revolver like a madman. Natasha feigns an attack, hopping back as Sin swings at her and under-handing the knife over to Jeremy who uses it to make two cleaves into our enemy's back. He somersaults away when Sin spins and swings at him. The knife finds its way back into Natasha's hand as she makes another advance. She slides between Sin's legs as it pivots back around. She chops into Sin's calf and leaps away, tossing the weapon into Sin's back. Jeremy jumps up and latches onto the villain's backside, planting a foot over the top of Sin's tail. He rips the knife out and makes repeated chops into the back of its neck and shoulders while Olivia steps up and clashes blades with Sin. I rush forward to hopefully keep the momentum going. Our forces can't afford to get much smaller so the time to finish this is now or never. Jeremy propels off of Sin's back before it can reach back and pull him off. I stomp Sin's tail down as it tries to whack me away and chop off the tip of it before stepping forward and driving my sword through Sin's lower back and out its abdomen. Pointing my revolver at an upward angle, I blast holes through its back, neck, and skull.

The villain's elbow swings back to connect with my temple. I lose grip on my sword—leaving it stuck in Sin—as I crash to my side. Sin twists, tripping Olivia with the nub of its tail. Jeremy flings the knife to Natasha. She catches it in time to shove it up in defense of Olivia when Sin's fin blade comes crashing down on her. Natasha's arms shake as Sin puts its weight into her, but Jeremy comes in with a leaping side kick to knock it aside. Natasha lobs him the knife and helps Olivia to her feet. Sin comes back to retaliate. It brings its tentacle down on Jeremy who blocks it with the knife, but is forced down to a knee by the strength of the blow. I come around while Sin is distracted and grab the hilt of my blade, giving it a good twist and shoving it further up the creature's back. Sin howls, jerking forward. The torque pulls me up over Sin's curled form and sends me crashing onto Jeremy. Olivia steps up to deflect Sin's next attack on us and Jeremy slides the knife across the floor to Natasha. Sin shoves Olivia back, but I feel like it might be losing some of its strength. The forcefield holding Jasmine flickers, offering further proof of this. Our strength is also waning, though.

Lightning dances nearer to us. Our arena is getting dangerously compact. Up above us, Sheera and Shirun sail between the flashes. They trade blows with their opponent. Sin's sickly green eyes light up like radioactive poison and its body steams from its wounds.

"I... will not be undone!" it clangs.

"Stand firm," Olivia encourages us as she lunges forward.

Sparks fly when her sickle clashes against Sin's fin blade. Our enemy hops away from her only to have Natasha run behind it and slice into its back as she passes. Sin falls to a knee, but spins around in time to sling its tentacle down—the tip ripping open Natasha's back. She shrieks as she crashes to the floor. The knife skids to the edge of the room where a bolt of lightning comes down to decimate it. I get to my feet and rush to retrieve my sword from where it's still stuck in Sin's back—refraining from shooting my gun in hopes of sneaking up to him. I'm mid-reach when Sin turns about and catches me by the throat. It lifts me up off the floor with a smirk. I punch and shoot into its arm while my air is mercilessly cut off. Olivia comes to my aid, but Sin fends her off with its tentacle. I think I'm about to go out when I see a blurry image of Jeremy flipping over Sin. I hear a howl as Jeremy withdraws my sword and then see a golden streak in front of me as Jeremy cuts off Sin's remaining arm at the elbow. A deafening cry rattles my eardrums as I shuffle backward, gasping for air.

Sin shoves Olivia away and Jeremy steps back as Sin's nubby tail swings at him. Looking over, I see that the cage holding Jasmine dissipates. She marches forward with her crossbow firmly aimed.

"Step back," she gently commands before she fires two

bolts.

We all do as she says as the shots plunge through the back of Sin's topmost kneecaps. The monster braces itself with its tentacle and twists around with a snarl. Jasmine's next barrage plunges into the shoulder that Sin's tentacle is fused to. The appendage melts and evaporates off of Sin leaving the creature literally unarmed. When it looks up hatefully, Jasmine sinks a bolt into each eye.

"Finish this," Jeremy says serenely as he heaves my sword to me.

I catch it and twirl it beside me as I march up to our ruined enemy. "Not the outcome you were looking for?"

"Oh, Mister Daley, this isn't the end of our story together. Even if you strike me down today, I shall never be fully eradicated. I am the devourer of souls, the disease of the heart, ruiner of minds, shadow of hope, and destroyer of worlds. As long as you breathe, I shall have power over you. Resist it if you must and challenge me if you dare. My solemn promise to you is that I shall never leave you."

I stand over this beast, chilled by what it's saying. Olivia's eyebrows are pinched together and her lips are pursed, but her eyes meet mine and I find resolve in her gaze.

"Maybe you can't be kicked out of this house," I reply, looking down at Sin, "but you're sure as hell going back to your room and you're never coming out…"

Sin cackles as I rear back and lop its head clean off. It bounces and rolls over the floor. I exhale deeply while I watch what's left of Sin's broken body slump to the floor and dissolve into a disgusting, dark sludge that slowly seeps off of the platform and flies into The Calamity. The lightning comes to a sudden halt, but our surroundings remain darkened. Jasmine rushes back to Samuel, Jeremy scoops Joanna up in his arms, and Olivia kneels beside Natasha, immediately going to work at stitching up her back. I stand in the middle of it all and look up to the battle still raging above us. Sheera and Shirun zip to either side of their opponent. They encircle the beast, their shoulders square and their weapons held in front of them. They move as one, crisscrossing the hound-man who struggles to defend against their gleaming cuts. Flakes of ash flutter into the air each time the creature suffers a hit. It's chain maces cracks lose force and its bone-wings start to slow. My heart thumps at the possibility that this might all finally be over.

The enemy manages to catch one of the Shiran by the ankle with his weapon, but its quickly disintegrated with the swing of a sword. Sheera and Shirun shoot up above the beast and come crashing down upon him. I trot backwards as the trio smash down into a flurry of black dust. A dark, stringy corpse is all that remains of the once mighty villain. His body levitates as it peels apart and is pulled up into The Calamity's swirling gales. Sheera and Shirun straighten, turning to me. The radiance of their bodies in this form is hard to look at this close up, but if this is what they really look like, then that's pretty incredible. Their brightness fades as they shift back into a more human shape. The storm around us dissipates, letting a gentle, cream colored light fall upon what's left of my mansion.

The remaining guests encircle us. They wear weary smiles and have a relieved sparkle in their eyes. Jasmine helps Samuel hobble over and keeps him propped up as he clutches his torso. Olivia leads Natasha over by the hand. She's wincing in pain, but at least she's not gushing blood anymore. Jeremy sets Joanna down on her feet and steadies her by the shoulders as she wobbles.

"We did it." Olivia beams.

"It cost a great deal," Jasmine laments.

"But we also saved so much," Jeremy adds.

"There's something left to rebuild on," Samuel agrees.

"And that is what makes all the difference," Natasha concludes.

I'm getting a little misty realizing that these are probably goodbyes.

"You did well," Shirun congratulates me—pulling my attention to him.

Sheera steps forward, looking from me to him. "I can see the beauty in his hues now," she tells him. "I can't condone what you've done—what you've risked—but I can at least see what you were so fucking desperate to save."

"Thank you, sister," he replies.

I catch a glimmer in the corner of my eyes and turn to see little pink orbs of light bubbling off of Jasmine. My stomach drops as I rush over. She smiles sweetly and hands Samuel over. I help him stand, but grab Jasmine's hand.

"It's okay," she soothes, "It's time we put ourselves back together."

Her body fades like a ghost and bursts into the bright orbs that float and flutter about. I turn myself and Samuel around to see Natasha fading as well, silver orbs popping off of her. She tosses and arm out to the side in an elegant bow before she's gone.

"What's happening?" I ask in a panic.

"Everything's going to be alright," Jeremy assures me.

"They're gone!" I protest.

"They're right here," he corrects, motioning to the silver and pink orbs around us. "This is much closer to what we really are."

Olivia steps over and places a hand on my shoulder. I feel Samuel getting lighter and look to see him turning into holiday green orbs.

"Hold me close, but share me often," he requests.

I don't understand, but I say, "Okay, I will."

His face is bright right before it disappears. Jeremy leads Joanna over to me as ocean blue spheres shoot up off of him.

"Breathe easy, my friend," he instructs before departing.

I catch Joanna in my arms as she stumbles forward. Already, bright yellow balls of light ascend off of her.

"Thank you…" she manages to say though she's still dazed. "Thank you for believing that William and I could be different. Thank you for not giving up on us even when we failed you."

"I…" is all I get out before she's gone too.

I try to stay calm, but I really don't understand what's happening. I thought I saved them. Olivia twists me around and pulls me in for a hug.

"Things will be much clearer in just a moment," she says into my ear. "This is a happy moment for you. Here, look…" She releases the embrace and leads me by the hand into the swarm of dancing colors. "See how beautiful they are?"

I look at her to see crystal clear orbs replacing her. "You're beautiful as you are now," I protest.

She grins warmly, "I know… try to never forget that. I can mend what's wounded or cut through what burdens you. Don't forget me."

"I won't," I promise as she joins in with the others.

Sheera and Shirun approach while countless other orbs rise up through the floor and drift from other floating sections of my tattered mansion. They form a symphony of colors—some light, some dark—some bright, others faded. I spin around to take it all in and make myself dizzy. The Shiran catch me by the back of my arms.

"It's really all over then?" I ask breathlessly.

"The worst is over and the darkness has passed," Shirun confirms though his tone is as melancholy as ever.

"The days ahead will be hard," Sheera cautions. "You're in a vulnerable state. It will be like you have only just recovered from a serious illness."

"You'll need to take care of yourself," Shirun agrees. "Surround yourself with good things and good people."

"Why does it sound like you won't be there to help?" I ask.

"Because we won't," Shirun answers heavily.

I step forward and turn around to face them. "Why not, where are you going?"

"I came to take Shirun back to The Light," Sheera answers. "I told you that was my intent."

"I must be judged for what I have done here," Shirun explains. "Although I do regret putting you in so much danger, I'm afraid forgiveness will be difficult to come by when I feel so unrepentant for doing what I thought I must."

"I still don't understand any of this. I'm not even sure if all this is real or just in my head."

Shirun comes up and places his hands on my shoulders. "Nothing I say will help clear that up for you, I'm afraid. Your beliefs must be your own, but please know that this really is the end of your ordeal here. Hold onto this triumph in the days that are to come. Seize your second lease on life and make the most of your time."

"Will I ever see you again at all?"

"Probably not," Sheera replies for him.

"At least not like this," Shirun amends. "We Shiran have many forms. You can see us if you know how to look. We might come as what you'd call 'luck.' We might be that song that plays at just the right time, a sudden warmth that calms you against the chill of the world, or perhaps even a friend who shows up with words of encouragement at just the right time. Look for us in every sunrise, sunset, and in all the beauty between. Do this, and we'll never be far from reach."

My head swims as I try to understand what these guys even are. "Okay… I'll look for you then."

"Good," he says—a tear dripping out of his eye. "Now, there's someone you should meet before you depart."

The colorful lights around us suddenly cluster close together. They spiral up into the air and gather down over the floor, merging together like water droplets. They build up into the shape of a man that's abstract at first, but slowly gains definition until it looks like… me. I approach my semi-transparent double, unsure what to make of him. He's wearing the same body armor as me, but from head to toe, his whole form is made of up colors that ripple like light on water. He's mostly shades of blue with some greens, reds, and greys mixed in. Ebony flecks float about along with inky droplets that squirm like pollution in otherwise clean waters. There are also streaks of radiant white crossing over each other. Sometimes a bit of orange, purple, yellow, or brown will wash up for a moment before giving way to the more prominent colors. The whole appearance is otherworldly. The interest with which he eyes me probably mirrors my own astonishment, but he wears a relaxed smile whereas I can't seem to unclench my jaw.

"Hello," he says.

He sounds like me, but his tone is deeper and warmer. It also reverberates as though there are multiple voices speaking at once.

"Hi," I reply, not sure what to say—I'd mostly just like to know what he is, but I'm not sure how to ask that.

"I'm you and you're me," he states, I guess my confusion is that obvious…

"I guess so… But what are you really?"

"I'm The Collective." Before I can ask, he adds, "You are The Source."

"What does that mean? Where are the others?"

"I **am** them—all of them. Or if you'd rather: they are parts of me. Because of that, we can never manifest at the same time. I apologize if it startled you when I pulled them all into myself, but many are in need of mending and besides, I wanted to meet with you face to face."

"So, they're all here with us right now?"

"I'm those that stood with you at the end like Olivia and Jeremy as well as those that fell along the way like Myles and Margaret. Regrettably, I am also what remains of The Eclipsed that you cut down. I am courage and kindness, but also cowardice and cruelty."

"And Jack?" My chest tightens as I ask.

The Collective shakes his head slowly. "I'm sorry, but no. Innocence once lost can never be regained."

"I see..." I think I knew this already, but I had to ask.

"Most will lose their 'Jacks' at some point or another," Sheera tries to comfort me.

"The choices I made undoubtedly cemented his fate," Shirun offers. "You did well to bring him along as far as you did."

"The others who did not accompany you at the very end are fragmented within me," The Collective explains. "As we speak, those that fell are trying to reform. Some will come back quite similar to how you knew them, others will be unrecognizable, and the rest may never return. In most cases, this will all be for the better, but this is a formative and fragile time for us. We should take care."

"This is ... a lot ..." I tell him.

He smirks and looks at Shirun. "The truth can be complicated at times."

I find Shirun nodding repeatedly with a bashful smile.

"You should say your goodbyes now," The Collective suggests. "I have one more thing for you to see and then this journey will be over."

I turn back to Sheera and Shirun. Sheera steps forward first and wraps me up in a hug.

"Thank you for finding me," I say. "I wouldn't have made it without you."

"Yeah, no shit!" she chimes. "It felt good to be able to save someone again though." She squeezes the back of my neck tenderly. "I think you're gonna be fine, but be mindful of the shadows inside you."

"I will," I promise her, surprised to see her a little misty-eyed when she steps back.

Shirun comes up and takes a firm hold of me by the sides of my face. "I can never fully express how sorry I am that my move to save you very nearly resulted in such a tragedy."

"I know you did everything you could for me, even if you weren't supposed to do it." I do my best to console him.

"I did and I would still do anything that I felt I had to."

"Such is the bond between Shiran and their charges," Sheera explains.

"Any maybe even someone who isn't their charge?" I tease her.

"Some of us are more benevolent than others," she retorts.

"I hope you're judged fairly," I say, turning back to Shirun.

He chuckles, "To be judged fairly would be to be judged harshly, but I appreciate the sentiment."

"Can you just tell whoever's making this judgment that I'd like to see you again."

Shirun laughs even though I wasn't trying to be funny. "The desires of your kind hold little sway in the matters of ours."

"Well then…"

Both of them chuckle at my feigned offense.

"One way or another, I must make this right, but I will miss you, Mister Daley."

"And I will miss you … Mister Shirun"

He laughs in my ear as he pulls me in for a hug. "You will be protected even if I'm not with you, that much I can promise you." He releases the embrace and finishes with, "Take care of yourself now."

"You too."

The Collective comes up beside me, offering an outstretched hand. I feel a little weird taking it—in a way it's like holding hands with myself. It feels even weirder when my feet lift off the ground. I'm lightly dragged up into the air where I can start to see the other remaining fragments of the manor. There isn't very much left and none of it remains fully intact. The remaining sections have no roof or ceiling whatsoever and most don't even have four walls around them. Down on what's left of the dining hall, Sheera and Shirun morph into their slender, radiant forms again and fly upward. I notice they're headed for the observatory. I didn't even realize it was there since it actually hovers above us. It's also still fully intact somehow. The Shiran give us as wave as they soar up into it.

"This house will need to be rebuilt," The Collective states. "For that to happen, what remains will need to be broken down."

"What do I have to do?"

"The process has already begun." He tilts his head down to where the fragments of the manor are gently breaking apart. "This may hurt from time to time, but it's important that you stay steady in the walk that's ahead."

"How?"

The Collective tugs me up and twists me around to face him. He takes hold of my other hand and makes uncomfortably intense eye contact with me that I have trouble holding, but also can't escape from.

"You have to love me—you have to love yourself—you'll never really love anyone or anything else until you do. Be kind to yourself, forgive yourself, embrace yourself, and above all, try to know yourself. The rest should fall into place if you do."

"Sounds easy enough." I look down to the dissembling ruins of the manor.

The Collective laughs—it's a hearty, familiar laugh. "No, it's not. You can't even look me in the eyes and you're only holding my hands because if you don't, you'll fall."

I look back to him, surprise and embarrassment pulling my eyebrows up. "Sorry, it's just—I was just—"

"You were treating me like I'm some strange man getting overly friendly with you. But I'm not, am I? I'm just you. Yeah, I'm a little broken and mixed up at the moment, but I can get there—we can get there. There's plenty to like so just try and like me a little more, okay?"

"You're right, I'm sure you are. I'll try." I promise him—or me—this conversation is confusing.

"Try to take a little quiet time when you can and use it to understand who you are, not just who people think you are. I shouldn't be a stranger to you."

"What if I can't?"

The Collective shrugs, "Then ask for help."

"Right."

"Nothing about this will be easy or convenient."

"I'll do my best."

"Good, don't want to fuck up our second chance."

I grin, feeling like this "Collective" sounds a lot more like me now than I originally thought. "No, we wouldn't want that," I reply.

"It was really nice to meet you, I hope we'll know each other well one day."

"I think we will," I'm finding it much easier to maintain the eye contact now.

"On we go, then," he concludes, beaming.

"On we go…"

With that, an intense white light closes in around us. It wraps us up in an overwhelming warmth that carries me home.

# Chapter 4

I wake up to the sun streaking through my living room window. I'm alone on my couch with no signs that Sheera was ever here. Her sword is no longer fused into my door and there's no traces of any darkness trying to get in. I sit up and lean forward, suddenly feeling exhausted and rejuvenated all at the same time. It's like there's this fullness in my chest that I can't quite describe along with a feeling of fragility totally unlike anything I've experienced before. I'm both happy and sad—healthy and sick. I sit back against the sofa, but have no idea what to do with myself so I just stay here for a while. Eventually, I shift my weight and pull my phone out from my pocket. 11:40 AM, I guess I slept through half the day already.

I remember I'm supposed to meet David for dinner tonight, so I reach out to him with a message asking, "ARE YOU STILL GOOD TO MEET TONIGHT?"

A few minutes goes by and I'm content to spend them right where I am. I think I stay perfectly still until my phone comes to life with a message from David.

"YOU BET! WHAT TIME ARE YOU THINKING?"

"5:30?" I send back.

"SOUNDS GOOD. THE PENINSULA, RIGHT?"

"YES SIR"

"GREAT, SEE YOU THERE."

I put my phone down on the coffee table and think about how the poor guy probably has no idea what he's walking into tonight. To say I was irritable and ungrateful the last time we saw each other might be putting it mildly. I don't even fully grasp the level of moodiness I've exhibited toward him in general these last six months. The only good news is that I feel like I'm finally in control of myself again. I can finally try to make it all right. It's sad that it took an elaborate series of nightmarish events for me to finally wake up, but at least something did the trick. I decide I have some work to do before I show myself in public so I use this as motivation to get myself off the couch. It occurs to me that I don't feel ready to go outside, but I've committed and it probably wouldn't be healthy to stay cooped up by myself like this anyway.

A shower, a shave, and some light hair styling later, I feel a little more enthusiastic about entering into the outside world. I spend a bit of the afternoon just doing some light cleaning: running the dishwasher, wiping down the countertops, doing some dusting, and running the vacuum. There's definitely more to do, but I hit a point where I need to get myself ready. I find a nice shirt, some stylish slacks, and a silver Kolex watch. Then I get my wallet, phone, keys, and a pair of black leather slip-ons as I make for the door. The Peninsula is less than a mile away, so I just walk there. The city looks so different somehow. The light from the descending sun seems brighter, but the shadows also look deeper and sharper. The contrast makes everything feel bigger, bolder, and so much more real. There's a similar effect on all the people on foot and in cars that I pass. There are so many of them all going about their own business. I guess I'm just glad they're normal people and not monsters.

I arrive at The Peninsula a few minutes before five-thirty. A young blond woman greets me at the front.

"Hi there!" she pips.

"Table for two, please," I tell her. "My friend should be here in a few minutes." It feels nice to refer to David as my friend.

"Sure, I'll take you right over here."

I'm led over to a corner table and find myself swimming in the indulgent scents of surf and turf.

"I HAVE A TABLE IN THE BACK RIGHT." I text David once the hostess leaves me.

A moment later, a waitress swings by. "Hi, my name is Carrie and I'll be taking care of you tonight. There anything I can get you to drink?"

"Sure, could I get a North Shore Stout. Actually, two please."

"Sounds good, I'll be right back with those!"

She sails off—ponytail bobbing from side to side. A few moments pass in solitude when I see David enter the dining area and walk over to me.

"Hey," I greet him.

His eyes widen ever so slightly at the ease and warmth in my tone.

"How are you?" I'm about to answer when he quickly adds, "You look well."

"Thanks," I'm relieved he doesn't think I look exhausted anymore. "I think I'm on a sort of upswing."

"Good, that's great, actually. All done with the dreams then?"

I look down at the table. "All done with a few things, I hope."

"That must be a relief? You can finally sleep a little easier, at least."

I nod a few times before answering, "It is, but it also feels like there's a lot I still need to deal with. It's like I feel easy and uneasy at the same time. I guess I'm just unsteady is all."

"I think that's just part of life sometimes, right? You have to take it step by step," he offers brightly. "There anything in particular you feel like you need to do?"

"I've just had a lot I needed to realize and that means there are some things I'll need to think about, maybe do something about too."

"Do you want to tell me about it?" Of all people, he probably deserves to know about everything.

"I'm not sure where I'd even start," I answer honestly.

"Well, we have a whole dinner ahead of us," he jests. "Start at the beginning, tell me the whole thing if you want to, even the parts we already talked about."

The beer arriving gives me a moment to collect my thoughts.

"Thank you," I say to the waitress.

I realize that there's no coherent or even sane way to explain it all. I'm just going to have to go from top to bottom if I talk about it at all. So that's what I decide to do after David orders the salmon fillet and I get a steak topped with shrimp. I tell him everything, starting with my very first trip to the manor—describing all the confusion and disorientation that I felt. A few times in the beginning he encourages me to keep going by asking what came next or how I felt about a particular detail, but once I get going, the story just kind of tells itself. I detail the following day and how out of sorts I felt at work, how I felt like he made life difficult for me, but couldn't come up with any examples of how he'd wronged me. I shared my dinner with Kayla that night and then describe my second visit to the manor. I refer to all the manor's guests by name and tell him all about Shirun. I spare no gory detail in the violence that occurred and I don't bother holding back on any of the crazy stuff that happened while I was supposedly wide awake. Sheera, my shadowy hunters, even Dr. Drakeson all come up. I also mention all the strangely coincidental encounters with people from our friend group and how I thought David was behind some well-intentioned conspiracy to deploy them on me at just the right times. Through it all, he just listens, sometimes nodding, sometimes smiling. He never interrupts to defend himself, to judge, or even to call the nearest mental health facility—which is a relief. By the time the story is finished, our meals are half digested and we're several stouts deep.

"Sounds like it's been a long week," he comments, probably still trying to absorb half of this.

"I think we both know it's been more than a long week."

His brow furrows as he replies, "I don't think you should be so hard–" he's cut off by his phone. "Sorry," he says, pulling the device up to his ear. "Hi Kendall," he answers. After a pause he replies, "Oh, okay, sure. Hey can I call you back later? I'm out with a friend right now." Another pause, "Yes, it's Bryan."

I polish off my beer and order us another round while he finishes the call.

"Thanks, I will, and you too. Talk to you later!" He looks back at me once he's hung up and says, "Sorry."

"Who's Kendall?" I tease him with an adolescent antagonism, hoping that will lighten up the heavy mood I've set for the evening.

"Oh, I've been seeing her."

"That's awesome," I congratulate him. "How long have you guys been together?"

"Well, we met online a little before I took on my current role and had a couple of dates here and there. I guess you could say we've been official for a few months now. She doesn't live in the city so we've mostly just connected on the weekends, but we're trying to figure out how to spend a little more time together."

"Oh, wow…" my heart sinks at realizing this is not at all a recent thing. "I'm sorry, David, I guess this shouldn't have been news to me. I know I've been a shit friend, but this is next-level douchebaggery."

"No, you—" His face reddens at my self-accusation. "You've just been going through some stuff."

"I've been going through being an asshole," I retort after the waitress has delivered our beers and left.

"I think that's being a little harsh…"

"I told Kevin to fuck off, David. What kind of a sick monster tells that guy to fuck off? It doesn't matter if I was hurting after Julie, I don't get a free pass from that or anything else I did that I conveniently wiped from my memory until recently."

David's mouth opens and closes. There's really not a ton he can say, he knows I'm right. After some contemplation he replies, "Maybe what matters is that you're working on it. We still love you and we're still here for you—hopefully you know that. As sorry as I am to hear about Kayla, I really do think you made the best choice as far as that goes. I think starting fresh with everything will help a lot with whatever you need to do."

"Thanks, I appreciate that—all of it. Plenty of people would have given up on me by now."

"I'm just glad you're not giving up on yourself," he says with a supportive grin.

"I'll drink to that," I reply with a big smirk.

"This is the last one though." He chuckles, raising his glass to mine.

"I'm lucky to know you, man."

David takes a long sip before responding, "Oh, don't worry, I know you are!"

We laugh and we drink like old times turned into new times. When we leave, I go home feeling less unsteady in spite of the light buzz I have going on. As I walk up to my living room windows and look into the dark cityscape, I can't help but feel a whole lot brighter about what the future has in store.

# Epilogue

It's been three months since my final visit to the manor. A lot has changed during this time. I went back to work with a renewed energy and a resolve to support David as both my manager and my friend. A part of me still harbors a little resentment, but I try to push past that. I'm probably not right for that kind of a role yet anyway and nothing is worth more than getting a friend back. I've even met Kendall a few times now. She's a pretty redhead who's reserved and respectful, but also seems like she can provide the right kind of trouble for David.

I've been reconnecting with the others too. Devon comes over every Saturday afternoon for beer, snacks, and a game of some sort. He sounded surprised when I reached out about it, but he hasn't missed a week. Sometimes other people join us for the new tradition too. He and I join Kevin and Erin for concerts and movies from time to time. David and Kendall show up when they're both in the city. Julie even makes an appearance occasionally, sometimes bringing her fiancé, Nathan, along. He seems like a good guy—driven and decisive, just like her. It's not all perfect all the time. There are points where I feel intensely lonely, maybe just because I'm not seeing anyone, but I'm grateful to have all these people back in my life. I'm also grateful that none of us ever bring up my random encounters with them during the week of my visits to the manor. Only David knows what I really went through during that time and I think I'd prefer to keep it that way.

In the last month or so, I've started seeing a therapist—a real one this time, not some crazy demon-shrink. We don't talk about my trips to the manor all that much. Instead, we've been focusing on factors in my life that may have led up to them. It turns out that I had a lot of misconceptions about how the whole therapy and mental health thing works. Never once have I been made to feel like a crazy person or judged in any way. That said, I am learning that I have to work through when it comes to how I regard women, managing feelings of anxiety, dealing with various phobias or biases, balancing personal happiness with material success, and how I relate to others in general. It's a lot to unpack, but we're taking it one step at a time. It's also nice just to have someone to help with it all.

Randomly, I also go to church now. I'm hardly a convert, I'm still not even sure whether I went through some profound spiritual battle, a temporary lapse in sanity, or something else entirely. I guess I just go for me—I go because I like it. There are worse ways to spend a Sunday morning and I make a whole thing out of it. I head to a parish a bit outside the city and then stop for coffee and breakfast at a little mom-and-pop shop down the road before heading home. I guess I gave it a shot because of my mom. She wasn't super religious, but she'd go visit a church when she needed to think or if things got tough. After everything I've been through, I wanted a peaceful place to escape to—a place away from everything.

Once I started, I realized I liked it. I don't participate. I just find a spot in the back to sit and listen. A lot of the sermons are about reflecting on your own actions or how to love one another— stuff I know I need to hear and it's nice to be in a building full of people who feel like they need to hear it too. An added plus is that the statues and stained-glass images of angels remind me of Sheera and Shirun. I do my best to look for them like they told me to, but it's easier here. Somehow, I feel like they're happy that I come here. Fortunately, none of the other churchgoers seem bothered by me crashing their weekly celebration either. No one has welcomed me, but they also haven't tried to kick me out or give me the stink eye— well there was that one old lady at first when I "took her seat," but I've found the congregation otherwise amenable to me.

Today's sermon is on forgiveness. I've been on the receiving end of a lot of that these last couple of months. I listen carefully about the importance of forgiving not just once, but as many times as you are asked too. I feel like you've got to draw the line somewhere—I mean someone could just be using you—but I get the message about being patient with people. I guess we're all bound to mess up over and over again even if we're trying our best. Maybe this applies to forgiving yourself as well—I should probably think about that over coffee later. The rest of the celebration takes place and I remain where I am in my corner while the rest of the church receives the sacraments. I stay where I am even once it's all over. I like to let people funnel out before I leave. I can handle city driving just fine, but there's something about the old folks fleeing the church parking lot that has me terrified for both me and the Wercedes. In the interest of not ruining my Sunday Zen, I just wait for them to do their thing—I'm not in any huge rush anyway.

When I take my leave, the sun is shining down bright and hot. The air is crisp and I swear the birds always perform an encore of the church tunes. The chugging sound of a car that won't start breaks through their chorus though. I look across the lot to see a woman hop out of her car and hurriedly open up the hood of her hatchback. I walk over, feeling sort of nervous to actually talk to someone that goes here. There aren't many people left in the parking lot though, so I really should get my Good Samaritan thing going.

"Need a hand?" I ask tightly as I approach the car.

The woman pulls her head out from under the hood. She's clearly a little stressed, but she tries to smile when she sees me. The daylight gleams off of her bronze skin and glossy, pink lips. Her blue and yellow sunflower dress sparkles as it sways in the gentle breeze. Her hair is clipped up so that it sways up and behind her head, pulled away from her artsy, stone earrings that dangle beside her cheeks. She's not super familiar to me, but I know I've seen her before—I think she usually sits in the front somewhere.

"I think the battery is dead, I'm fine though, I have Roadside Assistance."

"I can try giving you a jump real quick," I offer. "It'd be faster than waiting for Roadside."

She hesitates, looking to her car and then back to me. "Okay, sure, thank you."

"Alright," I catch myself grinning, so I try to casually wipe that off my face. "One sec."

I leave her and walk to the back of the parking lot where my Wercedes is parked. She's pulling jumper cables out of her trunk when I roll up in front of her.

"So, this is yours, huh?" she comments once I've stepped out and popped my hood. "I've been wondering who that fancy thing belongs too."

"It helps me compensate for a small personality."

Her eyebrows shoot up until I trade my serious scowl for a playful smirk.

"Oh … you're funny." She laughs uneasily, "Good, that's good."

"Sorry," I say as I prop open the hood of my car.

"No, no, that's alright. I grew up with two older brothers, so I know how to take a little joking," she replies as she attaches the clamps to her battery. "May I?" she asks, holding the clamps of the other end of the wires apart.

"Of course." I step aside and take a seat in my car.

I wait for her to step away and then turn it on. She gets into hers and tries to get it to start. It doesn't take the first time, but on the second attempt, her car comes to life. She leaves it on and hops out so I do the same.

"Thank you so much," she exhales as she comes to retrieve her cables. She gives me a measured look before returning them to her trunk. "You're sort of new here, right?"

"Yeah, I live in the city, but I've started to come here to get away from things, you know?"

She comes back around giving me a knowing nod. "I think I get what you mean. Were you always religious?"

"I'm not even sure if I'd describe myself as that now," I admit.

"Well, maybe you will be someday, just don't fool yourself into thinking that coming makes your demons magically go away."

"Noted. I've got no intention of running from them anymore."

"Good," she dips toward me with a grin. "Sorry, I didn't catch your name.

"I'm Bryan."

"Sofía," she extends her hand and shakes mine.

"It's good to meet you."

She glances back at her car, "Better for me probably," she jokes. "I should probably take this somewhere to get it looked at, but maybe next week you'll let me buy you a coffee or something— I don't love feeling like I owe someone."

"You don't owe me anything, it was no problem. I've been

going to Takami's Tea and Coffee Shop if you ever want to join me though."

"I think I'd like that," her smile sweetens and something about her amber gaze is so warm and so cool at the same time. "See you next week, then?"

"See you then." My heart races as she gets back into her car and I turn toward mine to shut the hood.

I mean, what am I even doing? Am I okay to be flirting with a church lady right now? I try to hold it together as I get in my car and drive off. I guess this isn't really anything just yet. I'll take a breath. I'll take it slow. I'll see where all this goes.

You found me in the dark, didn't know I was falling,

With voices everywhere, I couldn't hear you calling.

.......

But you reached out to me and took me by the hand,

I held onto you, cause without you I couldn't stand,

And we sailed through the night:

Cutting through all the lies,

Fleeing demons in disguise,

Sparks lighting up our eyes,

Chasing down brighter skies

.......

Shadows of my past always creeping and crawling,

My future was unclear, so vast and so sprawling.


Rushing all around, didn't know I was lonely,

Then you came crashing in, so bright and so lovely.

.......

And you reached out to me and took me by the hand,

I held onto you, cause without you I couldn't stand,

And we sailed through the night:

Cutting through all the lies,

Fleeing demons in disguise,

Sparks lighting up our eyes,

Chasing down brighter skies

.......

It's been a long way down, down a very dark place,

I could never find my way and I didn't know your face,

But when you brought me to the light, I knew I'd be alright,

I'd be alright....

.......

Cause you reached out to me and took me by the hand,

I held onto you, cause without you I couldn't stand,

And we tore through the night:

Cutting through all the lies,

Fleeing demons in disguise,

Sparks lighting up our eyes,

Chasing down brighter skies

.......

You found me in the dark ...

didn't know I was... falling.

# Voidwalker

# Acknowledgements

While this is an independently published work, there are a number of individuals who are owed thanks for seeing it through to completion and for ensuring that it was released at the best possible quality. Without their assistance, the final product would not have been the same:

**Jeff MacMillan**: For his thoughtful edits and feedback on the first half of this series.

**Nathaniel Mellor:** For his thoughtful edits and feedback on the second half of this series.

**Fellow Indie Authors:** For their correspondence and support (a special thanks to Ann Andrews and Derek Edgington).

**Robin Bailey:** For being such a big supporter of everything I do and just being a great mom in general.

**Nick Dolan, Nathaniel Mellor, and Robin Bailey**: for providing feedback on the end theme, "You Found Me in the Dark."

**Joseph Umali & Co.:** For unrivalled consulting services, especially in regard to providing feedback on the new cover design for this collection.

**All of my family and friends:** For always inspiring me and for making life so worthwhile every day of the week.

# About the Author:

Derek Bailey is a graduate of Southern New Hampshire University's Game Design and Development Program (BA) where he also completed minor in Creative Writing. He has a passion for storytelling in all forms and across a number of genres. He spends his days happily employed as a Digital Product Owner, but enjoys writing on the side as a means of expressing himself and sharing his thoughts on life whenever he can find the time and energy to spin tall tales. His first novel, <u>Digitarum</u>, was self-published in 2015 via Amazon's Kindle Direct Program.